RECORDER

RECORDER

CHILDREN OF THE CONSORTIUM | BOOK ONE

CATHY MCCRUMB

Published by Enclave Publishing, an imprint of Oasis Family Media.

Carol Stream, Illinois, USA.
www.enclavepublishing.com

ISBN: 978-1-62184-199-9 (hardback)
ISBN: 978-1-62184-201-9 (printed softcover)
ISBN: 978-1-62184-200-2 (ebook)

Cover design by Emilie Haney, www.EAHCreative.com
Typesetting by Jamie Foley, www.JamieFoley.com

Printed in the United States of America.

For all the stars who never shone,
and for the ones who did.

PROLOGUE

I did not have a name—none of us did—but once when I was young, I had a friend.

Early in my tenth year I slipped away from the other girls of my cohort. Their approved games did not interest me, and since I had fulfilled my physical activity requirements, I took refuge at my favorite place near the artificial brook.

Light sparkled on water rippling over smooth brown stones. Either the brook's engineers or its gentle flow had sculpted rounded banks in the loam, and lavender and thyme grew between orange lilies. The self-pollinating plants bobbed and dipped in the breeze created by the giant fans in the lofty, domed ceiling. It was a close approximation of a real brook, from what I had read, and its murmur muted the subdued noise of the other children.

Without regard to whether my action might stain my grey uniform, I sank onto a bed of moss and breathed in the lavender-scented air, concentrating on the water's burble until footsteps interrupted my solitude. Shoulders tensed, I closed my eyes briefly and inhaled before turning toward the sound.

A child from an older cohort threaded his way through the lavender and rocks. Though taller than I, his face was still rounded, so perhaps he had not yet reached puberty. Thick black lashes curled around silvery eyes that glanced from me to the brook. He sighed, then lowered himself onto the moss. We sat together and watched water ripple over rocks.

At length, I said, "The brook is quiet."

"Yes. I prefer quiet." He picked up a pebble and turned it over and over in his hands before tossing it into the water. "Did you—have you ever made a boat?"

I shook my head. He plucked several long, wide lily leaves and showed me how to weave them into shapes. For nearly forty-seven minutes, we made boats, affixing lavender stems for masts and setting them free on the water. I had never been so content. The bell tolled twice, and he left the way he came. I returned to my own cohort.

The boy and his boats occupied my mind the following day. During free reading time, I skimmed through old texts until I found the correct word. After mathematics, I slipped away to the brook again, where he sat, apparently awaiting my appearance. He inclined his head once in my direction, and I nodded back before kneeling beside him. We plucked lily leaves, carefully selecting them from different plants to avoid weakening any one in particular, and he sorted them by size. We sat side by side and wordlessly resumed building boats.

It was almost time to return before I summoned the courage to ask, "Have you read about friends?"

"Yes." His silver-grey eyes met mine, but the bells rang, and we separated to rejoin our cohorts.

The next day was a Tour Day. I disliked Tour Days. The citizens who came through stared at us as if we were laboratory specimens and spoke in poorly constructed sentences. Our Recorder had explained that most citizens believed their tightly fitted, brightly colored clothing expressed individuality, though I did not understand their reasoning. They had names and chose their own destinies. Surely, such distinctions of personality should have sufficed. Hair covered their heads, and their eyebrows waggled up and down when they talked, like matching caterpillars crawling across their faces.

While studying life cycles in biology, we had raised real caterpillars. One Recorder had disciplined me when I refused to touch them. Recorders and Elders discouraged imagination, but the similarity between those woolly creatures and citizens' eyebrows made me shudder. How could citizens think with all that hair coming out of their heads? It disturbed me not to see the clean, natural shape of their skulls.

That day, the dark man with angled eyebrows and long, thick cords of black hair returned. He had missed only three Tour Days since I first noticed him. Despite his hair, he dressed respectfully, though his charcoal tunic was darker than the grey we wore. The man did not prattle and point, as others did, but watched the cohorts carefully while we played or exercised quietly on the turf near the botanical gardens.

This time, however, his nut-brown eyes met mine, and his mouth tipped upward. I cocked my head, trying to remember the appropriate response, then forced my lips up in return. His smile grew, but his eyes held steady and did not crinkle around the corners.

"Hello." His voice was so deep it startled me.

I glanced back. No Elder intervened, so I assumed I had permission to speak.

"Hello," I said.

The man searched my face but did not appear to find what he sought. "Are you . . . happy?"

"'Happiness is irrelevant,'" I quoted.

An Elder stepped to my side, placing a hand on my shoulder and motioning back at his drones, which hovered behind him, long tendrils moving slowly beneath their bellies. I peered at the tall, dark man, to study his face, to memorize it. The man stared at the Elder's hand, and his eyebrows pulled together over his nose. A muscle ticced in his jaw. The Elder positioned himself between us, though I peeked under his arm to watch the man, whose long cords of hair swung out when he turned around.

The tour moved along. The man was leaving. Suddenly, the need to speak outpaced the need for permission. I stepped in front of the Elder, ignoring the way his grey, pupilless eyes were shifting from the man to me.

Though the man did not see me, I raised my hand. "Goodbye!"

He spun around. The Elder's grip tightened, and his three drones whirred behind us. The man walked backward to keep his eyes on mine while he and the rest of the citizens passed into the Consortium's low, grey buildings squatting under the faded blue of the riveted ceiling high above.

I wanted to tell him something, but there was nothing to tell.

Once the solid doors slid shut behind the tour group, the Elder released me. Still, I watched the building.

"You did not have leave to speak to the citizen." The Elder's tone was gentle. "You knew not to do so."

I turned to face him, the protest rising to my lips without forethought.

"But, Elder, you said nothing. I could not have known when no one told me to remain silent."

The Elder's eyebrowless forehead furrowed, and his mouth pinched into a tight line. For five seconds, his eyelids dropped to hide nanodevice-covered corneas. His eyes moved as if he read, or perhaps as if he dreamed. Perhaps he consulted other Elders over the Consortium network. I did not know.

Behind him, the children from my cohort stared at us, wide-eyed, and Recorders attempted to redirect their attention.

The Elder exhaled slowly. "I have consulted records and two other Elders. While what you say contains an element of truth, our consensus is that you did indeed know. Falsehood is not tolerated. There is no place for untruth in the Consortium. Dishonesty and infidelity are abominations."

The spherical body of his larger slave drone descended silently, and I braced myself. One of its long, narrow appendages slithered around my shoulders, the end resting lightly on my throat. I gritted my teeth, and my mouth went dry in anticipation.

Pain shot through me, and my fingers went numb.

The reprimand was the worst I had ever received.

When I had wiped the moisture from my cheeks, the other children were filing away, only one or two risking a peek in our direction. The Elder knelt in front of me, one hand at his side, the other fisted tightly over his abdomen.

"You must learn," he murmured softly, and it was difficult to hear him over the ringing in my ears. "You show promise. Perhaps, with greater focus . . ." His fingers flexed, and he sighed before blinking once. The grey nanodevices spiraled back from his eyes, revealing irises as dark brown as my own, darker than the sandy loam by the brook.

My breath caught. I had never seen an Elder's eyes.

"You must take care, little one. I, myself, do not wish to reprimand you again." The corner of his mouth drooped briefly. "On subsequent Tour Days, you will work in the Scriptorium. You will not interact with citizens."

His slave drone released me, and I fell back a pace. Nanodevices once more shrouded the Elder's irises, and after he dismissed me, I returned to our dormitory, my thoughts shifting from the man to the Elder and his drones, and then to the boy and his boats.

That night, in the deepest dark, while the other children slept, I allowed myself to cry.

Throughout the next day, my inattention merited several mild reprimands before I escaped the Elders and my cohort. I again sought the brook's solitude, and its peacefulness quieted me.

I was pleased when the boy arrived.

Before we built anything, I spoke. "Yesterday was a Tour Day."

He inclined his head once. "Yes. I am sent to the Scriptorium on Tour Days."

"Have you seen them?" I asked. "The citizens?"

"No, I have not, though I have seen documentaries."

I shuddered. "They have *hair.*"

He waited. The Elders taught waiting allowed reluctant communicators time to complete their thoughts.

"I saw a man."

"Oh." He was not questioning, merely making an appropriate conversational response. I appreciated his courtesy.

"He has toured before, but this time, he spoke to me."

"Why?" The boy's eyes remained on mine while he plucked the lilies' wide leaves. Their faint pops momentarily distracted me.

"I do not know. He appeared sad."

The boy was losing interest. I should have known my story would interest no one but myself. Still, I needed to clarify. "He smiled at me."

"But . . . smiles indicate happiness."

"He asked if I am happy, but happiness is irrelevant. Then, an Elder noticed our conversation. I said goodbye."

"Oh," he said again, but I knew he understood what had followed.

"He did not issue a reprimand immediately."

The boy did not comment on the delay in discipline. A shadow, as if from a cloud, crossed his face, but the council had not added clouds to the programming. Emotion. It must have been an emotion.

"I wish I were not reprimanded so often. I wish you were not, either." His mouth turned down. "I dislike reprimands."

"I also dislike them."

We gathered materials in silence and built more boats.

When the bells sounded, the boy placed his last boat on the water. It traveled past the low rocks and rich brown loam of the bend, and we stood side by side, watching it disappear.

"I have read about friends." He faced me. "Having one could prove beneficial."

"I confess a secret." My words spilled out as I wiped my palms dry on my leggings.

His eyes widened at the audacity of my statement.

"I want to have a friend. Someday."

A smile crept across his face, crinkling the edges of his silvery eyes. "Having a friend is a good plan."

At every opportunity over the next ten-day, I waited by the brook. I made no boats, since the boy never came. An unfamiliar listlessness slowed my steps and drew consequences when I once again lost focus on my lessons.

The last day I went to the brook, I saw him on the paths winding through the botanical gardens and understood at once that he would no longer build boats.

A personal shadow drone—*his* shadow drone—hovered a meter behind him, one long tentacle extending from under its jellyfish-like form, resting around his neck to establish a proper connection with his neural implant. He started toward me, but the drone issued a reprimand. The boy stiffened with pain.

I stared, eyes wide.

He mouthed the word, "Friends."

To spare him further discipline, I said nothing. Instead, I offered a smile.

I understood sad smiles, then, and I did not return to the brook.

If not for my neural implant, I would have slept poorly the night before my first solo assignment. My concern was neither for my ability to execute my duties, nor the impending flight and long climb into the bowels of Krios's moon, Pallas. Rather, I found myself preoccupied with thoughts of the sky.

For the first time, I would stand on solid rock and behold an expanse unbound by domes and rivets. Only a frigid, comparatively narrow band of oxygen, sulfur, and nitrogen would separate me from the vastness of space, and with my own eyes, I would see the stars.

Before our departure, an Elder had cautioned me to spare only the briefest moment for the sight. My purpose remained to maintain the integrity of the records, ensure the colonies' safety, and defend the rights of citizens. I would not betray my training.

And yet, to stand, free, under the openness of space and see the stars . . .

I exhaled. Leaning against the wall in the Consortium quarters aboard CTS *Thalassa*, I waited for my drone to charge. Although my favorite subsonic sonatas played, I could not relax. The ultraviolet fractals my neural implant projected onto my visual cortex did little to calm my rapid heartbeat, and on the opposite wall, the Consortium's daily aphorism seemed to mock me: *Clarity of mind is the gateway to personal peace.*

I rose and performed a kata, drank a cup of herbal tea, and dressed. Twenty-four years of grey clothing made the mottled black and charcoal of the lightly armored suit seem unnatural. The Consortium's triangular patch decorated my upper right arm, but wearing the emblem was not the equivalent of wearing the tunic and leggings I had worn since childhood. My stomach fluttered, as if I had swallowed a chrysalis, and somehow the butterfly had emerged and attempted to escape.

"Perhaps," I said aloud, "I am apprehensive, after all."

I received no answer save my drone's steady hum as it emerged from its charging alcove.

Selecting infrared for my predominant invisible light, I stood for a moment, rereading the aphorism, then exhaled slowly and released a small dose of neurotransmitters. Though anticipation of standing under a sky still gripped me, my pulse steadied. The drone's slender tendril slid around my shoulders, and its comfort brought a faint smile to my lips.

I linked to the Consortium network. The sole message reiterated orders I had received previously: *Locate the station's Recorder. If dead, retrieve her body and drone. Should any citizens still live, record their extraction.* I acknowledged the transmission, but such repetition of my orders was unnecessary. Surely, the Elders knew I would abide by the Acquisition and Verification Act, that I would redeem my gifting.

I gathered my datapads, gloves, and helmet, then drew a deep breath. It was time.

The doors slid apart, and my drone whirred behind me, one steadying tendril draped over my left shoulder. I waited until the doors closed and locked before heading to the briefing room.

The crew avoided me—most citizens did—their attention shifting down and away when I passed. But, halfway to the room, long strides behind me paused, then sped up.

"Recorder."

I stopped near one of the bland art pieces on even blander walls. Citizens believed monochromatic renderings made hallways soothing yet found our quarters stark and clinical. They were mistaken on both counts. I tamped down a hint of pity at their binocular, seven-color world, and my drone did not reprimand me.

"Nathaniel Timmons," I said as he joined me beside the art.

His green eyes flicked from me to my drone and back. "Going to the conference room?"

"Yes."

He grinned down at me. "I'll join you."

I recognized neither the need for accompaniment nor the need to refuse, so I merely nodded.

We had walked six meters when he said, "Haven't seen you around much."

"No."

"Usually see Recorders on the bridge and in the lounge, is all."

For the next five strides, I considered an appropriate response. "The Elders selected me to document the trip to the station. My primary purpose is not to serve as *Thalassa*'s Recorder."

Timmons raised one eyebrow and hummed, whether in agreement or only in acknowledgment, I could not tell. He had a vaguely musical, tenor voice. "But we don't have another Recorder."

"I am able to review daily activity from my quarters. An additional Recorder would be redundant."

As we turned the corner, he glanced up at the Consortium recording device on the ceiling and back at me.

An explanation seemed necessary. "Most Recorders interact more frequently because they are neither trained to observe multiple feeds, nor granted access to do so. A ship's Recorder is trained in public sector documentation. My training emphasis has been in observing and analyzing Consortium staff activity."

Timmons's attention shifted to my drone. His jaw clenched. I cross-referenced my database of facial expressions and body language. I had not intended to make him uncomfortable, but to clarify would, perhaps, exacerbate the matter.

"Why would Parliament and the Consortium send a Recorder with that specialty to a dead research station?"

"For internal reasons. I shall explain during the meeting."

His forehead furrowed, and Timmons ran fingers through his short blond hair. "Guess I'll wait." He offered me a quick, thin smile, which did not reveal his dimple. "Tell you what. I'll wave at you now and then through the cameras when we get back from Pallas."

"You need not."

He slowed, and I matched his pace. "It has to be a little lonely, sitting in your quarters, watching other people. It's the least I can do."

"On the contrary, the least you can do is nothing." My drone's weighted tendril encircled my shoulders, but I kept my eyes on his. "Additionally, I am not alone."

His gaze shifted and narrowed, following the tendril from my shoulders to my drone, but he merely motioned for me to precede him through the conference room's open doors. I set my equipment on a cabinet in the corner under a painting of an ancient Earth sailing ship and turned to acknowledge the woman waiting for us.

Venetia Jordan pushed a datapad aside and stood in greeting, long braids spilling over her shoulder, their amber beads clattering against her light armor. The standard issue suit made her appear taller than usual, although I knew her height had not changed. She was still only fifteen and a quarter centimeters taller than I, not quite as tall as Timmons.

"Good morning, Recorder. Stars, Tim." Jordan focused her golden-brown eyes on him. "You're not changed yet?"

He dropped into the chair next to hers. "Nah. I'd rather be comfortable a little longer."

She huffed and sat back down. I remained standing, though my drone left my side to hover over the long, rectangular table. Footsteps sounded in the hallway.

Jordan picked up the datapad and closed her document. "You picked the wrong line of work for comfort."

"Guess we both did." He checked the readout on his identification wristband. "Alec and Zhen are late."

"No." Alexander Spanos stood in the doorway. "You're early for once. J, we ran into North at breakfast. He'll be along in a few."

Timmons smothered a yawn. "Too bad we can't start without him."

"That would make for a more pleasant meeting—" Zhen DuBois had followed Spanos into the room but broke off abruptly, dark eyes narrowing at me, and stepped closer to Spanos, capturing his hand in her own.

One of Jordan's delicate eyebrows rose. "Zhen."

"I know," she snapped, still watching me.

"No sense having another blasted meeting," Spanos muttered. He settled across from Jordan, and Zhen DuBois slid gracefully into the chair next to him. Despite her suit, her movements were smooth, like flowing water. He kept her hand in his and avoided my gaze. "We've been over this how many times? They'll all be dead."

"Of course they are," Timmons said. "Two years without a word after that first biohazard alert, then radio silence until the nuclear warning? Unless it's the most ridiculous surprise party of all time, they're gone."

DuBois fingered the end of her thick, black plait. "Did they say what the biohazard was?"

"Not that I know of." Jordan turned to me. "Recorder, do you know?"

I did not share my personal dissatisfaction with the lack of information. "Nothing in any transmission received by either the University of New Triton or CTS *Ontario* explains the conditions leading to the nuclear reactor's destruction. There has been no clarification of either the distress signal or the radiation warning. I was not informed of the parliamentary committee's reasons for refusing to allow additional bots to scrub the area. Although *Ontario* was dispatched to watch over the moon and the station—"

"Ha!" Timmons tipped his chair onto its back legs. "That had to be the most boring job in the system—watching an empty rock for almost seven quarters."

I did my best to suppress a frown. "*Ontario*'s scans indicate the immediate danger has waned, or you would not be allowed to go. Safety for citizens is our priority."

"Just citizens?" Timmons watched me. "Didn't include yourself in that."

DuBois rolled her eyes.

"People matter." Spanos threw a sidelong glance at me. "Should've done something."

The corner of Jordan's mouth twisted down. "Not our business. We just need to get the data, check for survivors—however unlikely—then head back."

The captain's signature heavy footfalls in the corridor brought further conversation to a halt. The other four stood when he entered, though none greeted him. He waved a hand, and they sat back down. His grey queue swung behind him as he lowered himself into a chair and steepled his fingers.

"No need for meeting minutes with that thing present." He gestured broadly toward me and my drone. "I reviewed your orders."

Jordan's eyebrows rose again, but she said nothing.

"Isn't Genet coming?" Timmons asked the captain. "Or Smith?"

"No."

Since the captain was not forthcoming, I explained, "Officer Smith is finalizing the communication system. First Officer Genet is"—I closed my eyes briefly and checked my drone's feed—"on the bridge."

A muscle in the captain's jaw jumped. He glared past me to the oil painting and grunted in acknowledgment. "*Ontario* is on the way back to New Triton. You all know what you need to do. Get the data, seal the place, and we'll destroy it from here. The Recorder will go with you to make sure everything's aboveboard."

Spanos bolted upright. "What? I thought she was staying on the ship."

DuBois drew a quick breath, glanced at me, then whispered in his ear, "Alec, please don't."

Did they not realize I could hear them?

Jordan watched me, not Spanos. "Of course she's coming with us, Alec. I don't know how you missed it before."

Timmons shifted. My drone registered a fluctuation in his body temperature, which in conjunction with his pupils' dilation and his body language indicated either anxiety or dishonesty. "I did, too. Not sure it's a good idea if she goes with us."

Jordan turned to him. "Because?"

"Stands to reason." Timmons leveled his gaze on me. "You haven't done much of this sort of thing before, Recorder. Liability."

Whether or not he had lied before, he spoke truly then. I forced down my trepidation. "You are correct, Nathaniel Timmons. I will endeavor to observe unobtrusively."

My drone whirred over to where I stood and wrapped one thin arm around my shoulders. Timmons turned to Spanos, who had pulled a loop of wooden beads from a pocket. They clicked as he flipped them between his fingers.

"Alec?" Timmons said.

After three seconds, Spanos shrugged, and the tension in Jordan's shoulders eased. She entered a code into her datapad. Its soothing, programmed voice read regulations and assignment details, then the others signed their final releases. I notarized the signatures, then cleared my throat. Five pairs of eyes turned to me, wearing varying expressions of what my database indicated was surprise.

"I will fulfill my role in documenting the events on the station, but I must also ascertain what befell the station's Recorder. All communication from her ceased more than four ten-days before the distress call. I am to retrieve her and the drone."

The captain's nostrils flared. "The Consortium wants its property back, so they send you? A double risk, isn't it? A liability?"

His comment focused my attention on him. My jaw tightened, and my drone rose ten centimeters higher into the air and extended its arms, tentacles, and tendrils, like dendrites. Everyone at the table drew back.

"No, Captain North." I kept my tone even. "We do not want our *property* returned. We want our *Recorder*. She is a valuable member of the Consortium, and her drone an expensive piece of equipment."

Jordan set her palms down on the faux wood between us. "It's safe to say she was indeed a valuable and well-trained Recorder, if they trusted her out here on some hidden research station."

The captain stood and checked his wristband. "That covers everything I need to know. DuBois—that's your name, isn't it? If you need to talk to anyone about additional links, Smith will be at her post until you return." He turned to Jordan. "I'm off in four hours. The trip takes ninety minutes down, then who knows how long underground, and another ninety minutes back. If you finish before I go off-duty, comm me. Otherwise, talk to Genet. Timmons, Spanos, check the chem backup system before you go."

Like mirror images, both men crossed their arms and sat back. Timmons answered for them both. "Already done."

When the captain's attention landed on me again, he froze. For eleven seconds, he stood in silence, then strode out of the conference room.

Timmons kicked back in his chair. "Guess that went better than it could have."

Jordan shook her head. "I don't know who had the stellar idea to send North on this assignment. He was touchy enough before his son died."

"No one ever claimed Parliament is clever, Jordan. Their sole motivation—" DuBois broke off with a look in my direction.

I considered reminding DuBois that her opinions were her own as long as she did not violate the anti-obscenity regulations, but my database indicated telling her might not allay her concerns.

Venetia Jordan pushed back her chair and stood. "You'd better change, Tim. Let's get that shuttle on the ground and get this over with."

They left.

I was not truly alone with my drone hovering at my side.

Once this assignment ended, I could return to the Consortium Training Center on New Triton, receive my infusion of nanodevices, and resume my training and my duties.

I would not be alone there, either.

Taking my helmet and datapads from the corner, I started for the ship's hangar bay, suppressing the desire to sigh at the prospect of retrieving the other Recorder's body and drone—if she had indeed died.

We would return with the data, any survivors, the Recorder, and her drone.

But I would see the stars.

The moon's moon gleamed clear and bright, and I stood transfixed by the canopy of stars, their faint colors shining against the velvet vastness of space. Ceres hovered above the horizon, a pale, blue speck, while *Thalassa*'s lights flashed overhead, only a few degrees below the orange point of New Triton. My drone's tendril gently twined about my shoulders, and my implant magnified the deep sounds of space. The stars' dissonance rumbled underneath the team's voices and my own pounding heart. I smiled at the beauty of it—

Jagged pain shattered the stillness.

I staggered slightly, and for half of a second, anger splintered through me. The blame, however, was mine. I had allowed the sky to distract me from my task. Turning away from the heavens, I dimmed the invisible light and muted sounds inaudible to human ears. My drone hovered at my side, a delicate tendril still wound about me.

After triggering a calming release of neurotransmitters, I checked my connection to the six additional drones. All functioned properly, and their perspectives created a kaleidoscope of light and shadow in my internal feed. Satisfaction with the successful check almost erased the mortification of the reprimand.

Almost.

I clenched gloved hands and crossed to the metal access point. Sand and rock crunched under my boots when I passed Timmons, whose shadow reached across Pallas's red-orange crust toward the dimness beyond our lights. My drone released me when I stopped three meters from the heavy, sealed hatch.

"Already told you," Timmons was saying. "Not a moon."

"Of *course* it's a moon, Tim." Zhen DuBois gestured up at the sky. "Just because it's a moon's moon doesn't make it a moonlet."

Spanos kept his attention on the hatch. "Who knew chem engineers and comm specialists were such astronomy experts? D'y'think maybe we can stop arguing about the moon and get on with this?"

"Moonlet," Timmons said. "And the hatch's too corroded. Have to blast it."

DuBois snorted. "Moonlet isn't even a real word."

I did not correct her. A faulty understanding of astronomical terms was immaterial to our assignment.

"Never mind, Zhen." Jordan made another attempt to open the locking mechanism. "You're right, Tim. We'll need to blow the hatch. Grab Alec's pack."

Her voice crackled slightly through the communications assembly, which it should not have done. Accessing the network through my implant, I modified the feed, and the static disappeared.

Timmons crossed into the shuttle's lights and grabbed the pack. "Time to work your magic, Alec." He tossed it to Spanos, then bowed with a flourish, despite his armored suit. "Blow something up and get us in there."

Spanos dropped the pack, disturbing the oxidized surface. Red dust and fine, black sand billowed up like a miniature nebula, shimmering in the shuttle's lights. The interplay of shadows and light momentarily distracted me, even as the sky had. I wrestled my thoughts under control, focusing on Spanos as he connected wires and explosives to the metal.

"Hate working in a suit and gloves," Spanos muttered. "I can't hear the thing set. Can't feel it, either."

"It's your choice." Jordan straightened, gloved hands on her lower back. "There's enough oxygen, but if you don't mind frostbite and the smell of sulfur, maybe some residual radiation, go ahead. Just don't expect any sympathy."

"Don't do it, Alec," DuBois interjected.

Not even my drone deciphered Spanos's incoherent reply.

"You do know he's not stupid, right?" Timmons asked. "Although sometimes—"

"Don't worry, Zhen." Jordan hit Timmons on the shoulder. I did not believe she intended violence, so I did not tag the incident.

"Of course." DuBois did not clarify whether she spoke to Jordan or Timmons. "We just need to be careful. They didn't stock Max's infirmary very well."

Timmons scanned the horizon and checked his weapon again. "No need for a full hospital when this isn't really a rescue mission. Same reason they didn't bother sending marines."

"Should've just sent drones," Spanos said under his breath.

"They sent *her*."

Jordan spun to face DuBois. "Enough, Zhen," she snapped. "We've been over that already."

I inclined my head. It might not have been the correct motion, for she frowned in response.

The communications link magnified Timmons's huff. "This is a waste of time, J. It's a safe bet no one's alive down there. It's an even safer bet it's not going to be pretty. Like I said, she'll slow us down." He tipped his head at me. "No offense, Recorder."

Body language was a strong determiner of meaning. I stood tall to project confidence. "I do not take offense."

Someone exhaled sharply in what my database indicated was most likely disbelief, which was unfair. I had been truthful.

The glare from the floodlights obscured Jordan's facial expression. "Survivors? No, probably not, but their families deserve to know."

Timmons shrugged. "As long as we're getting paid."

"Done," Spanos announced as he tucked the equipment back into his pack. "Clear back."

We took shelter next to the shuttle, and I modified the communication assemblies to muffle the sound. A cloud of dust rose, and small shards of plastic and metal flew out, landing short of where we crouched. As expected, Spanos had efficiently set the charges, only destroying the hinges and locking mechanism. I reset the communication links while he and Timmons hefted the metal disc and set it on the sand.

Unjustifiable apprehension rose inside me, so I released another small dose of neurotransmitters and stole another peek at the sky before triple-checking the drones' coding and mechanical systems. Everything was operational. I focused on the hole in the ground.

Shadows within the access tube were deeper than the blackness of the horizon. They seemed to leech into the light more than the light penetrated the darkness. At Jordan's nod, I sent down the larger drones.

"I'd never want to live underground," Spanos said. "Domes are bad enough."

No one spoke for a moment.

"Let's get this done." Jordan pivoted and stepped onto the ladder. With a casual salute, she disappeared into the darkness. DuBois followed.

Timmons secured his weapon's strap on his shoulder. "Go ahead, Alec. After you."

With a groan, Spanos started down.

"Recorder?" Timmons asked.

I lowered myself into the dark.

The drones' light gleamed in a shrinking circle below, and thick shadows swallowed me as I climbed down and down. At last, I stepped off the final rung, swinging my arms to restore feeling to the fatigued muscles while Timmons and the remaining drones finished their descent.

The floor was level, the walls precisely smooth and perfectly plumb, although they arched three meters above us to create a seamless ceiling. The tunnel extended into darkness so deep it appeared solid. Light from the drones brightened only the immediate space, and dust motes drifted in and out of the shadows, glimmering in the air.

"Welcome to the bowels of the beast," Timmons growled.

Spanos snorted and continued inspecting his weapon.

"Keep your helmets on," DuBois reminded us unnecessarily while she checked the drones' panels and synchronized her datapad with the smallest of the six. "The system seems to have maintained the seal from the outside, but filters and scrubbers aren't working right. There's a lot of particulate matter in the air, and we still don't know what went wrong."

"That really clears things up, Zhen. Thanks." Timmons sounded sincere, though given my database's interpretation, I suspected he was not. "Forward, then?"

"Where else?" Jordan finished adjusting a few buckles. "This leads straight in. We'll be able to make it to the control room from here."

Spanos turned from watching DuBois and scowled at me. "Just keep those evil, mechanical jellyfish out of my way."

I did not respond.

Jordan stepped forward. "Simmer down."

"Those drones give me the heebie-jeebies."

"Heebie-jeebies?" With a bark of laughter, Timmons moved between me and Spanos. He put a gloved hand on the other man's shoulder. "Alec, Alec. Where'd you dig up *that* term? Or is it demolition jargon I haven't heard?"

"You know what *people* like her did to my family." Spanos shoved Timmons's hand away. "Recorders—"

"I said simmer down," Jordan ordered over the protests of the other three.

Spanos stalked away, and Timmons sped up and caught him by the arm, forcing him around to meet his eyes. Neither spoke. Then Spanos nodded once before he crossed to wait at the edge of the dark.

My drone pulled up his file. His perception of a familial misfortune explained his antipathy, yet I found no evidence of actual mistreatment. Perhaps the confining darkness triggered his emotional outburst, but whatever the cause, I made an official recommendation of clemency in my ongoing log.

After consideration, I directed the other drones to stay a greater distance from the group but to compensate with a tighter zoom. Antagonizing team members would unnecessarily alter the group dynamic.

I would not interfere. I knew my purpose and my place.

Taking a deep breath, I followed Spanos and Timmons into the shadows.

03

PERSONAL RECORD: RECORDER ZETA4542910-95451E

PALLAS STATION
478.1.7.06

The dark was oppressive. It should not have been since several drones were broadcasting full-spectrum light, but even with my shadow drone's interface, the predominant color remained grey. Our suits' mottled colors blended into the shadows, and the thermoregulatory material masked the team members' heat signatures. Not even my ability to interpret infrared light made the darkness less impenetrable.

We continued in our mobile sphere of illumination through the passage, angling down, turning several times, winding deep into Pallas's interior. Color-coded hatches and doors with old-fashioned hinges appeared at regular intervals on both the left and the right. We had traveled one and a third kilometers when we encountered our first difficulty. Debris from the collapsed ceiling blocked the way.

Jordan glanced back at Spanos. "How long would it take us to dig through here?"

"Not too long, but . . ." He gestured at me. "Can she send drones to take a look at the ceiling?"

"What are you thinking?"

"This wasn't an accident."

I sent two drones to inspect the blockage. As their thin, metallic arms collected material for testing, they dislodged tiny pieces and triggered a cascade of dust and debris.

"Alexander Spanos is correct. Neither the precise scoring on the ceiling nor the debris in the passage indicates a seismic collapse. This was intentional, although structural integrity appears intact."

"Not that a Recorder has any business having an opinion," DuBois said.

Spanos ran his fingers up and down the strap securing his weapon. "Someone did this on purpose, but we should be able to shift it. Shouldn't take too long."

Jordan nodded. "Let's get this cleared. We'll figure out the whys later."

All four of them set to work moving the larger pieces, and within seven minutes, they had created an opening.

Then, Jordan's eyes studied me. I searched my database and decided she was concentrating. "Recorder? Can your drones get through?"

"The largest will not fit."

"I don't think we can make it much larger without destabilizing the whole pile."

Leaving any of my drones did not please me, but I said, "You are correct. However, the Elders wisely allowed for redundancy."

She and Timmons stepped back, and I sent the smaller drones through the opening. We crawled after them to the other side, deeper into the darkness, leaving the damage behind, but the debris and fine, silty dust grew thicker as we progressed. Larger flakes, which either shimmered like mica or dully swallowed the light, varied from smooth to rippled and ranged from three millimeters to as large as my hand. What might have once been white fabric protruded from one drift, but since it was not Consortium grey, I did not send a drone to investigate. Clusters of oval-shaped matter, each approximately a quarter meter long, lay at random intervals. The air vents—some empty, some not—angled down into the tunnel, quiet and still, save for our passage.

Spanos glowered at me, though the sediment was not my doing. "Dust's deep."

"Don't know why it's so thick." Timmons squinted into the shadows ahead. "Place went dark only two years ago."

Jordan stopped and pointed at the tunnel floor. "What does this look like to you?"

The silence stretched out even as the darkness did.

Timmons cleared his throat. "Looks like tracks, J."

"Not funny," Spanos sputtered.

"He's right," DuBois said. "And if those are tracks, something else was in these passages, too. Or is. Something pretty large. Not bipedal."

Spanos spun to face DuBois. "What sort of 'not bipedal'? I don't want to run into the wrong sort of—"

"Wrong sorts? Like, what, exactly? There isn't any 'wrong sort' here, Alec." Timmons snorted. "I doubt they brought 'wrong sorts' on purpose, and there weren't any life forms on this rock to begin with. You watch too many vids."

Jordan told me to move to the center of the group, and the four of them again raised their weapons. I sent the smaller drones further ahead and behind. My shadow drone's presence should have been reassuring, but uneasiness prickled through me.

The dark stretched on. Delicate clouds drifted upward with each footstep, sparkling in the weapons' targeting beams, shimmering around the edges of the drone's light, and lending an eerie beauty to the emptiness of the tunnel. Only the hum of mechanical devices, our muffled steps, and the metallic jangle of equipment broke the silence.

DuBois checked her datapad. "Access to administration areas coming up on our left."

We reached the door, and Timmons spun the heavy steel wheel to access another set of dark corridors. Very little dust had accumulated, and I detected no evidence of recent human presence. Following the corridor toward the research and administrative areas, we reached the massive doors to the station's central control room. Jordan pried open the panel and inserted an override device.

The doors swung open, exposing another well of nearly tangible blackness. At Jordan's signal, I sent in the drones. Their beams could not penetrate the room's depths, but when the motion sensors detected them, overhead lighting flickered on with an electrical buzz.

Timmons whistled.

The engineers had left the natural formations on the ceiling, and stalactites hung like teeth over the abandoned access terminals. From what I could see, the room, like the second set of hallways, was clean, though shadows obscured its corners.

Jordan held her weapon ready. "Recorder, central station is over there. Go ahead and plug in. We'll do a quick sweep of the room first, then check for survivors. Let's move."

I proceeded to the center console's data port, and pulled smooth black coils from my pack, attaching them first to a drone. If the system had not been so old, I could have accessed the data from the ship. However, given the cost of creating an underground research station on an uninhabited moon orbiting a gas giant, and given the sophistication of its individual computers, budgetary constraints seemed improbable. The scientists must have chosen the archaic system to limit external access.

The last of the cabling in place, initialization screens flickered, and projections glowed, further illuminating the vast control area. A three-dimensional display rose over the flat workspace next to me, twisting upward like a strand of DNA. Computers throughout the chamber flashed briefly, then went dark again, but the drones successfully accessed administrative and scientific records. Information sped across the AAVA drone's translucent screen as files streamed to the ship and through my implant into my shadow drone's external storage. With all the data coursing through my mind, Jordan and DuBois's approach failed to register until Jordan spoke near my ear.

"How's it going?"

"Having just established the connection—"

"I should be the one doing that—"

"Ease up, Zhen," Jordan said. "The Consortium is authorized to access the data. Get what you can, Recorder."

"DuBois's assistance will speed the process."

DuBois did not reply but powered up a display near mine. Jordan made her way to the center of the room, while the two men investigated the perimeter and outer consoles. Timmons prowled the walls as Spanos wove in and out of freestanding consoles, their flickering displays casting warped yellow and cyan images on his suit.

Numbers, letters, words, sentences, paragraphs, and diagrams raced through my mind while I tracked the station's Recorder. She was dead, as the Elders suspected, her death but a note only mentioned in passing. Indignation with a tinge of regret flashed through me. Why had she been afforded so little dignity? She was as human as I—as anyone else. After her years of service, did she not merit more than a mere footnote?

Her body had been placed in a medical pod and secured in her quarters with her drone. I needed to retrieve them before we left.

My drone placed a weighted tentacle on my shoulders, and I rested against it while I stored the information in its memory and sent the files to my computer laboratory on *Thalassa*. I turned my focus to the information Jordan had requested. I found it. *Only five?* After a brief internal debate, I sent the information to Dr. Maxwell, without waiting for direction.

Keeping my tone even, I said aloud, "There are survivors in the medical bay, Jordan. The station director sent personnel into stasis."

Spanos's footsteps slowed. "Anyone *not* make it?"

"Most everyone did, Alec," DuBois answered. "There won't be bodies all over the place."

When Spanos appeared unsettled, I verified her statement. "Records state the seventeen individuals who died immediately prior to the incident were recycled properly. Since the directors stayed behind to trigger the self-destruct, they will not have been processed. Finding their remains is a distinct possibility."

Spanos was not mollified by my assurance, if I correctly interpreted the glare he cast in my direction.

Timmons whistled again. "Seventeen dead before? From what?"

DuBois's fingers sped over the controls. "Unknown virus?" she exclaimed. "Moons and stars!"

"Get Max on the line," Jordan ordered.

"Already here." Dr. Maxwell's deep voice rumbled over the link from *Thalassa*'s infirmary. "The Recorder pinged me, sent me her preliminary information. It does seem like a virus took them out. Keep those helmets on. First question is, pods or tanks, Zhen?"

"Mobile stasis pods."

"After two years of potentially poor conditions, how many do Edwards, Williams, and I need to prep for? How many can we keep asleep in the cargo hold?"

There was a pause while DuBois searched. I did not speak, though I knew the answer.

"Eighty-three pods, only five still functioning. And the power's fluctuating."

Dr. Maxwell's voice rumbled, "Two years in stasis with fluctuating power could have damaged internal organs past the point . . . This infirmary only has three medtanks. But we can't just let people die."

"We'll do what we can, Max," Jordan said sharply. "They should have planned for that when they stocked *Thalassa*, even if they didn't expect survivors." Her tone grew sharper still. "They implied lives were the priority, but they really only wanted data and equipment. Not your fault, not our fault."

"I'll need any specific information not available in the main logs," Dr. Maxwell added.

"All right. Tim, you head over. Recorder, pull up maps and go with him. Leave the drones behind to collect the data. We'll finish up here then join you. Zhen, check for alternate routes out. Stasis pods won't fit the way we came in."

Spanos rounded another console. "There's not much to do here, Jordan, since her drones are handling the data. I wonder if—"

He froze, staring at the control panel on his left, so I sent a drone to check. My stomach tightened. I knew my duty. Leaving the terminal and the attached drones, I forced my feet to where he stood.

"Moons and stars!" DuBois whispered. She, too, must have seen the feed.

Spanos cleared his throat, the communication link amplifying the sound. "We've found someone."

The first body sprawled across the control panel; the second lay tumbled on the floor. While the room's low temperature had prevented complete decay, the Elders' warning about the possibility of finding remains had not adequately prepared me for withered, leathery skin, or for empty, clawlike hands grasping at nothing but air.

Focused as I was on the still forms before me, I startled at Jordan's voice. "Can you ID them?"

Spanos backed away. "Go ahead, Recorder."

I fought an inclination to run but forced myself to concentrate on what I needed to do. Stepping resolutely to the body stretched over the console, I reached for the ID badge clipped to its—*his*—jacket. My hand stopped shaking, and I felt a shallow burst of pride at my control. Perhaps no one had observed the trembling. Perhaps it was not even recorded.

"John Westruther, Station Director," I read.

Jordan fingered the butt of her weapon. "And the other?"

I sent my drone to flip the corpse on the floor. It . . . *she* landed with a hollow thud, and her lab coat tore under my boot. I knelt to read her badge, trying not to look at her face while I gently pushed back the long, auburn braids, their vibrancy mocking the corpse's condition. She frowned in her ID picture, but according to my database, her eyes were not unhappy. I angled the badge, and her image shifted to profile, bearing little resemblance to the face on the ground.

"Dr. Georgette SahnVeer, Director of Research."

Dr. Maxwell's voice sounded. "Biopsy samples, please."

I summoned an AAVA drone. Timmons joined us, though DuBois remained at the computer.

Spanos shifted. "Shouldn't we recycle them or bury them or something?"

Timmons snorted. "Bury them where?"

The drone extended long needlelike appendages from metal arms attached to its underside and began to collect the samples.

"Our priorities are data and survivors, so no," Jordan said. "Zhen, got anything for me?"

"Not yet, J. There's too much data coming in."

The corpses drew my gaze as a magnet pulls iron. I found it difficult to look away. The light seemed tinged with green, and the room dimmed around the edges. I could hear the others talking, but my heart pounded in my ears.

Someone said, "Shut it, Tim."

My shadow drone whirred near my head and administered a brief reprimand. I snapped upright.

Timmons tapped my shoulder. "We should head out, Recorder. Got those maps yet?"

Stepping away from him—from them all, living and dead—I accessed the maps through my implant, reviewed the path, and waved an arm in the appropriate direction. "It is this way."

He shook his head and moved to the door.

Only my personal drone accompanied me to the medical bay. The others remained behind to transmit information to the ship. Jordan and Spanos began another sweep of the immense cavern, and DuBois continued to sort data.

The smooth hall was not lit, and with my drone the only light source, our shadows threw sharp shapes onto the concrete floor and over the walls' intricate murals.

"Your drone shocked you," Timmons started without preamble. "Why?"

I cringed, then stifled my response. His observation would, most likely, exacerbate eventual consequences for my reaction in the control room. It was not, however, his fault. I should not have visibly reacted to the reprimand.

Measuring my words carefully, I said, "The correction was necessary, due to my emotional response."

"What? An 'emotional response' to touching dead bodies?"

Fear trickled through me in anticipation of the Elders'

disappointment. I tamped it down. "Emotion influences the record. I must remain neutral."

His mouth tightened. "Emotions are normal. One of the things that makes us human."

"She's a Recorder, Tim," DuBois said over the communications link from the control room. "They aren't quite human."

"Aren't quite—" Timmons glared back up the hallway, though DuBois would be unaware of it at such a distance. "She's as human as you. Actually, right now—"

"That's enough," Jordan intervened. "Both of you."

We continued in silence for a tenth of a kilometer before he spoke again. "Don't know how anyone'd want to live underground like a worm, surrounded by nothing but grey." He cast me a sidelong glance. "Doesn't seem to bother you, though. Or do they punish you for liking color, too?"

I ignored his reference to the reprimand but was pleased at the opportunity to correct his misconception. "Contrary to what most citizens believe, members of the Consortium appreciate harmony and art. Have you not toured and seen our conservatory, which was designed to be aesthetically pleasing? However"—I looked from him to the ornate scrollwork on the corridor walls—"we see what you do not." I could not help smiling as I sent a few commands to my shadow drone.

"You smile?" A grin spread across his face. "Stars, I didn't—"

The light shifted abruptly from full spectrum to black. Timmons swore. Then, in hushed tones, he cursed again. I did not know if his outburst would be sufficient to incur fines for violating anti-obscenity laws, but my assignment was to record, not interpret.

"What's going on?" Jordan snapped.

"My apologies. I should have warned you."

DuBois spat, "What did you do, Recorder?"

"You could see this before . . . ?" Timmons's words trailed into silence.

"See what?" Jordan demanded.

"Art." Timmons had stopped in the middle of the hall and was staring at the intricate spirals bordering delicately painted line art of creatures from history and legend. "And it's beautiful."

"Art? We don't have time for *art*," Jordan snapped over the communication link. "And Tim? Watch it."

"Sure." Timmons remained focused on the murals.

I suppressed a sigh. My attempts to keep from negatively impacting the team had failed. I alerted Timmons before easing back to the visible spectrum. We were striding down the hall again before the light returned to full strength.

"How'd that get there? The station's Recorder?"

"I do not know," I said. "Her file did not indicate that art was one of her personal interests."

"Recorders have personal interests?"

"Yes." I did not elaborate.

"What else can you see?"

For approximately four and a half seconds, I considered my response. "The drone enhances aural and visual input and superimposes invisible light on my visual cortex, which is useful in a variety of situations. Information can be used to determine physical well-being or to ascertain the veracity of testimonies, though that is not as reliable as other measurements. While synchronization can—"

"You can chatter away to your heart's content once we're back on *Thalassa*. Keep the link clear." Jordan's verbal reprimand stung almost as much as a drone's.

My face grew warm at yet another mistake, but I triggered transmitters too late. My drone misinterpreted my fluctuating readings and disciplined me before I saw it move.

Timmons grabbed my arm and pulled me to his other side, away from the drone. His eyes flashed. "What was that for?"

Swallowing personal dissatisfaction, I slid my arm from his hand. "A mild correction for another emotional reaction."

Somehow, his smile did not seem sincere, though it did reveal his dimple. "I'll take your 'emotional reaction' as a compliment."

Jordan growled another admonition.

If I believed I was mortified before, I was wrong. Addressing him without invitation, I began, "Timmons, I meant nothing improper . . ." I trailed off when the drone approached for a third time.

"Not your fault. I have that effect on—" He stepped around me and addressed my drone. "There's no call for that."

He cried out. Disciplining of citizens was rare. It could not have been accidental. It was also the first time anyone had attempted to stand between me and a reprimand. I did not know how to interpret his action.

"Tim! What's going on?" Jordan demanded.

The drone then reprimanded me twice. Avoiding discipline always increased the consequence, which Timmons would not have known. During the seven seconds it took to even out my respiration, Jordan's inquiries grew more insistent. Timmons did not immediately answer. Unaccustomed to even such a mild reprimand as he had received, his breath came in ragged gasps. He leaned against the wall, watching me and my drone, eyes narrowed.

"Her drone—"

"Nathaniel Timmons did nothing wrong," I said. This was not, strictly speaking, a true statement. His actions, however, were well meant and should not be further punished, so I amended my ongoing report to recommend clemency again. "He attempted to assist me."

"Assist you?"

"I have entered his kindness into the record."

"Tim, you all right?" Spanos asked.

"I'm fine." Timmons still watched me, his expressions shifting rapidly.

Cross-referencing them to files in my database, I identified the most likely emotions as surprise, pain, anger, and admiration. Surprise, pain, and anger were reasonable. Admiration was puzzling, but immaterial. I looked away.

"If you're fine, Tim, just get to the medbay," Jordan said. "No point in Alec and me walking this room again. Zhen, you about finished?"

"Yes. Done all I can here. Got the maps on my datapad."

"Then we're on our way."

"Sure we shouldn't, you know"—Spanos hesitated—"do something with the bodies?"

"No."

"It feels disrespectful to leave them," he protested. After a moment of silence, he added, "Well, it does."

Timmons and I reached the medical bay, and although the inhabitants had been in stasis for years, my uneasiness returned. I triggered calming neurotransmitters and stepped to the control panel outside the double doors. I could not continue self-administering transmitters at this rate. The Elders would be certain to mention it, and the probability of receiving either further training or desirable assignments would plummet. My drone rested one tentacle on my shoulder, and I closed my eyes for two seconds, accepting its comfort, watching the shadowy world in restful, invisible light.

I opened my eyes and stepped through the wide doors into the medical bay. It stretched like a hallway, curving to our right, fading into darkness beyond the reach of the drone's single light source. Once inside, I used the main access port to locate the five functioning pods and activate the thin, blue safety lights at the base of the walls. After stabilizing power by diverting resources from units no longer registering nanoactivity, Timmons and I followed my drone past three-meter cylindrical pods, now darkened and dull, which protruded from their alcove-like slots. Single rows lined each side of the hall, reminding me of the retractable beds in my childhood dormitory.

The newer pods had transparent windows, but my drone's light was insufficient to reveal what, if anything, remained inside. The further back we went, the older the models, and those with windows gave way to solid metal canisters. A few control panels still emitted faint light, indicating the nanodevices and enzymes had not yet finished breaking down the remains. Perhaps, had Parliament approved a trip even a few ten-days earlier, the malfunctions could have been prevented and those lives saved. I swallowed.

"It's a display of coffins," Timmons said under his breath.

Spanos gave an incomprehensible reply, which I did not bother to replay. There would be time on our return trip to decipher his words.

Timmons and I continued. Only the uneven rhythm of our boots broke the silence. We rounded the bend, but the blue safety lights disappeared ahead of us, obscured by shallow drifts of fine dust. My chest tightened. The silt's presence made me uneasy. I pulled my attention from hidden lights back to the active pods' glowing controls and the section's command node, nestled between the final section of pods. Dr. Maxwell required more precise medical information than the main computers could provide. Ignoring Timmons, I set down my pack and pulled out another black data cable.

Dust dimmed the console's main display, and while my attempt to clear the screen only smudged the panel, I managed to pry open a small port and connect the cabling. The display brightened as my drone communicated with the system.

I had done at least this much correctly.

While the information streamed to the ship, I activated a secondary unit and studied the power logs, which indicated that shortly after people had entered the pods, geothermal power had been redirected from the pre-programmed sequence. I was adding the anomalous files to my data queue for further study when the blue safety lights flickered.

"Did you do that?" Timmons said sharply.

I shook my head but added for Jordan's benefit, "I do not know why the power to the floor lights fluctuated. I will investigate."

The lights flickered again, then dimmed, but before I resumed my work, I caught a glimpse of movement in my peripheral vision. In the shadows beyond Timmons, several meters beyond the last pod, a large shape separated itself from the darkest corner, rising slightly from the floor where the emergency lights were buried in silt. I attempted to overlay information from my drone, but it sent me nothing useful. I stepped toward the shadows.

"Going somewhere?"

"I thought I saw . . ."

"Where?"

"Over there." I gestured behind him, toward the deepest patch of darkness.

He turned, his weapon's targeting beam sweeping the medical bay's farthest reaches, and when it found the shape, he let out a hiss of profanity.

Over the communications link, DuBois asked, "Do I need to switch feeds?"

I did not answer.

Timmons held the weapon steady. "J, Alec, we got company. Get over here. Hustle."

The impossibly large insect cocked its head, its eyes refracting the light, and my throat constricted. My drone, still connected to the medical systems, responded to my fear by feeding data on invertebrates straight to my neural implant. I fought to swallow.

"What's going on?" Jordan's voice rose in pitch. "Tim? Recorder? Update! Now!"

Their respiratory patterns changed, and the communication link picked up the sound of pounding boots.

"Switching feeds to her drone." DuBois's words came unevenly.

Timmons held his weapon ready but did not fire. I wrenched my shadow drone from the computer terminal and, my hands trembling, shoved it toward the thing waving antennae at us. Only the drone's gyroscopes and artificial intelligence kept its trajectory accurate.

DuBois choked. "Moons and stars—that's a cockroach!"

"A *what*?" Jordan demanded. "Tim, what's going on?"

DuBois reiterated, "A roach, J—a giant, spacing roach! Drone says it's close to two meters long!"

My mouth was too dry, throat too constricted, for me to confirm her analysis. A Recorder should not panic. My neural implant attempted to adjust my brain chemistry without guidance and triggered sudden nausea.

The giant roach's antennae twitched as it watched my drone approach. It clicked its . . . mouthparts. I had read the relevant terminology moments before, but the words evaporated into nothing.

The creature did not move until my drone struck it with a brilliant beam of light. Then, it snatched my drone out of the air and crushed it. A blinding flash flooded my visual cortex, and I screamed.

Pain ricocheted through my skull, and I dropped to the floor, my lungs seizing up. When the agony subsided, I lay gasping for oxygen. Tremors prevented me from standing, so I rolled over to my front and watched the creature from between Timmons's tall, black boots, my pulse thundering in my ears.

Without my drone, darkness pressed in, and the blue lights illuminated only the creature's underbelly, jointed legs, and serrated feet, though its smooth exoskeleton gleamed in the targeting beam. It reared up on its back four legs, then dropped onto all six and started toward us.

Timmons fired several rapid bursts, which only slowed it. Shifting the heavy weapon, he switched rounds. A blazing incendiary blast hit the cockroach straight between its great compound eyes. Momentum carried it forward, skidding toward us over the concrete floor, stopping several meters away. As the thing began to twitch, a detached part of my brain recalled data about roaches surviving without heads. Cursing under his breath, Timmons fired once more. With a small explosion of matter, the roach stilled, steam rising in tendrils above its carapace.

"Report!" Jordan called, dull and muffled, over the communications assembly.

"I'm all right, J. Not sure about her, though." Something was wrong with Timmons's voice.

Targeting beams flashed. Jordan and Spanos rounded the corner as I pushed myself up to a sitting position, shaking with the effort. DuBois skidded to a halt behind them.

Timmons knelt beside me, attention shifting between his teammates and the twitching form. "See that thing?"

"Stars above . . ." Jordan kept her weapon trained on the smoking shape which oozed thick, yellow fluid onto the tiles. "I see what's left of it."

"Yeah." Timmons touched my arm. "You all right?"

I blinked up at him. He tried to wipe my faceplate clean, but a thick smear obscured the lower left-hand side.

"Your nose is bleeding," he said.

Dr. Maxwell's voice rumbled, but I could not understand the words.

Jordan answered, "No, Max, it's not too bad. But my ears are still ringing from that scream. Recorder, status?"

My throat felt raw, so I shook my head. Blood trickled down my upper lip into my mouth. I licked my lips and gagged.

Keeping hold of the weapon's grip with her right hand, Jordan tucked the butt under her arm as she and Timmons hoisted me to my feet. I shut my eyes to block the way the hall swam. Jordan let go, but Timmons gripped my elbow to steady me.

"What happened?" Jordan asked.

I could not summon the words to explain that nothing sounded right. Their voices lacked clarity and depth. I opened my eyes. Nothing looked right, either. Colors were duller, and the invisible light—

Anxiety pinched my chest. The light was gone. How could I function without infrared and ultraviolet?

"It tore her drone apart." Timmons's smooth tenor sounded less bright. "Seems to have done something to her."

"It must have sent some sort of shock through her implants," DuBois sneered. "*I* wouldn't want those things."

Jordan glared past me. "Not now, Zhen."

I needed to focus, to redirect their attention. The medical bay's system was failing. I managed to rasp, "The pods."

After a short delay Jordan answered, "Yes," and Timmons's fingers tightened on my arm.

"Alec, Tim, keep an eye out." She gestured back at the encroaching shadows. "Recorder, we need those drones."

And suddenly, I understood my lack of clarity—why nothing was right. Panic threatened to crush me like a black hole. I whispered, "No."

She took a step toward me, scowl visible through her faceplate. "What do you mean, 'No'?"

"I cannot." Fighting down a flood of panic as intense as the pain, I babbled, "I cannot—I cannot sense the drones. I cannot record."

I counted ten seconds before DuBois laughed. "Of all the useless things! A Recorder who can't record?"

She was not incorrect.

Dr. Maxwell's voice cut through my thoughts. "Clarify, Recorder."

"I cannot access any of the drones. Everything is dull."

"What does that mean?" The doctor's deep voice rumbled. "How do you feel? Any pain?"

I exhaled slowly, then swallowed. "I am dizzy and nauseated. Pain is receding." The statement was not untruthful, but to explain further would have distracted attention from the survivors.

"She's pretty shaky," Timmons added.

"For right now, then, stay out of the way," Dr. Maxwell ordered. I closed my eyes and tried to see his voice, to feel the wavelengths. I could not. "Head straight to the infirmary when you get back. Bring what's left of the drone if you can."

Spanos skirted the dead insect and walked over to my mangled drone. He kept his weapon raised as he nudged a limp, metallic tendril with the toe of his boot. "It's too big."

"Eject primary memory," I said. "There is a small panel under the main screen."

DuBois appeared in my line of sight. "It's all right, Alec. I'll get it."

While DuBois pried my drone's panel open to retrieve its memory, Jordan glanced back at Timmons. "See anything else?"

He released my arm, stepped to my right, and peered into the shadows from whence the roach had emerged. "No."

"All right," Jordan said. "Let's get those functional pods to the ship. Max, the Recorder stabilized them before she lost her drone, but if we have issues, you'll have to talk us through it. Recorder, sit. Over there, out of the way. Alec, check the pods. Make sure nothing's jammed. Tim, keep an eye out for more of those things. Zhen, find that alternate route."

"On it." DuBois stepped over my feet to tuck the memory core into the pack, all without a glance in my direction, then she took my place at the console.

Bracing my back against the wall, I slid down, facing the small drifts of silt which obscured the blue lights while DuBois tapped on the keyboard beside me and Spanos inspected the five pods with glowing screens. Jordan and Timmons stood alert, watching the shadows in either direction. The shape on the floor drew attention. The steam had dissipated, and the oozing had slowed, though its abdomen pulsed slightly. I shuddered.

Timmons had been right about me. I was a liability. Mentally cataloguing the distinct discrepancies, the differences without my drone, I tried to ignore the metallic taste of blood. Visual acuity had decreased by at least twenty-five percent. Everything was flatter, greyer, blurrier. Even worse, I was not disciplined for my anxiety, for my drone . . . my drone was gone. Panic swelled in my throat as I squinted into the medical bay's shadows, so much deeper, so much darker than before. I shut my eyes to block out the smear on my faceplate, the shadows, the pods, and the spattered mass in front of me. But with my eyes shut, for the first time in nine years, I saw nothing.

The others' voices waxed and waned, but my pulse pounded in my ears, overlaying their words. I . . . I could not release neurotransmitters . . . How else was I to regain control of my emotions?

"I don't know, Jordan!" DuBois was saying.

"Just do it, Zhen."

"Looks like they just have maglocks, J. No bolts to throw. Computer should release them. But how are we going to get these pods out of here?" Spanos asked. "They won't fit through that cave-in."

"I told you I'm on it." DuBois's fingers made tiny taps on the keypad. "Good thing I managed to finish uploading the information."

"The Recorder's the one who set it up," Jordan said.

"Well, she can't access anything, and now we can't even get her blasted drones out."

"Focus, Zhen." Jordan's boots stepped further away. "Stop sniping at the Recorder. Find the way out."

Though dull, their voices stabbed my head like knives. I had no drone to mute them. But Zhen DuBois was not incorrect.

I was a Recorder, sent to retrieve information and keep records. I opened my eyes. Swallowing bile and bracing one hand against the wall for stability, I forced myself to stand. Another wave of pain crashed over me, and everything swam. I drew in a breath, held it, and released it.

"I must redirect the drones."

No one responded. While DuBois continued to type, the other three remained focused on the shadows, and so I repeated myself.

Jordan did not look back at me. "Sure."

"Just don't mess up what we're doing," Spanos added. "Or anything else."

I attempted to ignore the throbbing in my head and the trickle of blood dripping ferrous salt into my mouth. Using the softer side of my glove, I scrubbed dust off the smaller projecting display. Accessing the input pad, I began a trace to the drone in the control room. The process was inordinately slower than thought. I needed my interface.

Alone, all gone, echoed in my mind while the others' words pummeled me like meteors. I could not filter out their dialogue. My fingers lagged.

"Is she up to it, Tim?" the doctor was asking.

"I don't know. She's not looking good."

"Let's hope she doesn't make things worse." Spanos knew his words were clearly audible over the link, that they could be recorded. Perhaps he did not care.

Jordan's voice was crisp. "You just worry about getting these pods out of their alcoves in one piece, Alec. Tim, anything?"

"No."

I heard someone pivot, and then Spanos muttered, "Is there any way to tell if there are more of those things nearby?"

"Afraid of a few bugs?"

"Not funny, Timmons," DuBois said. "I can't track them, but I found a way out that bypasses the cave-in. There's a hangar, and—"

"A hangar?" Spanos demanded. "You've got to be kidding. Why didn't we use that in the first place?"

DuBois huffed in response. "We could have, if whoever designed this station hadn't been so paranoid. Trying to enter the hangar from outside triggers a self-destruct sequence."

He pressed, "But from inside we're good?"

"I . . ." She hesitated. "I wouldn't have mentioned it otherwise."

I traced a connection to the AAVA drone plugged into the main console. Data blurred, and it was difficult to focus on the words which flew across the screen. I reduced its speed. If I completed this, perhaps I could redeem myself.

The drone that was physically wired into the control room's computer had to be left behind, but it would continue to stream data back to the ship. Such a loss on my first assignment was undesirable but unavoidable. I directed another drone to retrace our route, retrieve the one we had left in the tunnel, and return to the shuttle. The remaining three would join us as soon as possible.

Jordan's boots sounded in the hallway, out of synchronization with my throbbing temples. Her focus still up the hall, and her weapon still in hand, she nudged Spanos. He startled. "Alec, trade places. Let me try to get the pods free, and you go keep an eye out. Zhen, now that you've found a route, work on those pods. Still clear, Tim?"

"Far as I can see."

The pods had not disengaged, so I accessed the data. While the readout of the second and fifth pods held steady, the fourth indicated erratic life signs. Power for the remaining two flickered unevenly. My earlier estimation that the backup systems were capable of sustaining life support for several hours might have been inaccurate. I glanced back at my mangled drone, clutching at the console when vertigo hit. Before I had lost my drone, I had begun the sequence for release from long-term storage. DuBois had only to activate microantigravity and detach the pods. It should not have taken this long.

Blinking to clear my vision, I entered the final release command myself, then rested against the wall. The five units with life signs detached from their moorings.

DuBois said, "Got it."

Irritation rose at her comment, but I choked it down. Whether she truly believed she had done it or not was immaterial.

Microantigravity systems whined as the windowless metal cylinders slid from their alcoves. Datascreens on the ends displayed vital signs, but my head hurt too much to examine them.

Before I could suggest utilizing my pack's straps to tether the pods together, I heard the comforting hum of drones. For a fraction of a second, I forgot mine had been damaged beyond repair. I spun toward the familiar sound, then staggered against the pod closest to me when another wave of dizziness hit. It careened into one of the docked units, bounced back, and nearly hit Timmons, who dove, rolled, and sprang to his feet. Jordan helped him steady the pod while I shuffled onto my hands and knees, unable to stand.

"What happened?" Dr. Maxwell's voice echoed in my head.

"Nothing," Jordan said. "The Recorder fell."

"Is she all right?" he asked. "And the pods?"

Jordan stepped over and skimmed their flickering screens. "There doesn't appear to be any damage."

Timmons pulled me to my feet and searched my eyes. "Can't tell if she's any worse, Max, but her nose is still bleeding."

"At least the readings haven't changed," DuBois said.

I swallowed another hint of blood and gestured down the hall. "Drones. I heard drones."

Spanos lowered his weapon as the AAVA drones rounded the bend. "You can't have heard them. Unless . . ." His eyes narrowed. "You sure those things in your head aren't working?"

"Are they?" Jordan demanded.

"I do not lie."

Someone made a rude noise. I suspected DuBois, although I had no evidence to support my assumption.

Jordan tilted her head to one side, contemplating the veracity of my statement. "At least you managed to get some of them here."

"I can program them to assist with moving the pods."

Timmons shook his head. "You aren't too steady on your feet."

Jordan stepped close and squinted down at me, as if to see me better, though her records had indicated perfect vision. The light from her helmet sliced painfully at my eyes. "Her pupils aren't dilating properly, Max. What do you think?"

"That she needs to be in the infirmary and off her feet. Stat."

"We'll move faster using the drones." Jordan paused. "All right, Recorder. Give it a shot."

I lurched forward. Spanos stepped out of my way, but Timmons caught my elbow. He helped me to the nearest drone, and I pulled it down to a more accessible level.

Opening the top panel near the camera, I keyed in a code with shaking hands. I had to enter it twice, after which, all three drones obediently unfolded jointed, mechanical arms and grabbed the fronts of the pods.

"Good job," Jordan said. "Let's get out of here. Which way?"

"Through the doors and turn left."

Jordan took the lead again, followed by two drones pulling two pods each. Spanos and DuBois walked in front of the drone pulling a single pod. Timmons and I brought up the rear. We were passing through the double doors when I remembered Spanos's description of the drones as evil, mechanical jellyfish.

The idea of our procession resembling an ancient Earth parade struck me as amusing, with jellyfish drones and pods in place of plumed horses pulling carriages, and the five of us escorting them like honor guards. A low, uneven laugh broke from me, and everyone stopped.

Jordan turned to face me, her eyebrows rising. "Recorder?"

I laughed all the harder.

"Moons and stars," exclaimed DuBois. "She's broken."

And just as suddenly, laughter transitioned into great, gasping sobs. Air singed my lungs, and I stumbled and fell to my knees.

"Max! What do we do?"

"Describe what's happening." His deep voice was a heavy, soothing blanket. "Is she—"

Like a maelstrom in my head, my thundering heartbeat and ragged breath clashed with DuBois's melodic soprano, Dr. Maxwell's rumbling bass, Jordan's sharp commands, Spanos's staccato outbursts, and Timmons's soft croons.

The noise—my head, oh, it hurt. I tried to hold my head to keep my skull intact, but the helmet prevented me.

Timmons knelt before me and grabbed my shoulders. He held me still while Jordan adjusted controls on the front of my suit. My breathing and heart rate slowed. Everything went dark.

I traveled in a moving puddle of light under a dizzying procession of unlit ceiling fixtures, ductwork, grids, and fire suppression units. My head throbbed. Dried tears crusted my cheeks, and my lips tasted of blood. A yellow smear impaired my vision, but rapid blinking did not banish it.

Footsteps and a low mechanical whirr competed with the pulse pounding in my ears. I turned my head and realized I wore a helmet. The smear was on my faceplate. I tried to sit up, but, no, I was tied down.

Panic supplanted pain, and I fought the straps binding me.

"Max?" A man's smooth tenor spoke inside my head. "She's waking up."

"She shouldn't be," a bass rumbled in response.

"Check on her," said a slightly husky, feminine voice.

A man placed his hand on my shoulder, and through another faceplate, green eyes met mine. When his features split in two, I blinked again, forcing myself to see only one image.

"Easy now." The man's mouth moved in time with the voice in my ears.

Communications assembly. The voices were transmitted via a communications assembly in my helmet.

"Look at me, all right?"

I should have recognized him. Or did green eyes matter? I licked my lips and tasted salt. "I am looking."

A dimple flashed. "There you are. How're you feeling?"

"I cannot move." My voice felt gritty. "My head hurts."

"I would guess so. You collapsed, so we strapped you to a pod. We're getting you to Max fast as we can."

"Doors just ahead, on our right," said a second woman.

"She has a pretty voice," I said. "Like sweet tea. Or satin."

"What?" she said. "Moons and stars! You're kidding, right?"

The man's brows drew together. "Do you know where you are? Who we are?"

"I do not . . ." Thinking was like chasing vapor. "You have nice eyebrows. I . . . I do not."

The green eyes widened.

"What's wrong with her?" asked the beautiful soprano voice. "Tell me she's not flirting with you. That's—"

"Enough!" the deep-voiced man and the other woman commanded in unison.

The dimple reappeared. "No eyebrows, but you've got fantastic lashes. Zhen's just jealous."

Someone snorted.

The deep voice rumbled, "She needs medical attention. How much longer?"

"Not sure," said the first woman.

The smooth-voiced woman said, "Through the hangar, to the shuttle, then maybe another kilometer and a half."

"First we have to get through these doors," added yet another male voice, and we slowed to a stop.

There were too many voices.

As the green-eyed man moved away, I remembered. "Timmons. You are Nathaniel Timmons."

He returned to my side. "Yes. Do you remember—"

"Not now, Tim," interrupted the first woman. "Zhen, do you have access codes yet?"

"Not yet," said the soprano. "Alec, I need the extra cables."

A second man appeared in my line of sight and retrieved a pack from next to my head. His lips pinched tightly together, he glared at me from under thick eyebrows before moving away.

The first woman spoke. "The *other* port." Sharpness edged her voice. Jordan. Venetia Jordan.

"There isn't one!" The man had no reason to react so emotionally. He was not the one strapped to a pod.

"There has to be."

"Then *you* find it."

"Fine. Keep an eye out," Jordan snapped. "Tim, I saw movement again, over there."

I stared up at the grey ceiling, images filtering through my mind in a trickle, then a violent flood—CTS *Thalassa*, the team, corpses, stasis pods, the roach, my drone. A tear slid sideways down my temple.

"Blast," Jordan said. "It's not working. Tim, suggestions?"

"You know me and computers, J."

Something slammed against metal. Spanos cursed.

"Easy, Alec," Timmons said. "Zhen? Anything?"

"If the Recorder hadn't fried her brain, she could do something."

"Not helpful." Jordan's rebuke went unanswered. "You said you had access codes."

"Only to the outer doors. They were in Westruther's files."

"Then search someone else's files, for colony's sake. The pods' resources are running low, and those bugs in the corridors have us cut off from any other exit."

"I'm looking!"

"Then find something and get us out of here."

A weapon fired.

Timmons said, "Good eye, Alec."

Training mandated that I remain silent, but I spoke. "Drones."

"What?" Jordan demanded.

"Drones can interface with the doors."

"Or I could blast them," offered Spanos.

"No, thanks," Timmons said. "Zhen told us a blast big enough to clear the doors would trigger the self-destruct."

"How, Recorder?" asked Jordan.

"The AAVA drones are linked to the system through the one I left in the . . . the control room. I must key it in, myself."

"Zhen, can't you—"

"Her stupid drones won't let me in."

Firm footsteps sounded, and Jordan was beside me. Her gaze darted between my eyes before she nodded. "Let's get her down, Tim. She's our best bet."

They unbuckled the straps which held me, but when DuBois called out, Jordan left. Timmons steadied me, and I grabbed onto the hovering pod, as if it were an anchor.

I concentrated to avoid slurring my words. "I will be fine."

Staccato bursts of weapons' fire startled me. I lost my grip and slipped toward the floor.

"Got the voided thing," Jordan said.

Timmons scooped me up and carried me to the nearest drone. Once I was stable, he turned to face the corridor. My gaze followed his.

Not five meters off, several dark masses on the floor oozed thick, yellow matter. Beyond them, on the edges of the light, shadows twitched. I turned back to the drone, opened its access panel, then rested my helmet against its domed top to try to focus.

Timmons gave a short laugh. "Surrounded by gargantuan roaches. Never done this before."

Jordan said, "First time for everything, Tim."

Ignoring the pain and the noise to the best of my compromised ability, I fumbled commands on the tiny keys. The drone tugged its hovering stasis pod to the control panel and pulled me along with it. One long arm extended from its polymer underbelly, connecting with a tinny click. The lights flashed above the massive doors, and with a low metallic growl, they crept open.

"Alec, get the pods in there, now."

Still focused on the dark shapes moving in the hallway, Spanos retreated into the hangar. The drones followed with their pods. I tripped after them. While Jordan and Timmons fired into the corridor, DuBois backed toward the open doors, then they followed. Once inside, Jordan slammed her fist on the control panel, and the doors began to grind shut. Timmons fired at a charging shadow. Clinging to the pod that had pulled me in, I turned to face the hangar's interior and froze.

"Jordan?" I managed.

"Not now!"

Behind me the doors shut with a muffled boom. I choked out her name, "Jordan!"

"What?"

The sudden intake of breath told me the others had turned, had seen the contorting shadows as the insect colony scattered. Dr. Maxwell, monitoring the drones' feed from the ship, uttered what might have been a prayer.

Brown and black carapaces, the smallest a half-meter long, glistened as the insects skittered away from the weapons' targeting beams. The roaring whisper of thousands of pointed feet filled the hangar. Roaches climbed and crawled over each other, layers upon layers of legs and shells and mandibles and antennae and dull black eyes.

Jordan was the first to speak, her voice still and soft. "Zhen, if you start babbling and panicking like before, I will kill you myself. Quickly now, where do we go?"

"Personnel doors are in the back . . . all the way in back." DuBois's voice was barely audible. "We go straight through."

Timmons invoked a deity.

"I saw what just one of those things did to her drone." Spanos's voice cracked. "How can we possibly get through *this*?"

"Tim?" Though Jordan's voice was tight, it remained steady. "Too many for target practice?"

"'Fraid so."

There had to be a way. In my mind, I again saw the roach crush my shadow drone. A wave of pain and nausea rippled through me. But then, I knew. "Fire."

After a brief silence, Timmons chuckled. "Brilliant. If you weren't a Recorder, I'd kiss you."

Jordan moved in front of me and turned to face the others. "Alec, get your pack, see what you and Tim can do. Zhen, you're with me. We'll hold them back if they close in. Recorder, make it brighter, if you can."

"I will try." I disliked that my voice shook. "It will place a heavier load on the power cells."

"Power cells won't matter if we don't get out of here."

The giant room spun, but I maneuvered myself over to the nearest drone's access panel. While the men pulled supplies from their packs, my fingers fumbled commands. Jordan stood at my side, gaze fixed on the multitudes of jointed legs, the pale, almost luminescent young, and the moving, rustling darkness beyond our light.

"Zhen DuBois," I said. "Are you able to access geothermal power and activate hangar lights?"

"I couldn't in the hallway." She did not rebuke me for addressing her out of turn.

"Will you make another attempt now the drones have reestablished connections?"

"On it. It should only take a minute, J," she added.

Jordan did not look over, though she inclined her head. "Good idea, Recorder."

The drones' light brightened, driving the insects back. Within two minutes, DuBois activated the safety lights, which had little effect on the roaches. Instead, it expanded our view of the hangar's infestation. At that moment, the absence of my drone's visual, aural, and olfactory amplification was a comfort.

A distant part of my brain insisted on sending a drone to gather samples. Since I could not, I took comfort in the probability that the dust consisted of decomposed exoskeletons. I attempted to step back, away from the shifting insects, and stumbled.

"Easy." Jordan caught my arm. "Time to buckle you back on a pod."

"No, please, I cannot." My already nauseated stomach churned.

"I can't have you underfoot, and if you fall, they'll overrun you." She tilted her head at the moving, writhing mass. "You get on that pod when I say so and without a word of protest."

My brain rattled in my skull when I nodded.

Her grip on my arm tightened, and behind the reflection of the overhead lights on her face plate, she gave me a tight smile. "I don't leave people behind. We're getting out of here. All of us."

I leaned against the wall while she and DuBois kept the roaches at bay and the men worked on Spanos's pyrotechnics. Both women fired several times, which did not prevent the insectile behemoths from returning. Dr. Maxwell remained strangely quiet, and though I counted each second, ten minutes seemed to stretch beyond the actual scope of time.

Finally, Jordan spoke. "Once we're out, can we secure the doors? The bugs probably won't come after us, but let's not take any chances."

"Maybe," DuBois said. "I think I can."

"Thinking you can is not enough. Alec, we need a backup plan."

Spanos made an affirmative sound, and three minutes later, he stood. "That's the best I can do."

"Ready?" Jordan asked.

Timmons gave his weapon a last inspection. "Another one for the books. Exploding a path through an intrusion of cockroaches. Should be fun."

Jordan huffed but kept her weapon trained on the undulating shadows. She waved Spanos toward me. "Alec, help her onto the pod and secure her."

Spanos slung his weapon back and grabbed me by the waist. He lifted me onto the pod with greater ease than I would have anticipated, since he was merely twelve centimeters taller than I. Once again, waves of nausea washed over me.

He tapped my arm before he fastened the straps. "If you lie face down, you can cover your neck and still see to one side." He left my arms free. "And Recorder?"

"Yes?"

"Fire is a good idea."

Though I wished to acknowledge him, I could not reply. The idea of traveling through that crawling mass terrified me. Recorders were not supposed to feel fear, but I did. Then, for a fleeting moment, my dread lessened. My drone would have reprimanded me. But, I no longer had a drone. I would not be disciplined.

Left cheek pressed against the faceplate, I shut my eyes and clasped my hands behind my neck. Standard issue gloves were thin, but my fingers felt thick laced together. The suit's thermoregulatory unit must have failed because I alternately overheated and shivered.

I took measured, rhythmic breaths and tried to visualize the lavender growing in the Consortium's gardens. Instead, I saw the control room's flickering displays reflecting on the bodies of John Westruther and Dr. SahnVeer. I saw my drone's destruction by a creature which should not exist. I swallowed bile.

DuBois said, "Alec, you know I—"

"I know."

"Good luck," said Dr. Maxwell.

Jordan drew in a breath. "Stay focused. Let's move."

The pod lurched as the drone started forward.

Lying face down with gloved fingers behind my neck, I squeezed my eyes shut, acutely grateful for the absence of external smells. The musty scent from the accumulation of insectile infestation and the sharp musk of human stress would have been overpowering. Only the sounds penetrating my helmet and the movement of the pod beneath me gave any indication of our progress.

As the drone's speed evened out, the pod's motion smoothed. Muffled footsteps sounded on either side of me, most likely belonging to Timmons and Jordan, whose strides were longer than those of Spanos or DuBois. The even rhythm of their steps comforted me. I visualized them, illuminated by drones and hangar lights, casting small shadows on the concrete floor. Through the insects. Through the dark, shifting masses of cockroaches.

I inhaled slowly, and tried to recall the stillness of the brook where I had sought respite as a child. In my mind, green eyes supplanted botanical gardens, until the susurration of thousands of two-meter cockroaches shattered my attempts at calm.

Prime numbers.

Prime numbers were steadying. I reviewed them under my breath. "Two, three, five, seven, eleven . . ."

Jordan's voice broke in. "Hold steady, Tim. Alec, light it up."

A loud snap cracked through the scurrying sounds, then a deep, resonant boom grew to a roaring crescendo. My helmet's noise reduction was insufficient. Red-orange light penetrated my eyelids, and sudden heat stopped my shivering. The creatures' rustling increased to a scratching thunder as they fled the explosion.

". . . ninety-seven, one hundred one . . ."

"Tim, spray down that liquid and burn it!" Spanos yelled over the roaring fire, the scuttling thunder of insects, and the pounding pain in my head.

Timmons must have been the one on my right, because those foot-steps sped up.

". . . two hundred seventy-one . . ." I could not remember the next, though it was but the fifty-eighth prime number. I had not even made it through the first sixty. My chest constricted. I started over. I kept my fingers laced tightly over my neck. The heat of the flames grew uncomfortable even through the suit, but the light penetrating my eyelids changed. ". . . thirty-one, thirty-seven . . ."

DuBois's voice rang out. "Lost geothermal power."

"No kidding."

"J, ten o'clock!"

Weapons' fire shattered my concentration. Was sixty-one prime? I should have known.

"Tim!" Spanos shouted.

The pod faltered and dipped. My eyes flew open. Walls of flames towered over us. The light hurt like a physical blow, but I could not bring myself to look away. Timmons's tall, black silhouette stood against a nightmare of orange. He raised his weapon and fired.

"Almost through," DuBois's words resounded faintly in my ears over the cacophony.

The drone pulling my pod did not sound right, a high-pitched whine replacing its gentle whir. I forced out a warning: "The drone."

"What?" Jordan's voice echoed slightly, but I could not fix the feed.

"Drone sounds off." Timmons disappeared from my range of sight. "Yeah, something's wrong. Let's cut this short."

"That's the idea."

As he reappeared in my line of sight, a terrific noise shook the air, and a pillar of glowing smoke billowed up from beyond the wall of fire on my right. Someone's yell stabbed my ears. Smoking insect parts and steaming carapaces showered down on us. Something landed on my legs, and I bit back a cry at its heavy heat. Jordan shoved it off.

"Got it, Recorder. Hang on."

"What was that?" DuBois demanded, her voice huskier than usual.

"Don't know, don't care!" Jordan shouted over the roar.

The noise of the conflagration increased, nearly drowning out footsteps and mechanical sounds. The pod dipped, tilting me toward the left until I faced the hangar roof, where uneven rock glowed, reflecting the inferno below. My vision doubled. I shut my eyes and groaned.

"We're almost out." Jordan placed a hand on my back. "Just another little bit. Zhen, open the door!"

With a mechanical pop, the primary antigravity unit on the stasis pod faltered. Metal screeched on rock, the pod hit the hangar deck, and the straps securing me tore. Momentum slammed me into Jordan.

I swallowed back bile and pushed myself up on shaking arms.

"Jordan?" I began, but the drone caught my attention.

Damaged by flying debris, it continued to strain, struggling to pull the pod. The weight of the gravity-bound object and its sleeping cargo proved too great. A thin stream of smoke issued from a side port, and the drone caught fire. Its melting underbelly dripped onto the floor. I pushed myself over onto Jordan right before the drone exploded in a phosphorescent flash.

Afterimages lanced through my skull, and fragments of superheated metal rained down on my back. Several melted through my suit, and I bit my tongue in an effort not to cry out. Blood flowed, but I would not spit into the helmet, so I swallowed and gagged.

The flashes continued, even though I closed my eyes to block out the cavern. Voices echoed in my head, but I could not discern who spoke. I had hit Jordan hard, but when I tried to call her name, tried to ascertain her status, a moan was the only result.

One of the men picked me up, threw me over his shoulder, and set off at a run. Intense pain exploded in my abdomen. Each step jarred me, and I struggled to breathe.

When the heat subsided and the red light burning through my eyelids disappeared, I knew we were out of the hangar. I hazarded a peek. The sky and the horizon swam before me, so I shut my eyes again.

Timmons and Jordan babbled words I could not understand. Searing afterimages lanced across my vision, and the gut-wrenching pain would have doubled me over, had I been standing. My stomach knotted and heaved, and I vomited inside my helmet.

My rescuer lowered me to the ground. Someone wrenched my helmet off, and I emptied my stomach onto the frigid, red sand. I lay for a moment, coughing. When I opened my eyes again, double images of

Jordan squatted beside me. They resolved into one as she used her glove to wipe the acrid bile off my face before it froze.

So, Jordan was not badly injured. I would have sighed with relief if my body had permitted.

Timmons picked me up, cradling me to his chest as he jogged further from the hangar entrance. Shards of metal and rock and billows of smoke erupted from the doorway before it collapsed. He lowered me to the ground near a rocky outcropping some distance from the entrance, and I slumped over, my cheek pressed against sand so cold it burned, and watched my breath form sour clouds in the thin, sulfurous air. Each breath was icy fire as intense as the heat in the hangar. Each heartbeat was a blow. Another wave of pain shattered through me, and I could not leverage my weight to sit up. I wanted to see the sky one last time, but everything went black.

Rushing wind of the shuttle's engines threw red and black dust in my eyes. I coughed, then vomited again. In a random sequence like that of dreams and nightmares, voices echoed, Jordan hovered over me, and Spanos appeared. He carried me to a blue seat next to three drones which hummed steadily at their stations. I wanted to sit, to rest, but when I tried, the pain flared, obscuring the beige and blue around me. Staggering to my feet, I grabbed at a storage compartment handle for stability. After Jordan removed her helmet and cap, she helped me pull off my suit. It clattered to the floor.

She gasped. "That tunic—hold on, Recorder. We need to get your tunic off."

When she tugged it over my head, melted fabric peeled off my back, and I cried out.

"Sorry, Recorder. I'm . . . Stars, Max," she hissed through clenched teeth.

"Let the nanites take care of it," Dr. Maxwell said, his voice coming from everywhere and nowhere. "Just get her in the tank."

"Right." Mouth tight, she checked my pupils then led me to a chair, but I refused to sit.

"How is she doing?" Dr. Maxwell rumbled.

Jordan shook her head, her beaded braids sliding lethargically. "Looks like burns and frostbite."

Pain flared, obscuring most of Dr. Maxwell's reply. ". . . nanites . . . capillaries . . ."

Jordan steadied me while Spanos and Timmons secured the pods. When they pulled off gloves and helmets, she limped out of sight, and I heard her drop into a seat and heave a sigh. The shuttle's interior seemed to ripple. I wobbled. Timmons caught me, lifting me toward the emergency tank and its pale green medical gel. It was too much like the pods which stored corpses. I fought him.

"Alec! A little help, here."

I fought them both. With every gram of strength remaining, I pled and flailed, hot tears streaking down my cheeks. Spanos clenched his jaw, and Timmons murmured incomprehensible sounds as they held me down and the lower part of the tank slid into place, encapsulating my legs and hips.

The viscous gel seeped around me, through my leggings and my tight undershirt, and I thrashed even more wildly with complete disregard for the burns and the pain in my abdomen.

When DuBois called out from the front of the shuttle, Spanos left. Timmons settled beside the tank, pushing sweat-dark hair from his brow. He touched my head, and I stilled. Citizens did not touch Recorders.

"Hey, look at me."

"I am looking," I said.

"It's just medical gel. Nothing much."

"I know, but . . . I am afraid . . ."

"It'll be all right," he soothed, his hand still gently resting on my head.

"You . . . should not lie." I shivered. The gel had oozed up to my chest.

"Recorder? What color was your hair? When they let it grow?"

DuBois's voice sounded from the cockpit. "Tim, get up here now."

"Just a moment," he called back.

I forced myself to answer, though panic choked my words. "It does not grow."

"Too bad." He kept his hand on my head.

"Thank you for carrying me," I managed, glad the communications assembly was gone, and no one else heard me.

"You're welcome."

"Tim," Spanos shouted. "Get up here and fly this thing!"

"Hold on!"

The cooling gel had begun to work on my back, seeping through, numbing the burns, but he stayed beside me.

I kept my eyes on his and quietly began, "Two, three, five, seven, eleven . . ."

For a split second, he frowned, then his expression softened. "Ah. Prime numbers." Without hesitation, he joined me, and when I faltered, the numbers lost again, he continued, ". . . forty-one, forty-three . . ."

The gel covered my chin. Timmons had not reached sixty-seven when the viscous liquid filled my mouth, nose, and ears. I tried to relax, but fear again edged out reason. I resisted, coughing, swallowing, thrashing while the gel filled my lungs and stomach, and the nanodevices began their work.

A feeling of well-being flooded me, and my pain dwindled to a dull ache in my head and gut. The sour, acrid smell and taste of bile were replaced by delicate lavender and a hint of pine. The nanodevices triggered memory centers to calm me and endorphins to mitigate pain and promote relaxation, so my terrifying memories faded.

My vision rippled and blurred as the gel covered my face, but I kept my eyes on his while he continued reciting the numbers, even after he no longer touched my head.

I did not remember exactly when he moved away.

Lavender, boats, and green eyes spun together in contrast to fire, shriveled hands, and the mandibles of giant roaches. I was drowning in the images.

I needed air, but each inhalation was a battle. Oxygen burned my lungs, and pain fulgurated through me, driving back the nightmarish contrast of peace and fear. My back arched as I fought for breath after agonizing breath.

"Steady," rumbled a low voice. With a subdermal jet injector's audible pop, the torture faded.

My eyes scraped open, but the world doubled and swam. I could not rub the grit from my corneas, for my arm was too heavy to move. Beyond the stabbing pinpricks of light, everything bobbed up and down in a dizzying swirl of blue and green. Infirmary colors.

I tried to summon my drone, but as if I had hit a solid surface, my thoughts slammed to a sudden, painful stop.

My drone was gone. How had I forgotten?

Panic surged, propelling me up, but hands lowered me back onto a bed.

Pale blue eyes hovered over me. I blinked back tears, and the eyes settled into an equally pale face under receding, pale ash-brown hair. "Maybe another dose, Max?"

"Go ahead, Edwards. Recorder, slow deep breaths."

I managed to turn my head toward the second speaker. He stood at my bedside with another man. Both seemed familiar.

The slightly shorter, broad-shouldered man with long, thin ropes of dark hair smiled at me. "You're safe."

"I know you." The words hurt my throat.

He nodded. "Of course you do."

"She'll be all right, won't she?" the tall blond man asked, his voice smooth and musical.

The pale-eyed assistant—Edwards?—returned, blocking my view of the others, and the brief chill of a jet injector stung my skin. Tension and fear dissipated, and quiet peacefulness wrapped around me like a warm, heavy blanket. Edwards moved away.

My eyes slid shut.

"It takes a while." The doctor's voice faded as he spoke. "Her heart rate is . . ."

Even before the infirmary's pastel walls blinked into blurry focus, my drone's absence was a gaping hole. The comforting hum of its microantigravity unit had been ever present, and without it, the thrum of circulation fans and the low throb of medical tanks rang hollow. Anxiety swelled, yet no tendrils draped my shoulders to calm me, and my attempt to release neurotransmitters failed.

Struggling up, I braced myself on my elbows. Transparent doors showed neatly organized supplies, and equipment lined the room. Cyan and navy displays twisted upward from the standard medical computers, though I could not read them from the bed, and across the room, lights flashed on two of the three medical tanks. The clean stainless door to the closet-like diagnostic medicomputer gleamed. But there were no drones at all. I dropped back onto the bed.

"Hello, there!" An unfamiliar young woman appeared at my side and pulled the white bed linens up to my neck. Her cheekbones were sharp, giving her a fragile appearance. Although she appeared as bald as any Recorder, a teal tunic, not Consortium grey, hung loosely on her small frame. Like an Elder, she had neither eyebrows nor lashes, yet no nanodevices filmed her hazel eyes. A smile lit her face, and when she turned her head, light gleamed on a faint growth of light brown hair. Not bald, then. She said, over her shoulder, "Max! She's awake."

"I told you she'd be up soon." Dr. Maxwell made an adjustment on one of the tanks' controls, and when the medgel burbled, he straightened and crossed to my bedside. He had tied back his long dreadlocks, and his eyes were puffy. He offered me a small smile. "How do you feel?"

"I am not certain."

"Does your head hurt?"

"Yes, but not sharply."

"It'll probably bother you off and on for a while yet. Any abdominal pain or discomfort?"

"I, no . . . I have minimal discomfort. Have I been ill?"

"In a manner of speaking." He did not smile as broadly as the young woman had. "You've pulled through a rough spot. You'll be fine, considering . . . Do you remember what happened?"

I shook my head, grimacing at the consequent pain. Then, in brutally quick succession, memories flooded in. Gasping, I struggled upright, but vertigo knocked me back onto the sheets.

"Easy now." Dr. Maxwell lifted me slightly and propped pillows behind my head. "Coming back to you?"

I licked my lips before speaking. "I have lost my drone."

"Yes," he said.

I inhaled, held the breath for seven seconds, then exhaled slowly and closed my eyes. No ultraviolet or infrared images glowed. Sound was both quieter and louder than before. I lacked my previous range, but I also lacked a way to mute dull, irritating noises like the lights' high-pitched buzz and the low throb of the medical tanks and circulation fans.

But, I was not dead.

I glanced at the young woman, then back at the man next to my bed. "It appears you have saved my life, Dr. Maxwell. Thank you."

"Max," he corrected. "You're welcome."

When I asked for a comprehensive explanation, he held up a hand. "That's enough for now. I'll fill in the details when you're a bit more yourself."

A yawn disrupted my response, so I merely nodded my assent.

The young woman cleared her throat and stepped close, extending her right fist. "I'm Kyleigh Tristram. You saved my life. I've been waiting to thank you."

Watching Dr. Maxwell from the corner of my eye, I tapped her fist with my own, which I believed was the appropriate response. He smiled faintly.

"You are welcome."

"I know you did everything you could for . . . I mean, you saved me and Freddie, and Elliott and Ross, and the cats."

I did not understand, so I said nothing.

Dr. Maxwell's steady nut-brown eyes met mine. "As you no doubt surmised, Kyleigh was in one of those pods you rescued from the station. She's been up for a few days. Ross has, too, but the other pods were damaged. Both young men are still here." He motioned across the room to the medical tanks.

Extended time in stasis could atrophy internal organs. A knot tightened in my throat. "Were there not five?"

"Yes, there were." Dr. Maxwell leaned back and crossed his arms, brows drawn together in a dark line. "The other pod was a bit of a surprise. Full of cats."

"Cats?"

"Cats."

"Oh." I tightened my hands. Perhaps the destruction of my drone had caused more damage than I had feared.

"Evidently, the rats had died," Dr. Maxwell said, "and the enzymes broke them down. Only the cats remained."

I glanced from him to the young woman.

"It was my doing. Well, mine and Freddie's and Elliott's." Her gaze fell to her clasped hands. "When Freddie's dad ordered us into the pods, we couldn't bear to let Dr. SahnVeer euthanize them all. So we smuggled them into an extra pod. Jenny, my favorite, didn't survive stasis because she was pregnant."

Although not the most lucid explanation, her words triggered another memory. "I did not imagine the erratic life signs from that pod? I thought my confusion resulted from losing my drone."

"You were right." The doctor regarded me closely. "Why didn't you say anything?"

"I had spoken out of turn earlier. I did not want to repeat my mistake."

Kyleigh Tristram fingered the teal tunic's hem. "I did all the calculations. The extra pod shouldn't have stressed the system."

I tried to call up the data. Without a drone, only fragments surfaced, but they sufficed. "Nothing you did caused the malfunction. There is evidence someone tampered with the power."

The young woman's lashless eyes widened, and she opened her mouth to speak, but Dr. Maxwell forestalled her. "It can wait, Kye. It's bound to be a long story, and our patient here needs rest." He studied the small readout next to my bed. When he briefly touched the back of his hand to my forehead, I tried not to flinch. "Your numbers are holding steady, so you should be up and about in no time. Try to sleep. I'll be back in a bit." He turned to face the young woman. "And you, Kyleigh, need to check on those blasted cats."

She gave me a small smile before she left.

I stared at the quiet blue walls until sleep claimed me.

Discomfort prodded me awake.

I was alone. Above me, in a clear rectangle of glass surrounded by white ceiling tiles, my reflection stared down, thin under the cotton blanket, my head swathed in a bandage and my eyes like dark smudges.

Near the double doors, pale, almost grey, light gleamed from recessed fixtures. Mechanical systems droned. A faint chime rang. Medical tanks burbled, and indistinct masculine voices murmured from the hallway. Footsteps retreated, and the voices faded away.

I was alone, but frustration at enforced solitude soon overtook the feeling of emptiness. I plucked at my blanket, resenting the absence of my drone.

Thirty-one minutes later, Dr. Maxwell entered the infirmary. His ashen skin and the dark, puffy circles under his eyes testified to his fatigue. He had aged in the fourteen years since he had toured the Consortium Training Center and spoken to me in the gardens, but although grey wove through the roots of his dreadlocks, he still moved with the same confidence. When I first boarded CTS *Thalassa* and reported to the infirmary for the mandatory medical scan, I had hidden my pleasure at seeing him again. He, of course, did not recognize me, which was as it should have been.

I voiced none of these thoughts as he activated the multicolored projection to display my vital signs above the datapad near my bed. Other than monosyllabic acknowledgments, he did not speak as he propped me up for a cup of reconstituted broth, which I gulped.

"Whoa, slow down." He gently pulled it away. "You need to take it easy for a while."

"I am hungry."

"Of course you are." The doctor refrained from commenting on my whining, which was kind. "But your small intestines nearly ruptured. We've patched them up, but you still need to be careful."

"But I received no injury to my abdomen."

Dr. Maxwell said nothing as he handed back the broth. He remained silent until I finished and returned the empty cup. Then he set the mug down with care. "Nothing about anatomy is simple. The damage to your implant affected your entire body."

The infirmary's double doors slid apart.

"Is she awake yet?" Kyleigh Tristram asked.

"Now's not the best time, Kye."

"Sorry." She flashed me a broad grin. "They were asking after you at dinner."

"Kyleigh," said Dr. Maxwell, "would you please go back to the dining commons and get Jordan?"

Her grin melted, and her gaze flew between the doctor and me. "Of course."

While her footsteps faded, he moved toward the sink and washed his hands. "I need to check that skull of yours."

He returned to my bedside and unwrapped the bandages. I concentrated on remaining still to tolerate both his touch and the sudden chill of air. Unusual tenderness amplified the faint pressure of his fingers, as if he tugged infinitesimally at my skin.

"Hurting a bit?"

"Yes."

"The incision site is healing nicely, but you'll have a scar. I'm afraid your hair won't grow there."

"I do not have hair."

"You will." Dr. Maxwell's voice was gentle.

Offended, I drew back from him, though the sudden movement caused my discomfort to flare into pain. "Recorders do not have hair."

"Give me your hand." He held out his own, and I hesitated before complying. He set it on my head. "Feel that?"

Fine, scratchy, prickles met my fingertips. I jerked my hand from his, shaking it to lose the tactile memory. Heart pounding, I stared up at him, unable to look away, even when others entered the room. Dr. Maxwell acknowledged them before he sat next to me again and caught my flailing hand in his.

"You've lost your implant." His deep voice seemed to grow farther away as he spoke. I was dimly aware of Jordan standing beside him, and Timmons behind her. "I removed the damaged chip and wiring from your brain. It took hours to get it all out."

"What do you mean?" I whispered.

Dr. Maxwell's eyes met my own. "I'm sorry. You're not a Recorder. Not anymore."

10

Dr. Maxwell held my hand, as though he believed his words did not undermine everything I had ever known. He would not intentionally deceive me, but he was mistaken. He had to be.

I was a Recorder, and Dr. Robert Maxwell was wrong.

"I know. It'll be an adjustment. It's a lot to take in." He gave my fingers a light squeeze and fell silent.

Venetia Jordan, tall and strong, stood beside my bed, with Nathaniel Timmons on her left, his brow furrowed. Neither spoke.

No. Maintaining the record, ensuring the integrity of facts, preventing manipulation or distortion of events—these comprised the purpose of my existence, the redemption of my gifting, the reason I was alive.

He had to be wrong.

"I ran several scans, and you're going to be all right."

Without my drone's input, I was empty. I yanked my hand from his, shook my head, and fell back into the pillows. "Explain."

The doctor's voice was low and smooth. "How long did you have the implant?"

"Irrelevant," I snapped. "Please describe the excision."

Dr. Maxwell shot a quick glance at Jordan, then his gaze again met mine. "Humor me. How long?"

My jaw clenched, and I answered through gritted teeth. "All Consortium members receive our neural interfaces at gifting."

His nostrils flared. "Gifting? You've had a chip in your head your whole life."

"Yes. As our callings become clear, we receive training to best utilize our skills. I fail to understand the relevancy of these questions."

He tugged at his earlobe. "The implant grew."

"The implant is nonliving," I stated flatly. "It cannot grow."

"Nevertheless, it did. Infusions of nanodevices probably added to its scope, but however it expanded, microscopic tendrils had spread throughout your brain. They reached from your prefrontal cortex through temporal, parietal, and occipital lobes. When the implant was damaged, it began destroying itself, like it was progr—"

"Max!" Jordan said, her voice sharp.

He frowned.

"Max," she repeated, narrowing her eyes.

Dr. Maxwell cleared his throat. "When your implant was destroyed, the wiring began to short out. By the time you got back here, the damage was triggering reactions through almost every system in your body, from cardiovascular to pulmonary to gastrointestinal. It was killing you."

"I must review the records."

Dr. Maxwell nodded and reached for the datapad. Closing the projections of my vital signs, he pulled up other files before handing it to me. I read slowly—at a mere fraction of my previous speed—then studied the room. The details, the clarity, the precise measurability of everything had vanished. My lagging, empty senses confirmed the veracity of his documentation.

"If I hadn't removed it all, you would have died," he said softly.

Tension wrapped through me like a drone's tendril, and my mouth went dry. "Yes . . ." I forced myself to work through the idea aloud. "A master chip stimulating senses and interfacing with memory and perception might need to extend throughout the brain. Should such a connection become compromised, it could provoke a chain of events similar to the one you described."

The logic of this line of reasoning failed to comfort me.

I tapped the relevant section before handing him the datapad. "Based on your reports, removing the damaged materials saved my life, and I am grateful. Upon my return to New Triton, I will request a commendation for you before my debriefing, disciplinary action, and repair."

Timmons's protest distracted me momentarily, but I returned my attention to Dr. Maxwell. "I shall regain optimal functionality again when they install a new implant."

Dr. Maxwell rubbed the back of his neck. "Successful integration relies on early introduction. As your brain developed, the implant expanded. That kind of seamless synthesis can only be achieved in infancy."

"I do not accept your assessment." Even I heard the anxiety creeping into my voice.

"Stop dancing around it, Max." Jordan's comment made little sense. The doctor did not dance. He sat next to me on the bed. "Tell her straight."

He shook his head.

Jordan glowered down at both of us.

"Recorder." She paused. "Or whatever you want to call yourself now, what Max did could land him in a whole lot of trouble. To my knowledge, no one outside the Consortium has ever saved a Recorder. When one of you is sent on assignment, the crew is informed that should an injury occur, the Recorder is to be 'granted minimum emergency care and returned for assessment.' Max took a huge risk, at his own expense."

The doctor shifted.

Jordan pursed her lips. "If he wasn't a genius and the kindest man in the system, you'd be dead."

He shook his head. "Venetia."

"No, Max." Her jaw tightened. "She needs to understand that by saving her life you might have risked your own."

Timmons crossed his arms. "Don't be melodramatic, J."

She spun around, and the beads on her long braids clattered. "Melodramatic? You've heard Alec's story. And you remember Gervase."

"What's your cousin got to do with anything?"

"Not now." The doctor stood and placed a gentle hand on Jordan's shoulder.

Both she and Timmons fell quiet, but I broke their silence. "I thank you again, Dr. Maxwell. I am confident you will be rewarded rather than punished. The Consortium will share my gratitude. My own actions precipitated the destruction of my drone and my implant. Though the fault is entirely my own, I appreciate your concern."

"Call me Max," he told me again. The corners of his mouth tipped up, but his eyes did not smile. "And this is quite enough for now. You need rest to heal. It's been a rough seven days."

This startled me. "I have lost seven days?"

Timmons exhaled. "Yeah. It's been rough on Max and Edwards. Williams, too."

I blinked. "Edwards and . . . Williams? Your . . . assistants?"

Dr. Maxwell nodded. "They're Consortium staff, which you probably knew."

"Edwards, I remember, but Williams . . ." I had forgotten. How many other things had I forgotten as well?

"She usually takes nights," Dr. Maxwell said. "And fortunately, you slept well."

"You've been in good hands, between the three of them." Jordan lowered herself into a chair at a computer terminal. "Max handpicked them for this trip."

Dr. Maxwell stifled a yawn, and Timmons followed suit. "Don't do that, Max. It's catching. Although, you should get some sleep."

The doctor shook his head. "Somebody has to be here, and I sent Edwards to his quarters about an hour ago. The man looked ready to drop."

"Tell me what she needs, and I'll take care of it. Besides"—Timmons checked the time—"it's about eight fifteen, and Williams is on at nine, right?"

"Yes." Dr. Maxwell yawned again. "You might be right. Everything looks fine, and I'm just down the hall."

Max helped me to the water closet then back to bed, where I shook from even that minimal exertion. He checked my vitals and the tanks' screens one last time, then told me to have some more broth and cautioned Jordan and Timmons to let me rest. One hand on the door frame, Dr. Maxwell gave us a tired smile and said good night.

Exhausted, I leaned back onto the pillows and closed my eyes.

"Recorder," Jordan said suddenly, and my eyes flew open. "I need to thank you. When you threw yourself over me down there in the hangar, you took a fair amount of debris."

Unsure of what to say, I simply nodded.

"Why did you do it?" She rested her left elbow on the chair's arm. "Recorders aren't supposed to interfere."

I hesitated, glancing first at Timmons, then back at her. "You might have been injured. Further injury was undesirable."

"It wasn't your fault, though."

"Perhaps not, but—"

"No." Jordan stood and shook her head. "There's no 'perhaps' about it. Accidents happen. True, they happened a lot this mission—"

Timmons snorted. "An understatement if I ever heard one."

"But it wasn't your fault."

The circulation fan's sound deepened, and even cooler air blew through the vents, cold on my damaged head. I shivered. "In reality, it is I who owe you a debt of gratitude for removing my helmet. Had you not done so, I would have died a particularly ignoble death. Additionally, you remained beside me to ease my discomfort. This was unexpected. You were kind. Kindness," I added, "is a beautiful gift."

Jordan's forehead puckered, and she tilted her head to the right. I wanted to cross-reference her expression in my database, but the absence of my drone and implant crippled my understanding. I sighed and then wondered if they would misinterpret it as sighing over kindness rather than over my inability to analyze appropriately, though neither my personal feelings nor their perceptions of my feelings mattered.

"You're welcome."

"Who carried me out?"

Jordan nodded back at Timmons, who watched me from the foot of my bed. "He did."

"Then I thank you, as well, Nathaniel Timmons, for carrying me out of danger."

"Yeah." He studied his fingernails. "And nearly busting your guts by flinging you over my shoulder."

"I could not walk, so your action was necessary. And as you heard, Dr. Maxwell asserts my failed implant precipitated subsequent difficulties."

Jordan glanced back at Timmons, then at me. "We should let you sleep."

As if he had not heard her, Timmons continued, "Then you're

welcome. It was worth the effort of hauling your not insubstantial self out of there. You might only be a smidgen taller than average, but you weigh quite a bit, you know."

"Stars, Tim." Jordan rolled her eyes. "Consortium or not, that's bad form. Recorder, I apologize on his behalf."

Timmons winked. "It's a compliment. You work out, don't you?"

"I have indeed had extensive training to build stamina, strengthen core muscles, and improve neural connections, although I fail to see the relevance—"

"Second"—his grin faded—"we owed you one. If you hadn't opened those hangar doors, we would've been chewed to death or had to abandon the stasis pods and fight our way through that intrusion of bugs."

"True enough," Jordan added.

I could almost see the insects again, as clearly as a recording. My mouth went dry.

Timmons continued, though his voice echoed oddly in my ears. "Plus, you're the one who found a way out, though I'm a little disappointed in Alec. Blowing stuff up is one of his favorite things. He should've come up with it first." He paused and tapped the blanket over my foot. "Recorder? You all right?"

My heart sputtered, and the air pushed me down, felt thick in my throat. Without neurotransmitters, I was insufficient to regulate this—

"Just breathe," Timmons said. "In and out."

I wanted to answer him, but no words came.

"You'll be all right." Jordan's voice seemed to come from far away. "Try closing your eyes."

So, I did. I inhaled, waited, and slowly released the breath. Then again. And again. The pressure in my chest receded, and my heart rate slowed.

"Hey," Timmons said. "Recorder. Look at me."

I forced myself to say, "I am looking."

He tapped my foot again. "Good. You okay?"

I nodded.

"Don't worry about it," Jordan added. "Things hit people differently. Exams do the same thing to me."

"I do not know what you mean."

Her lips twitched. "No, you probably don't."

Timmons brought me a cup of water, which I appreciated, though I did not say so. He grinned at Jordan. "Go on, J. I'm gonna stay a bit, like I told Max. Make sure she's settled."

Jordan shot him a look.

He grinned. "She's perfectly safe with me, and you know it."

I counted eleven seconds before her shoulders relaxed.

"Fine. Recorder, Max will have you back on your feet in no time. We reach New Triton and Lunar One in a couple of ten-days, but you'll be better long before then, what with your stint in the tank and Max's nanites." She paused at the door. "Good night, Recorder. And Tim, behave."

"Always do, when it matters."

She did not acknowledge his remarks, only left.

Timmons rubbed the back of his neck. "Need anything?"

"May I have some more broth?"

He crossed the room again and poured me some from the thermal carafe. After handing it to me, he dropped into the chair by my bed and leaned back, hands behind his head, long legs extended. I sipped the broth.

"You okay with all that?" he asked.

"With what?"

"With what Max said. That you're not a Recorder."

I hesitated for only half a second. "But I am."

He raised one eyebrow. "Is that an 'of course you're okay with not being a Recorder,' or is that an 'of course you're still a Recorder'?"

"I am still a Recorder. Facts have not changed."

"You lost your implant and your drone."

"Yes, but I have trained to record and document objectively since my assessment as a child. It is who I am."

"I don't buy it. For an impartial observer, you were pretty involved in things."

My reflection rippled weirdly on the golden liquid inside my cup. "Yes. This is a concern."

Timmons sat up straight in the chair and braced his arms on his knees. "Don't go back."

"As a Recorder . . ." I drew in a deep breath to ease the tension in my chest, but it did not help, so I exhaled slowly. "As a Recorder, I will acknowledge my mistakes and make compensation."

"Recorder—"

"I am finished with my broth." This statement was not entirely true, as some remained in the cup, and I knew I needed the nutrition, but my stomach knotted.

His eyebrows drew together as he took the cup from my hand, and I suddenly recalled commenting on those eyebrows during our escape. I was correct, of course, based on the golden ratio for human faces, but I should not have spoken so. My cheeks heated. I withdrew my hand quickly, and the dregs nearly spilled on my blanket.

I watched his black boots cross the floor. "I must face the consequences of my failure," I said to the boots, as they returned to my bedside. "But I do not regret what I did, apart from irrationally destroying my drone by hurling it at the . . . into danger. I . . . I did not think clearly. Had you not intervened, that . . . thing . . ."

"Hey."

I looked up.

He stood at my side, green eyes studying me. "It's okay."

I swallowed. "I do not regret any of my other choices on Pallas . . ."

"But?" Timmons pulled the chair closer to my bed and sat down, leaning forward with his elbows on his knees.

"Although the Consortium would not endorse such actions, they were the right thing to do. How is it possible two such contradictory ideas can coexist?"

"Maybe the contradiction isn't what you think it is."

"All my life I have trained, but in a moment of crisis, all that training is for naught."

"I wouldn't say that. You're the reason we made it out." He nodded in the direction of the medical tanks. "The reason we *all* made it."

A shudder coursed through me. "Thus, I would not make any other choice."

"Exactly." He offered me a lopsided smile. "Want my company a bit longer?"

Grateful for his attempt to change the subject, I allowed myself to smile back. "That would be another kindness. I do not know why, but tonight, solitude is an empty thing. I do not welcome it."

His dimple peeked out. "I understand."

Approximately four minutes later, I said, "Timmons? Perhaps . . ."

"Yes?"

I shook my head, unable to explain the emotions which lurked like shadows at the edges of my mind.

"Go to sleep," he said quietly. "I'll stay for a bit."

I nodded, then tapped the small bedrail panel room controls and dimmed the infirmary lights. Their buzz faded, but without invisible light and despite the medical tank's green glow, darkness surrounded me, almost like a physical entity, reaching into my mind and squeezing out thought and reason. My breath came in gasps. I could not move.

A button clicked at my side, and gentle, red light bathed the room, pushing back the emptiness. His eyes, dark in the soothing light, found mine. My mouth was too dry to speak, so I could but nod my thanks. Timmons settled back in the chair and hummed quietly to himself before he, too, fell silent. The steady thrum of the air circulation fans lulled me to sleep.

I woke once to the sound of someone checking the medical tanks. Timmons was sprawled inelegantly on the chair, snoring a little, which made me smile. I fell back asleep to dream of brooks and pine forests. When I woke again, his chair was empty, but a glass of cold water dripped condensation onto my bedside table.

Dreaming of dark tunnels and insects, I slept fitfully afterward.

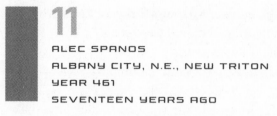

Arianna squealed when the swing hit its apex and her body was momentarily weightless. Alec rolled his eyes. She always did that. He climbed up the ladder to the top of the slide, squinted up at the riveted dome above, and sighed.

"You sigh too much, Alec," she called.

When he glanced over, she let go of the swing and threw herself into the air, landing on her feet like a cat in a vid.

"Aria!" He jerked upright and glanced back at the park bench where their mother was chatting with her friend from the symphony. Relief coursed through him. She must not have seen Arianna jump.

His sister climbed up to the top platform, sat beside him, and thoughtfully chewed the end of her braid. "Alec?"

"Yeah?"

Her voice was quiet. "What do you think a real sky is like?"

He lay back down and tucked his arms behind his head. "On Ceres it's smooth and purply-blue with white clouds, or grey ones, when it rains. Saw a vid in school with a real sunset. It's a lot like ours, only brighter. Sometimes you can see the moons in the daytime."

"I'd like to see a moon." From the corner of his eye, he saw her mimic his motions and fold her arms, too. "Someday I'll see a real sky."

Alec snorted. "Good luck. You gotta get rich first."

"I will be. I'm gonna be the richest ever."

"And how're you gonna do that?"

"I'll think of something." She rolled over, then sat up quickly, pointing across the street. "Alec? There's more of those people."

He pushed himself up and turned around. Several figures in pale grey stood between the columns of the tall, pillared symphony hall.

Alec tapped her shoulder and, when she looked over, reassured her, "They're just Recorders, Aria. We studied them in school before Founders Day, remember? They keep people safe."

"They don't look like it." Arianna wrapped her arms around her knees. "They give me the heebie-jeebies. They're like spiders that don't blink."

"Spiders *can't* blink." He counted three more Recorders standing near the squat government building on the corner. Two more watched the playground. Alec jerked his attention back to his sister. "Anyway, when've you ever seen a spider?"

"In school." She held her hands a decimeter apart. "It's this big!"

"Liar."

Aria glared at him. "It's in a cage. For science."

He shook his head. "Mama says the best part of Albany City is no spiders."

She waved one hand in the air like Mama did when she thought something was ridiculous. "Those drones are like their pet flies."

"See?" he said. "You don't know anything. Spiders *eat* flies."

She stuck out her tongue but fell silent again and leaned against him, watching the Recorders. An eighth one walked around the corner. And then another. So many in one place made uneasiness creep up his spine, like insects on thin, prickly legs.

"Alec," she said. "I don't like them."

He patted her shoulder. "Be right back."

Alec slid down the bright yellow pole and jogged over to his mother and her friend. When there was a lull in their conversation, he asked, "Mama? Can we go home?"

His mother cocked her head. "We haven't even been here an hour, Alec."

"It's just . . . there's lots of Recorders across the street."

A little crease appeared over her nose. "If they are really bothering you, go get your sister."

As he walked off, the lady said, "He's a good boy, Sophi. Eleven now, isn't he?"

"Yes, and Arianna just turned seven."

The woman murmured, "My children would be nine."

"I remember." The sadness in his mother's voice made Alec slow down momentarily. "We had just moved here from Trinity South, and Alec was tiny. I'm sorry, my friend."

From atop the play structure, Aria glanced back at him, her big brown eyes widening, her mouth a round O, and something prompted him to break into a run. He had almost reached the slide when an explosion across the street threw him to the ground. The world around him vanished in a storm of light and noise. Heat seared his face.

Mama was calling him, calling Arianna, but he couldn't see anything. Aria was screaming. He tried to crawl toward the sound. He hadn't gone far when someone caught him around the waist, pulled him backward, shoved him into Mama's familiar arms.

Couldn't they hear Aria crying?

"Alec, stop fighting me, honey." Her arms tightened. "I've got you, Alec. I've got you."

The roaring noise faded, and everything disappeared.

That first evening home from the hospital, Alec snuck into Arianna's room and sat in the dark, holding her stuffed bear.

The door slid into its pocket, and his father crossed the room. "No reason to sit in the dark, son," he said gently, but he didn't turn on the light.

"It's my fault, Papa." Alec hugged the bear tight. "I should've made them leave earlier."

"No, son." His father lowered himself onto Aria's bed. "If it's anyone's fault, it's those Recorders'. They could've stopped the men planting explosives or cleared the area. They saw what was going on, but they just watched and did nothing."

"I'm still sorry," Alec whispered into the quiet.

"It's not your fault, any more than it's mine or Mama's. It'll be okay, son. She'll be home soon."

"What happened to Mama's friend, the lady who pulled me and Aria out? Was she hurt, too?"

"She's still in a tank, but they won't tell us more than that."

Indignation simmered. "They should."

"Maybe."

"I want to thank her."

His father hummed in agreement. For several more minutes they sat quietly in the dark, but the words Alec had hidden in his heart finally tumbled out. "I didn't make her leave, and Papa, I said she lied about spiders. Practically the last thing I said was that she was a liar."

"She wouldn't think you meant it." His father's voice grew soft, and he wrapped an arm around Alec's shoulders. "She knows you love her, and she loves you. Your mother and I do, too."

"She'd been telling me about wanting to see the sky. What if she can't?"

"Take it a day at a time, son."

They sat together in the emptiness of his little sister's room until Alec fell asleep, but he woke in the morning on his own bed, his father's warm robe, still smelling of aftershave, tucked around him.

Time crept into days, then ten-days, and still Arianna stayed in the medtank. Vague impressions of being imprisoned in one, himself, haunted Alec's nightmares. Even during the day, everything was different. Their flat felt hollow without Aria in it. A growing, angry silence replaced his father's deep, rolling laugh. Instead of telling stories, Papa would sit with his worry beads, running the smooth olive wood through his fingers over and over again. Mama no longer sang while she cooked, and dark circles shadowed her eyes. She rarely played her violin, though when she did, the music seemed to cry.

Their parents argued at night, though they'd never fought before, at least, not that Alec remembered. When his father grumbled, his mother shushed him, but Alec understood. He wanted Arianna back, too. And it was all the Recorders' fault.

The fourth ten-day after Alec came home, his father stopped going to work, but if Arianna wasn't back, at least he had more time with his father. When his mother cut off all her hair, Alec missed the way it curled into long ringlets when she steamed vegetables, and his father was upset. She said it had to be done and she'd gotten a good price, so he cut off his hair and sold it, too. Then, she sold her violin, insisting she would buy it back before the season started, she and his father argued over that, too. Without music, the rooms felt even emptier.

Eventually, the steamed vegetables gave way to dinners of beans and rice, and Alec hated beans. The three of them ate in silence, and when Alec pushed the food around his plate, his father would scold him for not finishing his dinner. He would snap back, though when tears started in Mama's eyes, they both grew quiet.

One evening as he was clearing the dinner dishes, the door chime sounded. His father answered it, and from the kitchen, Alec saw his father's back stiffen right before he ordered Alec straight to bed. He opened his mouth to argue, but when he saw the color drain from his mother's face, he folded his napkin and slipped down the hall without a word.

Unfamiliar voices rumbled from the front room, so Alec waited a few minutes, then tiptoed out to peek around the corner. His father sat with his back to the hall, but Alec could see his mother's pale profile. A man in a green tunic sat across from her, and a Recorder stood behind him. The Recorder's drone hovered above his ugly, bald head, one of its tentacles draped over his shoulder, and a second drone hung in the middle of the room like an evil moon.

Alec craned his neck to hear what they said, but he was too far away. He snuck into the room, out of view of the others, and hid behind the sofa, still keeping an eye on Mama's profile.

". . . your seditious language," the man was saying. "We are sorry for the anguish your family has suffered, but you've been warned repeatedly to discontinue your wild allegations. You've fallen further and further behind in your share of the costs of your children's medical care since you lost your position at the mine office, and I am here to warn you the hospital will no longer fund your daughter's treatment as of next ten-day unless you can apply for aid."

Mama gasped. Her face grew blotchy, like it did before she cried.

"You know we won't qualify if I'm under suspicion," Papa muttered.

Alec shrank back behind the sofa, then crept to the end behind the potted plants and peeked between the leaves.

"You have been warned numerous times." The green-tunic man gestured at the Recorder.

"We have fifty-three recordings documenting your violations." The Recorder's dull, monotonous voice made Alec's skin crawl.

The man leaned forward. "The panel has reviewed the records provided by the Consortium. But, we are not unfeeling. We don't wish your daughter to suffer for your misconduct. And so, with the governing authority's permission, I am offering you a choice. If you submit to removal and break contract, your partner may apply for aid. Or . . . you may reject our assistance, in which case your entire family will suffer, and your daughter will die."

Mama grabbed Papa's arm when he stood.

"You're telling me—"

"No," the man interrupted. "I am presenting you with options."

"My life or my daughter's? Give up . . ." Papa's voice faltered. "Give up my family—my freedom—to save my daughter?"

"No one has threatened your life."

Papa barked a short, angry laugh. "There's no choice here." He was silent for a moment. "Can I have another day?"

"Of course." The man stood. "But bear in mind that the window for applying for aid closes soon. It will take several days to process the application. If funding your daughter's care is a priority, you need to decide quickly."

Alec shrank even further back.

"I've already decided." His father's voice was low, almost hard to hear. "I need time to say goodbye."

Mama made a small, injured noise.

The man gave them a thin smile. "We'll leave the observation drone until your decision is final."

While his mother sat frozen under the faint mechanical whir of the moon-drone, her breathing shallow and fast, his father accompanied them out. At the door, the Recorder turned to where Alec hid behind the potted plants and looked directly into his eyes. Alec's blood froze, and he couldn't move. The Recorder inclined his head in Alec's direction, then left.

The door clicked shut, and Papa returned to Mama's side. "I have to, Sophi, love. I can't let Aria die. With the aid, you'll not have to worry about . . . anything."

Her face flushed. "I told you! I warned you, and you wouldn't listen! What am I supposed to do now?"

It was like there wasn't enough air in the room. Breathing hurt. Alec glanced at the moon-drone, and his stomach churned.

"You wouldn't listen." Mama burst into tears.

Papa, his jaw tight, wrapped her in his arms. She grabbed his tunic with tight fists and kissed him.

Alec tiptoed back down the hall to his room. It was a long time before he fell asleep.

He stayed home from school the next day and spent the morning playing chess with his father. His mother stood in the kitchen doorway, watching them, quiet and still.

Papa left after lunch. For an appointment, he said. The hovering moon-drone went with him.

He never came home.

Neither did Arianna.

12

My reflection stared back at me self-consciously.

Although the Elders mandated tidiness of appearance, they did not tolerate vanity. Personally, I could not comprehend why citizens would strive to present a false portrait of health, beauty, and vitality. Such self-aggrandizement was superficial at best and deceptive at worst. Nevertheless, the mirror over the sink drew my attention. The seven days I had spent in the emergency medical tank had accelerated my healing and the growth of hair. A shadow of sable brown covered my head, and eyebrows—*eyebrows*!—crawled across my face. I raised and lowered them, watching them arc up and down. They were asymmetrical, but at least I would only rarely be subjected to the sight.

Tilting my head, I studied the angry pink scar wrapping around my skull and the small, puckered welts left on my shoulders by the burning debris. The marks continued down under the scratchy white gown and scattered over my back and legs. Although the healing skin was still tender, the scars—reminders of my failings—caused me more emotional than physical discomfort. I frowned, and my eyebrows moved over my puffy, shadowed eyes. Staring again at my pallid face and my stubble-covered head and the pink scar, I sighed in irrational discontent.

Only one of my outfits had been in the laundry while we were away. All my remaining garments were locked in my previous quarters, accessible only with a drone, and the standard issue medical gown's stiff seams and inconvenient snaps slid uncomfortably across my skin, rubbing the tender, new scars. I struggled out of the puzzling medical gown and into my sole remaining tunic.

Emerging from the infirmary's water closet, I walked cautiously across the room to the chair by my bed. The task of straightening the bedding seemed too immense, so I merely leaned against the armrest, thinking about moving, when Kyleigh Tristram entered the infirmary, one hand behind her back.

"You're up!" she observed, unnecessarily. "How're you feeling?"

"I am unsteady."

"Right." She hesitated. "Um, I don't know your name."

"Recorders do not have names."

"Well, I knew *that*. I mean, we had a Recorder on Pallas." She plunked down across from me on the foot of my bed, tucking something behind her. "I just thought you must have secret names, ones only the Consortium knows, or else how do you know who does what or who goes where?"

"We have our roles. Names are inappropriate."

"But what if you want to talk to, or about, someone specific? To chat? What do you call each other? I mean . . ." She flushed.

"We do not 'chat.' When we are newborns, we are assigned identification numbers, even as citizens are, but we do not use them to refer to each other. To identify a fellow Recorder with a number would be naming and therefore inappropriate."

Dr. Maxwell tugged on his ear. "Recorders aren't supposed to have a personal stake in anything."

"But you don't have a drone," Kyleigh Tristram stated, "so you need a name."

I stiffened. "No, I do not."

"I'll be thinking about it, all the same." A grin spread across her face. "You're moving into your new room today, right?"

"Yes," I said, attempting to mask the dissatisfaction I had with nonConsortium quarters.

"I can help you move your things."

I did not see the point of explaining how I had no things to move, so I did not respond.

"You know"—she tapped her chin several times as she studied me—"grey isn't really your color."

"I have always worn grey. It is, therefore, my color."

Kyleigh Tristram pulled a bag from behind her back. "Ta-da!"

"I am unfamiliar with that term."

She grinned. "It's for you."

I glanced at Dr. Maxwell. His dreadlocks slid over his blue-green scrubs as he shook his head. "She's probably never had a gift, Kye," he said quietly. "No personal stake, remember?"

I took the proffered bag, pulled out a very large russet sleep shirt, a pair of black leggings, and a rose-colored tunic, and laid them flat on the bed in front of me.

Kyleigh Tristram shifted her weight. "They aren't new, and they probably won't fit right. They were Zhen's and Jordan's."

"Really?" Dr. Maxwell's voice rose in tandem with his eyebrows.

"Well, last night after dinner, Zhen, Alec, and I were watching a vid, and Jordan stopped by and said she'd found out you only had one tunic. I don't have anything, really, except the two Max scrounged up for me and the teal one from Zhen. Anyway, Jordan asked Zhen to pull out something for you. The sleep shirt was Jordan's, but she's so tall, she figured her other tunics wouldn't work."

"DuBois gave this to me?" Jordan's generosity did not surprise me, but DuBois's did.

"She likes to be called Zhen, you know, not DuBois."

I doubted that Zhen DuBois would accept such an impropriety on my part.

"Anyway." Kyleigh Tristram fidgeted. "Jordan insisted, and I told Zhen this color didn't look good on her. You should try it on."

The idea was unappealing. "It is rose. I do not wear rose. I wear grey and always have. Thank you, Kyleigh Tristram, but—"

"Just Kyleigh."

I blinked. "That would be inappropriate."

"How can it be inappropriate when it's my name, and I don't mind?"

Dr. Maxwell laughed. "I know, Kye. I've been dealing with the same thing."

"Kyleigh . . . while I thank you, this tunic has buttons on the side. I do not intend to be ungrateful, but perhaps it is best if—"

"If you don't want to be an ingrate, then take it. Really, it's the least we can do." Her eyes lit up. "Oh, I know! I'll take you shopping when we reach port. Since you aren't a Recorder anymore, you'll need something to wear."

"There is no—"

"Max!" Her nearly lashless eyes went wide. "I haven't been declared dead, have I? Do I still have credits?"

"You're still legally alive, Kye, or at least you were when we left. Any credits in the accounts should still be there."

Kyleigh flashed him a smile before turning back to me. "Just wear it?"

I appealed to Dr. Maxwell. "Is there no possibility of my securing grey garments to replace those locked in my former quarters?"

He shook his head. "You're the only one on board who wore Consortium grey." He appeared to be attempting to suppress a smile.

"Then I have little choice." I tried to keep resentment from my voice. "With access to only two tunics, it seems I must wear *rose* after all."

Kyleigh grinned again and began folding the tunics into surprisingly precise rectangles.

Dr. Maxwell checked my vital signs. "Do you feel up to trying something besides broth?"

My stomach growled in response.

"I'll take that for a yes." With a deft flick of the wrist, he straightened the covers on my bed. "Kyleigh, I requested some pureed soup for her. Would you go fetch it from the galley?"

She put her hands on her hips. "I may have slept through my last two birthdays, Max, but I'm not a child. You can ask me to leave without sending me on errands."

His eyes crinkled at the corners. "Understood."

She slid the clothing back into the bag and paused to rest a hand on the medtank closest to my bed before she left.

The doors had barely closed behind her when Dr. Maxwell began to elaborate on his plans for my recovery. He prescribed all manner of nutritional supplements, as well as injections of nanodevices programmed to facilitate healing, and a physical regimen to rebuild my strength. After I had been assigned a new room, I began low intensity training in the gymnasium. For several hours I crawled, spun, swung, and balanced on beams and boards. It was all gentle enough not to impede my recovery, and I disliked the entirety of the program, from the bitter supplements to the boring, repetitive exercise. I preferred the slow grace of my cohort's katas to such tedious drills.

And I missed my drone.

The next day, in the privacy of my new quarters, I had no other option, save the rose tunic. The small pearlescent buttons down the side rubbed against my arm, and the seams chafed my skin, just as the pale, undecorated walls irritated my mind. The tunic's color was not all that disturbed me. It was much shorter and tighter than anything I had ever worn. Though I was but two centimeters taller, DuBois, it seemed, had a slighter build than I.

I said as much to Timmons while he walked with me and Kyleigh to the small gymnasium where I had my therapy sessions, as he had done the day before. Several crew members stared while we passed, and their whispered comments made me uncomfortable.

"I don't know." Timmons grinned. "It suits you."

"I fail to see how a garment which restricts movement can be suitable."

"It looks good. What else do you want?"

"My grey tunic. *It* suits me. This one is *rose*," I said with growing irritation at both the color and Timmons.

His grin widened, but before he answered, Kyleigh broke her silence, "Here's the question, though."

I waited, but Timmons did not. "Which question? Out with it."

Her hazel eyes settled on me. "Yesterday you said someone tampered with the power source and lines for the pods in the medbay. Back home, on Pallas."

Timmons stopped suddenly. "What?"

I paused as well and inclined my head. "I believe my interpretation is accurate, but I have not verified the information, since Dr. Maxwell wishes me to take time before resuming my duties. I caution you to wait until I am able to review all the data. Without my drone . . . since I lost . . . since that . . ."

As clear as a recording, the memory flooded me—the roach crushing my drone—the flashes of pain—

"Easy now." Timmons caught my elbow.

Kyleigh grabbed my other arm, and they walked me to the bench outside the gymnasium, where I sat down heavily.

Her voice echoed dimly in my ears. "Is it the roaches? Zhen told me they wrecked your drone. They weren't there before, you know. We had a few species in the labs, and Dr. Johnson was letting Freddie and Elliott use them for their senior project. I *told* them to do more research, not just copy the research on isopods and use it without understanding it, but no . . . They aren't keen on science, but I know they didn't design giant roaches."

"Not now, Kye," Timmons murmured.

Her babbling stopped abruptly. They waited with me while I took deep breaths and attempted to regain control. At length, she sat on the bench beside me and rested a hand on my shoulder. I flinched.

"It's okay, Recorder-that-isn't. You're safe now."

"My apologies." Had my drone been present, I would have been penalized for such an overreaction.

"Nothing to apologize for," Timmons said gently. "And I'm glad that drone of yours isn't here to contradict me."

Surprised he, too, had thought of my drone, I looked up. When he extended his hand, I stared at it, uncertain of his intent, and eventually, he dropped it back to his side. I rubbed my palms on my leggings to dry them. Though my heart still hammered in my chest, I stood.

"Yes." I cleared my throat. "At this moment, I am glad of that as well."

The next day, Captain North granted Kyleigh permission to transmit a message to her mother, who researched isopod farming methods for a biotech development team on Ceres. A reply would most likely be waiting for her at New Triton's Lunar One base, and Kyleigh lamented the fourteen-day delay. I did not blame her. I, too, waited with uneasy anticipation to what the Elders would say about my failings.

After Dr. Maxwell's other assistant, Williams, finished testing my cognitive abilities, I sat with Kyleigh as she drafted several versions of the message before an ensign escorted her to the communications center.

Soon after she left, Timmons arrived. As was his habit, he leaned against the wall by the door, arms loosely crossed. "Ready?"

"You need not accompany me to the gymnasium."

He pushed off the wall. "I don't mind. Already ran the check on the chem system, and I don't have to relieve Johansen until after lunch. They'll call me if they need me. I'm good."

I nodded. He chatted about small, inconsequential things while we walked, but when we passed my old quarters, I interrupted to tell him I had tried to enter but could not unlock the door without my implant.

His eyes crinkled slightly. "Like I said. Not a Recorder."

"You do not understand." I struggled to explain. "My room is where I review and verify information, program my drones, exercise, sleep, and eat. It is my . . . my sanctuary."

He slowed, so I did as well.

"Do you miss it?" His voice softened.

I reflected for approximately nineteen seconds. "Yes. Until my fifteenth year, I lived in the dormitories. After I received my drone, I had my own room."

"Must've been lonely."

I shook my head. "I was never alone."

"Never alone? In a room by yourself?"

"I had my drone"—I tried to smile but failed—"access to information from any time and place, and an entire network linked me to other Recorders should I require company."

"You're not alone now, you know," he said.

This was not precisely true, but I could not find the words to explain my exile from the person I was meant to be.

The dumbbell slipped from Kyleigh Tristram's hands, and I jumped out of the way as it crashed to the rubberized decking. I grabbed at the equipment rack to keep from falling over.

"Sorry." She retrieved it and dropped it carelessly into its slot. "Stars above, but I hate exercise." She made a face. "I know, I know. It's good for me, but if either you or Max say so one more time, I'll quit. Forever."

I tried to raise a single eyebrow, as Jordan did, but a quick glance at my reflection in the mirrors behind Kyleigh showed me I had failed. After I straightened the smaller weights, the magnetic seal activated with a click.

"Are you going to do it, then?" she asked.

"Telepathy is still fictional, Kyleigh Tristram."

"Dinner. Are you joining us at dinner? Max says you need to start interacting more."

"As a Recorder, I should not—"

"I'll let you help me with the cats."

I had never seen a live cat. Other than biology classroom mice, Consortium Training Center Alpha kept no mammals. Cats served no practical purpose. Pets were luxuries, and luxuries were not permitted.

"I . . ."

She waited as well as any Recorder, save for the smile creeping across her face, while I weighed the benefits of seeing a cat against the prospect of a communal dinner. Her hazel eyes smiled, though her expression was otherwise neutral. "It'll be worth it."

As a Recorder, I had a responsibility to expand my understanding. Increasing the range of experiences enhanced the ability to record, so I nodded. She grinned, and after we had changed out of our provided white exercise attire, we left the gymnasium for the small storage room set aside for the animals.

"There's something happy about a cat," Kyleigh said as we walked. "Although, Macavity is a bit of a monster. It's not like they were pets, though. Dr. SahnVeer brought them for research."

Her words brought me to a halt. "Kyleigh Tristram, animal experimentation is not sanctioned by Parliament."

"They cleared it before Dad . . ." She looked away and drew a deep breath. "Before we got there." She pulled out a wadded tissue and blew her nose. I cringed inwardly when she shoved the used tissue into her tunic pocket. "Anyway, Dr. SahnVeer presented the case before a closed parliamentary committee. She even met with the Eldest, and he wasn't at all like she'd expected. She told me he wasn't old, either, maybe only thirty-five. How can you have a young *Eldest*?"

"If the experimentation was approved . . ." I started again. "It is a title. Three years past, we received a new Eldest, who is but Jordan's age. Most Eldests serve only four to seven years. The office is taxing, and the weight of the Consortium rests heavily on their minds."

"That's an odd way of saying it."

"It is a gift to serve, yet it is also a burden." We resumed our walk, and after five paces I asked, "Have these cats been subjected to experimentation?"

Kyleigh made an indeterminate noise. "No. Freddie's dad ordered us into the pods before anyone had done anything to them." She fell silent.

Many people found stasis pods and medical tanks unsettling, claustrophobic, but it seemed probable Kyleigh was discomfited by the unjustified fear she had precipitated the disaster.

"There is no evidence suggesting your actions placed undue strain on the system. Dr. Maxwell has approved my return to work tomorrow, and I shall investigate the incident as I am able. However, the system failure was not your doing."

"I know." Her face seemed paler than usual, but she gave me a tiny smile. "It's just . . . it bothers me to think I probably lived because someone else died."

I did not respond. When resources ran low, nanodevices in the closed stasis system would have directed micro and macronutrients converted from dead matter to the active pods. Kyleigh's conclusion was not inaccurate.

The door to the storage room opened, and a warm, musky scent with a sharp hint of ammonia stopped me as the door slid shut behind us. My nose wrinkled.

Five small, mottled, nearly naked creatures scattered at our entrance. Somehow, despite our conversation thirty seconds prior, I had forgotten how well nanodevices worked. Having lost the soft fur and thin, wiry whiskers in stasis, the animals were wrinkled, ugly creatures more reminiscent of evil mythological beings than sleek felines. Kyleigh gave me a quick smile but said nothing.

We sat on the floor, and the animals came to investigate. One seemed interested in me, though I did not want to touch the fine, new growth of black-and-white fur. After rubbing against my legs, the cat crawled onto my lap and made a peculiar noise.

"This one might be injured."

"No. He's purring. You know they purr, right?"

I had forgotten. I would not have forgotten, had I not lost my drone.

The naked cat put his forepaws on my collar and snuffled my face. I snuffled back, assuming that to be the appropriate response. He rubbed his head against my jaw and nudged my hand.

Kyleigh grinned. "He likes you."

After three minutes, I decided the Elders were incorrect. A purring cat, even an ugly, mostly hairless one, had value. I asked Kyleigh if he had a name.

"Dr. SahnVeer wouldn't let us name them, because she didn't want us getting attached, but I called him Bustopher when she wasn't around."

I sat with Kyleigh, Bustopher, and the other cats longer than I had intended. It was the most peaceful afternoon I had experienced since I was a young child, when my friend and I built boats beside the conservatory's brook. Dinnertime approached, so we changed the litter—an unpleasant job—washed our hands, fed and watered the cats, then thoroughly washed our hands again.

When we arrived at the dining commons, I stopped at the door, immobilized by the steady murmur of conversation and clink of flatware on dishes. The peacefulness of the afternoon evaporated.

"I am unprepared to dine here." I drew back. "I shall eat in my room."

"A deal's a deal." Kyleigh grabbed my arm to pull me forward. "Don't be a coward."

Recorders were not cowards.

I tugged the rose tunic down over my hips and squared my shoulders. Kyleigh gave me a slight smile and an even slighter nod, and together we stepped through the door.

I forced myself to observe as I should. Thirty-seven people, nearly two-thirds of the ship's complement, filled the dining commons. Support staff occupied one of the three white tables running down the center of the pale orange room, the crew sat at another. Jordan's team, a few officers, and a large, thin man I did not recognize sat at a third. The apparent social stratification surprised me.

Kyleigh and I each collected a tray from the stainless-steel counter between the galley and the dining commons, selected our meals, and joined the team at the third table. Jordan and Dr. Maxwell nodded to us and continued their conversation, but when we set down our trays, Communications Officer Adrienne Smith stood abruptly and left. DuBois scowled at me, and Spanos stared, his fork hovering in front of his mouth. She rapped his fingers with her spoon, then he muttered something about looking almost normal and resumed eating.

Timmons raised his ceramic mug at us before finishing his drink, and I slid into the chair between him and Kyleigh, opposite the man I did not know. Keeping my eyes on my dinner, I focused on my soup for several minutes, then risked a glance at Timmons.

He winked.

"So," said the man across from me. His warm baritone was deeper than Timmons's but not as deep as Dr. Maxwell's. "You're the Recorder."

Timmons narrowed his eyes. "She was."

I frowned at him, then nodded at the man. "Yes, I am."

"I'm Julian Ross."

"Indeed."

For a moment, his face was unnaturally still, then the corner of his mouth rose. Julian Ross added, "One of the station survivors hauled out by Jordan and company."

"So I surmised."

He extended his fist, though reaching across a table during a meal was impolite. When I did not tap it, he picked up his glass of water instead and took a slow sip, still watching me.

The beginnings of dark lashes faintly outlined deep blue eyes under growing eyebrows. His hair was growing in, as Kyleigh's was, and the short stubble would most likely be a rich brown if he grew it out as most citizens did. The shadow of his beard emphasized high cheekbones.

And then I realized I had been staring. My analysis had taken more time than it would have with my drone, and the resultant violation of social etiquette was unprofessional. My stomach twisted. I watched the steam writhe above my soup. "Excuse me—"

Julian Ross laughed. "It's all a bit much, isn't it?" For one horrible moment, I believed he spoke of the way I had stared at him, but he continued, "You've never eaten in the dining commons before, have you? Don't Recorders eat alone?"

Relief at having been mistaken enabled me to say, "Yes, we do."

"Well, don't let all this chaos get to you. We're not that bad, if you give us a chance." He smiled broadly. One of his eye teeth was crooked, and the slight imperfection emphasized the regularity of his features.

"You can leave off the charm, Ross," Kyleigh said.

"With two such beautiful young women, how can I resist?"

I knew then he meant to belittle me, and I ducked my head as my cheeks heated.

"Oh, leave them alone, Ross," Jordan called from down the table.

He snapped a salute in her direction. "Yours to command," he said before grinning back at us. "My apologies, ladies."

Kyleigh rolled her eyes. He laughed and resumed his meal.

If I had not lost my drone, I would not have stared. If I had my drone, he would not have dared to belittle me. But then, if I had my drone, I would not have been in the dining commons at all. I managed to swallow a little more soup, though my appetite had evaporated.

"I have finished," I managed to say, "and shall return to my room."

Kyleigh cocked her head at me. "Do you want me to—"

"No," I interrupted, another social etiquette violation, yet I could sit across from Julian Ross no longer. "Do not trouble yourself. I shall see you tomorrow." I stood but immediately sat again and whispered, "What do I do with my dishes?"

"They go over there." Kyleigh pointed to a cart next to the galley door.

Timmons touched my arm. "I'll take care of it. You've had a long day. Get some rest."

I thanked him and left the dining commons, almost relieved to escape its pale orange into the beige of the corridors, but dizziness slowed my steps before I had gone far. While I steadied myself against the wall, footsteps drew my attention, but it was only Julian Ross. Irrationally disappointed, I resumed walking.

"Listen, I'm sorry if I made you uncomfortable," he said when he caught up to me. He was quite tall, perhaps ten centimeters taller than Timmons. "I didn't mean to."

I said nothing.

"I'm still not myself," he continued, "but I—we—owe you and the rest of the team a huge debt. You got us out of a rough spot and fought through an insectile nightmare to rescue us. I appreciate it."

Pushing down a rush of anxiety at his allusion to roaches, I stopped and leaned once more against the wall.

He halted beside me. "Are you all right? Can I help you to your room?"

I shook my head and forced out the words, "No, thank you. There is no need."

A slow grin spread across his face. "I saw the way you looked at me earlier." His attention dropped to the tunic, then lifted to my face. "Anyone ever tell you you've got beautiful eyes?"

I fled to my room with as much alacrity as I could, given my dizziness, and his chuckle followed me down the corridor. Shutting the door, I leaned against it and recited prime numbers before changing into my too-large nightshirt and hurling the rose tunic into the laundry bin. I scrubbed my teeth with more force than strictly necessary. When I finally curled up on my bed, it occurred to me that Bustopher the ugly cat was better company than I had been.

There was a knock on my door. I did not answer.

"Hey," Timmons called softly. "If you're still awake, I brought you some tea and crackers. Thought you'd still be hungry."

With a sigh, I slipped out of bed, flicked the blankets back into place, and opened the door.

"You okay?" His eyes searched my face. "You left in a hurry."

When I motioned for him to enter, he set the snack on the bedside table and sat down at the computer desk on the other side.

The childishness of my concern bothered me, but still I asked, "Why was Julian Ross mocking me?"

Timmons raised an eyebrow. "He wasn't." He leaned back in the chair. "Look, Recorder-that-isn't, he was flirting. He thinks you're good-looking. He's not wrong, you know."

"Physical beauty," I said, lifting my chin, "is immaterial."

His dimple flashed. "If you say so."

After a moment, I picked up the tea and inhaled the steam. Lavender-peppermint. I smiled at him over the brim. "Thank you."

"You're welcome." Timmons put his elbows on his knees. "So . . . down in those tunnels, you said you like art. 'Members of the Consortium appreciate harmony and art,' or something. If that's true, how's physical beauty immaterial?"

"Beauty is subjective, but symmetry and craftsmanship are measurable. When I have free time, I strive to meet those standards in my own work. I often fail." I sipped my tea. "However, such aesthetics are immaterial when evaluating people. Outward appearance is not indicative of worth. To say otherwise is to invalidate the individual."

"True enough." He leaned over and took a cracker from my plate and winked. "Though, for someone who doesn't care about appearances, you sure seem to be picky about pink."

I bristled. "The tunic is rose, and the color is not my primary objection."

A corner of his mouth lifted.

"Grey is a comforting color. It is familiar. We—Recorders, Elders, and staff—believe in cleanliness and tidiness, but citizens seem to place greater value on maintaining unnatural appearances. I do not understand. Do not friends know the value of the person underneath?"

"I would hope so, though some people, even family . . ." He snatched another cracker, but his grin dissipated. "That's not always been my experience."

That he had been unfairly judged by anyone, but especially by family, bothered me. I set the mug of tea next to the plate of crackers and folded my hands. "Timmons, I do not value you any less because your physical features do not align as well with the golden ratio for beauty as others' do."

Timmons choked on the cracker. "What?"

Concerned I had misspoken, I clarified. "For example, although Julian Ross's features more closely follow the ideal for human faces than yours—"

He coughed.

I bit my lip. "Do you need something to drink?"

"Nah." Timmons rubbed his hand over his jaw. "Just took me down a peg or two."

I hid my unfamiliarity with the phrase by sipping my tea, then offered him another cracker. He shook his head.

"Your eyebrows, however, are more precise."

His mouth quirked. "That's something, I guess."

"Yet your eyebrows are not why I prefer your company." Immediately, I stiffened, expecting a consequence that did not come.

He watched me for three seconds before he said, "Same here." Then he slapped his hands on his knees and stood. "Drink your tea and rest up. Max said you're cleared for work tomorrow, right?"

"Yes. Jordan has asked me to assist DuBois with Pallas Station's information."

Timmons walked to the door. "I reminded J at dinner how you managed to get into those systems with a concussion and all. Told her you could probably use your computer magic to straighten it out."

"That is the nicest thing you have ever said to me."

A lopsided smile crept up his face. "Guess I need to work on my compliments, then."

The door clicked as it locked behind him.

I finished the tea and crackers, brushed my teeth again, and went to bed. Although my mind wandered from the dining commons back to lavender-peppermint tea, the prospect of sorting the information without my drone brought my thoughts around to the cats. Neither they nor I had names, and we had outlasted our original purpose.

We had that much in common.

Skipping breakfast the next morning after so small a dinner the night before was, in retrospect, unwise. I was so pleased to return to work, however, that I went straight from my quarters to Jordan's office and waited in the hallway for forty-five minutes before she arrived, if the analogue clock on display was accurate.

"You're up early," Jordan said in greeting. "All right, then, let's go get Zhen."

DuBois was in the dining commons with Spanos. If my memory of their files was accurate, their two-year personal contract had expired during the trip from New Triton to Pallas, but if close physical contact indicated anything, their relationship had not deteriorated.

"Zhen." Jordan folded her arms. "Whenever you two are finished."

"Coming." DuBois slid away from Spanos and kissed his cheek. "See you later."

A smile softened his features. "Lunch?"

"Of course."

When DuBois joined us in the hall, Jordan said, "We've got a lot of information to dig through today. The Recorder will be helping us out."

I added, "I am glad for the opportunity."

DuBois did not respond.

"We should have transmitted this information last ten-day," Jordan continued, "but so far we've only sent a basic summary. There's still a lot to sort out. Zhen's already started, but you two working together should make a good dent in it today. If either of you have questions about what was going on at the station, Ross might be helpful." Her eyes narrowed at DuBois. "And Zhen? Play nice."

I kept a hand on the wall to steady myself, and Jordan shortened her stride to match mine. DuBois walked ahead of us with such grace that she seemed to float, long black hair falling straight down her back.

"Jordan," she said without turning around. "It'd be best if I work from the other lab."

Jordan paused, then consented, and DuBois took the right turn when the hall branched and was soon out of sight.

I stared down the empty hallway. "I do not believe she prefers my company."

"Choose your battles, Recorder." Jordan gave no further explanation, and I asked for none.

When we reached my computer laboratory on the port corridor of Deck B, the door slid open quietly. I preceded her, but paused. Having only visible light made the room unfamiliar.

As the parliamentary committee which spearheaded the mission had suggested and the Eldest had approved, before leaving for Pallas I had disabled the Consortium recording device in the upper corner near the door. Its dark lens still stared blindly down at the three adjustable workstations, the desks, and the single charging station on the back wall. The water closet remained in the back corner. The same posters advised citizens about proper workplace behavior and regulations, and the same monochromatic print hung on the walls. The table and four ergonomic chairs still occupied the center of the room.

However, without ultraviolet light, there were no patterns, no mosaics. I drew a deep breath and slowly released it. The colors did not reappear. I had known they would not.

"I will do my best, Jordan."

"Yes." She nodded. "I'd be surprised at anything else. I'll be by this afternoon to see how you're getting on."

With a sense of renewed purpose, I adjusted the height settings at my favorite workstation—someone much taller than I had stood there previously—and immediately began to sort the files.

There was a plethora of information, and it was strangely jumbled. I had been very precise when I programmed the drones. It was possible that the destruction of the drones and my neural link had scrambled the data, but there was no obvious explanation for the disarray. I skimmed the files, creating a semblance of order, and tagged the information on the station's dead Recorder for later review.

Less than five ten-days after her death, Security Chief Gideon Lorde and Dr. Christine Johnson had been the first to succumb to the illness that had taken the lives of seventeen more people. Two days after the illness's onset, the director had sent the station's staff and their families into medical stasis.

But then, I read that Kyleigh Tristram's father had been murdered before the sickness struck. My stomach seized. I had not known, had not realized. For seventeen seconds, I stared at his identification picture—at the hazel eyes so like hers. The murder remained unsolved. Perhaps, if I . . .

No. I could not afford distraction.

I tagged those files as well and resumed my duty. As I shunted information into the proper places, the image of Dr. Charles Tristram's eyes and his untamed hair seemed superimposed on the words and numbers flashing before me. My drone would have reprimanded me for such inattention, and rightly so.

I set my jaw. I had failed to recover the body of the station's Recorder or her drone. The loss of two of my own drones was an even greater misstep. I would not fail in this task. I forced myself to focus and began cataloguing the security files.

Lost in my work, I only gradually became aware of someone behind me. I turned, expecting to see Jordan, but Julian Ross stood near the door, hands in his pockets, watching me closely.

"Good morning."

He was clean-shaven, which made the stubble on his head seem darker. His skin appeared smooth, almost soft, although soft seemed a word unsuited to Ross. Even after two inactive years in a stasis pod, his arms retained a degree of definition. He must have spent an inordinate amount of time in the gymnasium prior to the disaster.

"May I be of assistance?"

He shook his head. "Just wondering how things are going. If you need anything, you can ask me."

"Jordan told me as much. And, no, thank you, I am simply organizing data today, though I might have need of your expertise later."

He pushed away from the wall. "I didn't mean to upset you yesterday, though I guess I managed to do so twice. Most people enjoy compliments."

I accepted his admission as a tacit apology. "Recorders are not 'most people.'"

"Point taken." He loitered silently for another ninety seconds, so I asked if he needed anything else.

"I just want to know what happened down there." He gestured at the lower right-hand corner of the room, which puzzled me until I realized his motion referred, inaccurately, to the station.

"Of course. The information will be accessible once I have completed my work."

His gaze focused on the corner. "We'd been on that station two years, me and Elliott. Most of my friends were there. I've lost just about everyone, although Max insists my brother will pull through. I'd like some answers."

"I will do my best."

The corner of his mouth turned upward. "A not inconsiderable feat, if Jordan is correct."

My cheeks grew warm, which irritated me. I had not blushed so frequently when my implant regulated my emotions.

"Keep me informed?" he asked.

"As I am able."

"Recorder. Ross." Jordan's voice startled me, and I accidentally moved a file to the incorrect section. I moved it back.

"At your service." He half bowed with an athleticism belying his years in stasis.

She raised an eyebrow at him, then turned to me. "How's it going?"

"I am making progress." There was nothing else to say, so I resumed my work.

"Have you had lunch?" Ross asked.

I almost replied, but when I glanced over my shoulder, he was looking at Jordan.

"Just finished," she said.

"Too bad." He grinned down at her. "What about tomorrow?"

"Maybe."

Ross left, and Jordan watched him walk down the hall, a faint smile on her lips.

"Jordan," I said.

"Yes?" She turned back to me, her smile slipping away.

"Was there anything else?"

"No. Just checking in. Keep at it," she said, and left.

Involved in my task, I lost all sense of time. The work was not a true challenge, but without my implant and drone, it required concentration. My progress was slow since manual dexterity lagged behind thought. I focused intently in an attempt to compensate, reading more slowly than I had before, which compounded my frustration.

I only noticed Jordan in my peripheral vision when she joined me at my station.

"That's incredible progress." She opened another projection and skimmed the information. "You should take a break. You've been at this for a while."

When I turned away from the screens, my vision blurred. I blinked, suddenly aware of a growing headache.

"Recorder?"

For a second, her image split in two before I managed to focus.

"You're done for the day. Log off."

I nodded and began to close the programs, but my fingers were clumsy, as if the headache's onslaught had triggered an inability to control myself.

She put a gentle hand on my arm and said, "I'll get it."

When the room spun, I realized I had locked my knees, though I knew not to do so. I grabbed the desk to maintain my balance.

"Easy, now. Have a seat."

I heard the chime of her communication piece, heard her speak with Dr. Maxwell. Light hammered my head. I closed my eyes and slumped into a chair. The tapping of Jordan's fingers finishing my task was like weapons' fire.

The doctor's low voice announced his arrival, but I was too tired to open my eyes and greet him. With a cool pop, a jet injector fired microparticles and nanodevices through the skin of my neck. The pain receded, and my eyelids felt less heavy. I could almost taste lavender and pine.

"Sit up, Recorder," Jordan ordered, though her voice was soft.

Hands helped me straighten, and I opened my eyes. Dr. Maxwell knelt before me, Jordan tall at his side.

"There you go." He seemed to study my face. "What's going on?"

"My apologies. I am tired and have a headache," I rasped, my throat dry.

He pulled out a portable scanner.

Jordan glanced from me to the doctor. "She was waiting for me this morning around six thirty. I don't know if she's had anything to eat or drink or taken any kind of break. From the looks of it, she's been hammering away for the past nine hours."

Footsteps sounded in the hall, and someone entered, halting behind her.

"What happened?" Timmons's voice demanded. I could not see him from where I sat.

Jordan kept her eyes on me. "Max has everything under control. Not your concern."

"Go easy, Jordan." Dr. Maxwell, too, spoke without taking his eyes from mine. "She'll be fine, Tim. She just overdid it." A small crease formed between his brows. "Recorder, you need to accept that you don't have that blasted neural implant anymore."

"I do not understand."

He gave me one of his slightly sad smiles. "You've always relied on your drone to monitor your vitals, but now you have to do it yourself. Eat, drink, rest when you need to. You can't wait for a reminder or reprimand anymore."

Dr. Maxwell was correct, and I was mortified. "Yes."

"Maybe we can help, though," Jordan said. "I'll get you a commlink, or maybe a wrist monitor?" She glanced at the doctor. "Max, do you have any in the infirmary?"

"I should."

"You worked all day without eating or drinking? That's the stu—"

"Not helpful, Tim," Jordan snapped.

"All right, then." Dr. Maxwell stood. "We'll get some electrolytes in you. You'll bounce right back. Tim, could you get—" The doctor turned, then broke off abruptly. "I assume that's your blood?"

Jordan spun around. "Stars above, Tim."

"Relax, it's a scratch. Alec and I were sparring. I was on my way to get patched up and overheard Thacker say something about the Recorder, so I came to see for myself. Face wounds always bleed more than they should."

"Get back to the infirmary," Dr. Maxwell ordered. "And apply pressure on your way."

"And change your shirt," Jordan added. "You look like you're auditioning for a horror vid."

Timmons laughed.

"Tim! Void take it, man! Leave your shirt on until you get down there!"

"Max said apply pressure. It's efficient. Direct pressure and a more exciting sort of audition."

"Infirmary, now!" Jordan ordered, pointing toward the door. She added, "Show off," under her breath as Timmons left.

Whistles and applause echoed in the hallway. I heard his voice, though I could not discern the words, and then more laughter and another whistle.

Jordan and the doctor helped me to the infirmary. Timmons, in a clean shirt, sat on the edge of an exam table while Edwards applied a gelatinous bandage to the cut on his right cheekbone.

"That should do it." Edwards pulled off his gloves and pushed a strand of ashy brown hair behind his ear. As Consortium medical staff, Edwards had not received the specific nanodevices to suppress follicle growth, and for a second, I envied him. "We can remove the bandage tomorrow morning. The nanodevices should have knit the edges by then."

Timmons prodded the bandage, which rippled slightly under his finger. "Thanks, Edwards." He glanced at me. "You still don't look too good."

I ignored his personal comment and sat on an exam table. Dr. Maxwell checked my vitals and handed me a glass of foaming green liquid. I forced myself to ignore the color and take a sip. It tasted both salty and sour.

Jordan stood just inside the doorway. "Why don't you call it a day? Let Zhen check out what you've done so far."

"You will find everything in order." I tried not to take offense at the implication of substandard work. "While I am much slower without the implant, the quality of my work was not inferior."

"Slower?" Jordan's eyebrows rose. "You moved more information today than Zhen and I moved in the past ten-day. I haven't been working on it full time, but still . . ."

I waited five seconds, but she did not complete her sentence. "Since Zhen DuBois reads an average of 593 words per minute—"

"Really? That's faster than most people." Dr. Maxwell's dark eyes narrowed at me. "And how do you know that?"

"I have read her file."

"Her file?" Jordan asked quickly.

"Yes. I received dossiers on your team, although information regarding the ship's crew was minimal. I was expected to understand the people with whom I would interact while on Pallas." Edwards did not react, but the others exchanged glances. "Only data relevant to this assignment is in the files, and I can no longer access them, since they are in the data banks in my old quarters."

"You said '593 words per minute' dismissively." Jordan narrowed her eyes at me. "Like it wasn't much."

"I did not mean to do so."

Dr. Maxwell leaned back. "How fast do you read?"

"I am no longer certain. With the implant I could easily maintain a rate of 11,279 words per minute, but I suspect it has fallen to a bare quarter of that now, or I would have finished sooner."

Timmons whistled.

Jordan's golden-brown eyes widened. "What?"

I shook my head. "Without the ability to manipulate information through the implant, I am slower."

All four fell silent.

"My reading speed is not all that has changed," I added. "I cannot see as well, and some things bother me which did not concern me before."

"Such as?" Dr. Maxwell picked up an ophthalmoscope and checked my eyes.

"Sounds, smells, and the lack of access to facts when I need them. I sometimes feel there is a hole in my mind through which my memories have fallen. My responses have grown more emotional, and I cannot release neurotransmitters. And"—I lowered my voice—"my clothing bothers me. The seams are uncomfortable."

"Well, you could—"

"Tim." Jordan glared at him. "She doesn't need you spouting rubbish."

He winked at me, then winced as his cheek moved beneath the bandage.

Jordan steepled her fingers. "Max, you know more of *Thalassa*'s crew than I do . . ."

Dr. Maxwell nodded. "I'll ask around. There are bound to be a few people willing to give you something that'll fit better."

"Thank you."

"Un*seem*ly comments aside," Timmons began. The doctor and Edwards grinned, but Jordan shook her head. "Shouldn't she have something to eat?"

"Yes." Dr. Maxwell patted my shoulder. "Get some food into her."

Jordan's beads made a soothing clatter. "I'll go track down a commlink. Take it easy, Recorder. Work on something else tomorrow. Give me some time to catch up with you." She flashed me a smile then glanced at Timmons. "Don't forget we've got a meeting with North and Genet."

He groaned.

Jordan grimaced. "Agreed. Drinks are on me after this."

"North's been beyond tetchy since Pallas. There aren't enough drinks on board."

"When we reach Lunar One, I'll owe you. See you at dinner, Max."

Jordan disappeared down the hallway while Dr. Maxwell walked over to the emergency tanks in the corner of the room. He did not comment on the status of their occupants, and I did not ask. Timmons steered me to the door.

With the dining commons empty, we continued through to the galley. He searched through the refrigerator for a snack while I brewed two large mugs of tea, and we settled at the table nearest the back.

He pushed the plate with a sandwich toward me, took a huge bite from an apple, and made a face. "Mealy. You'd think I'd remember that apples get grainy and dry, but no. Ever the optimist, I suppose. Go ahead. Max's orders."

The sandwich was haphazardly made. Condiments oozed from between the slices of bread and fell with squelches onto my plate. I swallowed mouthfuls of tea to wash it down but managed to not cringe at the texture. "Timmons, I looked up the meaning of your idiom."

He raised an eyebrow. "Idiom?"

"'To take you down a peg or two.' You used the phrase last night, in my quarters." I stared past him at the stainless counter shining against the orange wall. "Did I indeed damage your self-esteem?"

A faint flush tinted his cheeks. "No more than I deserve."

"But if your family—"

He set the half-eaten apple on my plate. "No, it's fine. My grandfather is . . . a difficult man. We haven't spoken since university, to tell the truth. J, Alec, and Zhen are more like family than anyone else, which is fine by me. Add in Max, and I'm good." He reached for his tea. "Feel kind of lucky, really. After I turned twelve, home was Alec's place. You would've liked his mother."

My own tea was tepid, so I put it down and studied him, uncertain of how to respond.

He, too, set down his mug. "My class toured Training Center Alpha when I was about nine. That where you grew up?"

"Yes. I spent most of my free time in the Scriptorium and in the botanical gardens. We have a brook."

"I remember that." He grinned. "Got in trouble there, too. Ran off and tried to get some novices to play. Turns out Elders and their drones don't approve of playing."

"But that is untrue." The protest tumbled out before I thought to stop it. For a second, I held my breath, but again, the punishment did not come. "We play."

He waved his hand. "Organized sports. Not the same thing."

"But that is also untrue. Little ones have enrichment areas." A small smile rose at the memory. "The rooms are full of age-appropriate toys and music, even art supplies. That is where I learned to draw as a child, with the Caretakers—"

"The what?"

"Caretakers are Recorders who tend the little ones. We serve with them when we are slightly older, to help determine our callings. It was my favorite assignment."

"Caretakers . . ." Timmons regarded me for eleven seconds with an expression I could not identify. "That clears up a few things."

"When we are older, we are assessed for our callings." I swallowed the last of my cold tea. "I remember once a very loud citizen came to evaluate our capabilities for possible co-training with the military. His talk of how we looked the same angered me." If I closed my eyes, I could see him still. "He wore one thick braid with black synthleather woven through it, and the way in which it hung down his chest reminded me of a thin, dead snake."

Timmons's perfect eyebrow arced.

I clarified. "It was not that I disliked snakes. I did like them. However, when my favorite one in the biology laboratory died the day before, I discovered that I did not like death."

He nodded. "Neither do I."

"Oh. There you are."

I turned in my seat. Kyleigh stood on the threshold, then took two hesitant steps into the room. Timmons motioned for her to join us, then rose to fetch mugs of hot water and a selection of teas. She picked one at random and dunked the tea bag up and down.

"I missed you today, Recorder," she said.

"Your day proved difficult?"

"Yes and no. It's not like anything went wrong, and I'm thankful to be alive, but"—her voice faltered—"they're all gone. All of them. All but Freddie and Elliott and Ross. My dad, then Freddie's dad, and everyone . . ."

A solitary tear trickled down her cheek, followed by several more. Timmons pulled a square of cloth from his pocket and handed it to her. An unaccustomed helplessness swallowed me as I watched her cry. Then, sudden understanding assailed me. I, too, had lost everything. Answering tears gathered in my eyes, but I blinked them back. Tears were unproductive, and Recorders did not cry. However, Timmons's actions reminded me physical touch was reassuring. I took her hand, then let go, appalled at my audacity.

She sniffled.

"All will be well," I whispered.

Kyleigh's tears slowly subsided. She wiped her cheeks and the tip of her nose with the cloth, then cleared her throat. "Thanks."

We sat in the quiet until Timmons's communication link chimed. He closed his eyes, as if checking an internal chronometer, and stood without answering.

"Gotta go. Don't want to keep the captain waiting or show up dressed like this. It'll be all right, you know," he said to Kyleigh. "Though it won't feel like it, from time to time. Just ride each wave as it comes."

She wordlessly offered him the damp cloth, but Timmons shook his head. "Keep it a while longer, Kyleigh, just in case."

My reports could wait another day. "Would it help if we went to visit Bustopher? Or Freddie and Elliott?"

A small smile appeared. "I already checked on Freddie. We can go see the cats."

So, we did.

Kyleigh hated those first moments when the ship left dock, before artificial gravity kicked in. The weightlessness reminded her of how ships were nothing but fancy metal canisters, drifting through the emptiness of space. It was worse than it must have been for ancient Earth sailors, journeying into unknown seas where they might spill over into the nothingness of the world's end. At least they could swim a while, before the sea monsters took them. Space granted no such luxury.

She clenched her teeth. When Dad tapped her hand, Kyleigh opened her eyes, and he blinked at her from behind his thick glasses.

She forced a tight smile for his benefit and sighed with relief when her long, light brown braids fell to her shoulders and her weight settled back in the seat.

The only other passengers besides Kyleigh and her dad were two Recorders and two brothers. The scientist brother—who must be clever if they wanted him on the project—obviously believed he was too handsome for his own good, which she had to admit he was. The scrawny younger brother introduced himself as Elliott when they boarded. He was taller than she was—who wasn't?—but not nearly as tall as his brother, who towered over everyone.

The scientist noticed her attention. His blue eyes twinkled, and he nudged his brother with his elbow. The older brother raised an eyebrow and nodded toward Kyleigh. The younger one glanced over, turned bright pink, and shrank back into his seat, but the scientist winked at her. When she rolled her eyes, he only chuckled, pulled out a datapad, and started reading. Elliott didn't look up from his shoes.

Kyleigh frowned. Poor guy, living in his obnoxious brother's shadow.

The two Recorders sat opposite her and Dad. The female was traveling to the research station, but the other would remain with the ship.

Recorders didn't bother her. They were only doing their jobs, keeping everyone honest and safe.

The older female Recorder unbuckled and stood, studying them, and Kyleigh studied her right back. The Recorder's eyebrowless forehead puckered, and when she held up her left arm to her drone, it twined a vine-like tendril around it. She left the seating area at a brisk walk, the drone whirring softly beside her.

Dad touched Kyleigh's arm again, and she startled, though he didn't notice. He peered at her through his hideous glasses. "I'm heading back to our rooms, kiddo. I'll see about lunch after I check on my equipment."

In spite of everything—leaving Mom and home and all her friends—Kyleigh had to laugh. "Dad, you'll forget once you open those crates. I'll get us something when I join you."

He gave a sheepish grin, lightly tugged a braid, and ambled off.

The other Recorder's drone hovered over him like a cloud. He seemed young for a ship's Recorder, maybe five years older than she, with a complexion so smooth she felt a pang of envy. The ugly grey tunic stretched tight over his arms and shoulders. Thick, dark lashes curled around his eyes, which were silver-grey in the bright, cool light of the seating area. What would he look like with hair on his head and a smile on his face? He wasn't technically as handsome as the arrogant scientist, but he certainly was—

Kyleigh blushed. Stars! What was she thinking? A Recorder, handsome?

Silvery eyes met hers. She knew at once he was seeing her, not merely observing. For half a second, she suspected he knew exactly what she was thinking. Then the ridiculousness of the idea made her smile. Recorders could do a lot of things, but reading minds wasn't one of them. He narrowed his gaze, as if trying to recall something, and after several seconds, his lips tipped upward.

The Recorder was *smiling*. She blinked in surprise, then his expression faltered and fell, and he inclined his head once, then turned away.

Kyleigh's face grew hot enough to power a ship. She jumped up and headed to the door, stopping to ask directions to the galley, where she grabbed two prepackaged lunches, then found her way to their quarters.

The long, dull trip out to the research station lasted nearly three ten-days.

Kyleigh made friends with Elliott, but he wasn't interested in science or math, or even poetry. In fact, he was kind of boring. She read a lot, and Dad supervised her studies.

She avoided the female Recorder but watched the other one, surreptitiously. The staff and most of the crew ignored them both, but Elliott's brother was dismissive and condescending. Halfway through the trip, she grew so incensed about Elliott's brother's rudeness that once he left the common area, she stepped in front of the young Recorder to block his exit. His face did not register surprise, but he cocked his head in question.

"I'm sorry he's so . . . stupid."

His voice a pleasant though monotonous rumble, the Recorder answered, "He is who he is. You cannot change him. Although, Julian Ross has no mental deficiencies, as his accreditations attest."

Kyleigh put her hands on her hips. "He acts like he doesn't know you're a person."

"I am a Recorder."

She glared up at him. "That doesn't mean you aren't a person, and it certainly doesn't justify rudeness."

Another unpracticed smile spread across his face. "It might not, but you will be—what is the term? Hard pressed?—to prove it to him. His opinions are set."

Kyleigh moved aside. He passed her, his drone hovering behind him, and she followed him into the hallway. As he turned the corner, the drone wrapped a narrow tentacle around his neck. The Recorder paused for a second, straightened slightly, then rolled his shoulders before he disappeared around the corner.

"I wouldn't go there if I were you."

Kyleigh jumped. A blond officer with unfashionably short hair leaned against the wall. He and the shorter one, who resembled an ancient Greek statue but with long, thick lashes and tumbling dark curls, must have overheard her conversation with the Recorder. They'd clearly seen her watching him. The darker one scowled, his arms tightly crossed.

"Can't trust them, you know," the blond said apologetically. "Not when they have those machines floating around their heads. Drones record everything."

"Excuse me?"

He gave her an insinuating wink. "He'd probably be a nice enough fellow, if he weren't one of them."

Her face heated.

The other one uncrossed his arms. "They aren't safe. Trust me, I know. If you care about your family, you'll stay off their radar."

"Easy, Alec," said the taller man. "Look, kid, you and your dad seem like decent people. Actually, so does he." He gestured down the hall after the Recorder, and the other man snorted. "And ignore Ross. Don't call attention to yourself or that Recorder. Play it safe."

Kyleigh stormed off, temper rising at a low laugh behind her.

When the door to the suite she shared with Dad slid open, she marched over to where he sat, all attention on the three-dimensional model rotating above the datapad's screen and on the graph paper littering the table. He had one stylus tucked in his hair behind his left ear, and another twirled between his fingers as he tapped his heel against the ugly, serviceable carpeting.

When he looked up, she plunked into the chair opposite him and rattled off what had happened.

Dad pushed aside the datapad. His three-dimensional model pixelated and disappeared, and he took off his glasses and rubbed his eyes. "That young man has a point."

"His hair is stupid," Kyleigh grumbled and immediately regretted it. Being irrational made her cross.

Dad's eyebrows vanished under his unruly bangs. "Well, the stupidity of his hair is not reflected in his advice. Don't try to be the Recorder's friend, Kye. For your sake and for his." He gave her hand a squeeze, then pulled the datapad back, and the projection flickered back to life.

Kyleigh ran her long braids through her fingers and chewed on a bead. "I wish Mom was here."

"Sweetie, we've been over this. Your mother and I had reasons—very good ones, but ones we won't share with you." He shoved the glasses back on, his hazel eyes magnified through the lenses. "Your mother couldn't walk away from the project on Ceres. It was this or break contract, which we can't—we *won't*—do. I know it's hard to understand, but trust us. She'll be finished and back with us before you know it."

"But, Dad, two years?"

"It's not as long as you think, Kye. And Dr. SahnVeer is a giant in nanotechnology. Studying under her is an undergraduate's dream." He hesitated. "But maybe I've been selfish to keep you with me."

"Don't say that."

He rubbed his temples. "Why don't you do a few nice calculus problems and relax?"

She grimaced and tugged on his long grey hair, which defied gravity and stood up like a frazzled halo. "Sure, Dad. And really, why would I listen to someone with such bad hair?"

Dodging the crumpled napkin he tossed at her, she pulled out her math while he settled back to his work.

Everyone else had boarded the shuttle for the ninety-minute transport down to Pallas. Kyleigh hung back, hoping to talk to the Recorder again before they left. It was hard enough to start over, friendless except for Elliott. She couldn't imagine how hard being actively disliked by everyone would be.

She double-checked Dad's crates, then fidgeted outside the shuttle doors. The Recorder's drone hovered at shoulder level, instead of the usual two meters above the floor. One of its extensions plugged into a port inside the shuttle's doorway, and the translucent screen on its top flickered with data streaming faster than Kyleigh could read.

She paused next to the Recorder. "I'm leaving."

He glanced up, and the screen continued to flash. "It would appear so."

She probably imagined the twinkle in his silvery eyes. "Was this your first solo assignment?"

"Yes."

His drone detached itself, and the colorful screen faded to opaque grey. The extension telescoped into the drone's sidewall, and it rose to its usual position, following him out the door.

"Hey," she called after him, "I'm glad you were here. Maybe, in a different world, we could have been friends."

The Recorder stopped by the shuttle's door and turned to face her. "Friends?"

She nodded and shuffled her foot on the entryway's rubberized flooring.

He smiled, a real smile this time. "Yes. It would have been possible."

"Kyleigh?" Dad called from the seating area. "We need to buckle in."

"I have to go." She bit her lip and edged past him through the drab beige entry to join her dad.

Behind her, she heard the Recorder say, "You remind me of a friend I played with when I was a boy."

Kyleigh spun around, but the door closed, and he was gone.

Thirteen days after our disastrous assignment, on the sixth day since I had awakened, I could no longer avoid filing my report to the Elders, which meant I needed to meet with Captain North. After informing the captain I would join him and the first officer in the conference room, I notified Dr. Maxwell of the delay to my daily checkup. Despite the appropriateness of my grey tunic and leggings, I felt almost naked without my drone. Reminding myself once again that body language was a strong determiner of meaning, I straightened my shoulders and strode purposefully through the halls.

First Officer Archimedes Genet, his appearance precise and his dark hair in the single braid favored by most officers, reached the captain's door just ahead of me and motioned for me to precede him. I nodded to acknowledge his courtesy.

The conference room was still the same beige, navy blue, and steel grey, and the same mediocre oil painting of an ancient ship still hung on the wall. The same rectangular, faux wood table crouched in the center. Yet, like in my computer laboratory, the unmutable noise of the circulation vents and the absence of invisible light made the room unfamiliar.

I remained standing while First Officer Genet took his seat across from Communications Officer Adrienne Smith. Captain North leaned back into his synthleather chair and studied me as if I were a laboratory specimen.

"You spaced this one," he said without an appropriate salutation. I elected not to be offended by his vulgar language. "No drone, no current records. And hair? It's unsettling."

"None was done intentionally, Captain North."

He snorted. "And you still think you can do your job?"

I studied him, unblinking, trying to replicate the heavy, weighted stare of the Elders. The loss of my drone diminished the effect, but eventually his gaze faltered.

First Officer Genet spoke up. "Please excuse us, Recorder." His baritone should not have surprised me, as I knew his slight frame had no correlation with the depth of his voice. "Your accident was unprecedented and has been disorienting."

Again, I inclined my head toward him, then faced the captain. "I am reviewing the information from the station, and my report must include pertinent ship's data. I am here as a courtesy. I will be accessing the records. You will provide the same transparency as you would for any agent of the Consortium."

Communications Officer Smith ran her thumb across her fingertips while she kept her gaze on the floor at my feet, then said in a rush, "Of course, Recorder. We will comply with any requests you make."

Since I had eyebrows, I wished, for a moment, I had mastered the art of raising one to express disdain. "You misunderstand. This is not a request. Until such a time as a replacement arrives, I bear the Consortium's authority."

Her face paled, and Officer Smith froze, then turned to Captain North.

"We didn't know if you'd recover," the captain said. "Since our Recorder was effectively out of commission, I had Smith pull the logs and recode them."

"Coding is not a difficulty for me," I stated without condemnation, "but a lack of compliance would be a difficulty for you."

"Is that a threat?"

"It is an observation."

"Sir, let's not make this a bigger challenge than it already is." Genet rose and approached me. He was close to my own height, so we stood eye to eye. He extended his hand, palm facing up. "Welcome back to the land of the living, Recorder."

I missed my drone's ability to measure physical responses and the honesty of statements. For fifteen seconds, we faced each other. Then, we formally clasped each other's wrists.

The captain rose and extended a datapad. "If you're going over records, start here."

Officer Smith jumped to her feet. The errant thought that she had not meant to stand but had been ejected from her seat by an unknown force nearly made me smile, but training asserted itself.

"Very well," I said, accepting the datapad.

Captain North's mouth compressed into a tight line. He leaned over the table, one hand behind his back, the other splayed on the faux wood. I wondered briefly if he chewed his nails, for they did not extend to the ends of his fingers. "Aren't you going to ask what is on it?"

"No, Captain. Either you have complied, or you have not."

Officer Smith rubbed her palms on her thighs. "When Captain North had me inquire about your prognosis, Dr. Maxwell signed affidavits assuming all responsibility for his actions, both moral and financial."

Captain North began, "I will not be responsible for what that man did—"

"Captain," I interrupted, "I will review the data and obtain any clarifications necessary. However, this is your ship. You are indeed responsible."

Officer Smith needlessly straightened her jacket before edging to the door. "Let me get you the codes."

With a nod to both North and Genet, I followed her out to her station on the bridge, which grew quiet when I entered. I waited for her to retrieve the information, hands clasped behind my back. Alexander Spanos, who had been leaning over and pointing to a dataprojection at an ensign's desk, straightened. While other crew members merely cast sidelong glances my direction, he nodded at me.

"Recorder."

"Spanos."

For a second, a slight smile lifted the corners of his mouth, then he resumed his previous conversation, although the ensign watched me from the corner of his eye.

Officer Smith handed me a micro datapad, then escorted me back to the hallway.

"Recorder." She paused. "About the data North asked you to validate . . . Everything the doctor did was done without the captain's approval or consent. All resources were carefully logged and will be reimbursed from his personal account. He, Dr. Maxwell, said he wouldn't sit by and let someone die on his watch simply to 'placate the captain's prejudices.'"

"Are you concerned I shall judge your participation in the events in question? I assure you, such judgment is not my purview, but that of the Elders."

She simply stood, opening then closing her mouth, so I left.

Back in my computer laboratory, I fed the codes into the system and let the recordings play, viewing and certifying the testimony on the datapad, but my mind was not entirely focused on the information. The growing familiarity of my laboratory did not offset my mood: even without my drone's database, the captain's overt rudeness seemed to indicate antipathy.

Making assumptions about a citizen's motivations led to faulty records, so I tried to clear my thoughts. His attitude might not be personal, but it was difficult to take it any other way.

17

For one hour and thirty-one minutes, I stood at my station and accomplished nothing. I wrote my summary, deleted it, and started over, only to delete it again. The sequence of events was undeniable, but my thoughts churned and tumbled over each other, and my sentences did not flow. With a sigh, I rested against the smooth surface of my workstation and attempted to wrestle my words into order.

"Hey."

I startled, accidentally erasing what little progress I had managed. Pivoting, I frowned at Timmons, who grinned as he sat down at the workstation next to mine. Failing to keep the irritation from my voice, I snapped, "You caused me to delete my work."

"Nope. You did that yourself." He propped his feet up on the desk. "Did you know your nose scrunches when you're mad?"

"Whether or not my nose scrunches is immaterial." I then added, somewhat inaccurately, "I am not angry."

Timmons had the audacity to laugh. "It's all right to be angry once in a while. What's the problem, anyway?" He balanced the chair precariously on two legs. The gelatinous bandage had been removed from his cheekbone, and I could not help noticing his cut was healing remarkably well.

"There is no problem," I began, but the impropriety of my emotional outburst struck me. "My apologies, Timmons. I should not have blamed you for my misstep. A Recorder must display greater self-control."

He snorted. "Quit apologizing all the time. And the whole Recorder thing? You aren't one anymore."

"We must agree to disagree. I will concede, however, given my inadequate performance—"

The chair legs hit the floor with a sharp crack. "Max says you're not a Recorder, and he would know. But inadequate? I don't think so."

"Excuse me." I turned back to the computer.

His proximity should not have made any difference, but when he walked up behind me twenty-three seconds later, I was acutely aware of his presence.

"What're you working on?" he asked quietly.

"My report to the Consortium, which is even more difficult to write with an audience." I turned to ask him to leave, but the unfamiliar expression on his face stopped me. Without my database, I could not identify it.

"You've been through a lot," he said. "Max warned you to take it easy, remember? You need rest if you want to make a full recovery."

"I remember. I apologize again. I have been irritable of late."

"We all have." He shrugged. "Headache gone?"

I nodded.

"Your hair is growing in." The timbre of his voice changed, deepened.

My hand flew up to my head, but I was not thinking of my own hair. Inexplicably, I thought of his. Did the shorter hair on the sides and in back have a different texture, and why did the hair at the nape of his neck curl slightly while his bangs fell straight?

I clasped my hands behind me.

"Max says it is better to allow my hair to grow while my scalp is healing." My own voice did not sound right, either. I swallowed and changed the subject. "I need to write this report."

After seven seconds, which somehow seemed longer, he asked, "What are you planning to say?"

"I will tell the truth. The team retrieved the information and rescued Kyleigh, Ross, and the others."

"And what you did—"

"I shall admit that as well."

"You don't have to, you know. You're not a Recorder anymore. You have a choice now."

I did not answer him.

He seemed to search my face for something. "You have no idea, do you? What a brave, uncommon woman you are? Few citizens would put themselves at risk for people they hardly know. You took twice the punishment I did, down in the tunnels, when I interfered with your drone. I could see it, and I knew it was my fault. Then you covered for me to Jordan and never said a word about it, never even looked crossways at me."

"No, I–"

"You had your drones back off after Alec's outburst. You didn't have to. Most Recorders wouldn't. Threw yourself over J when you were in bad shape. Max says you might have saved her life. Stars, you're even kind to Zhen." His voice sounded thicker than usual. "I think–"

"I am a Recorder," I interrupted, tapping my fist on my thigh and stepping away from him.

He growled a curse in the name of a deity.

I stiffened. Losing my drone made a difference, for our words would not be recorded, but he needed to curtail his violations. "Please stop."

He blinked. "Stop what?"

"You should not invoke deities. Deities and religions are not sanctioned for public discourse. You should speak of religion only in the privacy of your personal space with like-minded people."

The corner of his mouth quirked. "And how would a citizen find like-minded people if no one speaks of their faith?"

I sputtered a protest, but he held up his hand, scowl sliding into a lopsided smile. "No, never mind. It wasn't an invocation. I was only cursing. No god'd want me anyway."

"I do not want your words to be misconstrued."

"Why?" He leaned against my console. "Isn't that manipulating the record or something?"

"I had not . . . I do not . . . Perhaps."

"So, why?"

"I . . . It is contradictory to Consortium protocol." I involuntarily checked the inoperative recording device near the ceiling. Though there would be no record of my own violation, relief did not ease my discomfort. I drew a deep breath. "I consider you my friend, and do not wish you to suffer negative consequences. I do not want you to be hurt." I touched his sleeve, but when his gaze dropped to my hand, I lowered it and moved away. Recorders did not touch citizens. My words, wholly insufficient, stumbled out, "You are important to me."

His eyebrows drew together. "What's your real name? I can't keep calling you 'Recorder' when you aren't one."

"I have no name." I clasped my hands behind me again. "Identification number aside, none of us do. The absence of my neural implant does not alter the fact that I am still a Recorder. When we return, they will repair me. Dr. Maxwell is not a member of the Consortium, and his assertion that my neural implant cannot be replaced has no basis in our internal procedures."

"You don't need to be repaired. You're not broken."

"How can that be true when part of me is gone?"

"Recorder . . ." His jaw ticced, then he cursed again under his breath, spun on his heel, and left the room.

I stared after him, rooted in place by the feeling I had done something—said something—terribly wrong.

I needed my implant, needed it to regulate the painful buzzing in my chest. Instead, I attempted to finish the report, but my mind wandered, and my clumsy fingers garbled the words. Inability to interface with the drones had crippled my usefulness.

Timmons was correct. I was no longer a true Recorder.

18

Seventeen minutes after Timmons's departure, Jordan entered my laboratory and demanded, "What happened between you and Tim?"

"Nothing of consequence."

She narrowed golden-brown eyes at me. "Don't interfere with my team."

"I did not intend to do so."

At length, she said, "I know this has been difficult. You certainly didn't have an easy first assignment."

"No." How insufficient that word was. "Although I attempt to redeem my errors."

"When I file my final reports, I'll . . ." She fixed her gaze on the ceiling. "I'll do what I can to help you."

"I appreciate—"

But Jordan left the room.

Had I again said something wrong? I tapped my fist on my thigh several times before I returned to the report.

Five minutes after Jordan left, as I deleted my opening paragraph for the eighth time, my communication piece chimed. The novelty of someone choosing to communicate with me had not worn off, so I was quick to answer.

After all, the interruption had not disturbed any progress.

"Good morning," Kyleigh Tristram said in a rush. "Would you be interested in helping with the cats?"

The incomplete document flickered at me. I deleted it and closed the program. "Yes."

"I'm heading over there in a bit." She paused. "Does . . . does your scalp itch?"

"At times."

Her low laugh floated, disembodied, from the communications link. "It does, doesn't it?"

I began to confirm my arrival time, but the communication piece chimed again, ending the connection.

Timmons had left, possibly angry. Jordan had left while I was speaking. Kyleigh had ended the link before I had given an estimate for my arrival.

The odds of these three events occurring in such a tight time frame indicated the probability of my behavior as a factor.

The silent computer seemed to stare back at me from under the Parliament- and Consortium-endorsed posters detailing workplace regulations. Citizens were even more complicated and unpredictable than I had been taught, and maintaining relationships was a challenge for which I had neither the resources nor the experience necessary.

Timmons and Kyleigh, Dr. Maxwell and Jordan, were my friends. I would miss them. Leaving them behind to resume my life would be difficult. Perhaps this was yet another reason Recorders distanced themselves from others.

While I walked to the storage room, I reviewed my meeting with the ship's officers and then the three abruptly ended conversations. My confidence dwindled, and my steps slowed. Consortium training advocated conflict resolution. I needed to repair what I could, to find Timmons. Kyleigh would understand if I arrived late. I was more confident of my ability to interpret situations in person, so I turned toward the lounge.

I heard Jordan before I reached it, and her voice snapped with an energy I had begun to associate with anger. Recorders did not interrupt emotional conversations and disputes. Personal drones administered discipline, offering a sense of absolution and closure. This, however, was not the Consortium.

". . . known each other too long. You don't fool me, Tim!"

"Forget it." His tone matched her intensity, if not her volume. "Just leave it alone."

I stopped on the threshold.

Timmons and Jordan stood next to a table under the viewport. Since they were approximately the same height, their eyes were even, and it struck me again how well matched they were. Neither noticed me. Jordan grabbed his arm, but he shrugged off her hand.

"Tell me it's not what I think it is, and I will."

Timmons's jaw clenched.

"Stars above! Are you out of your mind?"

He growled an answer I could not hear.

She took half a step backward. They fell silent, eyes locked on one another.

I should have announced my presence or slipped away, but I did neither, only stood immobile, just outside the doorway.

"You've made some wicked mistakes before, but, honestly, this one takes the prize."

He ran his hand through his hair, and his bangs fell haphazardly over his eyes. "Jordan—"

"After what . . ." She lowered her voice. "Look, Tim. No matter what you and Max want to believe, she's theirs. There's no telling what they'll do about her interference, not to mention the loss of her thrice-blasted neural implant and some extremely expensive equipment. You really think they'll just let that all slide? Not to mention that she interfered."

"We'd be dead if she hadn't—"

"And that's my point! Her choices saved our lives—and I'm grateful—but they were *choices*. There's no way she'll be reinstated."

Sharp pain squeezed my chest. Was it indeed possible the Consortium would not repair me? I tapped my thigh, then fisted my hands at my sides.

"Good!" Timmons paced the room. "If they don't reinstate her, she can leave."

"Don't be stupid." Jordan stood with her back to the viewport, the burnt orange of her tunic almost glowing in the blandness of the lounge. "They won't let her go, and you know it. You don't hear of Recorders acting like that, thinking for themselves—and it's not because they don't. They might be Recorders, but they're people. They're removed, Tim."

"And you'd know that how?"

"I know for a fact it's true. They won't let her back in, but they won't let her go free. Recorders disappear, just like citizens. Like Alec's father."

He fell, rather than sat, into a chair, scrubbing his hands over his eyes. "You don't know that."

"Yes," she hissed. "Yes, I do."

Timmons raised his eyes to hers, but Jordan merely shook her head. He crossed his arms. "Like I thought."

Jordan slapped her hands down on the table, her braids clattering over her shoulders. "Void take it, Nathaniel! Will you just listen? They won't 'repair' her."

"If you're so worried, talk to Max—"

"Stars, you think I haven't? Max is seizing the moral high ground on this, and it's going to space him, too."

When he did not refute her words, a thread of fear wrapped around me like a drone's tendrils. Surely the Consortium would not reject its own, and surely Dr. Maxwell was not in danger for helping me.

I shrank back further into the hall, but I did not leave as I ought.

"Walk. Away."

Timmons let out a stream of profanity.

"Knock it off!" Jordan's voice came sharp and fast, like steam under pressure, then lowered. "And keep it down. She might not be prowling the ship with that cursed drone, but she's still a Recorder. You can't trust her."

Her words sliced through me. I considered these people my friends, but she was right. Friendship required trust and respect. Citizens trusted the veracity of records, but they neither trusted nor respected Recorders. How had I forgotten so quickly that with or without my implant and my drone, my status precluded friendship? And how could the absence of something I had not truly had hurt me? How could it make it so difficult to breathe?

"She thinks they're going to 'fix' her, J, like she's a spacing drone. And, if you believe all that, how can you stand there and tell me to walk away, like she's nothing? Like she didn't risk her life for you?"

"Tim . . . I don't know. Maybe we can figure something out. We still have time before we reach Lunar One, but whatever happens, you need to walk away."

Sliding further into the hallway, I pressed myself against the cool wall. Each inhalation was work, each exhalation, difficult.

"I know I should, if that's any consolation." His laughter sounded short and sharp, somehow reminding me of broken glass.

She growled, "Then do it."

I truly had not meant to eavesdrop. Recording was one thing. This was different. I needed to leave. I needed to think. One hand on the wall to steady myself, I wiped my cheek dry and retreated. Something in me had indeed malfunctioned. At that moment, I was glad I did not have my drone.

19

The door slid shut behind me, and Kyleigh smiled up over a cat's mostly naked head.

"I wondered when you'd get here." Her smile melted away. "Are you all right? Your eyes are red and puffy."

"I apologize for my tardiness."

She studied me. "Do you need to go to the infirmary?"

"I do not." Avoiding her gaze, I sat on the floor next to her, and Bustopher bounded off a sealed storage crate and onto my lap. While he nudged my hand, I carefully selected a true sequence of events. "I had difficulty with my report, and I talked to Jordan."

"I saw her maybe an hour ago. She was looking for you, and I told her to try your lab."

"Yes." I focused on Bustopher. "Have you fed the cats?"

She ignored my diversionary tactic. "She said something about Timmons. What'd he do this time?"

My face heated. "He did nothing wrong. I spoke with him earlier, and though I do not understand how my words created a negative response, Jordan suspected I had upset him." I did not attempt to suppress my sigh. "Societal interactions present greater challenges than I had anticipated."

"Yes, they can." She grimaced. "I met him before, you know, him and Alec, on the ship that brought me and Dad to the station four years ago. Did you know he reads? Timmons, I mean. Dad did, too, of course, but only really about—" She began again. "Dad read about math and science. But Timmons reads everything. I even saw him with a banned book once, though I wasn't meant to. Oh!" Her hands flew to her cheeks, and her mouth widened in an oval. "I shouldn't have said that."

Perhaps he had acquired his propensity for violating anti-obscenity laws by reading unapproved texts, but I merely nodded.

"It was a long trip." She laughed but avoided meeting my eyes. "Long and boring. Ross and Elliott were there, too, and two Recorders."

"Two?" Confused by her random statements, I reached for the most appropriate conversational response. "That is unusual."

"I know. Pallas didn't have one, so she stayed, but the other one was the ship's Recorder."

While she focused her attention on the cat she called Hunter, I silently berated myself. I had temporarily forgotten about the Recorder stationed there, the one I had failed to bring back.

"And . . ." She glanced around, then leaned forward slightly and whispered, "Well, I had a bit of a crush on him."

My hand stilled, and Bustopher nudged me. "Oh?"

Kyleigh blushed furiously. "He was nice."

Citizens did not describe true Recorders in such complimentary terms. As I was damaged, Timmons's exaggerations did not signify, but nonetheless, a lump formed in my throat. I cradled Bustopher to my chest.

"He had broad shoulders and beautiful silvery-grey eyes. We talked a few times, and he said it was his first assignment, but Ross was always so horribly rude to him." She made a face. "Anyway, when we left, I told him we could've been friends if things were different, and he agreed. Then he smiled. He had a nice smile."

I knew someone like that. A bubble of happiness pushed my earlier turmoil aside.

"He said he'd played with a friend when he was a boy, which I thought was odd. It would've had to have been someone from the Consortium." She sighed. "This might sound strange, but even though I remember all that, I can't recall his face, not really. Just his smile and his eyes."

Recorders never gambled, but I would have wagered she had met my friend. I suppressed a grin. "Oh?"

"Anyway, Timmons overheard me talking to him and warned me not to try to be the Recorder's friend. You know how he stands, leaning against the wall, smirking." She huffed slightly, and her gaze returned to the cat. "He said you can't trust Recorders. Or Alec did. One of them did. My dad agreed, but I didn't really understand. Not then."

She continued to speak for several more moments, but her earlier words echoed in my mind, and I wished I had not heard them.

Timmons had been so kind. In some people this might have seemed duplicitous, but I did not believe he was. He had been respectful and helpful. The loss of my implant and my drone had unsettled my emotions and clouded my perceptions. I had misinterpreted his considerate behavior as friendship. That was all.

I wrestled my thoughts under control and focused on the tan paneled wall behind her. Fortunately, Kyleigh's attention had remained on the cat on her lap, and she did not see whatever my face might have revealed.

". . . maybe it doesn't count. Besides, Dad was like that." She hugged the cat close, and Hunter's smooth, contented purr filled the room. Kyleigh smoothed her hand over the cat's head. "Dad used to distract me with math problems."

Focusing on her last statement, I said, "I, myself, recite prime numbers to settle my mind, but solving equations would also be beneficial. He sounds like a good father."

"Yes, he is . . . He was. You . . . know about my dad, right?"

"You speak of his murder?"

Tears filled her eyes, and she dashed them away with her sleeve. "Gideon never found out who . . ." She stood abruptly, to Hunter's dissatisfaction. "But I guess it doesn't matter now, since everyone is gone."

I could not say why, but I did not believe her assertion that the lack of closure was immaterial. The security chief should have found the perpetrator.

Kyleigh paced the room. "In a twisted way, I'm luckier than Freddie. Dad was already gone before we got in the pods. I knew—and even though I was technically asleep in stasis—I dreamed. I worked through it, somehow. I mean, you aren't asleep-asleep in a pod."

A memory of the roach-dreams shuddered through my mind, but Bustopher nudged my hand, pulling my attention away from the nightmares. I managed to say, "Yes. I know."

Kyleigh leaned against the tan paneling, slid to the floor, and wrapped her arms around her knees. "Thing is, Freddie's dad wasn't gone when we went into stasis. Freddie doesn't know yet. John, his dad, used to say all things worked together for good, but it doesn't feel that way just now."

"No," I said, thinking of Timmons's opinion of Recorders, of the argument I had overheard, of my failures. "It does not."

"Feelings are like shadows . . ." She stopped.

I waited.

"There's a certain solidity to shadows," she finally said. "A certain weight and heft. All the fears and dreams we carry—the silent, intangible things—they aren't completely intangible. They can weigh you down like solid objects."

Tightness closed about my chest again. "I do not understand."

She chewed her lower lip. "Those things we can't even see act like an invisible force. Maybe . . . like a black hole? Bending light, destroying matter." She held up a hand to forestall my commentary. "I know, Recorder, I know. Energy in a closed system, and all that. But that isn't the point: all analogies have flaws. I mean, sure, we all have thoughts and dreams and ideals that impact us for good or ill."

"Not all," I said without pausing to think I should not.

Her hazel eyes focused on me like lasers. "Yes. All. Even Recorders."

"Perhaps."

"Even you."

It took three minutes to collect my thoughts enough to change the subject. "I am sorry for your loss. I cannot understand, however, as I never had a family to lose."

"Do you regret that?"

Her question demanded too many answers. I found myself glancing over my shoulder for discipline. Thirteen days without a shadow drone did not erase eight years with one, especially since I had been in a medical tank for more than half that time. Still, losing a drone, losing who I was meant to be, might or might not have correlated to losing people. I did not know, and so I did not respond.

"May I tell you a secret?" she asked, almost inaudibly.

Once more, her question disoriented me. "If I am still a Recorder, you should not."

Kyleigh stretched her thin legs in front of her and tilted her head to the side. "Max and Timmons say you aren't. It isn't a real secret, though. I mean, Freddie knows, but not Elliott or Ross. I don't really like Ross. He has an ego the size of a moon, and it's irritating."

"Oh." My inadequate answers were beginning to irritate me.

"Something has always seemed off with him, you know?"

I pictured Ross's quick smile and deep blue eyes. The Consortium had not provided the dossiers on the personnel from the research station. Unfamiliar with her colloquialism, the appropriate response eluded me. "I am afraid I do not."

Kyleigh's faint eyebrows shot up. "You don't . . . like him, do you? I was sure if you liked anyone—"

"No, no," I interrupted hastily when I realized she implied a deeper bond than mere amicable tolerance. "I did not mean to imply any emotional attachment. Rather, I meant I do not see any particular trait indicating he is not a desirable companion."

"Desirable?" Kyleigh grinned and waggled her faint eyebrows up and down.

"Allow me to clarify," I said, scrambling for the correct description. "I have not experienced flashes of intuition which assist decision-making. I simply meant that I did not understand how you came to such a conclusion."

"So," she pressed. "Who do you find 'desirable'?"

Avoiding her question, I asked, "Is that your secret? You do not prefer Ross's company?"

"No, it's something else." She studied my face. "It doesn't matter. I suppose it isn't a secret after all, since it's already part of the record, and they can't do anything about it now."

Again, I waited.

"I was almost a Recorder, myself."

"I do not understand."

"My mother was Dad's sister. Blast. I said that wrong again. My birthmother didn't want me. She was going to give me to the Consortium, but her brother, my dad, convinced her to give me to him and Mom since they hadn't had children. But, when Dad got the offer to work on Pallas, Mom stayed behind on Ceres. She did send us letters, though, and she was supposed to join us . . ." Kyleigh frowned down at her knees. "Freddie's dad was supposed to tell Mom about Dad, but I don't know if he sent the message or not."

Bustopher butted his head against my arm, so I rubbed his ears, my thoughts spinning in my head. Had my mother's extended family known of the possibility of taking me, instead of gifting me to the Consortium? No . . . The fact no one had wanted me was as immaterial as whether or not my nose scrunched when I was angry.

"Theoretically, we might've known each other, maybe even been friends."

Friends.

It was difficult to speak past the tightness in my throat. "No. We would not have been in the same cohort, since you are younger than I. But, regardless, we would not have been friends. Recorders do not have friends." I paused, then asked, "Can you keep a secret?"

"From whom? You keep saying you're a Recorder. You shouldn't have secrets."

I forced a smile. "It appears I do. I am glad you were never a Recorder. I am glad you are not like me. You deserved to have a family, even though it came with loss."

Kyleigh's hazel eyes grew larger in her thin face. "I didn't—"

"I am glad you are not like me," I repeated. I stood suddenly, and Bustopher's loud protestations echoed in the storage room. "I must go and finish my reports. I apologize for not being more helpful with the cats."

"I didn't mean . . ." Kyleigh pushed herself to her feet. "I'm glad you're my friend. I only wish I'd met you earlier. Please, you don't have to go."

I paused with one hand on the door frame. "Do not be concerned, Kyleigh. Your history will not be part of any record I transmit."

Ignoring her protests, I left.

The words spilled from my fingers into the computer with ease, documenting the assignment. I elaborated on my less than professional uneasiness in the tunnels and around the bodies. I wrote of my mistakes and the thoughtless act that resulted in the destruction of my drone. After describing how Timmons, Jordan, DuBois, and Spanos saved my life by strapping me to the pod and how we escaped through the hangar, I described my failure to locate both our lost Recorder's remains and her drone, my loss of the AAVA drones and of data and samples, of being sick and nearly drowning in vomit until Jordan ripped off my helmet.

Confessing that I had no reliable memory or record of our escape, I wrote of how I had been incapacitated in the infirmary and thus failed to obtain a record of the station's destruction. I praised Dr. Maxwell for his skill and generosity in saving my life, but I also explained that my implant was gone.

My failures mocked me from the document, and I could not bring myself to send it. Not yet. Instead, I closed the programs and left for dinner. The dining commons were mostly empty, so I ate my meal in peace, then took the shortest route to my room, watching my boots and silently reviewing my lack of options. So involved was I with my thoughts that I nearly ran into DuBois and Spanos.

DuBois's dark eyes flashed, and she wrapped her arm through his. "Watch it."

I backed up several steps. "My apologies."

Spanos's thick, dark brows knotted. "It's all right, Recorder. You know, you did a good job with the computers."

"Thank you, but it was your expertise with explosives that enabled our escape." I had not instigated the conversation, but conciliatory behavior was, to my understanding, a functional part of societal manners. "My apologies for detaining you. Good night."

I had not progressed more than a few meters when I heard, "Moons and stars, she looks terrible!" Her words almost echoed in the empty hall. "Sure, her hair almost covers those ugly scars, but she's ghastly pale."

He answered her, his words indistinguishable, then she laughed.

"That's a change of heart."

Heartily sick of overhearing conversations, I accelerated.

Memories of the day's events churned inside me, from the meeting that morning, to the confrontations, to Kyleigh's revelation about both her Recorder and Timmons. Finally in my quarters, I changed, turned on my red nightlight, and sat on the bed, staring at my hands.

Kyleigh believed we were friends. I thought of Timmons, Kyleigh, and Dr. Maxwell as highly as I had before, although after Kyleigh had explained his feelings about Recorders, I realized Timmons would not describe me in a like manner. And, regardless of her feelings, I also valued Jordan.

There would be severe consequences for them should the Consortium hear of my perceptions. Timmons had been disciplined for merely interfering in my drone's duties on Pallas. What price would be exacted if any of them were believed to have undermined my unbiased neutrality?

I was accustomed to consequences. If I merited reprimands, I would accept them. I would not resist.

But nothing—*nothing*—must happen to Timmons. Or Kyleigh. Or Dr. Maxwell, Edwards, or Jordan. Or even Spanos and DuBois.

Not because of me.

Never because of me.

20

Only the quiet throb of the circulation fans broke the silence in my computer laboratory the following morning while I set down my tea and initiated the programs. After rereading my work from the day before and making several small clarifications, I drew a deep breath and transmitted the data over a secure channel, but instead of contentment in a job completed, emptiness swallowed any sense of satisfaction.

It was done.

Forcing down irrational discouragement, I accessed the data regarding the station's Recorder, attempting to lose myself in the information. But while correlating personnel files, I found myself caught up in people's stories, rather than numbers and patterns.

Unlike Kyleigh, Freddie was completely alone. His father—John Westruther, the man we had found in the control room—had been his sole living relative. At least Kyleigh's mother was alive on Ceres, but I found no record of any communication from Westruther regarding her father's murder. And though Elliott was still in the medical tank, he and Ross had each other. The magnitude of the survivors' losses slowed me temporarily, but I pressed on.

I completed my work, retrieved some water and a nonperishable snack, then made my way to the storage bay to perform overdue maintenance on the remaining drones. Though someone had changed the access codes, it took me but forty-one seconds to enter.

Ignoring the empty stasis pods which occupied but a fraction of the space, I continued to the side wall where the AAVA drones sat in their temporary nooks. I carefully wiped down casings and lubricated joints, then performed systems checks, modified minor programs, and processed the few surviving samples from the station. A service bot took the sealed containers of dust, rock, and biopsy samples to the laboratories near the infirmary.

When my wrist monitor chimed, I drank some water and ate my snack, then leaned back against the wall to rest. My mind raced through the previous day. Timmons storming away. Jordan scowling. Kyleigh blinking back tears.

Words and images spiraled like a vortex inside me. I tried listing prime numbers, but in my mind's eye, Timmons recited them, his hand resting gently on my head. My own hand flew up at the memory and met the bizarre texture of hair and welt-like scars, and my eyes snapped open.

This was unacceptable.

I needed normality. I needed restoration. My drone was gone, my implant was gone, and even the sanctuary of my old quarters was lost to me. When my gaze fell on the nearest AAVA drone, I straightened. If I could reconfigure one, even without my implant, it should be able to interface with the coded locks. I took a smaller, undamaged unit to my old quarters and spent the next two hours attempting, unsuccessfully, to open the doors. Crew members passed, their whispered comments buzzing like air through a broken vent.

Discouraged, I trudged back to the bay and returned the drone to its alcove.

My empty stomach churned, and my head throbbed. I collected a tray from the deserted dining commons and walked slowly to my quarters, but my mind kept returning to the concept of friendship. Shunting aside the images of Timmons and the others, I summoned the memory of my first friend's silver-grey eyes, the scent of lavender, and our boats, a scene much more vivid than *Thalassa*'s monotonous beige corridors.

I was convinced Kyleigh's Recorder was my childhood friend. It was ludicrous to entertain the possibility of anyone having genuine interest in a member of the Consortium, but a tiny thread of happiness ran through me. Four years ago, he had been well. Kyleigh had seen *him*— the person, rather than the drone—and had recognized his worth.

But before I reached my quarters, that tiny thread of happiness had vanished, replaced by my concern about consequences for losing my non-bias.

Footsteps sounded in the hall behind me. I had no desire to speak with anyone, so I quickened my pace. Nevertheless, Timmons caught up with me, though he remained quiet for the count of eleven seconds.

Then he said, "Want to tell me about it?"

My fingers tightened around the tray's rim. "Nathaniel Timmons, if you wish me to provide information, you must specify a topic."

Out of the corner of my eye, I saw his lips twitch. "All right. I want information about you."

"I have had a taxing day and require both food and rest." I made a careful study of the antistatic carpeting. The absence of full-spectrum color hit me again, and I drew in a sharp breath.

"If that's all, then why won't you look at me? I want to see what you're thinking."

We reached my room, and I turned to face him. "I have told you what I am thinking. To say you could *see* what I am thinking would be to grant you powers beyond human observation. If you will excuse me, I am tired and do not have the energy for a lengthy conversation."

He tried to lift my chin.

I stepped back, moving the tray to my left hand, and pushed his hand away with my right. "You do not have permission to touch me."

He shifted back slightly. "What's wrong?"

"Nothing is wrong." I told myself that this was not inaccurate.

"I don't buy it." His green eyes narrowed. "I mean, I don't think nothing's wrong. Talk to me."

I said nothing. My door opened, but I waited in the hall for five seconds before entering and setting my tray down. Still he stood watching me quietly, his head tilted to the side.

"Good night, Timmons." I closed the door.

I forced myself to eat my dinner, though my appetite seemed insufficient to the task.

Timmons had warned Kyleigh not to trust Recorders and had not refuted Jordan's denial of my trustworthiness. Yet, he regularly insisted on my company and expressed concern for my welfare. I could not reconcile these contradictions.

I did not fall asleep easily. It had been a thoroughly unsatisfactory day.

Jordan entered my computer laboratory and lowered herself into the chair next to my station. "I didn't see you yesterday."

"I was working."

Her right eyebrow rose, but she nodded. "You've accomplished a lot."

"I finished organizing the files, sent my report, and worked on the drones. Today I plan to review the data from the station."

Jordan folded her arms.

My own arms had never been that well defined. But, that, too, was immaterial. "Today I intend to examine details of the events preceding the station's disaster."

"I suppose so." She leveled her gaze at me, "Recorder, are you avoiding us?"

"That is an irrelevant, personal question which has no bearing on the task at hand."

Familiar footsteps sounded in the hall. I immediately returned my attention to the screen, and Jordan was at the door before Timmons entered.

"Leave her alone, Tim. She's working."

"I just—"

"Tim." After five seconds, she added, "Recorder, we'll leave you to it."

I did not look up. "That is, indeed, the best option."

I heard her depart, and when his footsteps eventually followed hers, I sank back against the chair, exhausted for no rational reason.

After two or three glances at the empty doorway, I rose to secure it before organizing the information from the research station, integrating the video feed by time stamp. The first item that drew my attention was the confirmation of Kyleigh's assertion that the station had no Consortium representative in residence for several years. This puzzled me. There was always a Recorder. Always.

Pallas Station's Recorder, who had arrived on the ship with the Tristrams, had died in her sleep three ten-days before Dr. Tristram's murder. Nineteen days after his death, people grew ill and died, and two days later, Westruther sent the remaining people into stasis before the station's nuclear generator malfunctioned. When the final supply ship arrived, they found the station had gone dark, save the automated warning signal. They were ill-equipped for exposure to radiation, and so they left.

No written record or summary, no final report of an autopsy existed for either the Recorder or Dr. Tristram, nor for that matter, was there any analysis of the illness that had prompted Westruther's medical stasis order. The station was a scientific research outpost. Scientists would certainly have performed autopsies and would most certainly have begun an analysis on the sickness.

I frowned.

The reports were incomplete. Either Security Chief Gideon Lorde did not keep good records, or I had erred in compiling the files. Nothing indicated he had found the guilty party. Dr. Allen, chief medical officer, had also left insufficient records. It seemed unlikely the AAVA drones had failed to retrieve all pertinent files. I had programmed them to do so myself. Unless . . .

I checked surveillance recordings, found some from the timestamp of Dr. Charles Tristram's death, and pulled one up on the display capable of projecting a small holographic version of the records.

The projection showed him studying a paper, pacing, then sitting down at his desk and staring at a data cube image, running his fingers through his long hair until it gave him a deranged appearance. He took off his thick glasses and pinched the bridge of his nose. From the angle of this recording, I could see papers on his desk, but I could not read them. He looked up, directly into the camera, and suddenly, the image disappeared. A grey blur took the place of the feed, but when the recording resumed, Dr. Tristram sprawled, unmoving, across his desk.

The wound could not have been self-inflicted.

Someone had tampered with the recording and deleted data. I tapped my thigh.

Criminal investigation was not my field, but information was. I had been sent to secure data, and researching Kyleigh's father's murder would be operating within assignment parameters. I wanted—I *needed*—to do this for her, to grant her closure and express my gratitude for her kindness. For the first time that day, a hint of a smile crossed my face.

So, in the interest of justice and for her sake, I checked encrypted time slots for virtual visual records. Resolving to do my utmost to uncover the facts, I scheduled one for the following morning.

Verifying information was one of my callings. Pallas research station might be gone and the murderer with it, but Kyleigh's father's murder should not remain unsolved.

Morning crept into afternoon. When Kyleigh invited me to assist her with the cats, I thanked her but declined. She had not yet realized it was in her best interest to avoid me. I returned to my solitary work on the AAVA drones in the storage bay, but the quiet was not comforting. Instead, it loomed over me like a storm.

For the second evening, I ate alone. Sleep was, again, difficult.

21

I stopped in the infirmary before breakfast for my required daily health check. Dr. Maxwell, however, was asleep, slumped over his desk, his mouth open and cheek resting on his arm. He snored more quietly than Bustopher purred. I watched him for a moment before I crossed to the linen closet. Removing a blanket, I returned and draped it over his broad shoulders, then carefully pushed the long dreadlocks off his face.

The first time we had spoken, in the botanical gardens when I was a child, he had seemed so large and strange. Now he was familiar, though his question echoed in my memory: *Are you . . . happy*? I had never answered him.

"Perhaps I will tell you someday," I whispered. "It was not important information then."

In the soft, green glow of the emergency tanks, the faint shapes of the two young men cast dim shadows onto the floor. Pausing, I glanced down at them. Elliott appeared a younger, thinner version of his brother, perhaps even as tall. Freddie, in the tank next to him, was on the handsome side of average, although his facial bones were sharp and his cheeks sunken. He was even thinner than Elliott, who was even thinner than Kyleigh. It was difficult to determine in the viscous liquid and its faint green light, but his skin tone appeared slightly deeper than mine, as my friend's had been. The nanodevices triggered muscle contractions. Freddie's hand tightened into a fist; his face contorted.

I dreamed in the tanks, and the dreams were not always pleasant. Despite the impropriety of the act, I reached through the gel and touched his head, as Timmons had done for me.

"Shh," I hushed. "Your doctor is one of the best, and Kyleigh speaks of you often. All will be well."

His face relaxed. I withdrew my hand and wiped it dry. The white noise of the fans and Dr. Maxwell's small snores blended with the mechanical whirs and clicks of medical equipment, like music. The morning's inherent stillness comforted me.

When the first shift-change bustle subsided, I walked to VVR and entered my access number on the panel to the door's right. A young crewmember wearing engineering blue cast a sidelong glance my direction, then sped past me. Finally, the light over the door turned green, indicating the footage had loaded, and I stepped over the threshold into Kyleigh's father's office.

Dr. Tristram's workspace was chaotic. Piled papers, data cubes, half-empty coffee cups, laboratory coats, sweaters, and plates of desiccated food littered the surfaces of the tables and cabinets. A large desk with a built-in computer occupied the center of the room, although uneven, precarious stacks of papers mounded over the expensive projectors, which would render them inoperable. Several chairs were tucked haphazardly into corners, and an antique typewriter rested on an uncluttered table. Next to the old-fashioned hinged door, a single tidy workstation held a small datapad, decorated with Kyleigh's name and pictures of flowers.

Even Recorders sometimes found it disconcerting to walk through projected images and avoided them as they would solid objects. I had no such difficulty, yet walking through the images to inspect the piles of documents was unproductive. The cameras had not captured the details, and Dr. Tristram's penmanship was illegible. I could decipher only a few handwritten words and some of the files' alphanumeric labels.

I stood by the center desk, faced the doorway, and said, "Play recording."

The virtual door banged open into the room with the disconcerting squeal of unlubricated metal. Dr. Tristram staggered in with an armload of papers, which he dumped on top of the right-hand cabinet. He sorted through the stack, plucked out one sheet, and kicked the door shut behind him. He traversed the room toward his desk, detouring around objects without tripping, despite paying attention to nothing save that piece of paper. After several minutes, he let out a shuddering sigh and fell into his chair, murmuring incomprehensibly.

I raised the volume.

The sound amplified, I could finally discern his words. "This can't be right. Do I say something? No direct evidence . . . But John has to . . . And Georgette. She'll know what to do. Oh, sweet stars above! Melody'll kill me if anything happens to Kyleigh."

Dr. Tristram lowered the paper and retrieved a data cube from his pocket. Shoving a few stacks out of the way, he set it on the desk next to his archaic keyboard. The image of a pretty, smiling woman of nearly three-score years glowed above it. He stared at it for roughly thirty seconds, running his fingers through greying shoulder-length hair.

He removed his glasses and pinched the bridge of his nose. A noise from the hallway startled him, and me. He glanced at the door. This must have been the point at which he stared straight into one of the cameras.

"Freeze image." I stepped close to reexamine the paper, but between the poor quality of the recording and his abysmal handwriting, I could still read nothing. I followed his gaze. The door was still shut. I turned back to him.

His hazel eyes were very like Kyleigh's.

"Resume," I said past the discomfort rising in my throat, for I knew what was coming.

Dr. Tristram glanced down and hurriedly shoved the document and several others into antiquated folders and buried them in the clutter on the floor near his desk.

"Who's there?" he asked.

Everything vanished in an overwhelming roar of static and pixelated, swirling grey.

The noise was too bright, and the grating, rasping sound incapacitated me. Dropping to my knees, I covered my ears and rocked back and forth but could not hide from it. I dared open my eyes once, but the flickering grey was blinding, and I squeezed them shut to keep it out. Curling into fetal position, I forced myself to breathe. In. Out. In. Out.

My hands over my ears and my eyes tightly shut, I forgot I could decrease the volume or stop the recording.

Eventually I became aware that the overpowering static had been replaced by a slow but steady drip. I opened my eyes cautiously to see that Dr. Tristram's room had reappeared. The sound emanated from the speakers in the ceiling, drawing my gaze upward. I forced myself to stand. I had forgotten: due to the poor quality of the recording, sound was not directional. I glanced around to find the source of the drip.

I stood in a puddle of arterial red. I jumped back, my heart pounding painfully.

My boots left no tracks—they were clean. Of course they were still clean. All of this was merely a projection. Once my breathing calmed, I made myself inspect the image before me.

Kyleigh's father's slouched over his desk. The speakers continued the slightly irregular rhythm of his blood dripping from the papers onto the floor. I looked away.

"It is merely a recording," I said aloud.

I punched my thigh with my fist several times as I recited prime numbers and forced myself to walk over and inspect him. A wound gaped across his throat. Human anatomy and physiology were not my areas of expertise, but from what I understood, this level of blood loss would have required a beating heart.

But, if his heart still beat, why had he not disturbed the stacks of papers?

A string of saliva hung from his open mouth and glistened in the light. His eyes, unnervingly like Kyleigh's, stared blankly. I could not close them—it was only a recording. Those empty eyes continued to stare.

My jaw tightened until my teeth ached. I needed to focus on the papers. Only the papers. Some were no longer readable, and others were missing. Someone had disrupted the recording, killed Charles Tristram, and absconded with the files.

The frequency of the drops hitting the floor slowed, then stilled. I knew I was safe, that all of this had happened over two years ago, but I did not feel safe. I backed through the typewriter until I bumped into a comforting, solid wall, and the recording passed the timestamp I had watched in my computer laboratory.

Dr. Tristram's door flew open, slamming into the virtual wall with a magnified boom, and a lanky man at least two decades younger than Kyleigh's father strode into the room.

My hands flew to cover my ears. "Lower volume! Lower volume to standard level!"

VVR complied.

The lanky man froze for but a fraction of a second before pulling a small sidearm from his belt and kicking the door closed. I could not help but draw back as he aimed the weapon at me—no, not at me. He sidestepped quickly through the room, scanning, checking corners, glancing behind file cabinets, kicking chairs to look behind and under them without toppling their uneven piles. Not once did he turn his back to the room. Once he had circumnavigated the office and ascertained no one else was there, he checked the floor between the blood puddle and the door.

I had not thought to look for footprints. There were none.

Weapon ready and mouth a tight line, he approached Kyleigh's father. The crisp slap of his boots was softened by the ever-spreading puddle, yet the lanky man did not hesitate. He bent to check under the desk and, when he saw it was clear, placed his middle two fingers on the dead man's wrist. He inhaled audibly, then hit the communication link on his chest. "John Westruther!"

"Here."

"Put us on lockdown and secure the recordings," he barked. "Now."

"Done." Even as the man who must have been Westruther spoke, an emergency warning light began to flash, alternating between red and yellow, and an alarm sounded. "Why?"

The lanky man's nostrils flared. "Murder."

"What?" a woman said.

"Charles is dead."

"*What*?" the woman and the man said in unison.

"Dead. Murdered."

The woman snapped, "Don't be ridiculous, Gideon."

Gideon Lorde. This was the security chief.

"We've got a murderer loose." A muscle twitched near Lorde's eye. "Get Brisbane and his team down here." Lorde rattled off more names and a list of equipment, then paused. "It's a bloodbath. Clearly a blade of some kind, but I don't see a weapon." There was a pause as Lorde resumed his circuit of the room, alert to details. "John, you'll need to secure the classrooms. Get someone watching those kids."

"Georgette, find Kyleigh," Westruther said. "But I'll tell her." She did not respond, but the sound of running footfalls faded while Westruther issued orders to a doctor and security teams. "Gid, I'll be right there."

Gideon Lorde glanced at the door, then fastened his gaze again on the body of Kyleigh's father. "Understood."

"Freeze program."

It was one thing to read of homicide, and another to see its aftermath. My uneasiness was compounded knowing Gideon Lorde had died two years before, because I saw him—moving, acting, speaking. It did not help that John Westruther was the man we had found in the control room. Freddie's father. Georgette, an uncommon given name, was surely Dr. SahnVeer, the woman we had found with him. These were the voices of the dead, some of whose bodies I had seen and touched. I shivered, then took a deep breath to shake off encroaching emotions. Emotions had no place in the record.

VVR reset to a previous time stamp, and I stepped around Kyleigh's father to examine the papers on his desk. My stomach churned as I advanced the recording to immediately after the static blur. Then, I returned to the earlier timestamp to compare the file numbers. The missing files seemed to be labeled with a series of numbers and Cyrillic, Greek, and English letters. I memorized the labels, berating myself for not bringing anything with which to record data.

Skipping ahead again, I watched while the security team processed the scene. Gideon Lorde directed his crew with confidence. I did not memorize the numbers they wrote on evidence bags, as it would be relatively simple to find them in the record. While two men lifted the body onto a medical hoverbed, another man arrived and stood watching from the doorway. Though he bore little resemblance to the corpse I had seen in Pallas's control room, I recognized John Westruther at once.

Lorde noticed him before the others did. He nodded. "John."

Westruther ran his fingers through his hair, which stood up in uneven, three-centimeter spikes, stepped into the room, and placed a hand on Lorde's shoulder. They watched in silence as the evidence was processed and a cleaning crew mopped up the blood.

They left and sealed the door.

I stood alone in the recording of the office and ended the program. The empty room flickered away around me, but the images remained, scorched into my mind.

My wrist monitor chimed, but I could not eat lunch after witnessing the events in Dr. Tristram's office. Instead, I visited the cats. Kyleigh was not present, but Bustopher seemed pleased to see me, perhaps because I brought him food. After feeding them, I changed the litter, which was particularly foul that afternoon for no discernible reason.

Solitary dining had been my life for over a decade, but the prospect of eating alone bothered me that afternoon. I needed normality; I needed a drone. Taking several bottles of water and a snack, I returned to the storage bay, resolved to program an AAVA drone to act as my shadow. I carried the smallest one to a counter, but fifty-nine minutes into my attempt to reconfigure it, my communication piece chimed. Dr. Maxwell requested my presence for the missed checkup. My shoulders sagged. The drone would have to wait.

When I reached the infirmary, Kyleigh was once again present, though she had neither an official position nor a volunteer one. Perhaps, as a Recorder, I should have asked why she was perpetually in attendance, but I did not. After all, I had not been assigned to be *Thalassa*'s Recorder, and the burden of completing my assignment was heavy enough. If Kyleigh and I could have been friends, perhaps the question would have been appropriate as well. If she grieved for her father or feared for the young men in the tanks, she did not need my impertinent, personal questions to reinforce her sadness or discomfort.

Since Dr. Maxwell remained focused on displays of rapidly shifting lists and images, Edwards checked my vitals. He hummed a monotonous tune while he tested my reflexes, nodding when my legs kicked as they should. With thinning hair and fine lines at the corners of his eyes, Edwards appeared to have reached his fourth decade of life. He would soon complete the thirty years of service required of non-Recorder Consortium staff. His gifting would be redeemed, the cost of his education and upbringing repaid. For approximately three seconds, I envied his future freedom.

"Edwards?"

He waited, his pale blue eyes steady.

Despite disliking personal questions, I continued, "Did you ever resent being relegated to service staff?"

Edwards shifted his weight. "When I was much younger, I did. We— all the children in my cohort—were jealous. The Elders never explained why we were not selected. Perhaps we had defects, or they had sufficient numbers. However, I eventually realized we were the fortunate ones." A smile lit his countenance. "In a few years, my duty will be fulfilled, and I will attain status as a citizen and officially have a given name. Selecting my name is a serious undertaking, though I have narrowed my choices to three."

"It does not seem fair," I said, but I did not clarify my antecedent, even to myself.

"Life isn't fair, Recorder." Edwards tilted his head. "But sometimes, that's a good thing."

I did not reply.

He stepped to the side but kept his gaze on me while Dr. Maxwell walked over and studied the digital display. The doctor made a noise in his throat, then stood quietly watching me for two minutes.

"Is there anything you want to discuss?" he asked. "Anything at all?"

"No."

Dr. Maxwell tugged his ear. "I understand you've been keeping to yourself, avoiding people. You haven't logged time in the gym, and I haven't seen you at meals."

"I have done katas in my quarters, and I prefer to eat alone, as befits a Recorder. However, I will resume my visits to the gymnasium. I will even eat in the dining commons, if you insist."

He placed his hand on my shoulder. "I'm not insisting, but you shouldn't isolate yourself. There's no reason to avoid us."

I shook my head. He did not understand. "Max, when we reach New Triton, I will be disciplined. It is possible that I will be repaired and reinstated, but if what you have said is true, if the damage is irreversible, I suspect I would face . . ."

He gave my shoulder a small squeeze. A muscle in his jaw twitched, but his voice was calm. "Then don't deprive us of your company for the short period of time we might have left. Some of us miss you."

"I am merely a Recorder."

Kyleigh spoke from behind the doctor. "You are our friend."

"No," I protested, pushing off the bed and backing away from them. "Your father and Timmons were correct, Kyleigh. It is not safe. Friends complicate the records. Bias contaminates information. If I receive a new implant, an emotional response to *friends* will cause pain or discipline, mine and possibly yours, as citizens are punished for compromising Recorders."

Edwards set the scanner down. "Yes, that has happened before."

"If they find a way to isolate my memories . . . forced memory downloads are painful. Recorders who lose neutrality face severe discipline. I do not relish such penalties, but they are an acceptable price for having known you. If, however, they suspect any of you has attempted to undermine my non-bias, the consequences for citizens are also extreme. I cannot tolerate that happening to people to whom I have injudiciously drawn close."

"We should be free to make our own decisions, don't you think?"

"You do not understand. You have never experienced . . ." I faltered. "I could not bear it. No one must suffer on my behalf."

Kyleigh's faint eyebrows drew together. "But you aren't a Recorder anymore."

"Perhaps not," I admitted. "Perhaps I am nothing. I am not a Recorder, and I cannot be a citizen. Kyleigh, Timmons was correct. You cannot trust a Recorder. But neither can you trust a nothing."

Dr. Maxwell crossed his arms. "What has Tim been saying now?"

Kyleigh's eyes widened. "Oh!"

He turned to her.

"This is my fault." Her face paled. "You misunderstood! That was years ago. I'm sorry! I didn't mean—that's not how I feel, or Timmons!"

"But do you not see?" My words tumbled out. "He was correct. I am concerned for you. Do not risk yourselves for nothing."

I spun on the heel of my boot and walked toward the door.

"Wait." Dr. Maxwell's quiet voice stopped me. "I might not know what exactly you are talking about, and I can't make decisions for you. But it isn't good to be alone."

My heart pounded, but I turned back.

"We care about you," he continued. "You are not nothing, and you have *never* been nothing. You have always been more than a Recorder. Every human in the system, in this blasted galaxy, is extraordinary, valuable." His warm, nut-brown eyes held mine. "Some people say we evolved from the dust of stars. Others say we are uniquely formed by a divine being. Stardust or Creation. Either way, you are exceptional. You are the only one of you in all of space and time. You cannot be nothing."

For several minutes, the silence was disturbed only by the fans and the mechanical burblings of the tanks.

"I will consider this, Max . . ." I stepped toward the door. "At your request, I will join you at dinner."

My work on the drone occupied the remainder of my afternoon, but my mind was not on the task. Instead, it raced through the events of the past ten-days. I kept returning to my growing discomfort with my assignment, to overheard conversations, to what Dr. Maxwell—Max—had said. His words whispered through my mind, and at length, my hands grew still. There, alone in the echoing room, surrounded by inactive drones, I decided. I returned the AAVA to its alcove and walked away.

No one else had arrived when I entered the dining commons, so I took my tray to one of the small tables in the back. Fatigue gave my utensils more weight than accounted for by their mass, and eating was a chore. I did not look up from my food until Jordan sat down across from me. Cradling my tea for its warmth, I scooted back in my chair.

"Recorder." She dug her fork into the reconstituted vegetables.

"Jordan." The knot in my throat tightened. "I must confess something."

She slowly lowered her fork, steepled her fingers, and studied me through narrowed eyes. "What could you possibly have to confess?"

"I was searching for Timmons, to correct any misunderstandings, as you advised me to do. I overheard your disagreement."

Her eyes became slits. "Eavesdropping, or recording?"

"I did not record anything. I did not intend to eavesdrop."

"But you did. What did you *accidentally* overhear?" Her voice was sharp, almost harsh.

I closed my eyes briefly out of habit, focusing on my memories as I had done when I had my neural implant, then opened them. "You believe the Consortium will not take me back and that others should distance themselves from me." Jordan's face paled slightly, and I wanted my drone, to gauge her response. "I . . . I suspect you are correct. Max, however, disagrees. He urged me to continue interacting with others. Balancing distance with interaction will be difficult."

Jordan sat completely still. Eventually she spoke. "Why are you telling me this?"

I sipped my tea to avoid her gaze, but the cup's heat no longer warmed me. "To apologize for overhearing private discourse in which I was not an invited participant. I have concluded doing so was wrong. I respect your stance and fear it may be true."

She tapped her fingers on the table. "Is that why you've been avoiding people?"

"Yes. My proximity could harm people to whom I have grown—"

"'Injudiciously close?'" Max's deep voice said.

I startled, spilling tea onto the napkin on my lap. "Yes."

Jordan glanced at Max, then back at me. "What do you intend to do?"

Perhaps I should have waited to tell Jordan the next day in the quiet of my computer laboratory, but the delay might have distressed her. "I will take meals here and resume assisting Kyleigh with the cats. I have decided against reconfiguring one of the remaining AAVA drones as a personal shadow. My initial records and testimony have already been transmitted to the Elders, and if—when—they send my replacement, I shall endeavor to protect you all from my indiscretions. I shall . . ."

Max moved around the table to stand beside Jordan, but both watched me.

Jordan asked, "You shall what?"

"I shall not reveal anything not already in the Record. Upon reflection, I am convinced extraction is only possible for memories accessible through an implant and drone. Since I have neither, this should pose no danger. The Elders will not know I lost my neutrality. Unusual emotional or physiological responses can be accounted for by unusual circumstances. I have hidden or suppressed my emotions for most of my life. I will do so again."

Jordan's eyes widened. "That's manipulating the records."

"No." I stood abruptly, leaving my tray on the table. "It is remedying error. But even if it were . . . I will do all I can to protect you from the consequences of my lapse. Excuse me. I am no longer hungry."

They did nothing to hinder my escape, but I met Kyleigh in the hallway.

"You're leaving?" When I nodded, her expression shifted. "You aren't mad at me, are you?"

"No. Why would I be?"

"You've been avoiding me and everyone else because of what I said."

Years of training enabled me to suppress a sigh. "I was attempting to keep you safe."

"That doesn't make sense, you know." Kyleigh bit her lip. "Are you sure you won't stay for dinner? I told Timmons you'd be here."

I almost changed my mind but shook my head.

"Can I stop by tonight after dinner? I need to talk to you." She paused, regarding me critically. "No, I'll talk to you tomorrow. You look beat."

"I may be tired, but that is a gross misstatement," I protested indignantly.

She grinned.

"Another idiom?" I allowed myself a sigh. "I miss my neural implant. I would have known."

Her grin disappeared. "Don't say that. Don't even think it. We wouldn't be friends. We *are* still friends?"

"As long as we can be," I said quietly.

"Then I'll see you tomorrow. Meet me in the infirmary when you can, sometime after lunch. Max has been letting me use one of their computers to finish the research I'd started with Georgette—Dr. SahnVeer—it was my thesis project, you know, and besides, Freddie and Elliott are there." She shook her head. "But my point is, I want to show you something I found. We'll take care of the cats afterward."

I nodded and returned to my quarters.

I was tired, more so than my activity level would have demanded, but I did not prepare for sleep as usual. Taking the blanket from the foot of my bed, I sat and stared blankly at the door. I only intended to rest for a moment, but I woke in the morning still in my clothes with the blanket twisted around my legs.

Being in the right place at the right time was an art Nate hadn't mastered yet, though not for lack of trying. But, if Todd and company planned to teach the new kid a lesson, that meant the hall near the gym. The magisters rarely went down that way, and even though the Eye of the School was watching, no one else would do anything. After all, when Todd had pummeled him two quarters ago, no one had cared. Not even their grandfather.

The distant sound of a datapad shattering reached him. Nate ran faster.

Todd's voice echoed down the polished hallway, ". . . pathetic, spacing trog."

"He's here as a *gift*." That'd be Sidney. Fine. Nate could handle Sidney.

"A *gift*?" Todd sneered. "Who'd waste credits on dross like him? Crawl back to the tunnels, trog."

"Him and his miner rat mother." *Oh, void it, that's Eloise.*

Nate took a moment to catch his breath. If his blasted grandfather taught him anything it was to look the part. He squared his shoulders and sauntered around the corner.

Stars, he was too late. Alec's lip was split, and a blackish-purple knot swelled on his forehead. Eloise was twisting his arms behind his back; Sidney was rummaged through Alec's shabby satchel; and Todd, of course, supervised it all.

Nate leaned against the wall and kept his voice light. "Seems like a disagreement is underway. I'm here to render my services."

Todd spun around. "Shove off, Nathaniel."

"Todd, Todd. Three on one? Bad form, mate, bad form. Might even be four on one if Eloise is counted twice, like she should be."

Eloise growled.

"You'd better watch it, Nathaniel," Todd warned.

Alec gagged and spat out blood, and Eloise jerked his arms higher.

Before Nate could do anything, his cousin grabbed Alec's braid and yanked his head back. "You spitting at me, miner rat?"

A grim smile flickered across the new kid's face. He took careful aim and spat at Todd, who wrenched him out of Eloise's grip and hurled him to the ground. Alec landed hard on his knees. Nate knew that look—he'd fought back enough tears of his own. He staggered to his feet and faced Todd, who was a good twenty centimeters taller. Todd wiped the bloody spit off his cheek.

Nate crossed to Alec's side. "Leave him alone."

"Or what?"

"Last chance to walk away, Todd. Very last chance."

Sidney laughed. "Like you're big enough to do anything."

Force equals mass times acceleration. Don't have to be a drilling platform, Nate. Just be fast.

Todd smirked. "*You* walk away, pretty boy. It'd be a shame to mess up a face Grandfather loves so much."

Nate clicked his tongue reprovingly. "Jealousy is *such* an unattractive trait." His cousin's fingers twitched. "To be fair, with a face like yours, you've got good reason—"

Todd lunged. Nate's fist slammed into his cousin's face, and the bully fell. Spinning around, Nate kicked Sidney in the chest, and he staggered back against Eloise. Arms flailing, they tumbled over.

Alec stood there, blinking, so Nate grabbed his arm. "Let's get out of here before *he* shows up—"

He pulled Alec into a run, but they weren't fast enough.

The Recorder caught them when they turned the corner. His drone rose behind him. "There will be no fighting. You will come with me to see Magistra Jones."

Nate snuck a look at Alec. He'd always been quiet in class, never smarting off to the magisters, minding his own business. He even did his homework during study hall. He'd probably never been called to the magistra's office in all his life. For a split second, Nate was jealous, but Jones wasn't bad. They'd be okay.

He smiled up at the Recorder, who only raised what should have been an eyebrow. Nate sighed. Once in a while, they smiled back, and he felt like he'd won a battle when they did.

The Recorder escorted them to the waiting room and left again. Nate sank into one of the chairs. The blue one in the corner was his favorite—he could see the whole room from there—but Alec fidgeted for a while before he settled back, swiping his sleeve across his oozing lip.

Maybe two minutes later, the drone showed up, tendrils wrapped around the bullies' wrists. Todd was even paler than usual. Positively ghostly. *Serves him right.* When the drone released them, they shuffled across the room to the remaining chairs. The drone headed back down the hall.

Todd's eye was darkening into a glorious shade of purple. It was a work of art, really.

Nate leaned back into the stiff synthleather. "Stars," he said lightly. "It's a shame to mess up a face Grandfather loves *so* much."

Todd's hands curled at the taunt, but Nate only grinned, ears pricked for the sound of footsteps and the drone. There, just barely. One one-thousand, two one-thousand, three. He winked.

Angry red replaced Todd's pallor, and he jumped up, fists clenched, just as the school doctor, then the drone and the Recorder entered.

"You shall remain seated and cease physically threatening the others, Todd Anthony Markham," the Recorder intoned, "or you will face further discipline."

Todd dropped back into the chair like Nate had hit him again. While the Recorder kept Todd pinned under his baleful stare, the doctor's gaze slid past Alec's split lip and the bruise on his forehead. When she only motioned for Todd to accompany her, Nate tensed. *Should've taken Alec, too.*

Magistra Jones finally emerged from her office and put her hands on her hips. "Nathaniel. What brings you in here this time?"

Nate pointed at Eloise and Sidney and said, cheerfully, "Bullies."

"Fighting will get you expelled."

"I didn't do anything to him at all," Sidney whined, "and he kicked me."

"I did not address you, Sidney."

Nate shot a glare at him. "Magistra, when I got there, they'd already stolen Alec's bag, broken his datapad, and busted his lip. Eloise was holding him, and then Todd grabbed his braid and threw him down."

Jones shook her head. "You know to fetch an adult, not dive into a fight."

"No, ma'am. If I'd run for help, they would've beaten him to a bloody pulp. And even if Alec did throw the first punch—which I doubt, but I wasn't there so I don't know—they started it. They've been calling his mom things like 'spacing trog'–"

"Nathaniel! We do not use that language here!"

"—and worse stuff. Honest truth."

She pursed her lips and turned to the Recorder. "Did they?"

"Yes."

Nate flashed a triumphant grin.

"Why wasn't I informed?" When the Recorder remained silent, she turned her glare to the others. "That language is completely unacceptable."

Press the point home, Nate. "It wasn't fair, Magistra. I mean, three against one? That's just wrong."

"I'll evaluate the situation." Magistra Jones rubbed her temples with her fingertips. "Sidney, Eloise. My office, now. Alexander, Nathaniel, wait here. We have already contacted your guardians. They will be here shortly." She glanced back at Alec. "And the benefactor."

Void take it. Todd's dad was off world, and that meant their grandfather was coming.

The Recorder followed them all into her office. The door closed.

When the two of them were alone, Nate cleared his throat. "Don't let Todd get to you."

"He'll be mad at you now." Alec's voice was lower than Nate had expected, and with a start, he realized Alec hadn't spoken before, not in the whole ten-day he'd been at school.

"He already despises me, just hadn't tried anything for a while." Nate shrugged. "Bound to happen sooner or later. He's always been like that. My—*his* whole family is." He chewed on his thumbnail, caught himself, and tucked his thumb into his fist. "I hate things that aren't fair."

Alec was silent.

Nate continued, "He shouldn't have said that about your mom, and they shouldn't have hit you."

Alec wiped his lip.

"Nothing'll help, though, if you're slow. Tell you what, you can try to hit me once in a while, when no one's watching." Alec didn't respond. Maybe he was in shock or something. Had a headache, probably. Nate forced a smile. "We'll just keep an eye out for Recorders."

"I hate Recorders," Alec muttered.

"Most people do." Nate nodded at the Consortium camera in the ceiling, but Alec didn't seem to catch on. Maybe he hadn't realized that cameras were everywhere. Maybe he just thought it was fire suppression or something, but it wasn't like Nate could say it outright.

"Well," Alec said through clenched teeth, "I have a good reason. My sister and I—"

"At least you have one." A sister would've been nice, unless his grandfather was beastly to her, too. So, maybe not.

"Have one what?"

"A mom. A sister."

"My sister's gone." Alec's words lashed at Nate. "So's Papa."

The flash of jealousy evaporated. "But you still have your mom. That's lucky."

"Lucky? That Papa never came home, and my sister died in a tank?"

Nate tightened his fist around his thumb. "That's . . . awful."

The door slid open, and a pretty woman in a wrinkled, baggy brown jumpsuit walked in. Alec bolted to his feet. The woman set a heavy-looking bag next to Alec's chair, placed small, chapped hands on his shoulders, and gently touched the bruise on his forehead. He flinched. Her brown eyes, a lighter brown than Alec's, widened.

"Alec?"

Jealousy and guilt both bit at Nate. He kept his eyes on a smudge on the wall under the prime minister's smug face as Sidney's mom, then Eloise's father arrived. Magistra Jones opened her door and motioned for them.

His cousin returned and sat in the chair across from him. Alec's mother looked at them uncertainly. The door opened again.

"Todd," their grandfather said sharply, "what happened?"

"Nathaniel hit me, sir."

"And you let him?"

Don't look, Nate. Don't acknowledge either of them.

Before his cousin answered, the magistra stepped out of her office. "Dr. Timmons. Todd."

They filed in after her. In the quiet waiting room, his grandfather's strident tones rose and fell behind the closed door. ". . . finished . . . should have been gifted and spared me . . . ruined my Lillian's life . . . send that parasite to the mines . . . No! Todd will . . ."

Alec's mother stared open-mouthed at the door. Nate glanced at Alec, who was studying him through narrowed eyes, his fingers curling and uncurling. Heat rushed up Nate's neck. He clenched his jaw and stared at that smudge on the wall like it could save him.

Shake it off, Nate. Lillian loved you. Not your fault.

The magistra's calm voice murmured when his grandfather stopped.

His grandfather barked something. The hinged door creaked, and the Recorder walked over to the closet camouflaged in the wood paneling. Nate braced himself. They were going to talk to the Eye. The Recorder had left the magistra's door open, and everyone in the office watched as the wall panel slid into its pocket.

The Eye, surrounded by drones with long, writhing tentacles, sat cross-legged on a cushion as grey as everything else in her closet room, hands resting palms up on her lap. She turned her wrinkled, old, grey-tinged face toward the door.

Nate shot a quick glance at Alec and his mother. His mother's eyes were lowered, and her hands twisted on her lap, but Alec's face drained of color. Maybe he hadn't seen an Elder before. The first time seeing one was always the worst, especially this one. She made Nate's skin crawl.

"The magistra requires the record of the remarks precipitating the altercation," the Recorder said.

She opened her eyes, and Alec flinched as she turned her solid grey, inhuman gaze toward them.

"The exact record of the event has been transmitted to the magistra's files, along with corresponding codes for the discipline of the three minors who initiated the conflict and the one who aggravated it." She focused on Alec. "You must learn not to respond to provocation,

Alexander Spanos. A stable community consists of citizens choosing to avoid confrontations." Then she turned to Nate. "Nathaniel Timmons. Refrain from behavior which violates social constructs."

She closed her eyes, and the panel slid shut.

Magistra Jones's voice floated into the waiting room. "She always knows. The Elder has the direct feeds for the whole school."

The Recorder locked eyes with Nate for a second before rejoining his drone in Jones's office, and his forehead creased. The door closed behind him with a click.

Alec whispered, "Direct feeds . . ."

He studied the ceiling's tiles and fixtures, and Nate saw Alec's eyes widen when he realized the camera was a *camera*.

The old-fashioned door flew open, and only the emergency hinge on top kept it from slamming against the wall. The Recorder preceded everyone and stood under the prime minister's portrait. Nate's grandfather stormed past the magistra without a glance her direction, Todd on his heels. The other four followed them out, though Sidney paused to murmur a short apology to Alec.

As Sidney left, another woman entered. Nate snorted. The place was a regular public transport station, with everyone coming and going.

The woman said, "Sophi."

Alec's mother stood slowly, but Alec jumped to his feet. The woman crossed the room as gracefully as Nate remembered Lillian doing, though she looked nothing like his mother had. This woman wasn't much taller than Alec's mom, and her hair was a mess of short black-and-grey curls, not Lillian's straight golden-blonde.

"It's you!" Alec exclaimed. "You're all right!"

"Hello, Alec." The woman smiled softly.

Alec's face grew somber. "It didn't all work out right, but"—he drew a deep breath—"thank you."

She tilted her head down. "Of course, Alec. And for both of you, I am so sorry for your loss."

"Thank you," Alec's mother murmured, then darted a glance at her son, then back to the woman. "Are you here for us?"

The woman nodded.

"It wasn't your fault, Charity."

"No." The older woman took off her delicate shawl and folded it over her arm. "But this is the easiest, best decision I have ever made. Alec can remain here until he goes to university. After all"—a smile flitted across her face—"everyone responds to donations."

The magistra, still standing in her doorway, turned a little pink.

The woman continued, "I understand losing people, Sophi. Magistra Jones, if we could finish, I have a concert this evening."

Magistra Jones nodded. "Yes, we can address this quickly. Alexander, your datapad will be replaced. I'm going to let this go with a one-day suspension, but I will not tolerate this sort of behavior. I don't want to see you in here again. Do I make myself clear?"

"Yes, Magistra." Then Alec asked, a little too loudly, "What happened to Todd, Sidney, and Eloise?"

The Recorder began, "Their judgment is not your—"

"No," Magistra Jones interrupted. "The students will know soon enough. They are no longer enrolled." She glared at the Recorder. "I should have been informed earlier. There is no excuse for such behavior."

Todd—*gone*? Relief hit Nate hard.

Alec spoke up. "And what happens to Nathaniel? He was only trying to help."

"I know." Magistra Jones's voice softened. "Nathaniel, this is your fifth school, and your grandfather has made it quite clear he is willing to take legal steps to remove you from his care should you be expelled. As of today, you are to board here year-round. Should you lose your position and his guardianship, your next stop would be a public boarding school with no opportunity to attend university. You are bright enough: do not ruin your future. One day's suspension in your dorm room. You are dismissed."

A second wave of relief washed over Nate. He might not have a home, but at least he wouldn't have to worry about his *family*.

"Now, if you please." Magistra Jones gestured to Alec's mother and the older woman.

"Wait. Did that man . . ." Alec's mother's mouth pinched, then she glanced at Alec, who nodded solemnly. She crossed the room and set her hands on Nate's shoulders. He froze. Keeping her gentle eyes on

Nate's, she said, "Magistra Jones, may he visit us over Festival this year? We may not have much, but—"

"You will have what you need," the older woman said quietly.

Nate managed to say, "I'd like that."

Jones murmured, "I'll grant permission."

Nate glanced at Alec, then back at Alec's mother. A soft smile bloomed, just for him.

Then, for the first time in years, someone hugged him. For a moment, it was like he forgot how to breathe. Then, before he realized what he was doing, he hugged her back, tight, his eyes scrunched to keep the tears from leaking out. She released him but kept a hand on his arm.

Nate dashed his sleeve across his eyes. He turned to leave but paused in front of Alec. "So, if you want, you can call me Nate."

Despite the swollen lip, a slow grin spread across Alec's face. "Well, only if you let me try to hit you now and then."

His mother gasped. "Alec!"

The older woman hid a smile, and Magistra Jones pointed at the door. "Nathaniel, to your dorm room. Tomorrow is quarterly inspection. Be prepared."

"Always am." Nate sauntered out, humming tunelessly, smiling until his cheeks ached.

24

PERSONAL RECORD: RECORDER ZETA4542910-9545E

CTS *THALASSA*
478.1.9.03

I had not known Julian Ross had been granted access to my computer laboratory, yet there he sat, lounging at one of the two seated stations, spinning a stylus through his fingers. Taken aback by his presence, I did not respond appropriately to his greeting. He made no mention of my rudeness, which I recognized as kindness.

"Jordan told me you're working on the information from the station, so I wanted to see if you needed any help," he offered. "And I thought I'd make sure you're all right."

"There is no reason to interrogate me regarding my condition."

He held up his hands. "You've been avoiding people. Other than turning up briefly at dinner last night, you've seemed more . . . Recorder-ish . . . lately."

"I have been working," I said.

Ross grinned, his one crooked tooth accentuating the symmetry of his features. "Having recently come out of the tank myself, I know how shaky I felt, and I didn't have to recover from brain surgery."

I attempted to raise an eyebrow, but this had no impact on his commentary. "Residual effects have faded."

"Your hair is growing in nicely. I'll be glad to have mine back." He ran a hand over the stubble on his scalp, then pointed at my computer. "So. What are you working on?"

I ignored the more personal statements, and after three seconds of internal debate, I decided to tell him. "I am attempting to organize the information from the station, to determine, if possible, what happened."

He stretched out his long legs and shoved his hands into his tunic pockets. "Those last few ten-days were tough. Charles Tristram, Kyleigh's dad . . . he'd been a little withdrawn, though he always was eccentric—the brilliant ones are. He was murdered. You knew, right?"

"Yes."

When he leaned back into his chair, I sighed. Determined to make the best of the situation, I settled at the table and asked him about his role on Pallas.

"Research! I'm good at it. Sounds immodest, I know, but facts are facts." He grinned. "We were investigating the effects of unusual strains of bacteria on endocrine function and the potential for genetic manipulation using nanites. Georgette made incredible strides with that tech."

Julian Ross grew more animated as he elaborated on his study of autoimmune disorders, focusing on treatment of diseases and genetic anomalies with nanotechnology, DNA, and bacterial and viral therapies. The ideas were controversial in light of the nanotechnology restrictions implemented after the attempted genetic cleansing one hundred thirteen years ago. Rewriting genetic code using nanodevices containing hidden viral therapies bore too many similarities to eugenics.

When we transitioned to discussing the research station's procedures and practices, I opened some sketches and diagrams on my datapad. Ross's communication link pinged. He turned it off and joined me at the table, edging his chair next to mine. He was pointing out discrepancies in one of my sketches when Timmons entered.

"Hey," he said in greeting, and my diagram lost meaning, devolving into stick figures and scribbles.

"Timmons." I bit back an involuntary smile, reminding myself that he did not trust Recorders, and more importantly, the Consortium must not discover that I considered him my friend.

His dimple appeared, then vanished. "Haven't seen you around."

"I have been working."

Julian Ross stood and put his hand on the back of my chair. It occurred to me again that he was extremely tall. "Really, Timmons, we're busy, and I doubt you'd add much to any rational, scientific conversation."

"Ross, you should not be unkind." I turned from him to Timmons. "Have your duties kept you satisfactorily occupied?"

One corner of his mouth quirked upward. "I suppose so. We have daily briefings now, until we reach Lunar One. Stopped by on my way there to, ah, check your status." The quirk expanded into a full grin.

I wanted to look away but could not. "I am well."

"You—"

"Enough, Timmons," Julian Ross interrupted. "We're busy."

Timmons's lips compressed, and a muscle jumped in his jaw.

"Ross," I said, "that is not—"

Rapid footfalls were the only warning before Kyleigh ran into the laboratory, face flushed and eyes bright.

"Ross, *there* you are! Elliott's tank—he's waking up!"

Without a word, Ross sprang up and bolted down the hall. Kyleigh remained at the doorway, bouncing on the balls of her feet.

"Go on," Timmons said to me. When I did not move, he gently took the datapad from my grasp and tipped his head in Kyleigh's direction. "She could use the moral support. I'll shut up your lab and stop by before dinner."

Kyleigh grabbed my hand, then pulled me along until we were both running. I had not gone far before my body betrayed me with cramps and nausea. Slipping from her grasp, I staggered to one of the benches which covered the ducting for the ship's backup chemical system.

"I cannot run, Kyleigh," I managed. "But do not let me hold you back."

Kyleigh flopped onto the bench beside me. "No, I'm sorry. Are you okay?"

"I shall be."

She stared at her knees. After six seconds, she said, "Elliott and Freddie and I, we do everything together. Freddie says I think too much, but I just care more about my studies. Dad wants . . . wanted me to finish my degree early. He—Freddie, I mean, not Dad—and Elliott are the fun ones. They did the paintings, you know. Timmons said you showed him."

"The elaborate murals in the Pallas station's corridors?"

She nodded. "They used ultraviolet paint left over from tagging everything and snuck down at night to work on them. Gideon thought it would complicate security, but Freddie's dad, John, said art makes life better. Freddie liked that the murals were hidden in plain sight. He's brilliant."

She did not speak of Elliott, which puzzled me, but when I agreed with her assessment of Freddie's skill, she fell silent. The cramp in my side receded, and we resumed at a slower pace.

"Freddie, Elliott, Ross, and me." Her voice shook. "We're all that's left, and Freddie won't have anyone. I suppose I still have Mom . . ."

When we reached the infirmary, she stopped abruptly. "I can't go in. What if he doesn't . . .?"

It took me seventeen seconds to say, inadequately, "Yes, you can."

She drew back.

"You will regret avoiding this, whatever the outcome." I reached out and tapped her arm. "We shall go in together. You shall not be alone."

Kyleigh swallowed. "All right."

She glanced at the ceiling. I, too, looked up, but nothing was there. The doors slid open.

Elliott's tank stood drained and empty, and the lights underneath flashed as it ran a purification cycle. Max, Edwards, and Williams, Max's other assistant, stood around a bed on the far side of the infirmary. Julian Ross gripped the bed's metallic railing, staring intently at the silent figure under the blankets.

"Elliott?" Ross's voice was rough. "Elliott, it's me."

"That's it. Let him hear your voice," Max said.

"Elliott, you need to wake up now, buddy. We made it out, and everything'll be fine." Ross's focus darted to Max. "Why isn't he responding?"

"His pod was damaged. The growth spurt strained its resources, but his vitals look good. It's simply a matter of his body coordinating everything while we wean him off the nanites. He's doing fine. Give him a reason to wake up. Keep talking."

Kyleigh and I made our way into the room, pausing a few meters from the bed. When Elliott started to thrash, Max, Edwards, and Williams held him firmly in place. Kyleigh rushed over and placed her small hand on Julian Ross's arm. His grip tightened on the railing, his knuckles white.

Elliott's thrashing stopped, and slow, shuddering gasps took its place.

"Elliott?" Julian Ross pled.

I could not see the young man on the bed but observed his waking, nonetheless, in the faces of his brother and his friend. Kyleigh beamed and leaned against Ross, but he did not acknowledge her, his focus on his brother. I had seen Ross smile, but never with such brilliance.

A hoarse voice croaked, "Julian?"

"Welcome back, Elliott." Julian Ross's voice was rounder and full of light. "I've missed you."

25

I slipped out of the infirmary and proceeded to VVR, where I spent a tedious morning. The recordings near Dr. Tristram's laboratory had been erased for fifteen minutes before and after Gideon Lorde's arrival. The only person present in the hallways before Dr. Charles Tristram walked into his office was Jean-Pierre Marsden, the station's chief of engineering. I reviewed all the recordings in real time, then spent the remainder of the morning caring for the cats. After lunch I stopped back at the infirmary, as Kyleigh had requested, but she was not there.

Certain I could eventually locate relevant information in the files, I returned to my laboratory where my afternoon crawled by with little progress. Evening brought Timmons's familiar knock, and I began shutting down the programs with a sense of relief. The door slid back into its pocket, and there he was.

I smiled. "Is it dinner time?"

He did not smile in return but simply nodded. "I stopped by the infirmary. Elliott's bouncing back fast, might even be up and about tomorrow. They moved him over to his brother's quarters, where Ross'll keep an eye on him. That'll take some of the load off Max."

His comment brought that morning's confrontation to mind.

"I do not agree with Julian Ross's earlier comments." When Timmons did not respond, I continued, "He did not speak for me. I did not mind that you were here."

Timmons made a small affirmative noise. "Jordan said you overheard us a couple days ago." He studied my face. "Were you going to talk to me about that?"

"Yes." I turned away to straighten the chairs at the table. "I intended to tell you this evening. I have not had sufficient opportunity."

"And whose fault is that?"

"Mine." I glanced at him, then resumed tidying.

"Why?" When I did not answer, he continued, "So you know Jordan doubts they'll let you back in."

"Yes."

After five seconds of silence, he said, "Care to tell me what else you heard?"

I picked up my datapad and turned it over and over in my hands. "You spoke well of my performance under adverse circumstances but did not accept that the Consortium will reject me, despite Jordan's assertions." I tried to manage a small smile, but it faltered as I reviewed the conversation. "The idea angered you. You argued briefly about a mistake she believed you were making."

He tilted his head, and my gaze fell from his green eyes to his black boots.

"I was relieved, however, when you resolved your disagreement." I motioned to his boots and added, "You wore similar boots on the expedition. Why do you choose nonstandard footwear?"

"Don't change the subject," he said.

"Such was not my intent."

"So that's what you thought we were talking about?"

Although I was momentarily confused as to whether he meant his boots or his argument with Jordan, I decided he meant their conversation, not ours. "Your concern that I overheard you is understandable. Citizens do not trust Recorders. I should not have listened, and I . . . Please know I will not report your violation of the anti-obscenity code. I will not compromise either of you. You are important to me."

Timmons rubbed a hand over his chin. "That's all?"

Ignoring the pinch of anxiety in my chest, I added, "I had done something that disturbed you, so I wanted to find you and make amends, but I could not bring myself to interrupt. I apologize for eavesdropping."

"You didn't get anything else? That can't be the whole reason you stopped 'interacting.'"

"No."

"Does it have to do with what you told Max and Kye? That you are trying to protect us?"

I blinked rapidly, uncertain as to whether irritation or dismay had the stronger grip on my emotions. "Is there nothing better to do on this ship than to gossip?"

He gave me a lopsided smile. "Tell me yourself, then."

I sighed. "You do not trust Recorders, Timmons. I cannot blame you for that."

He straightened. "And who says I don't?"

My face heated, and I turned my attention back to my datapad. "Kyleigh."

"And where'd she get that idea?"

Without taking my focus off the blue surface of the datapad, I recounted Kyleigh's story. Timmons suppressed an oath. He leaned out of the laboratory and looked up and down the hallway before stepping back inside. The door slid smoothly into its pocket, and the magnetic lock's small click seemed louder than usual. Taking four long strides, he crossed to where I stood and placed his hands on my shoulders, but I did not move away.

"Kyleigh's wrong. Alec might feel that way, but I don't. You should've asked me if you thought . . ." His hands slid down to grip my own for a moment. He held them briefly, then let go. "I don't have a problem with Recorders."

I tried to raise an eyebrow.

He shook his head. "No. I don't. It's the drones."

"There is not one without the other."

"Look, I haven't told anyone this in a while. J knows, because her mother was there, but Alec wouldn't understand." His jaw tensed, then relaxed.

"You need not speak of anything that causes discomfort," I said. "I accept your statement. I should have verified the testimony, as any Recorder knows to do."

"No. Or, yes, you should have, but blast it, I'd rather you understood. Sit down." Timmons motioned to the table and lowered himself into one of the chairs. "Please."

I hesitated before taking the chair on his left. He rested his elbows on the table and shut his eyes for two deep breaths. I waited as I had been taught, then those green eyes opened and met mine.

"I was six when Lillian died."

I sat straighter. "Lillian?"

"My mother. Thought you read our files?"

"Those files contained only data pertinent to the mission. You called your parent by her given name?"

He studied his fingernails, then shot me a look through his bangs. "Wasn't allowed to do anything else. We lived with her parents."

I waited.

"Stars, but it was like all light went out once she was gone. My grandparents took me to her services at the Center."

"The Center for Reclamation and Recycling?"

He nodded. "The Recorder stood off to one side, but that drone hovered next to her, those blasted arms swinging back and forth. For years, I'd heard my grandfather go on about Recorders and their drones, and that drone drew my attention. Even then I felt guilty for not watching Lillian, like if I had, she would've gotten up and been fine."

I could envision the Center for Reclamation and Recycling, as if it had been projected into my mind. All were built with the same template: vaulted ceilings; colorful, arched windows; the ubiquitous ferns along the walls; refreshment tables near the old-fashioned swing doors; the preparation room with its chemical smells and its buzzing filters; the furnace at the back with its whisper-quiet sliding door. The Centers were never without solemn guests wearing appropriate pale green arm bands or jackets.

It would have been frightening for any child, but to have his mother on the conveyor belt, with the crowds, and the drone . . .

"My grandparents sent me up by myself. They had cut off her hair, of course. She . . . I touched her hand. It was cold, and that scared me." He rubbed the back of his neck. "I started crying, and my grandfather rounded on me, in front of everyone, shouting about how it should've been me on that conveyor instead. No one said anything, no one stopped him, so I ran. Dashed through the people, wound up in the gardens. Lillian loved plants. I felt like she'd be there with me if I hid in the ferns. No one came to look for me. They just left."

A peculiar tightness restricted my breathing. I clasped my hands tightly on my lap. "Oh."

He offered me half a smile. "Eventually, the Center's Recorder came looking. She left her drone near the gate and crawled under the ferns. Didn't say a word, just held out her hand. I took it. She only smiled with her eyes, though. I can still see them. Lighter brown than yours, with a touch of green, and short, blonde lashes. She just sat under the ferns with me. Called me 'Little One.'"

"Yes," I said quietly. "That is what we call our children."

Timmons ran his hand through his hair. "When it got dark, she asked if I wanted to go home, but the last thing I wanted was to go back to my grandfather's house, and somehow, she knew. After she led me out of the ferns, her drone flew over and wrapped a tentacle around her, but she never let go of me. She said she had to take me somewhere safe, first."

I drew in a long breath at her risk. She was brave, that one.

"She brought me to her chapter house. I held her hand while we walked through what felt like kilometers of drones and Recorders. She and three Elders talked for who knows how long, and she held onto me the whole time. In the end, she knelt down and told me they verified her story, but I had to go back, although they'd watch over me by sending a drone, which scared me as bad as my grandfather did. They made her leave, even though I told them I wanted to stay with her, and I cried again. An Elder escorted me back to my grandfather's." Timmons snorted. "He was livid, but he couldn't say anything with the Elder there. She left a drone, and I was fine."

"If the drone kept you—"

"No." He shook his head. "The drone wasn't what kept me safe. Anyway, it wasn't a big deal. They sent me off to school after that. Every time I came home for Festival, though, I walked the four kilometers each way to the Center. She never talked to me again, just smiled with her eyes."

I reached out to touch his hand but caught myself and pulled back.

"Sometimes I'd just sit in the gardens, and once in a while, she'd sit on the bench next to the ferns. The last time I saw her I was about nine. She left the drone at the gate again and sat on that bench in front of the ferns where I liked to hide. Didn't say a word. But when she left, I found a scrap of paper under the bench."

Somehow, I kept the surprise from my voice. "She wrote you a note."

"Yes. Don't know how. Never figured that out."

"Recorders, if not selected for training on the path of an Elder, are allowed to disconnect their drones overnight." I had not had that option, but many Recorders valued the quiet when their drones charged. "What did it say?"

"'Be at peace, Little One. You will be whole.'"

The Recorder should not have done so, but it was a great kindness. I hoped she had not been caught and sent to the Halls. If not, perhaps she had been reassigned, or perhaps she had retired. I hoped it was so.

"I held onto that note for a while, but I destroyed it when it occurred to me that she shouldn't have written it. I didn't want anyone to know." He leaned over and tapped my hand. "So, your explanation about the Caretakers made sense to me. And it isn't the Recorders. It's their blasted drones."

He stood abruptly, so I did as well. We walked to the door, but before it slid open, I briefly touched his sleeve, then clasped my hands behind my back.

"I am honored you confided in me."

"Kyleigh was wrong." His posture remained stiff, though he smiled. "But even if she wasn't, I'd still trust you. You're different."

The door slid open, and we stepped in unison into the hallway.

"Allow me to express sympathy, Timmons. Causing a child to feel unwanted is unconscionable. Your grandfather was wrong. I have viewed such cases and records, but I never . . . Even as a child of the Consortium, who had but one friend once, I was valued. I am sorry you were not."

Timmons rubbed a hand over his eyes. "I didn't tell you to make you feel sorry for me. I wanted you to understand why I don't distrust the person."

"You were but a boy, drawing illogical conclusions, and—"

He huffed out a breath. "You're missing the point, and I don't know how else to explain it."

"Prosing on again, are you?" Alexander Spanos asked.

I started. I had never startled so easily before. The past ten-days might have placed excessive strain on my adrenal system, so I made a mental note to mention the possibility to Max.

Timmons cleared his expression before he turned to his friend. "Private conversation, Alec."

"Right." Spanos shrugged. "On your way to dinner, Tim?"

"We both are."

Spanos studied me before he spoke. "I'll walk with you. Zhen's probably already there."

The three of us reached the dining commons before DuBois, so we took our trays to the middle table. Spanos kept glancing at me.

After six minutes, he put his fork down. "You're different from other Recorders."

I straightened my clothing. I truly disliked the rose tunic. Perhaps the new ones—

"You changed the outcome of a bad situation. Broke a lot of rules to do it, too."

"Yes." I had not anticipated any remarks concerning my behavior, merely my appearance, although his observations were valid. Staring at the food on my tray, I said, "I anticipate being severely reprimanded for my actions."

"Reprimanded?"

"Yes."

"What does that mean?"

"Alec," Timmons said, and his tenor deepened. "This might not be the best time."

Spanos remained focused on me. "If you knew you'd get in trouble, why'd you do it?"

I drew a deep breath. "I reacted emotionally when I destroyed my drone—"

"You didn't destroy it," Timmons interrupted. "The roach did."

"When I accidentally destroyed my drone," I clarified, "only five of the station's medical stasis pods were functioning. I could not leave them. Neither could I allow the rest of you to be trapped when I could prevent it."

Spanos leaned toward me and stabbed the table with his index finger. "Recorders don't save people."

I struggled to suppress growing agitation. "It is true that few act as impetuously as I have. Recorders face tribunal and potentially severe disciplinary action for violating our codes of conduct, but we are of utmost use and assistance through maintaining records. We prevent social—"

Spanos slammed his fist onto the table. I jumped. With intensity unlike any I had observed in him before, he thundered, "Don't you dare spout those lies!"

"Alec," Timmons warned, half rising from his chair.

Once recovered from Spanos's outburst, I motioned for Timmons to be seated and asked Spanos, as mildly as I could, "Why do you call them lies?"

Spanos only ground his teeth and glared.

"Because." DuBois's voice startled me. She walked over and put her hands on Spanos's shoulders. "Recorders stood by while he and his little sister were injured. She died. They could've warned people of the potential danger, but no. They stayed silent and did nothing."

Spanos reached up and set his hand over one of hers.

My gaze flickered between them. "This, then, is the incident to which you referred on our assignment, when you said people like me had ruined your family?"

His face tightened, and he pulled his wooden beads from his jacket pocket. They clicked over and through his fingers as he flipped them in his left hand. "My father was given a choice. Turn himself in for 'counseling' or the hospital would stop Aria's medical care. So, one day we played chess all morning, and then he walked off with one of those spacing—"

"Alec." DuBois's fingers tightened around his.

"One of those observation drones, for his *counseling* appointment. He never came home."

"None of this was in your file." My words barely rose above the ambient noise in the dining commons. "Something that important should have been in your file."

His accusations were disturbing, but I also heard Jordan's voice in my memory: ". . . *they are removed, Tim.*" Small discrepancies in the records and other stories that did not match my training began to fit together into a pattern I did not want to see.

Everything I had managed to eat suddenly turned heavy as raw ore in my stomach. My hands shook, so I lowered them onto my lap. I felt as if I were a large pane of glass that had cracked and threatened to shatter, or as if a chasm had opened, and I had plummeted through it.

Timmons reached over and took my hand off my lap, but I pulled away.

Spanos closed his eyes and leaned against DuBois.

"Why?" I managed. "What had he done?"

"Nothing." Spanos clipped the word short. "Nothing except speak against the Consortium because their precious Recorders stood by and let us get hurt. I got better, but not even six ten-days in a medtank could save Arianna's life. She was seven."

Seven. Seven was so young.

"I did not know, Alexander Spanos, and cannot fault you for hating me."

"Maybe I don't," he muttered. "You're not like them."

I pushed away from the table. "I will excuse myself. Your pardon."

Timmons touched my shoulder before I stood. "Please stay," he said, his voice low.

"Thank you, but no. It is unfair to Spanos to have to eat at the same table with me this evening. If, in the future, any of you decide my presence is too difficult, I will refrain from joining you and will find other ways to accomplish Max's recommended social interaction. Excuse me. There is something I must do."

"You don't have to . . ." Spanos trailed off.

I glanced from him to DuBois. "As I told Jordan yesterday, memory extraction requires neural implants. I have already lost mine, so you need not worry. The Consortium cannot replay this conversation. I promise not to implicate anyone."

DuBois's knuckles grew white as her grip on Spanos's hand tightened.

I tapped my leg. "I will choose reclamation before doing anything to harm you. If it is in my power, you will be safe."

No one spoke as I deposited my tray in the proper bin. I nodded to Dr. Maxwell, Jordan, and Edwards as I rushed past, my stomach churning.

The door to my quarters slid shut before I threw up my dinner. I washed my teeth and face, then opened a link on the small terminal in the corner.

I found Alexander Spanos's story in the archives, how the sole surviving Recorder had documented his rescue by a local musician who had been speaking with the children's mother. The article and documentation expressed sympathy for the family's loss.

No one, of course, grieved for the dead Recorders.

Spanos was correct, Recorders had permitted events to proceed, had done nothing. It was possible his sister could not have been saved, but how had Recorders simply allowed the explosion to take place when it could have been prevented?

Then, all records of Spanos's father disappeared five ten-days after the incident. Nothing explained his absence—no death certificate, no notice in the newsfeeds, no indication of appropriate honorariums. He was gone, and even his identification number had been removed.

Other searches confirmed similar patterns in other families, including Jordan's. Her cousin—gone.

Alexander Spanos was right.

I was sick again.

Two hours after midnight, I fell asleep in my clothes for the second night in a row.

The sound of someone knocking on my door shattered my sleep. I yawned as I crossed my room and leaned my forehead against its smooth surface.

"Who is it?" I asked.

"Jordan," Timmons said.

I opened the door to scold him, only to find both him and Jordan standing in the hallway.

"Well." He cleared his throat. "You look awful."

Jordan shot a glare at him but said, "You're usually up early. You missed breakfast, and morning's nearly over. Everything all right?"

I covered another yawn. "I was unwell last night."

Her long black braids hung over her shoulder, new beads at the ends glowing like amber. For two and a half seconds, I wished for braids with beads like hers, and to be strong like she was. For two seconds longer, I wished I had tunics like hers, but perhaps in blue or a deep green rather than burnt orange and gold.

She was studying me. "Do you need to see Max, or will food suffice?"

I tapped my thigh, my stomach tightening at the idea of dining, but said, "I am not unwell now, though I should change before I eat."

"We'll be right here." Jordan assured me, but as the door slid shut, I heard her say, "Stars, Tim. Telling her she looks awful?"

I wore my one Consortium grey tunic again, disappearing comfortably into a Recorder's garb until the memory of my discoveries sent a shudder through me. I smoothed the grey fabric over my hips, where it hung loosely, and drew a breath. I could trust Jordan and Timmons. Couldn't I?

When I joined them in the hallway, Jordan eyed me critically. "Have you been skipping meals?" she asked.

"Not intentionally."

They both frowned.

In the dining commons, Timmons seated me and brought me a cup of tea while Jordan commandeered more food than I required. The staff nodded at us as they left for a short break between their endless rounds of food preparation. Timmons and Jordan sat and argued about sporting events and entertainment, and their apparent ease gave me hope.

I chewed slowly, thinking through what I would say. When their conversation ebbed, I wiped my hands on a napkin and folded it carefully. "It is unorthodox for a Recorder to ask citizens for information regarding her own kind. Nevertheless, I find I must."

Timmons set his coffee on the table but kept his eyes on mine.

"A Recorder's ultimate goal is to maintain an unbiased record, thereby holding government accountable to the populace, and citizens to one another. I have always believed our work creates a secure environment without bias or prejudice, in which people can thrive. Rendering such service redeems our gifting to the Consortium. It is the reason we exist. All my life, I have studied to this end."

Jordan's delicate eyebrows drew together. I did not look at Timmons.

"Last night"—I drew a deep breath—"I verified Alexander Spanos's story. Those Recorders did not act for the good of others. Maintaining records is not a higher priority than maintaining life, and so I do not know how much of what I have been taught is incorrect." I forced myself to look at them. "Will you share your thoughts with me, Venetia Jordan and Nathaniel Timmons?"

I waited.

"I told you," Timmons said slowly, "it's not Recorders I mind, so much as their tech." He cast a glance at Jordan before resuming. "Some are different. *You're* different. The one at Lillian's service was different, and so was the one at the university library. Gerry used to watch out for her, remember, J? Thought she was cute. Which she was—she smiled a lot for a Recorder."

Gerry. Gervase Singh. Jordan's cousin, about whom I had read in the early hours of the morning. I felt as though something had lodged in my throat, and my resolve to speak faltered.

"Yes . . ." Jordan leaned back, increasing the distance between us. "I grew up believing Recorders were there to protect citizens, but I was wrong. They exist to keep people in line. One wrong move, and it's over."

Timmons scowled at her. "A bit harsh, J."

I managed to ask, "Jordan, what have you decided about me? As a . . . person?"

Golden-brown eyes focused on me like targeted lasers. "Why?"

I surveyed the dining commons to ascertain that we were indeed alone, drew a deep breath, and said over the pounding of my heart, "I intend to complete my assignment, but I no longer wish to be a Recorder. The Eldest is unlikely to offer me the . . . opportunity . . . to leave. To do so, I will need help, yours if you will grant it. I do not know whom else to trust."

Nathaniel Timmons let out a low whistle, and Venetia Jordan jerked upright.

Regret struck like a physical blow, and last night's nausea returned. I should not have spoken. I should not have eaten.

Then Timmons grinned. "Told you, J. She's all right."

Jordan leaned forward. "Are you sure?"

"Forgive me," I whispered. "I was wrong to tell you. I should not have asked."

The galley staff returned, and with them the sudden realization that the recording devices all over the ship—the devices that had been so integral with my training, so much a part of who I had become, so ubiquitous and ordinary—now would testify against me. I sprang to my feet.

Timmons stood casually while Jordan took my tray to the counter. I fled to my computer laboratory, and they followed. No one spoke. The door slid shut. Timmons lounged against it, while Jordan balanced with controlled grace on the table's edge, her arms folded.

Still berating myself, I did not sit but stood next to my usual computer, my back to the posters about workplace safety. "I have erred."

Jordan shook her head almost imperceptibly. "I don't know."

"No," Timmons said simultaneously.

A glance up at the inoperative Consortium device in the corner only partially reassured me. "Since much of the station's information is classified, the recording devices in this room were deactivated before we left for Pallas's surface. You were right not to trust me. I was so accustomed to recording and observing through my drones, I failed to consider that the ship itself continued recording, even after I could not. I cannot explain such an obvious lapse, as I do not fully comprehend it. But I foolishly endangered you all. I deeply regret it."

I stood and paced the room as I considered how I could repair the damage I had wrought. "I shall review the morning's recordings from the dining commons and remedy my error."

"What do you mean?" Jordan asked.

"I will destroy the records of our conversation."

"You'll *destroy* records?" Her eyes widened.

"I was wrong to speak of it. Such an error was irresponsible." I shook my head. "I selfishly implicated you in my—my potential defection."

"You weren't wrong," Timmons said firmly. "You chose your co-conspirators well, as far as I'm concerned."

Jordan's fingers drummed on her arms. "What do you have in mind?"

"I believe my best course of action is to disembark at Lunar One. It may be possible to erase myself from the records by then."

"You can't go wandering off by yourself," Timmons protested, ignoring my potential crimes of altering records and violating Consortium rules. "You don't know the first thing about surviving out there."

"If I am to avoid returning to the Consortium, I have little choice." I stopped across the table from Jordan. "I must find a way to recode an identification band, but to do so, I need both a band and access to my former quarters and the equipment there."

"You know what will probably happen when they find you?" Jordan asked, her voice low. "And I'm sorry, Recorder, but they're everywhere. They *will* find you."

I did not want them to see the apprehension on my face, so I sat and studied the floor. "Alec's father was not the only one who criticized the Consortium and disappeared. And when records or Recorders are compromised, both citizens and Recorders vanish. I cannot resume my place in a system that . . ." I lifted my eyes to meet her steady gaze. "I would not leave children in the path of destruction. Recorders face primary reclamation when we err, and whether I return or not, I have erred."

"What are you facing?" Timmons's voice tensed.

My gaze fell to the smooth, white tabletop, and I quoted, "'Through service we redeem our gifting. And should we betray that gifting, we will yet continue to serve.'"

"That's not an answer," he growled. "It's a riddle, and a bad one at that."

Jordan's braids spilled down when she placed her palms on the table. "Are you facing execution?"

I would not lie, but if they knew, they would be at risk. For the count of ten seconds, I simply breathed. "Primary reclamation is but continued service."

Timmons strode to the table and glowered down at me.

Before either could question me further, I said, "Timmons, Jordan, what was meant to protect citizens and encourage acceptance has become a system of neglect and manipulation, of oppression. I cannot participate. I wish to leave."

The corner of Jordan's mouth lifted slightly. She pulled up a chair next to mine. "Well, then. Let's hear your plans."

Some of the weight lifted from my chest as we discussed scenarios and difficulties, ramifications and escape routes for the next hour.

Immediately after they left, I accessed the security records and found a useful incident to recode so that audio recordings in the dining commons appeared to suffer damage from a small galley fire. Video was fed from overhead cameras, so lipreading was unlikely, but I decreased the resolution, as a precaution.

My search for Kyleigh's father's murderer had taught me one useful thing. Altering records discretely drew less attention. It was probable that an Elder would find it if she thoroughly investigated the recordings, but I sat back, content with my circumspection.

The remainder of my morning was spent making additional alterations. As I wiped clean any trace of unapproved activity from the terminal in my quarters and from all tiers of backup, the probability of success increased. Happiness, excitement, and fear bubbled inside my chest like liquid nitrogen at room temperature.

After all, who better than a Recorder to manipulate the records?

Having spent the morning on personal business, my work for the day—reviewing the data from the station—still needed to be done. Time spent with Kyleigh and the cats would need to wait, and after lunch, I visited the infirmary to tell her so. Max welcomed me with a smile, then resumed updating his logs on a datapad, but Kyleigh did not turn away from the computer in the corner, though she held up her right index finger.

"Just a minute."

While they both worked, the burble of the medical tank lured me across the room. I studied Freddie. Submerged in the pale gel, his lashless eyes moved behind closed lids as if in REM sleep. I hoped his dreams were better than mine. At the very least, it was probable his did not include behemoth cockroaches.

The antistatic tiles muted Max's booted steps as he joined me, pulling my attention away from the occupied tank. "How is Freddie?"

Max shook his head. "Older pods don't have upgraded safety systems. If the nutrient pool hadn't increased as the other pods shut down, neither young man would have survived. Freddie grew a good twenty-one centimeters, and his pod wasn't equipped to support that growth rate."

Across the infirmary, Kyleigh sniffled, but when I glanced over, she still had her back to us, shoulders hunched.

"The problem with long-term stasis is muscular and cardiovascular atrophy, and current nanotech can only do so much to prevent it," Max said. "Freddie was in the worst shape of them all. Something had damaged the connections to his feedline. A day or two later, and he would've been gone."

In the tank, Freddie's chest moved as if he sighed. I sighed with him. "He seems very young."

Max snorted. "You all do."

Kyleigh spun her chair to face us. "We need to tell her about the nanodevices."

I made a mental note to add the infirmary and both their personal access points to my list of alterations, then spoke quickly to forestall Max's response. "Might we meet tomorrow in the computer laboratory, instead?"

He gave me a measured nod. "All right. Tomorrow after lunch."

Satisfied that I would have more time to finish my work, I turned to Kyleigh. "I shall not be tending the cats today."

She leaned into her chair. "I'll see you at dinner, though, right? We're having a small party for Elliott."

The prospect did not appeal to me, but I had promised to eat in the dining commons. I could leave if Spanos or DuBois did not desire my presence. "I will attend."

"Good." Kyleigh bit her lower lip. "Are you sure you can't spare a few minutes for me and the cats? It won't take long."

For two seconds, I was tempted.

My work of organizing the station files neared completion, but I was determined to track down Dr. Tristram's murderer, and surely, creating a plan for my escape could be considered work as well. "I have not the time."

"I suppose." Her shoulders slumped. "I—Bustopher will miss you."

Despite the immensity of the tasks I faced, I managed to smile. "I am sure you exaggerate."

Ignoring her protest, I left the infirmary.

Although I found no official written report, I did uncover video recordings taken during Charles Tristram's autopsy. Since my priorities were to search for missing information and modify ship records to keep my friends safe, I set those files aside. If I allowed myself to lose focus, I would end up circling around the information and making no progress at all.

Time ticked past, and despite having searched the data from the station three times, I only found records of Dr. Tristram's files in a few locations, and most of those pertained to mathematical formulae. Cracks in his state-of-the-art desk, whether from improper usage or intentional damage, had allowed his blood's salt and iron to wreak havoc on the processors and destroy the data inside. As a result, none of the information from his computer had transferred.

If the station had not been destroyed, someone could have returned to determine whether or not the data was stored in the station's backup. I pushed aside the thought of returning to the tunnels and the dark and the roaches.

For three minutes, oblivious to the computer laboratory around me, all I saw was the cockroach crushing my drone, the subsequent flash of light, the long hallway, the pods of the dead . . .

Prime numbers.

Prime numbers steadied me. Eventually, the memories faded, and ignoring my dry mouth and churning stomach, I drew in a deep breath, slowly released it, and resumed my work. Video records flashed at the highest comprehensible speed, but without a neural implant's additional search power, I had lost my efficiency. Forty-three minutes passed, and fatigue forced me to reduce the speed another twenty percent and eliminate the second feed. Twenty-three minutes later, I slowed yet again. At last, my head aching from the speeding images, I found visual evidence of Dr. Tristram's files.

After queueing the data, I jogged to VVR, keyed in my personal code, and waited. At length, a soft bell-like chime and a small green light indicated my selection was ready. The door slid open, and I entered a different office altogether.

If Charles Tristram's office was cluttered, John Westruther's was austere. A large, color-coded map of the station hung on the wall across from the desk, the office's sole decoration. His jacket hung neatly from the first in a row of hooks beside the door, but nothing else alleviated the room's bare precision. The desk was organized and tidy, without personal items or stacks of paper. Even his computer was centered neatly.

If I could have smelled the recording, I might have detected cleaning solution, electronics, and cologne—my experience with citizens led me to believe a man of John Westruther's appearance utilized products to accentuate his masculinity, though perhaps I misjudged him.

He sat at the desk with perfect posture, shoulders squared and back straight. Not a single wrinkle, not a smudge, not a speck of dust marred his crisp white shirt. Everything about his person was precise, except his hair. It was short—even shorter than Timmons's—but he had, most likely, run his fingers through the untidy, grey-flecked curls.

I walked around Westruther's office, familiarizing myself with the environment. The letter on his computer was addressed to Kyleigh's mother, Melody Jones, notifying her of Charles Tristram's death, discussing options for Kyleigh's immediate future, and asking her to join them before the moon went into the dark of its orbit and human transportation was less tenable. He did not wish Kyleigh to travel to Ceres alone.

I positioned myself across from his desk with the door on my left. "Play."

Gideon Lorde strode into Westruther's office, followed by a petite woman with long auburn braids carrying a stack of paper files. I attempted to reconcile Dr. Georgette SahnVeer's corpse in the control room with the image of the woman before me. In the recording, she gave the impression of being taller than she had in death.

Westruther's attention shifted away from the letter on his screen. "What is it?"

Lorde shut the door, turned the manual bolt, and stood at military rest, his hands behind his back.

"We need to talk." Dr. SahnVeer dropped her stack of paper files onto Westruther's desk.

He closed the document, minutely adjusted the computer, and leaned back. "You've got my attention."

"Pause." I walked through her to read the labels and was disappointed, though not surprised, to see that they were not the files that had disappeared from Dr. Tristram's office before Gideon Lorde had entered. I returned to my former position before telling VVR to resume play.

Dr. SahnVeer laid her hand flat on the files. "Gid gave me these to review while he investigated the murder. And I believe there's a link."

Westruther's mouth pulled to the side. "How's that?"

She straightened. "These aren't what Charles was supposed to be working on. He found something and traced it back, like following breadcrumbs."

"Breadcrumbs?"

"Stars above, John. As in Hansel and Gretel? Don't be dense."

"He was following a trail," Lorde said.

"Ah." Westruther's lips pressed tightly.

One of SahnVeer's braids slipped loose, and she tucked it behind her ear. "Someone's been using the empty lab in section seven."

"People are always using the labs." Westruther sat back. "It's probably one of the students. Or Ash and Brisbane, though they think no one knows what they're up to. If you think it's a problem, just check the vid feeds, or—"

"They've been erased." Lorde narrowed his eyes. "Georgette and I inspected the lab. Someone's been running viral therapy experiments."

"We're off the grid," SahnVeer said. "Someone is hiding something."

Westruther frowned. "That's a pretty big leap in logic."

"No. That lab is being used for unauthorized experiments." She lowered her voice. "It took years to convince the authorities to let us research nanodevices and viral therapies, John. What we're doing here has the potential for enormous benefit, but it could easily be twisted into something awful. If Charles was right—and I think he was—that's already happened. We've been compromised. Someone here is creating something outside our scope, something wicked. Charles found out, and they killed him."

Westruther's hazel eyes narrowed. "Back it up, Georgette. Where are you getting all this?"

She picked up a file, licked her fingertip, and leafed through it until she found the page she wanted. Folding the stiff manila paper backward, she shoved the file at him. "Not your strong suit, I know, but just skim it."

His eyes tracked back and forth across the page, and he stopped halfway down, marking the place with his index finger. His whole body went rigid, and he uttered a low epithet.

She nodded. "Exactly."

"Gid?"

Lorde stalked past me to the desk. He gave the impression of potential energy in a spring, ready to burst into motion at the least provocation, though I did not know why a man should remind me of a coil of metal. He stabbed a finger at the stack. "Whoever killed Charles is connected to this."

"This has the potential to be very bad." Dr. SahnVeer's precise diction accentuated her analysis. "The RNA manipulation indicates a pretty nasty bug."

Westruther pressed his lips together, then focused on Dr. SahnVeer. "What you're saying, Georgette, is we're harboring a murderer intent on instigating a biological disaster."

"Yes. And with a delivery system like the one I'm working on for the treatment of miners' tumors, it might even be undetectable by the medicomputers. Our system might have prevented external espionage, but it's been corrupted from within."

"This is not corruption," Westruther stated. "It's a threat to every human in the system. Any idea who's behind it?"

"Not yet," Lorde said harshly.

Westruther moved his computer to the side and pulled the stack to the center of his desk. "We need to find out. Fast."

"Pause." Pulling a small recording device from my tunic pocket, I stepped into, then through, Dr. SahnVeer's image to decipher Charles Tristram's illegible scrawl.

I had work to do.

I paced the breadth of my computer laboratory, as the concept of an engineered virus spun through my mind with dizzying and nauseating speed. Why would anyone design something with the sole intent of killing people?

Despite my desire to leave the Consortium, my drone's absence no longer seemed beneficial. I wanted it back, both to increase my information processing speed and to regulate my neurotransmitters, for fear squeezed my chest like a steel band.

If only I could review the situation with a colleague, but without my drone, without the Consortium's long-range device in my old quarters, I could not contact the Elders. The nature of the information made transmission over common channels inadvisable. I did not consider the captain a viable option, though perhaps my distrust was based unfairly upon his evident distaste for my company. No one else—

Venetia Jordan. She would understand the threat and the broader context.

Jordan, however, did not answer when I attempted to contact her. Reassuring myself that we could meet in the morning, I secured the computers, placed my datapad on the charger, and straightened the equipment. Since no actual proof of Dr. SahnVeer's suspicions existed, and her discovery was merely a possibility rather than a confirmed threat, there was no satisfactory action I could take at the moment.

Since I had rashly promised to join Kyleigh, I made my way to the dining commons, pausing from time to time to make room for groups of two or three crew members also heading in that direction. Noise stopped me in the hallway. I had forgotten the celebration planned in Elliott's honor. Attending a party seemed irresponsible while the possibility of that virus remained unverified, but I took a deep breath and entered.

People milled around, talking. Or sat in groups, talking. Or stood in clusters, talking. The din buffeted my ears. The guest of honor was not yet present, but his absence did nothing to stifle the celebratory nature of the evening. An extra table laden with treats and beverages occupied the room's center, and I suspected the punch bowl contained a mild intoxicant. Perhaps they were pleased our relatively unsuccessful mission had not been a complete disaster, but they did not know about the virus.

I tugged down the hem of my tunic and ventured into the crowd, which parted around me without making eye contact. No one except DuBois, who glowered at me, noticed my arrival. Kyleigh, Max, and Jordan were chatting near the refreshments. Being unnoticed was both disappointing and reassuring, and my contradictory emotions irritated me.

I eschewed the punch, took a tray of food, and found a seat at an empty table along the back wall. I had not taken my first bite before spontaneous applause announced the arrival of Elliott and his brother. Julian Ross was grinning broadly. Blue eyes sparkling, he stopped to clasp any proffered hand. Elliott, though steady on his feet, walked more slowly.

The family resemblance was strong. Ross stood approximately three centimeters taller than his brother, but Elliott slouched, so I could not be certain. His time in the medtank had left him gaunt. If he gained weight, he would be as handsome as Ross, though his pallor and sunken cheeks made him appear simultaneously older and younger than his twenty-two years. Perhaps two years in a stasis pod caused a delay in development. Perhaps it was unfair to credit him his full age.

When Elliott saw Kyleigh, his expression lightened. She rushed to meet him, but Jordan paused to drain the rest of her punch before following.

Kyleigh beamed. "Stars, but you got tall!" She stood on her tiptoes and pulled him down to kiss his cheek.

He blushed.

Grinning, Ross picked up Kyleigh as though she weighed nothing. Spinning her around in a circle, he kissed her forehead and set her down. She stepped back, took Elliott's hand, and led him over to the serving table, where someone handed him a cup of punch.

Ross bent slightly to kiss Jordan's cheek as well, but she turned, and his lips landed on hers. I froze, my spoon hovering at chin-level. I watched her eyebrows rise, and my stomach tightened. The conversations faded as the room's attention shifted away from the punch bowl and Elliott to the two near the doorway.

A slow smile crept across Ross's face. "I suppose manners demand I apologize, but, honestly, I'm not sorry."

"Well, if you aren't sorry, neither am I." Her hand slid behind his head, and she kissed him.

One of the engineers whistled, and several crew members laughed. A smattering of cheers reverberated in the dining commons, and the noise returned to its previous level. I set my spoon down and clasped my hands on my lap.

"Of *course* he's already found someone." An unfamiliar baritone drew my attention. Elliott scowled as he and Kyleigh passed me. He dropped into a chair at a table several meters away. "It never does take him long. He could've told me."

"It's news to me, too." Kyleigh took the seat next to him and stole a glance at the two near the doorway.

Having gathered food and drink, Jordan and Ross made their way over to Kyleigh and Elliott's table. Ross slid an arm around Jordan, and she leaned against his shoulder and smiled.

I could feel my cheeks warm again, so I returned my focus to my plate, only looking up when two cups of punch appeared next to my tray. Max took the seat across from me, murmuring something about timing. I did not ask him to clarify. I, too, found it odd that Ross allowed his attention to be diverted from his brother. Elliott had, after all, been in a medical tank until yesterday, and the welcoming party was in his honor. And Jordan . . . her behavior surprised me as well. She had always seemed so very rational.

"Thank you for the punch, Max," I said, though I did not touch it.

The doctor did not answer me.

Jordan's low laugh recalled my attention. Ross was tracing small circles on her upper back and waving his other hand for emphasis as he spoke. Eventually, the faint scowl on Elliott's face vanished, and he grinned.

Max asked me to pass the salt. I did, but he did not use it. We sat opposite each other in silence until Nathaniel Timmons arrived five and a half minutes later, setting a huge mug of punch next to my tray before he sat in the chair at my right. He set his black boots on the remaining chair and winked. My cheeks grew warmer still, and I gave him the barest of nods. His brows drew together, and his gaze flew between Max and me.

"Okay," he said. "So I'm late to the party, though I doubt that's the reason you two look like you'd rather be mining in the outer belt. What did I miss?"

Max pinched the bridge of his nose. "I'm not sure."

"Perhaps . . ." I shifted uneasily in my chair. "Perhaps you should ask Jordan."

He followed my gaze to the table behind Max, and his eyes narrowed. Ross noticed his attention, and the corner of his mouth quirked. Timmons's boots hit the floor with a thud. His lips tightened. He looked at Max, who gave the barest shake of his head.

"I thought she would be joining us for dinner tonight," I said. "But it appears she will not."

Neither man spoke, and the sounds of utensils on plates and the low buzz of other people's conversation grated on my nerves, though I could not say why. I pushed my vegetables across my plate, creating equidistant squares of color.

"So," the surprisingly deep voice of Archimedes Genet carried from Jordan's table. The first officer had circles under his eyes—he must not have slept well—but nevertheless, he smiled broadly at Elliott. "You're one of the young men we've had in storage. Welcome back. I trust you're feeling better."

Elliott stood quickly, and Ross steadied him with one hand. I could not parse why, because Elliott stood at least fifteen centimeters taller than Genet's slight frame, but he did not seem as solid as the older man.

"Yes." Elliott's face flushed. "Thank you."

I returned my attention to my own table.

Timmons drained his punch. "Stars, Max. I didn't—" He picked up mine and drained it, too. "Well. I'll talk to J in the morning. She seems a bit preoccupied just now."

Given the hour, waiting outside Jordan's quarters to catch her before she commenced her day was, in retrospect, bad manners, though no one had ever explained that aspect of social etiquette. It seemed reasonable to me at the time.

Her door slid open, and she stopped on the threshold. "Recorder. Good morning."

I ignored the growing sense of uneasiness buzzing in my chest and met her eyes. "Good morning, Jordan. Yesterday we agreed to meet this morning and discuss the data from the station."

"Well," she said calmly, "5:15 is a little earlier than I had in mind. My office, or your lab?"

"Your office will suffice."

We walked there silently, passing the old clock and pictures of ships, and she held her identification bracelet to the panel next to the door, which slid open. She motioned me to a chair and listened intently as I explained what I had learned, then watched the recording on the projector in her desk, reviewed my notes, and frowned at the wall for three minutes.

"None of this was in the data files?" she finally asked. "Only in the recordings?"

"Yes. I discovered it because I viewed the footage of Dr. Tristram's death, observed that some hand-labeled files were missing, and pursued them. I have not yet found evidence to substantiate Dr. SahnVeer's suspicions but will continue searching today. If the station had not been destroyed, it might have been possible to locate the missing information in its backup systems."

"It wasn't destroyed," she said, without looking up from my notes.

For three seconds, I felt as if my heart had stopped. How had I not known? Not been informed? Once again, I had lapsed in the execution of my duties.

"Jordan, the station was to be destroyed after we retrieved any survivors and the data."

She glanced up. "The captain overruled me. He insisted blowing up the hangar and the hatch we entered was sufficient to block access." She shut off the display. "You were in Max's medtank."

Only years of training kept my mouth from falling open. "Why was there no record made of his decision? If it had been properly documented, I would have known."

"No idea. He said he'd take care of it." Jordan drummed her fingers on the arm of her chair. "You've got more important things to worry about."

She was right. I set my reaction to the captain's brazen decision aside and nodded.

"I need a full report on this, as detailed as you can manage. Send me copies of the recordings, too. This should have gone out last ten-day. Keep digging."

"I will. But, Jordan, it could not have gone out last ten-day. We did not have it then."

"Immediately," she said, without clarifying her erroneous statement. "And what made you look into this?"

"While reviewing anomalies during my primary inspection, I found several data packets had been altered, and the investigation into Dr. Tristram's death had been compromised." I tapped my thigh. "A connection between his death, the potential threat, and the station going dark is highly probable."

Jordan leaned back. "Whatever that virus was . . . It could be theoretical or already destroyed. It could still be at the station. It could be nonexistent. I don't like not knowing. Keep digging. Given what you've found, I'm bringing Max in on this. He'll have a better grasp of the medical implications. I'll stop by your lab later. Write up that report."

She went to the door and opened it to find Timmons, hand raised to knock.

"Good morning." He flashed me a smile, but it faded as he looked at Jordan. "Got a minute, J?"

"If you will excuse me, I will take my leave." My eyes slid from their faces to the antistatic flooring. I slipped between them, down the hall, the idea of the potential virus still spinning in my mind, blotting out all other thoughts.

I was early for breakfast. Several people drifted in and out, some alert, some bleary with fatigue, while I finished my meal. Timmons entered, took a tray of food, slapped it onto the table next to mine. Coffee sloshed out of his mug. Dropping into a chair, he rubbed his forehead with one hand.

"Good morning again," I offered tentatively.

He glared at me without provocation, so I stared back and raised both eyebrows. I wanted to raise only one, but I had not yet mastered that skill. After several seconds—I lost count that time—I took his coffee, carefully wiped the bottom of the mug so it would not drip, and handed it to him.

"Perhaps you should have some caffeine before you socialize." When his own eyebrows rose, I added, sincerely, "Or perhaps you should sit in solitude, until you attain a more temperate mood."

Timmons gulped down the coffee and choked.

"The coffee is still hot." I repressed the unkind urge to smile at his discomfort. "Which is not my doing, as you poured it yourself."

I had not touched my juice, so I slid the small glass to him. Glowering, he lifted the glass in a mock salute. He set it down with a sigh, took a more cautious sip of coffee and began to eat with haste.

In between bites he said, "Any progress on your plans?"

"The dining commons during breakfast is an inappropriate location to discuss my progress," I said. "And eating that quickly is not good for your digestion."

"I'll keep that in mind." A glimmer of a smile dawned in his eyes. "Guess I'm a bit grouchy this morning."

"Yes," I said, "although I believe you will explain your mood, should such an explanation be necessary."

He snorted. "Right."

Mild disappointment—though at what, I could not say—propelled me to my feet. Timmons followed, and we deposited our trays near the galley entrance. I collected another cup of tea.

"By the way," he called, and I paused at the door. "You're getting better at that eyebrow thing."

I could not help smiling as I returned to my computer laboratory.

The familiarity of the room was soothing, and I relaxed as I started to work. After establishing several layers of security, I designed an agent capable of searching for keywords and images in the video records. Once it was running, I finished the summary Jordan had requested, but even after several more hours of searching, I found no further information regarding the virus or Dr. SahnVeer's suspicions. Either it had been erased in its entirety, or it did not exist at all, which I doubted. To calm my frustration, I stood and tried the meditative poses I had learned as a child. They were ineffective.

I drank my tea. It, too, was ineffective. I paced the room, tapping my thigh, trying to think.

Whoever had erased the data might have left accidental trails. The perpetrator's blatant carelessness might be the result of having altered the records in a rush, which meant mistakes. For the first time in my life, the idea of slovenly behavior encouraged me. I began to search for deletions and compare their timestamps, but my communication link chimed.

Jordan asked, "Are you available right now?"

"I have finished the report, so, yes."

"Good. I'll be right there to review it and anything else you've got. I received . . ." She exhaled. "I'm on my way. I'll explain then."

"I will be here."

The chime indicated the link had been terminated, but there was, simultaneously, a knock on the door. I rose, surprised at the immediacy of her arrival. It was not Jordan, however, but Timmons.

He leaned against the door jamb and grinned. "You were right. I should have coffee before interacting with people."

"Perhaps," I said.

Neither of us moved. When Jordan arrived moments later, we still stood in the doorway. Her eyes flickered between us. His smile disappeared, and mine faltered.

"Jordan."

"Timmons."

"What're you doing here?"

Though she was, in general, courteous, she did not immediately reply. Her lips tightened. I hoped that my early morning intrusion had not adversely affected her mood for the day. At least Timmons's demeanor had improved after his coffee.

"You might as well come in, too." Jordan stalked past both of us into the laboratory. "I'd rather get this out of the way all at once. You won't like it."

With this cryptic statement, she waited for us to clear the door before securing it, then turned to me. "Any more data on the virus?"

I shook my head. "I have several searches running. While it is possible the data was not properly uploaded, it is more likely the information was erased at the source, like the video records of Dr. Tristram's murder."

"You said this would be of interest to me, Jordan," Timmons remarked as he sat down. "I am, of course, as intrigued by the idea of a plague-inducing virus as I ought to be, but since you briefed me on it earlier, I suspect that's not what you meant."

Her eyes narrowed, and she raised her chin.

I stepped between them and said, "I summarized the details of this morning's work." Entering the security codes, I opened the document. "If you wish, you may peruse it before I transmit it to the Consortium. Surely, they will act on such a threat, rather than merely document ensuing deaths. I will also transmit the document to several government contacts and the university. Given my current state, I am concerned they might not see the information otherwise."

"No," Jordan said so sharply I startled. "I'll do it."

"She's not incompetent, *Venetia*."

Jordan's nostrils flared. "That isn't what I meant, and you know it." Her braids swung as she turned to me. "Don't draw undue attention to yourself or give cause for greater scrutiny than you're already under. I'll send it to some of my university connections and copy the Health Center, while I'm at it. My fath—*they* will be extremely interested." She squinted at the display, then pointed to several sentences. "You need to strike these lines. And these."

"Why shouldn't she send it herself?" Timmons demanded. "What's going on?"

She tapped her left foot but did not turn to face him. "I received a transmission, Recorder." She drew in a breath. "How solid are your escape plans?"

My stomach knotted. "I have made little progress in that direction. I have, however, managed to adjust the footage from the dining commons, dating the alteration to a small kitchen fire." Jordan opened her mouth, so I held up my hand. "It should draw attention away from our conversation. I also modified the recordings from the lounge."

Timmons's focus darted from Jordan to me.

"Both of you should review your personal logs," I continued. "They are not admissible, but the Consortium has access to everything, unless deadlocked. I cannot alter your logs without the Consortium's network, and even then, doing so might be noticed."

Jordan paced back and forth.

I rose to block her path. "Did the transmission address my present condition?"

She avoided my eyes. "Yes."

"Will you or Max be disciplined for saving me?"

"I don't think so." She hesitated. "But I was told to watch you carefully."

Timmons pushed away from the table and stood. "Did they say why?"

"Because they consider her damaged, Timmons," Jordan retorted. "Because they can't control her right now."

"She's not damaged. If anyone on this ship is damaged—"

"I don't know that? Keep your opinions to yourself, Nathaniel, and stick to facts."

"Facts? *Facts?* Like you have the faintest—"

Their argument spun, undefined, around something neither wanted to say, or perhaps merely did not want to say in my presence. Attempting to ignore both their disagreement and my growing anxiety, I made Jordan's suggested changes. I sent a copy to her and another to the Consortium, then erased the document from the computer's memory.

"Jordan," I said, and they both fell silent at my interruption. "I have sent it. What other news do you have?"

She sank into a chair. "Stars. I shouldn't let myself get distracted."

"It is well, Jordan."

"Not really, and I'm sorry." She let out a long breath. "Timmons, I'm apologizing to you, too, because . . . Because. Recorder, you need to put a priority on that escape plan."

"Why?" he asked hoarsely.

Jordan kept her eyes on mine. "We reach Lunar One in seven days. That's your deadline."

His hand flexed at his side. "Again, why?"

But I knew. I forced my voice to be steady. "They are coming."

Jordan nodded. "With your replacement."

The room grew quiet. I almost believed I could hear our heartbeats over the noise from the air circulation system.

"This is not truly a surprise," I said, eventually. "I will add this to my work schedule."

"No." Jordan stood. "This is your primary concern."

A spike of fear pierced the continual buzz of anxiety. "I will not ignore the threat of a bioweapon."

She shook her head. "A *potential* virus. On a dead station."

When Timmons spoke, his voice was raw. "It won't be ignored, just let other people focus on it. You need a way out of here."

"He's right," Jordan said. "Zhen can start tracking the virus. Look, I know I haven't always been supportive, and I still don't think you'll be able to run for long, but you're right. You can't go back. You're safer heading to the mines in the belt. I've heard you can get lost out there. They might not find you."

"No." Timmons compressed his lips. "That'd kill her, J."

Relief flooded me when he called her J again. The fact that he had not done so since they arrived had bothered me.

"What other choices does she have, Tim? The sanctuaries have been gone since 237. No one will hide her. Where could she possibly go?"

"I don't know." He faced me, green eyes intense. "Sweetheart, you've got to focus on getting out of here."

Sweetheart? He must not have realized what he said, though for half a second, I allowed myself to believe he had not misspoken. I knew he had, but nevertheless, my face heated.

Jordan's eyes widened, but before she made any comment, her communication link chimed. "Jordan here."

"Venn, you still up for lunch?" Julian Ross's voice asked.

The muscle in Timmons's jaw ticced.

Warm color rushed to Jordan's cheeks. "Yes. I'm in the Recorder's lab."

"I'll be right there."

She gave him an affirmative before chiming off. Her smile faded when she glanced at Timmons, whose shoulders had stiffened.

"Stars, Tim. Let it go. Whatever issues you two have, I'll be fine." She turned to me. "I meant what I said."

I turned off the displays and opened the door.

"Recorder . . ." Jordan darted a glance into the corridor. "Keep your priorities straight."

We waited in uncomfortable silence until Ross appeared at the door and flashed one of his brilliant smiles at Jordan.

"Ready?" He nodded at me. "Afternoon, Recorder. Timmons. Didn't see you there."

Jordan nudged Ross. "Leave him alone."

He gave her a light kiss. "Sure, Venn," he said, watching us over the top of her head.

They left, but Timmons did not relax.

"You do not like to see Jordan with him."

Still watching the empty doorway, he shook his head. "Not much."

"I have researched his behavior. I believe he enjoys provoking you. Perhaps—" A sudden thought made me tap my fist against my thigh, though there was no reason for apprehension over a simple question. I watched his boots and asked, "Have you had lunch? We could take something portable to eat elsewhere, which is what I do when I dine alone. The bay where I store my drones is quiet."

When he did not answer, I cleared my throat.

He turned around. One hand rubbed the back of his neck, where his hair curled ever so slightly. "Sorry. It's just . . ."

"Jordan will be fine."

"I know. My mind wanders sometimes." Green eyes met mine. "You were saying?"

I bit my lip. "It is time for lunch."

He sighed. "Dining commons it is, then."

I shook off the desire to be called by a mistaken term of endearment. "That will suffice."

30

Though I had never viewed an autopsy before, I could not bring myself to prepare by studying ahead of time, and it was with a degree of trepidation that I queued the recordings on the small projector in my computer laboratory. If it sufficed, I would not need to run it in VVR. I had not forgotten Jordan's admonition to prioritize my escape preparations over other work and was content to permit DuBois to oversee the search for the virus. However, I remained committed to solving Kyleigh's father's murder, as a parting gift to my friend.

I played the record, but after the preparation of the body, the feed disappeared into static, even as it had at the scene of the murder. Both relief and concern coursed through me. The damage could not be coincidental. I left it playing in a loop in case the repetition would trigger insight.

Without the cause of death, I lacked evidence to guide my search, although the deletion of information was, itself, material. Skimming the other recordings for patterns, I found Westruther and Lorde met every morning. I queued their meetings on the small three-dimensional display, even though the images suffered when the computer played the thready audio recording.

The sound itself decreased my efficacy. Since the loss of my implant, it was easier to watch several images than listen to several sounds. Although I could loosen my visual focus, without my drone to isolate the audio feeds, I could not separate the sounds to follow multiple conversations at one time. I doubled the playing speed, hoping to catch keywords. Recordings of the day before the incident were undamaged, but those of the five days immediately following the murder had been deleted. They resumed the sixth day, but Charles Tristram's death was not discussed.

I had decided to return to the beginning and follow the trail forward when an unexpected hand on my shoulder startled me. I spun around.

"Max! I did not hear you come in."

He said nothing, but simply stood beside me, eyebrows drawn together and a deep frown on his face. Kyleigh had stopped in the doorway, pale and shaking. Concern for her brought me to my feet.

"What is wrong? Please"—I gestured toward the table—"sit down."

He squeezed my shoulder.

"Max," I peeled my attention from her face, up to his. "I believe she should rest. She seems unwell."

He nodded at my display. It took a moment for me to realize her pallor was due to the autopsy playing behind me. I hastily blocked her view of the recording as it flickered to static.

"Kyleigh . . ." I faltered into an uncomfortable silence.

Without a word, she fled.

"Max, I forgot our appointment." I stumbled over my words. "I did not mean . . ."

Still, he said nothing, though he released my shoulder and crossed the room to pick up a chair. Placing it near my workstation, he sat down heavily. "What in the colonies did you think you were doing? You knew we'd be by this afternoon. That's her *father*."

I swallowed past the lump in my throat. "I did not . . . Had I considered it, I would have thought she would be pleased by my attempt to ascertain what had happened."

His frown deepened. "Seeing her father like that isn't going to help her. Even you could have figured that out! Don't they teach you protocols for assignments like this?"

"No." I pushed away from my computer, from the recording which flickered back to the body on the table, from Max. My voice shook, I could no longer meet his eyes, and tears sprang, unwanted, in my own. "It was not necessary. I was merely to document, not to interact. There was no training regarding grief or emotions. There was no training for error, or for losing one's drone. There was no training for when you are no longer who you were."

His shoulders fell. "I shouldn't have said that. Don't worry. We'll talk to her in a bit."

"You should speak with her now, Max. I erred yet again, and when I try to . . ." I faltered. "Too often I fail. But Kyleigh did not deserve this."

"And you do?" He touched my shoulder lightly. I flinched, for a split second anticipating a reprimand from my shadow drone. His face softened. "I'll be back."

He left quietly, but once he was in the hall, I heard him call Kyleigh over his communication link.

Blinking rapidly, I turned off the video as it once again displayed static. The computer laboratory had never seemed so empty before. Even when I had chosen to withdraw from my friends, its solitude had not mocked me as it did just then. Drawing a deep breath, I tried to focus entirely on the problem at hand instead of the memory of Kyleigh, staring in horror as the recording of her father's autopsy played behind me.

Twenty-seven minutes passed before Dr. Maxwell returned.

I said, "I should have locked the door earlier, as I usually do. I have grown lax."

Max shook his head. "I told Edwards I'd be here for an hour or two."

"That is unnecessary. I have uncovered no information requiring your expertise. Should you not be helping Kyleigh instead?"

He met my eyes directly, as he had when I was a child, and a sad smile crept across his face. "No, this is where I need to be."

He did not clarify but instead asked what I had been doing, and together we worked out a system. I skimmed for anything that could shed light on missing data and sent it to Max to review while I kept searching.

We had been working together for an hour and ten minutes when he exclaimed, "I found something." He moved aside so I could see.

The small display showed John Westruther's barren office. Westruther frowned over steepled fingers from behind his desk, and Gideon Lorde stood, his back to the station map, feet braced and arms crossed. Chief Engineer Jean-Pierre Marsden slouched against the wall while Dr. Oliver Allen, the chief medical officer, waved a paper and gesticulated wildly. Westruther and Lorde followed the doctor's frenzied movements with furrowed intensity, but Marsden scratched his ear, then studied his fingertip.

Max paused the recording. "Allen's saying it's a good thing he kept a printout in his quarters. His files disappeared after Tristram's remains were cremated. He can't prove what happened."

The frozen images of the men flickered slightly. Again, the knowledge I viewed the dead made me shudder, so I refocused on Max. "Marsden's presence would not be required at a meeting to discuss an autopsy."

"Allen interrupted a meeting about replacing the vid feeds. He burst in with that paper." Max glanced back at the closed door, perhaps to reassure himself that Kyleigh would not hear. "Tristram was subdued with a subdermal sedative, then injected with a mild neurotoxin directly into his spinal fluid. The murderer then used a scalpel, probably from a research lab, to open the carotid artery."

A prickling sensation crept up my spine, and I wrapped my arms around my waist. "This makes no sense. It was unnecessarily elaborate. If he had been subdued, why would it be necessary to cut his throat?"

He watched me for a moment. "I don't know. Does it bother you?"

How could he ask? I rose and paced the laboratory. "Yes, of course it does. Someone murdered the father of one of the few friends I have ever had, in an egregiously violent manner. The individual was never apprehended, although he or she died on the station and can no longer harm anyone. My friend"—I faltered slightly—"if she still cares to be my friend, did not have the closure of justice. I watched him, Max, when he was murdered—"

"You did *what*?"

"No." It was unlikely the pain in my chest was indicative of any medical ailment, so I ignored it. "That part of the recording was erased. I did not see the act itself, but his final concerns were for his daughter and protecting people from a potential security breach."

"The virus?"

"Yes. He was a good man." It was half a minute before I spoke again. "Why would you ask if his death bothered me? Do you believe I would be unmoved by the murder of my friend's father? Or perhaps you merely think the method itself would be insufficient to provoke an emotional response?"

He watched me silently.

I moved to the door, blinking back moisture. "I know I am not conversant in many aspects of social interaction and I hope my lack of perception has not caused lasting harm." I blinked faster. "I appreciate your assistance with my investigation, Dr. Maxwell . . . After securing the files, I will send this to VVR and record all I can from that document, then be sure to credit your actions in my report to Jordan."

He appeared at my side and handed me a tissue. I wiped my cheeks, blew my nose, and then stood there, holding the wad of damp, flimsy paper.

"Call me Max," he reminded me gently. "I'm sorry. This isn't easy for you. Nothing here is like the Consortium."

"No," I managed to say. "Emotions are a liability. This level of distress would be severely reprimanded. We are taught control at a very young age."

"Did you have friends in your cohort? Were you happy?"

It was the question he had asked me years ago, and it was still immaterial.

"I had a friend, once. He was older than I, approximately thirteen. We made boats together three times before he received his shadow drone. He must have been more stable than I. I did not receive mine until I was fifteen years past gifting. Several children—Oh stars!"

His eyebrows flew up at my language. "What?"

Oh, please, stars above, it could not be true.

"Easy, there! Sit." Max guided me to a chair and knelt before me. "Breathe. It's all right. Put your head down between your knees and breathe."

But it was not all right. Some of the children in our cohorts disappeared, and I never before questioned where they went. I did now. We had been told that sometimes children were shifted to different training centers, but were they truly? The pale boy with red eyelashes from my cohort, the obstinate girl with eyes like slate from my friend's . . . Where had they gone?

I drew deep breaths, whispered the periodic table of the elements, and slowly began to regain control.

"Tell me—what's all this about?" He reached out, then retracted his hand.

"No." I could not tell him. Exhaling slowly, I closed my eyes and tried to visualize something other than those children. "I do not feel steady. I wish I still had my neural implant. It prevented episodes like this."

Max's face grew very still. "People all have moments of instability. I forgot what a different world this is for you. But please, never wish for your implant again."

He stood, then handed me my cold cup of tea. I sipped it.

"Kyleigh and I meant to update you about her interesting progress in understanding specific nanodevices. She wanted to tell you herself, but given the circumstances . . ." He continued in a monotone, "How well do you remember the day you woke up? After the surgery?"

"Clarify." I put the tea down.

"Do you remember what I told you?"

I closed my eyes, pushing myself to recall our conversation. "The roach's destruction of the drone damaged my neural implant, which triggered systemic failure. You had removed the damaged material that had 'grown' throughout my brain."

"Yes. There was more, but Jordan stopped me from telling you. I said it was as if they'd been . . ."

The scene replayed in my head, and I remembered him starting to say— "Programmed?" My eyes flew open. "I remember."

He sat, watching. Waiting.

"But," I protested, "you cannot mean the malfunctioning implant purposefully triggered failures in other systems?"

"Kyleigh's the nanotech scholar and would be better at explaining," he said, "but I'll do my best. When your neural implant was destroyed, it sent signals to nanites throughout your body, either activating chemical reactions or targeting specific parts of your microbiome. Some of them punctured intestinal walls and others carried pathogenic bacteria, rather like the way Dr. SahnVeer programmed devices to deliver medicines to tumors. Whoever designed them didn't want anyone to 'go rogue' and survive."

I went cold. Not even two ten-days ago, this information would have been ridiculous. Now, I believed it.

"Are you all right?" Max touched my shoulder again, and I jerked away.

"You suggest my implant was designed to kill me, yet you ask if I am all right?"

"I know. It's hard to grasp."

"No." I choked out the words. "It is not difficult to comprehend. It confirms my fears. My head hurts, Max."

"I'm sorry." He stood. "Why don't you walk down to the infirmary with me? I'll get you something for your headache. You can see the data we have—"

The data. They had the data in the medical system. The Consortium could not discover what they had learned about my implant.

"No, Max, you cannot have that information!"

"Of course I can," he began, but I lurched to my feet.

"No! You must forget everything you found. I shall make sure no one knows you have seen it. You must tell Kyleigh she has not, either. Jordan was right. You cannot know." When he shook his head, I grabbed his arm. "Do not tell anyone what you will now forget. I shall stay here. I will fix this."

He stared down at me.

"Swear it, Max, swear you do not know, and make Kyleigh swear it, too. Swear by whatever star or deity you will, but I need you to swear. Promise me, oh please, promise me!"

"I—" His nut-brown eyes widened. "I promise."

The moment he understood, I turned away to the computers, initiating new programs. "If possible, have Edwards bring me something for my headache and to help me focus. I cannot spare the time. While I appreciate your help with the research, please leave. I have work to do."

Max still said nothing as I began to search for and purge evidence from the medical records. After I heard him leave, I lost all sense of time.

Edwards brought food and a jet injector for my headache. Nothing helped with the tension, though, and I found it difficult to eat. I still had my wrist monitor, but its constant reminders became a distraction. I turned it off.

Eventually, a knock at the door disrupted my fading concentration, and I checked the time. It was evening. My visitor had the access codes, for the door slid open without my invitation, but I recognized the footsteps.

"Hey," Timmons said. "Heard you've been busy."

I did not divert my attention from the computers, even for him. "Yes."

"Mind if I come in? I brought dinner. Need to make sure you're eating."

"I do not mind." For three seconds, dizziness pushed against the edges of my perception, as it had seven days prior, when Max had scolded me about taking precautions regarding my health. "Perhaps I am done for the day. I am slowing, and my lack of focus could contribute to mistakes. I cannot afford mistakes."

Timmons stepped into the laboratory, and the door slid shut. I heard him set something down. When I glanced over, he was sitting at the table. He motioned to the chair next to his.

"I don't particularly want to eat in the dining commons, either." He fell silent while I closed the programs and the computers and reinstated the security protocols, then joined him. "You okay?"

"No," I said, fighting tears of exhaustion. "It is too much, Timmons."

"Nate."

"Nate?"

"I'd like it if you called me Nate." His face appeared slightly flushed.

"Why?" I asked, distracted momentarily. "Because your name is Nathaniel Phineas Timmons?"

The flush deepened. "I'd appreciate it if you wouldn't go telling everyone the Phineas part."

"I have not done so yet. I knew your name. I also know Max's name is Robert James Maxwell, and Jordan's is Venetia Renee—"

He chuckled. "Really? Oh, she's gonna hate me knowing that."

"Nate," I repeated, savoring the sound and the way it felt to say it. "Why would you ask me to use your given name?"

He did not answer but busied himself with eating. After several bites, he spoke. "Any luck on figuring a way out of here?"

"Escape cannot be my priority. First, I must ensure that you, Max and Kyleigh, Jordan, Spanos, Edwards, even DuBois—that you are safe. I will not put a higher priority on myself if any of you are at risk."

"I don't like it. We'll be at the station soon. You don't have much time."

"I know." I rested my forehead on my palms. "I do not know if I can manage it."

"Hey. Look at me," he said.

Raising my head, I answered, "I am looking."

He held out his hand. I stared at it for a moment, then put mine in his. His grip tightened for half a second, then he let it go, reached over and gently traced my left cheekbone. I did not pull away, though perhaps I should have.

"If anyone can get this straightened out, it's you."

"You cannot believe that," I said.

"I do. And I'm never wrong when it counts." He flashed a tired version of his usual grin. "So, how about some dinner?"

And Nate handed me a sandwich.

31

Venetia studied her reflection in the full-length mirror, adjusted the fabric draped over her shoulder, and decided that regardless of Mother's demands, she wouldn't wear the pearls. Unclasping the elaborate strands, she laid them gently in the velvet-lined box, then looped her favorite rope of polished amber around her neck before applying a touch of scent to her pulse points.

Gold silk brushed against her legs as she triple-checked her packing. Everything she needed was nestled neatly in the small trunk on the bench at the foot of her bed. Jewelry wouldn't be an asset where she was bound, and other than the amber, that wasn't a loss. She stretched and checked the mirror again. The sari's folds still fell correctly. For a moment, she smiled with satisfaction, but that faded quickly.

Poise wasn't enough. Strength and perseverance weren't enough, either.

Well. His loss. *Their* loss. She unclenched her hands and exhaled slowly.

The door slid open, and her cousin slipped inside. Tabitha flopped her tiny self onto the four-poster bed and eyed Venetia critically. "Your mother'll be livid you're wearing that old thing, Neesha. And you aren't wearing her pearls."

"I like the amber. If she wants to display her favorite jewelry, she can wear it herself. Venetia tucked a spare datapad into her trunk, then latched it shut. "And, if she wants me here tonight, she gets me and my choices."

"She's still angry you're leaving?"

Venetia gave a short laugh. "Mother would never stoop so low as to be *simply* angry."

"I guess not, but I'll miss you. And, you look amazing, with or without the pearls." Tabitha fingered the lace on her sleeve. "Although, since you and Philippe . . ." She huffed. "Philippe is an idiot. Who's your date?"

"Tim."

"That'll get under your mother's skin."

"I don't care. She'd love it if I groveled at Philippe's feet, but that isn't going to happen." Venetia drummed her fingers on the tall bedpost. "I thought about asking Gerry, but your brother isn't around. I haven't seen him since graduation—"

"No one has." A little line of concern creased Tabitha's forehead.

"Tim and I checked his quarters earlier, but he wasn't there." She tamped down the worry. "Tim promised to follow up tomorrow afternoon, but since Gerry wasn't around, Tim said he'd show up tonight. It's not like I want to go, but he'll make the evening bearable."

"He's not bad on the eyes, either."

"He's just Tim." She crossed to the mirror and put on a final touch of makeup. "He came to my defense, fists flying, three years ago and has been inordinately obnoxious ever since to make up for any unintended chivalry."

Her cousin grinned and rolled over to grab the florist box from the nightstand. "Did he send the flowers?"

"Of course."

"Bet he didn't get the right ones." Tabitha tossed the box across the room.

Venetia caught it with one hand. "You'll bruise them, Tabs. And leave off. He's not stupid." She opened the box, revealing the perfect wrist corsage of tiny russet lilies and golden roses nestled in delicate, pale green paper. She hadn't told him what she was going to wear, but he'd got it right. Venetia slid it on and held out her wrist with an exaggerated flourish. "See?"

Tabitha shrugged. "I keep forgetting who his grandfather is. Turn around. One last check."

Silk flared as Venetia spun, the gold threads glinting in the fading window light.

"You do look lovely." Tabitha sighed. "I wish I was tall."

"No," Venetia said dryly. "You probably don't."

Tabitha didn't answer. She cocked her head to the side, then inspected herself in the mirror before they headed down to join the small crowd in the library and the sitting room. When they were halfway down the stairs, the murmur of voices stilled, making the harpist's music louder than it was.

Venetia paused, one hand on the scrolled banister, as the guests parted for a Recorder and her drone. An unfamiliar man in a lime-green tunic followed in her wake, and after they had left, people flowed back together, the sound of their conversation sharper than it had been. Tabitha raised a brow in silent question, and Venetia shook her head, braids clicking against her bare arms. She sped up to precede Tabitha into the room.

Tim lounged against a bookshelf, casually ignoring the sea of colorfully dressed guests ignoring him. He cleaned up nicely—Venetia would give him that—and bowed over her hand. Tabitha giggled, and Tim winked at her.

"Venetia!" Even from across the room, her mother's tone expressed rebuke. "A word with you."

Tim took her arm. They threaded their way through the crowd of family, politicians, and faculty members. At least she didn't see Father and his sycophants anywhere. There was that.

"How do you want to play this tonight, J?" he murmured.

"Let's just get through the evening."

"But do you want them to despise me even more? Maybe they can be so aggravated that you aren't welcomed back? Good guy, bad guy? Which one of us is which?"

"I'd appreciate it if we could both be good guys tonight."

"Fine." He gave her a mock salute. "Pick the most boring *and* the most difficult option."

When they approached, her mother set her empty champagne flute on a table and stared at Tim as if he were an isopod. With a swish of velvet skirts, she turned. "Venetia, what are you wearing?"

Tim answered for her. "I would say, ma'am, she is wearing a sari that makes her shimmer like a sunset."

Mother frowned. "Hyperbole is in poor taste, young man, especially when I did not address you."

"Tim . . ." Determined not to rise to Mother's barbs, Venetia said calmly, "Would you be so kind as to find us something to drink?"

"Of course." He sauntered off toward the bar, and Mother glared after him.

"Venetia, why must you encourage that boy? If you bring him to events, people will gossip. Remember Philippe."

She counted to three, then said, "Why would I want to remember Philippe? Besides, Tim's my best friend."

Her mother's golden eyes narrowed. "That boy's *friendship* is beneath you, no matter who his grandfather is. No wonder Philippe left you."

Heat rose in her cheeks. "Mother, *I* left Philippe when he found my cousin more appealing. She didn't mind settling for a two-year, nonexclusive contract. If I ever contract with someone, it's going to be exclusive. What's the point, otherwise?"

"And if you keep this up, no one will want to contract with you."

"What does that mean?"

"Venetia, dear. First, you declare you are not going to work toward a doctorate. You have potential. Your father and I spared no expense on your education. Even this"—she waved a hand to indicate the people milling around them—"is for you, dear. Your current behavior borders on discourteous."

Spared no expense. Venetia had earned every blasted grade, fought her way through every class, figured out workarounds when the letters were hard to decipher. She was the one who qualified for the scholarship, though she'd had to study twice as hard as everyone else. All without a tutor. Tutors would have embarrassed her oh-so-brilliant parents.

Venetia opened her mouth, but Mother continued, "Joining the riffraff and going to their—what is it?—boot camp? The very name is plebeian. This is due to that dreadful boy's influence, isn't it? Even his own grandfather—"

"No," Venetia said abruptly. "It's not. My decision has nothing to do with anyone else."

Tim reappeared, a cocktail in each hand.

"Regardless." Her mother accepted a drink without a glance at Tim, even as she brushed off Venetia's remarks. "You simply cannot run around with your arms showing. You have arms like a miner, dear, and you need to soften those lines with fabric."

Setting the other glass on an occasional table, Tim watched her mother for a moment, his expression flat, and then he smiled and placed a hand on Venetia's forearm.

"This arm," he said quietly, "is as strong as steel but as beautiful and delicate as a poem. And it's been out of mine for far too long." He bowed slightly. "Ma'am."

Stars above, Tabitha was right, and he played that smile for all it was worth.

Her mother's glare could have melted platinum when Tim guided Venetia through the crowd to the balcony, avoiding Father who strode through the crowd, artificial friendliness pasted on his face.

"You all right? I hope that wasn't too much. It was all I could come up with, at the moment."

She raised an eyebrow.

"I mean, it's true, J. I just didn't make you uncomfortable, did I? Didn't–"

Across the room, her mother screamed.

Guests gathered in a tight knot around the mauve chaise lounge onto which Mother had collapsed, artistically, of course. Her father, towering over everyone, rubbed his lips briefly, then knelt next to Tabitha at Mother's side. Tabitha jolted to her feet and disappeared into the crowd.

"Tim, at the risk of parental wrath, mind if we skip out early?"

He grinned and took her arm again, but they hadn't gone far when Tabitha, face unnaturally pale under her makeup, appeared at her side and grabbed her hand.

"Neesha! Gervase–"

"Gerry?" Tim asked. "What about him?"

Tabitha threw a frightened glance over her shoulder and drew them away from the writhing knot of people. "He's . . . he's gone."

"Gone where?" Venetia looked past Tabitha to her parents. "He would have told me if he was leaving."

Tabitha lowered her voice. "I don't know."

Across the room, her father dropped a quick kiss on her mother's head and then raised her to her feet, looming over her. Turning to one of the men nearby, he bent and spoke in his ear. The man nodded, then left.

This *had* to be staged.

Father's perfectly pitched voice cut through the noise. "My partner is unwell, but dinner will still be served in half an hour, so please feel free to stay, if you wish." He guided Mother through the crowd and paused in front of Venetia and Tabitha but pointedly ignored Tim. "Find your uncle and both aunts. Meet us in your mother's sitting room." He turned abruptly, and they left.

Tabitha's wide eyes met Venetia's, and her lips quivered.

"J, what do you need me to do?" Tim asked.

"I'll take care of Tabs. Find my aunts and uncle for me?"

"You need me to stick around after?"

She wanted to say, *Oh stars, yes, please stay*, but pinched her lips, then only said, "I don't know what's happened, but probably not?"

He melted into the crowd while she ushered Tabitha up the stairs. When they reached the suite, her father was waiting outside the door to the sitting room. He opened it without a word. The door slid shut behind them, but he remained in the hall. Crossing to the sideboard, Venetia poured a drink and offered it to Tabitha.

"What happened, Tabs?"

Before her cousin answered, the door slid back open, and Venetia's father stepped in with one of the university hospital's doctors, who was maybe fifteen or twenty years older than she. He wasn't as tall as Father, probably a few centimeters shorter than she was.

"I believe she's simply overwrought, Maxwell," her father was saying, "but I would appreciate you making certain of it. She has a delicate constitution."

No, Mother has a constitution and will of iron. Venetia ignored the doctor's indistinguishable, deep reply and masked her expression as they disappeared into her mother's room.

Minutes ticked by. Tabitha finished her drink and set the glass on the table. The door opened again, and Philippe, immaculate as usual, entered, a look of superiority on his tan, aquiline features.

"Oh, blast him. That's the last thing I need," Venetia said under her breath as her father and the doctor emerged from the bedroom. Her father ignored her and walked through to the hallway, but the doctor stopped and glanced from her to Philippe, then back.

Philippe's theatrical voice filled the room. "Venetia."

Suddenly, Tabitha's younger half-sister, Jeanette, flung herself through the door, nearly running into Venetia's father. She draped herself over Philippe, who absently caressed her back.

Venetia straightened to her full height. Nausea and anger churned when she thought of those long fingers on her back just before graduation five days ago. "What do you want, Philippe?"

"I heard something has happened to Gervase."

"None of your concern. Get out."

Footsteps and a rumble of voices sounded in the hallway. Her aunts and uncle entered the room, but instead of leaving, Tim froze when he saw Philippe and Jeanette.

"Venetia," Philippe said as if she were a recalcitrant child, "such vitriol has no place in civilized conversation."

Tim stepped forward. "I'll tell you what has no place in anything civilized."

A thin smirk spread across her father's face. He stepped back a pace, a gleam in his eye Venetia didn't trust. At all. Tim's propensity for rushing to anyone's defense could undo his future. If he did something rash, he'd lose his place at university. Her father would ensure it.

"*You* don't," Tim continued. "You're a waste of good carbon."

"Tim, it's fine." She stepped between them. "I need to give him something anyway."

Philippe leaned toward her, his usual smirk in place.

Venetia smiled sweetly then, like lightning, she punched him in the face. Jeanette shrieked. Philippe staggered backward and hit the table, knocking over the crystal decanter. Blood and brandy drenched his jacket.

"Consider yourself uninvited," she said. "Get out."

Her father said nothing to her but only held out a silk handkerchief. "Call my office tomorrow, Philippe. Try not to bleed on the carpet as you leave. Maxwell, if you don't mind, would you see to this young man?"

"Of course." The doctor's deep brown eyes twinkled at Venetia. "Admirable precision on that hit, but you might want to work on your impulse control."

Venetia blushed. Stars above! His velvet, mesmerizing voice was like magic. What on any known planet was wrong with her, reacting like this to a man she'd met once or twice before, just because of his voice?

While the doctor escorted Philippe out of the room, Tim quirked a brow at Venetia, and she shook her head in response.

"I'll let myself out, J," Tim said, "but I'll be back to take you to the shuttle around 5:45."

She nodded in acknowledgment, and he left her alone with her family.

Uncle Gustave's youngest contracted partner, Louise, emptied the remnants from the unbroken decanter into a glass and extended it to him. He downed it.

"Well," he said, "an interesting prologue, as usual, Jacques, but what's the problem? That young man didn't specify."

After carefully locking the door, her father led her aunt to an overstuffed chair. He knelt before her. "I'm sorry, Margaret. It's Gervase."

"No." She seemed to know what he meant.

Aunt Margaret's honey-colored eyes filled with tears, and Uncle Gustave sat frozen in his chair. They all listened in growing horror.

"Gerry isn't stupid, Uncle Jacques," Tabitha protested. "He wouldn't fall in love with a Recorder! That's impossible."

Jeanette shuddered. "It's disgusting."

Venetia's heart seized. Gerry had always watched the petite Recorder from the university library, whose occasional soft smiles lit gentle blue eyes framed by long blonde-brown lashes. The Recorder who saw them as people instead of data. She thought of Gervase, with his guileless grin and deep well of compassion . . .

"What happens now?" she asked, somehow not choking on the words.

Her father stood. "Gervase's actions corrupted the integrity of the records. The Recorder was returned to the Consortium for whatever discipline they administer. I didn't ask. Not our concern. He"—his voice broke, and for a split second, Venetia thought he might be sincere— "Gerry has been removed."

"Removed?" her aunt's voice wavered.

Father's square jaw tightened. "Yes."

Aunt Margaret's whisper was barely audible, "When can my boy come home?"

"He can't. You need to understand," her father told them all, "not a word of this can get out. This evening, a Consortium Representative assured me—"

"*Tonight*? Here?"

"Yes, Venetia, here, in front of our guests." His cheeks darkened. "He assured me that if our family complies, if we let this go, none of us shall suffer. If, however, a single word leaks out, we shall all lose our positions and be relocated to the mining colonies like common criminals."

Uncle Gustave finally spoke. "Is my son dead?"

"His identification number has been stricken from the records," her father said. "I suspect he will be sent to work off his crimes."

"Where?" Venetia demanded. "With no notice? Without being allowed to come home or contact his family? He loses his freedom with no recourse, no trial?"

"That is enough," Father barked, then his voice became smooth again. Venetia's skin crawled at his artificiality. "I would have done anything to save him, but as of tonight, Gervase does not exist. Do you all understand?"

Tabitha stumbled across the room and fell into the chair next to her mother, tears coursing down both their cheeks. Jeanette wailed loudly.

Venetia glared at her. Like that ignorant, self-centered brat cared about anyone except herself. "Gervase was the best of this whole family, and you throw him away for a mistake? No one even tries to help him?"

Her father rounded on her. "There is no help for a man who betrays his family as he has by turning against the Consortium. He signed his own papers when he seduced a Recorder."

"He fell in love. And she must have loved him, too—"

"Enough!" he snapped. "Recorders love nothing but their sacred records."

Venetia watched Aunt Louise, Uncle Gustave, and Jeannette swallow their grief, nod, wipe away their few tears. Her father stood, rigid as a statue while Aunt Margaret and Tabitha wept. Blood pounded in Venetia's temples. She crossed the room to squeeze Aunt Margaret's thin hand.

"I need to finish packing."

"Venetia," Father began, "my dear—"

"Don't you call me 'dear.'" She gained control and modulated her voice as he had taught her. "You say Recorders love their records, but at least that's something. *You* only love yourselves. You lot make me sick. Gerry deserves better."

"Neesha," Tabitha protested faintly.

"Love you, Tabs." She stooped to kiss Tabitha's cheek, then took off the wrist corsage and placed it on her cousin's lap. "You, too, Aunt Margaret." She squared her shoulders and met her father's cold eyes. "The rest of you can rot."

She walked purposefully from the suite, her braids swinging against her back, silk swishing around her ankles. She kept the amber necklace, but when Venetia Jordan walked away early the next morning, she left the golden sari folded carefully on the foot of her bed.

32

When Zhen DuBois saw me outside the dining commons before breakfast the next morning, her spine stiffened. Even with less experience with citizens than I currently had, I would have known she was livid.

"You aren't even human, are you?" DuBois spat out the words.

"I am human," I said mildly, backing away.

"I had dinner with Kyleigh yesterday. You knew she was coming to speak with you, and you replayed her father's autopsy? That's twisted. You shouldn't be allowed out. They should find a way to keep you away from people."

"I did not—"

"Didn't what? Think? Feel?" She advanced into the radius of my personal space. "You might have fooled the others, but you don't fool me."

I could smell the citrusy soap she had used that morning and the coffee on her breath. I retreated another step.

She jabbed her finger against my clavicle. "You need to stay away from her, away from Alec, away from me. You aren't human enough to interact with people."

I tripped and bumped into the wall. Her method of communication was outside the boundaries of acceptable social behavior, but escalating a confrontation would not create a better outcome. Agreeing with her valid points was my best option.

"I intend to apologize to Kyleigh, who did not deserve what happened yesterday. I made an error, an egregious error, for which I truly repent, although you might not believe me."

She shifted her weight onto her heels. "No. I don't. You—" She stopped abruptly when Jordan, Kyleigh, and Elliott exited the dining commons.

"Zhen?" Jordan folded her arms. "What's going on here?"

DuBois lifted her chin at me. "Someone should keep her in check, especially since she isn't bound to the Consortium anymore. She can't be allowed to run around hurting people."

Kyleigh's red-rimmed eyes shifted between DuBois and me. She did not speak. I did not blame her. Why would she? Although I wanted Jordan to explain that I would not hurt people, I knew she could not. She was too honest.

Instead I turned to Kyleigh. "I greatly regret any pain or discomfort I caused. It was unintentional. Should it be necessary to discuss this further, I will be pleased to make the time to speak with you. Excuse me. I will retrieve my meal, then return to my work. Jordan, we should discuss my progress later today in my laboratory, at your convenience."

Elliott's attention flickered between our faces, and DuBois snorted.

"Yes, Max explained what happened." Jordan drummed her fingertips on her arms. "I'll work it in. Zhen, my office, fifteen minutes. Kyleigh, Elliott, I'll check with my contacts at Brisbane University, see what I can do."

No one else spoke. No one moved. I waited for fifteen seconds, then slipped past them into the dining commons where I took enough food for the morning, though I did not wish to eat. As if projected by a drone, I saw Kyleigh's reddened eyes, the pallor of her face. How much of that was my doing? My walk back to the computer laboratory seemed inordinately long, and once the door was locked behind me, I went straight to work.

Dr. Maxwell was incredibly detailed in his record keeping, which made my task more difficult. Plumbing the depths of his medical databases was tedious, as each individual entry required evaluation.

It took until twenty minutes before noon for me to remove most references to Consortium nanodevices from logs, records, and journals. Subtly altering the visual and audio records had been difficult. I also deleted information and questionable searches regarding nanotechnology from their other files. In hopes of preserving her chances for a degree, I left Kyleigh's research with Dr. SahnVeer untouched and then finally drank my cold tea.

My friends were as safe as I could make them.

I rested my head in my hands, and when my rapidly growing hair slid through my fingers, an uneasy shudder made me clasp them on my lap instead. At the moment, the search for a way to remain free from the Consortium did not feel worthwhile. My timer chimed. I grimaced and stretched, doing my best to ignore the garish colors and unattractive designs of the workplace safety posters. My feelings of regret and disappointment were no excuse to fail my designated tasks. I resumed perusing the recordings, hoping to uncover further information, and eventually dull focus replaced my lassitude.

The Elders told us our work was our redemption, that in the completion of our duties Recorders would find a sense of purpose. They were not entirely wrong.

A knock disrupted my progress. I secured the computers but left my programs running, irritated with myself for not scripting this earlier. Apparently, I was not as clever as some people believed, although, after the past twenty-four hours, this should have surprised no one.

I released the lock, and the door slid open.

"Elliott Ross," I said with surprise. "My apologies for keeping you waiting. We have not been introduced."

"You're the Recorder who got us out of the station." Though he slouched slightly, he was still tall enough to block my view of the hall. He mumbled, "Kyleigh needs to talk to you."

A knot formed in my abdomen. "You are certain of this?"

"Yes. I mean—" His eyes, blue as his brother's, looked past me toward the charging station at the back of my laboratory. "She didn't say so exactly, but I can tell, especially after Zhen . . . after this morning. It's eating at her."

The concept of an emotion like a living thing devouring Kyleigh piece by piece disturbed me. "What do you mean?" He did not immediately reply, so I added, "I will not intrude if she does not wish to talk."

"She hasn't said much only that she should've known better. It isn't natural for her to be so quiet. And I miss . . . ." He shuffled his feet. "Well, could you talk to her? Enough things have gone wrong. You owe her that, so are you coming or not? I told her I had to do something and would be right back."

At his words, the memory of eavesdropping on Jordan and Nate resurfaced. Kyleigh had said that dreams and fears could weigh one down like a physical burden. The concept, though still confusing, seemed to have merit after all. I tapped my thigh then stepped into the hall and locked the door.

We went slowly, and he trailed his right hand on the wall for balance. I studied him. Elliott was taller than Nathaniel Timmons by several centimeters but gave the impression of being much smaller. His time in the stasis pod had left him thin, almost frail. He needed to regain muscle mass. The stubble on his head was barely long enough to catch the light and, if memory served, was most likely prickly.

He stumbled. When I reached out to steady him, he cringed, bracing himself against the beige wall. "Don't touch me."

"I will not, if you do not wish it." The comment should not have hurt, yet it did.

His almost skeletal frame shook.

"Elliott," I continued, "you have pushed yourself beyond your endurance, which is no shame. Your brother would—"

"No!" He wobbled on his feet. "Don't tell Julian."

The desire to call his brother for assistance battled with the need to respect his wishes. I paused, then suggested, "There is a small bench over the chemical ducting system around the next corner."

"I'll be fine."

"I understand you do not wish to be touched, but if you lean on me, you can make it to that bench and rest."

He swallowed, and his blue eyes flickered up and down the hallway.

"Although I make social errors, I do not intentionally harm people. It is in your best interest to accept my offer of assistance."

A faint smile crept onto his pale face. "You really do talk like that. I thought Kye was pulling my leg."

Ignoring the bizarre mental picture of Kyleigh Tristram tugging on Elliott Ross's legs, I stepped close, and Elliott hesitantly reached out one long, gaunt arm and placed some of his weight on my shoulder. He trailed his other hand on the paneling, and we proceeded around the corner, where he eased himself onto the bench, leaned back, and shut his eyes.

His pallor concerned me. "Are you certain you are not in need of medical assistance?"

He shook his head and motioned weakly to the other end of the bench, so I balanced on the edge, to allow him space.

"My brother and I don't have much to do with Recorders. We try to stay out of their way," he said. "There was one on Pallas, but she died. Before everything went wrong."

"Yes." I had retrieved neither her body nor her drone, and my failures echoed through my mind.

"It was scary, you know." His hands moved restlessly on his lap. "First, Kyleigh's dad. And it was awful knowing some psycho-murderer was running around. They tried to keep it quiet, but they never caught him. Or her. It could've been a her, I guess. And then Dr. Johnson died, and Captain Lorde got sick . . ." He rested his head against the wall. "Or was it the other way around? Anyway, more people started dying. Freddie's dad sent us to the pods, but now . . ."

I kept my voice soft. "You woke up, and everything had changed."

"Everything!" His lashless blue eyes flew open. "I'm the wrong size, and it's hard to learn to walk and balance and everything. And I'm completely bald!"

I suppressed a smile. "I am the wrong person to whom you should complain of baldness, although I do sympathize with your predicament. Imagine—I woke up to find I had hair."

His expression shifted, perhaps loosened. "Well, I suppose that would be a change. You know, I can't imagine you completely bald. You don't seem Recorder-ish enough."

Thinking it might make him smile, I said, "That is because I now have eyebrows. Eyebrows disturbed me when I was a child, as they resembled wooly caterpillars crawling over people's faces."

I was correct. He relaxed ever so slightly. A smile creased his face, and his resemblance to his brother strengthened. "That eyebrow-caterpillar connection never occurred to me."

"But I did not see anyone with hair until five years after gifting, when they allowed us out on Tour Days to help us acclimate."

He startled. "You mean, you never saw a normal person until you were five? Just other Recorders? What about your parents?"

"We do not have parents. Our genetic donors gift us to the Consortium for service. The Eldest is our parent."

"But . . ." He turned to face me. "I always thought you volunteered or something. You're telling me your parents gave you away to the Consortium when you were a baby? You had no choice?"

"No. Gifting typically occurs around the beginning of the third trimester of pregnancy, to assure a better survival rate for the fetuses and to avoid further emotional complications for the donors, who are compensated for their contribution."

He made a strangled noise. "Don't you ever wonder about your parents?"

I took but five seconds to consider the truest answer. "Perhaps we all do. But we have our callings. Curiosity is part of a developmental stage, so we are not reprimanded when we are young. And, although pride is generally discouraged, we are taught to take satisfaction in our status as gifted ones. Our service is the redemption of our gifting."

Elliott was silent. I studied the artwork fastened to the wall opposite us. Random ribbons of red and blue paint twisted meaninglessly across a cream-colored canvas that nearly matched the paneling. A frame would have made it more complete. I decided I did not like it.

I changed the subject. "This is my first solo assignment. It was a great honor, which I have failed. However, I have also learned a great deal, which I hope will help me become a better person."

"You think of yourself as a person? A normal person?"

"Yes, I am a person," I said indignantly, turning from the ugly painting back to Elliott Ross.

"But you're a Recorder. Sort of. Or you were one."

"Yes, and even then, I was a person. That, Elliott Ross, was a very rude remark."

He lapsed into silence for perhaps thirty seconds before saying, "Zhen doesn't like you much."

I attempted to raise my eyebrows, thinking that this might quell his line of questioning. It did not work.

"Why?" he pressed.

"It is not right to hypothesize about another person's feelings."

"But what do you *think*?"

"When I unintentionally hurt Kyleigh yesterday–"

His communication link chimed, and Kyleigh's voice itself came through. "Elliott? Are you all right? You've been gone a while."

"On my way, Kye. I had to rest, but I'll be up in a sec."

"Do you need help?"

He shot a sidelong glance at me. "I'm fine, Kye. Just had to get something."

"All right." The communication link chimed again as she signed off.

"Are you rested enough to continue?" I asked, but Elliott was already standing.

He kept his hand on the wall. I stepped closer, in case he needed my assistance, and we arrived at the cats' room without further incident.

The door opened, and Kyleigh turned from the sink across the room. Her eyes widened when she saw me, but then her gaze slid to Elliott. She dropped the cloth towel she had been holding, and in less than three seconds, she was at his side, wrapping an arm around his waist. Elliott swallowed and stood taller while she guided him to a chair, shooed a cat away, and gave him a gentle shove. He sat down heavily, and she returned to the sink to fetch him some water.

"Drink," she ordered, and when he took the glass, she faced me and took a deep breath. "About this morning . . ."

"My apology was insufficient given my error. Kyleigh, I am truly sorry."

"I checked my computer, and I'm missing data. Max said–"

"That is also my doing." I wanted to explain, but I did not care to reveal why I had erased so much of her hard work, not in Elliott's presence.

"I know," she murmured. "I talked to Max."

I studied Bustopher's black head while he wove between my ankles. The uncomfortable quiet was broken by his small noises. I picked him up, and he butted his head against my chin. His apparent affection made the awkward situation bearable.

"It's okay."

I raised my eyes to hers. They were still puffy and faintly red, making their hazel greener than usual.

"It's okay," she repeated. "It was shocking, and awful, and horrible to walk in and see . . . that. So, yes, I was angry, and yes, I told Zhen. I couldn't see any reason for it. Max explained later, but I should have known. You wouldn't do anything to hurt me. I should've trusted you."

"You have been crying."

"Yes. Not just . . ." Her voice trembled. "Well, I've been crying because it hit me again that Dad's gone. I could almost pretend he wasn't, and I was only going somewhere without him and that we'd be together soon."

"I understand." Elliott's baritone seemed thicker. "It was like that when my dad died, too. Honest, Kye, it'll never go away completely, but it does get better. It just takes time. I promise."

Kyleigh flashed Elliott a shaky smile, then turned back to me, so she did not see the expression on his face. Only three ten-days ago I might not have recognized it, but there was a softening in his overly thin features like that in Spanos's when he watched DuBois. I focused on Bustopher again. I did not believe he meant anyone to see that. I felt as if I had eavesdropped, though I had heard nothing.

She touched my arm. "What it comes down to is, it's all right. Apology accepted, and I'm not mad. *And* I need to apologize. I misjudged you."

I wanted to protest that she had not, that I had done the wrong thing, but to reject her apology was, perhaps, to reject her. A knot rose in my throat, but I managed, "It is well."

For a second, I was concerned she meant to hug me, but she only squeezed my arm.

"Timmons said you'd say that." Kyleigh gestured toward Elliott. "So. This is my friend, Elliott Ross, who is overly involved in other people's lives and interferes all the time, but I forgive him anyway." She flashed him a grin. "Elliott, this is my friend, who currently does not have a name, even though I'm trying to make her choose one."

"I am pleased to meet you, Elliott Ross." I paused, then switched Bustopher to one arm and extended my fist, as Ross had at dinner last ten-day.

"Recorder," he said with a nod. When he did not bump my fist,

Kyleigh raised one faint eyebrow. He stood awkwardly, then tapped mine with his own.

Bustopher jumped down and began to wind around my ankles again. It was odd that a small animal trying to trip me made me happier. I checked his food and water. He attempted to convince me his food supply was inadequate, which was clearly untrue, so I merely knelt to scratch his jaw.

"So." Kyleigh paused. "Did you find out anything? Gideon didn't. We never knew what had happened to my dad. If you didn't, that's all right. I mean, Gideon couldn't."

"I have found nothing Gideon Lorde did not know." I refused to relate my findings on how her father had died. If she was unaware of the cause of death, I would not tell her. This was not a lie. It was an omission. "I will continue to investigate the event, however, while I pursue the other things Jordan has asked me to do. I shall not forget."

She picked up the cat called Hunter. "I didn't think you would."

"You know, it could've been that weird guy who worked in the galley," Elliott suggested.

"Finley?" Kyleigh asked. "No, Finley was just, well, he'd been trapped in the mines on one of the asteroids for a few days, and he honestly believed ghosts would get him if he wasn't careful. That's who he was talking to. The ghosts."

Elliott frowned. "My dad died in one of those mines when all the oxygen leaked out. Ross was at university on scholarship, and he had to come and get me. I was stuck in that stupid child welfare center for two quarters. It was awful. The place smelled like stale crackers and dirty diapers. How come you know about Finley, and I don't?"

A sad smile flitted across her face. "I asked."

He fell silent, gaze fixed on his feet. I did not want him to feel worse, but I did not know what I could do to improve the situation. Kyleigh, however, did.

She studied me. "You skipped lunch again, didn't you? Were you avoiding Zhen?"

I did not answer, but my face must have conveyed the truth.

"She isn't mean at all," Kyleigh assured me. "We hang out and watch vids in the evening. She's teaching me to knit."

"She's been pretty nice to me," Elliott said.

Kyleigh laughed. "Sure. And I suppose that's why you've been staring at her. You'd better hope Alec doesn't notice."

He ducked his head.

"We'll head over to the dining commons and grab a snack." She tiptoed to the door, stepped into the hall, and checked both directions with exaggerated care. "It's all right, the coast is clear! Let's feed my nameless friend. Maybe Elliott can help us think of something to call you."

She tucked one arm through Elliott's and the other through mine and steered us toward the dining commons.

"Missed you yesterday." Nate swung himself into the chair next to mine at breakfast the next morning. "Heard it wasn't the easiest of days."

I set down my fork and watched the steam twisting above my tea. "No," I said quietly. "It was not. I hope your day was better than mine."

He shrugged. "Since we're closer to the populated sectors, we had drills all day. Had to run tests on the chem system. Finished up late, though you look even more tired than I feel. Maybe a cup of something stronger than"—he reached over and read the label—"ginger tea? You should try coffee."

I merely shook my head and wrapped both hands around the comfortingly warm ceramic. His dimple appeared, and he pushed his own mug across the table.

"Go ahead. It's fresh. I grabbed it when I saw you come in. Wanted to join you before I headed over to finish yesterday's reports." He pushed the mug closer. "You won't know what you're missing until you try it."

The coffee smelled good, but when I took a tentative sip, I gagged. I grabbed my tea and swallowed hastily, burning my tongue.

"It isn't that bad!"

"Now what?" Kyleigh slid her tray next to mine.

"That is coffee?" I asked. "Taste evolved to warn us of toxins in our foods, Nathaniel Timmons. Bitterness indicates toxicity."

He laughed outright. I glared at him.

"Really, it isn't bad with enough sweetener," Kyleigh said. "Like chocolate."

Still grinning, Nate took the cup and downed its contents, despite the fact I had taken a sip. "Sorry about that."

I did not entirely believe him, but somehow, I did not mind.

Spanos and DuBois joined us, and Spanos sat down across from Nate, liberally applied pepper sauce to his entire plate, and proceeded to eat while ignoring everyone. DuBois perched on the chair next to him and inclined her head at me. I found the lack of overt hostility encouraging. Perhaps Jordan had spoken with her.

"Those reports are calling my name, but I'll swing by before lunch, if you don't mind," Nate said to me. "You'll be in your lab?"

I did not know where I would be, so I explained that I might be in VVR, skimming records. He gave me a nod and left. Thankfully, no one spoke for five minutes, so I had almost finished my meal before Ross and Elliott sat down next to Spanos, who scooted his tray several centimeters toward DuBois's but otherwise did not acknowledge their arrival.

"Well, Recorder," Ross said. Elliott startled and turned slightly to look at him. "What is on your schedule for today?"

I finished my juice, folded my napkin neatly, and stacked my utensils in the center of my plate. I had an irrational, unkind desire to tell Ross that what I elected to do was not his concern, but I suppressed it.

"I will continue to follow up on the events on Pallas."

"And that entails?"

"I will not know until I finish," I said.

"Elliott and I are applying to university today," Kyleigh volunteered. "Freddie will, too, when he wakes up. There's a really good art school on Ceres, in Trinity North, but Jordan says she knows some people at Albany City University who can help us get in, even without a secondary certificate. All our academic records were left behind. Not," she turned to me, "that I'm complaining."

Elliott sat silently without eating, darting quick glances in my direction.

Ross followed his gaze, and a small frown creased his face. "Eat something, Elliott. Like I said yesterday, you'll be able to test out of some things." He motioned for the pepper sauce, and when Spanos ignored him, Kyleigh pushed the bottle across the table. "Kye, your father was in contact with several universities on New Triton. They'll have your academic records."

"Given the thoroughness of your father's work, I believe Julian Ross is correct." Not knowing what else to say, I stood, and took my tray to the receptacle and my tea to VVR.

Three hours and thirty-one minutes later, I rubbed my eyes with the heels of my hands. None of the recordings I had selected contained information pertinent to Dr. Tristram's murder, the engineered virus, or any connection between the two. I loaded my antepenultimate file, which pixelated into existence around me.

Before I instructed VVR to play the record, I prowled the edges of the laboratory. Several sparsely furnished workstations lined up in even rows, and medical equipment covered the tables around the periphery. Dr. Oliver Allen sat on the edge of a chair, datapad in hand, the end of his stylus between his teeth. Chief Engineer Jean-Pierre Marsden, however, stood on a neighboring workstation, arms stretched overhead, captured as the newly installed security camera activated.

After my previous failures, I did not hope for useful information, but still I said, "Play," and with a grunt, Marsden tossed the damaged security camera into a box.

"Be careful with that, Jean-Pierre. They might need it to"—Dr. Allen waved a hand—"check for fingerprints or the like."

Marsden's laugh grated on my ears. "What, are we back in Medieval Earth, Oliver?"

"Not medieval, I think. Charles would know."

The engineer jumped to the floor. "Charles isn't here, though, is he? Cremated last ten-day. Dust unto dust, and all that. Him and his special—"

"Oh, shut up!" Dr. Allen snapped.

But Marsden went on. "Now Gideon's insinuating my people messed with the blasted equipment. It doesn't take an engineer to damage a Consortium spying machine." Marsden slapped a lid onto the box.

"I'm sure Gideon wasn't insinuating anything of the sort," Dr. Allen said. "He's merely trying to ascertain the facts."

They must not have realized the camera was already recording, for Marsden, who had no respect for the anti-obscenity laws, interrupted Dr. Allen to speculate inaccurately on Gideon Lorde's genetic heritage.

"Language, Jean-Pierre," Dr. Allen said when Marsden paused for a breath.

"It's a good thing that thrice-blasted Recorder is dead, instead of prowling around, interfering." Marsden tossed the box and some tools into a crate atop a service bot. "You know the spacing Consortium will send more of their spies on the next transport. Gideon had better wrap this up before it arrives."

Dr. Allen drummed his fingers on his pant legs. "That virus—"

"I didn't want to be sent to the back end of the spacing system to begin with, and this pretty much closes the deal. If Georgette's right about this 'mystery virus'—not that I believe her—maybe it'll take us all out and end our misery."

"That isn't funny. Just turn on the camera and run the systems checks so Gideon can figure out what happened. Leave the hypothesizing to the scientists."

"That so-called virus isn't what killed poor, sainted Charles."

Dr. Allen shoved the stylus into its slot on the datapad with more force than required. "Charles was a good man, whatever your opinion."

"Good and dead."

I was thankful when they left the room and the recording terminated. I had listened to enough of Marsden's conversation. It angered me that he maligned Kyleigh's father, when his loss had caused her such pain. It took four minutes to regain control of my emotions before I began the next recording, which was even less helpful.

Summarizing the morning's work on my datapad, I sent copies to both Jordan and the Consortium. Anxiety tightened bands around my chest yet again. Unless I managed to escape before their arrival— and I had made no progress in that direction—I would face severe consequences. The very absence of the information indicated its existence, yet I had found no evidence. My failure to document and verify the virus might have put the system in danger. The Elders would not accept mistakes of this magnitude.

I slipped into the hallway outside VVR, my mind churning. Though Jordan had assured me DuBois would track the virus, my duties pressed down on me. My thoughts scrabbled over and under each other as the roaches had in that hangar: the virus endangering millions of lives, the incomplete data from Pallas Station, Kyleigh's father's murder.

Additionally, my defection loomed closer and closer as we approached Lunar One. I had not established the basis for a new identity, had not found a way to hide my escape from the Elders. Even if I mapped a route to safety, my appearance and mannerisms might very well betray me, while my absence of resources would make my flight difficult.

And through all these concerns, worry about my friends' safety thrummed as ever present as the rumble of *Thalassa*'s circulation fans.

Preoccupied with these thoughts, it took several strides to realize Elliott had joined me. I slowed as a courtesy. While he moved with more confidence than he had the day before, he was still ungainly, not yet having adjusted to his longer legs.

"Recorder," he said. "I . . . I was looking for you."

"You have found me."

He glanced up and down the hallway before he indicated a bench under more unframed artwork. It made no sense that citizens needed incomplete and poorly executed decoration. "Mind if we sit down?"

I acquiesced.

"It's Julian." He cleared his throat. "I mean, no, not Julian. It's Freddie."

His answer confused me. "You are concerned about your brother or your friend?"

He nodded, only briefly glancing up from the grey-flecked flooring.

"If you are concerned about Freddie, I cannot resolve your

understandable apprehension, but Kyleigh, you, and your brother have all survived. It was fortuitous you were in the same group."

"But we were . . ." He faltered to a stop, and his forehead wrinkled.

When he said nothing more, I resumed. "Other sections were not as fortunate. Evidence indicates the possibility that the disruption of geothermal power and supply lines to some of the other pod groups was intentional."

Elliott fidgeted. He glanced at me, then at his hands, which he opened and closed. "I hadn't heard that. Are you sure?"

"Yes."

"That doesn't make sense. Why would someone reroute the power and supply lines?"

"I do not know, but please excuse me, Elliott. Once again, I am too verbose. I meant to assure you that Max knows what he is doing. Freddie will be fine."

Elliott's blue eyes scanned the hallway again before he returned his gaze to my face. I imagined Kyleigh saying, "the coast is clear," and I suppressed a smile.

He licked his lips, then pressed them together. "I know he will. It's just . . ."

Citizens considered physical contact comforting, so I reached up and briefly tapped his shoulder. He stared at my hand, and I belatedly recalled how much he disliked my touch. He reached over and took it, swallowing convulsively.

Comforting people was not my forte.

"Recorder," he began, then paused and chewed on his lower lip again.

I attempted to withdraw. His grip tightened. I had not realized how much larger his hand was, though I should have. He was even taller than Nate, and his hand engulfed mine.

"Release me, Elliott."

"I think you're not . . . you're a good, a nice person, and I'm sorry." His voice trailed to nothing. He again looked up and down the hallway.

"Let go," I said, still attempting to pull free.

"Yes. No. I mean, I'm sorry."

Without warning or explanation, he wrapped his other arm around

me and pulled me against his chest. I could not free myself. Even in his
weakened state, he was too strong.

"Elliott, please."

He drew a deep breath and pressed his mouth against mine.

Panic billowed like a nebula. I jerked away, but he held fast. Needed
to get free. Threw my weight backward, but he was so much bigger than
I. How did one escape? I could not remember—difficult to breathe—my
arm trapped—

There was a roar of anger, and Elliott's grip loosened. I pushed as
hard as I could. I tumbled out of his grasp and off the bench, sucked in
a lungful of air, and staggered to my feet.

Nate had grabbed Elliott by the front of his tunic and shoved him up
against the wall. "How dare you!"

Nate pulled back his fist.

"Nate, no!"

He stopped.

I wrapped my arms around myself. "No, please."

Nate let go of Elliott, who slumped to the floor. Out of the corner of
my eye, I saw Ross turn the corner, then break into a run.

"Are you all right?" Nate asked me, his voice rough.

My heart raced, but I nodded, scrubbing Elliott's saliva from my lips
with my right sleeve. Why would he have done that?

Ross skidded to a halt and dropped to his brother's side. "Elliott?"

Elliott mumbled something, and Ross shot to his feet, spinning to
face Nate and me, glaring down his nose. "What happened?"

"Nothing he doesn't deserve," Nate growled.

Ross's handsome features contorted. "What did you do, Timmons?"

"Wrong question." Nate's hands flexed. "Ask your voided baby
brother what *he* did."

"Don't push this off on Elliott! He's only been out of a medtank for
four days, and he never instigates conflict."

Elliott scooted against the wall, his face redder by the moment.
When Ross looked back at him, Elliott's gaze flickered to me, and his
heightened color drained away. Nausea twisted my stomach. I wanted
to spit, to clean my mouth, to be anywhere else.

Ross started in my direction. "*You*. He'd better not have so much as a bruise."

"Leave her alone." I did not see him move, but Nate was there beside me, blocking Julian Ross's advance. I had never heard that harshness in his voice before. "Your brother's the problem, assaulting her like that."

Ross's shoulders stiffened, and his pulse beat visibly in his temple. He was too close. I stepped closer to Nate, but when I looked up at him, the corner security camera drew my attention. A chill swept down my spine: the whole event had been recorded. I could not allow the situation to escalate further, so I moved between them, arms extended.

Julian Ross turned his laser-like gaze on me.

"Take your brother away, Ross. Please, take him away from here." I wiped my mouth again.

Ross narrowed his blue eyes to slits. "Did he kiss you?"

"There was a misunderstanding." The words spilled out, and I silently begged them to listen. "I am sure it will not happen again. Am I not correct, Elliott?"

Without looking up from the floor, the young man mumbled, "No. It won't. Not again."

Ross hauled his brother to his feet. "I found your note," he said in an undertone, "and went looking for you, but really? You *kissed* her?"

At Elliott's faint nod, Ross stiffened and then shoved Elliott behind his back. In a voice that seemed louder for its quiet intensity, he said, "You'd better leave him alone. Keep this out of your spacing reports."

Nate gave a terse laugh. "Not a chance."

The recording device remained aimed at us, like a targeting beam. The ramifications of Elliott's behavior included more than personal disgrace and whatever consequences a citizens' court would mete out. Jordan's cousin had been removed and his Recorder sent to primary reclamation for similar, though consensual, behavior, and the thought of primary reclamation chilled me.

I clasped my hands to stop their shaking. "The repercussions are daunting."

Nate glanced down at me, green eyes as intense as Ross's icy blue ones, but my focus drew the men's attention to the ceiling. Their demeanors changed. Elliott shrank further down. Ross stiffened and sidestepped between his brother and the camera, although part of my mind registered the behavior as ludicrous. I swallowed, but the memory of Elliott's behavior surfaced. I gagged, wiped my sleeve across my lips and teeth, then scrubbed my arm against my hip.

"Elliott, Elliott." Ross smiled as if nothing unusual had happened. "I suspect an apology is in order."

Placing his hands on the younger man's shoulders, Ross rotated Elliott to face me. Elliott tried to shake off his grip.

"I'm sorry, Recorder," he mumbled. "You, you're a good person, and I wish I . . . You don't have to worry about future . . . about it happening again."

He seemed sincere.

Ross regarded me closely for several seconds before he winked.

My face heated. I dropped my gaze and saw Nate's fingers curling. He took a decisive step forward, so I put my hand on his arm to stop him. His fist did not relax. I dropped my hand to his, and his fist opened, fingers curling around mine.

Ross smirked. "Holding hands? I beg your pardon. Was this a property dispute? Tell me, Recorder, which takes precedence? First come first served, or possession as nine-tenths of the law?"

Nate's lips compressed, but when he tried to release me, I tightened my grip. Ross laughed and led Elliott away. Once they had disappeared around the corner, I dropped Nate's hand. My pulse thundering in my ears and my emotions roiling, I sank back onto the bench. Dimly, I heard Nate contact Jordan over his communications link. Her voice rose in pitch, then interrupted his response with a caustic epithet. The chime pinged softly as she ended the link.

Nate seated himself on my left.

"Did he hurt you?" His voice was somehow like an overpressurized system on the verge of rupture.

"I had forgotten he is so tall." I shook my head. "I shall be well. I am sure it was a misunderstanding. I am not adept at communication."

"It's not your fault. I know you well enough to know you didn't do anything wrong. He had no right, that son of a—"

I looked up. Tension etched lines on his face and made his jawline sharp. It had never occurred to me to be frightened of Nathaniel

Timmons, but for a moment, I saw why Elliott had quailed before him, and I flinched. His tension lessened slightly.

"I'm sorry." Nate's voice was softer, and though he did not clarify the subject of the apology, it did not matter. "Let's get you out of here." Nate stood, and I almost thought he meant to offer me his hand, but he did not. "Come on. Computer lab."

I nodded and shoved myself to my feet, arms wrapped around my middle. "I do not know that I shall be able to navigate society."

"You'll be all right."

The memory ran like VVR through my mind as we walked, and I stumbled. Nate caught my elbow, then let go. I wiped my mouth again, but the sensation, the physical memory, did not disappear. When we reached my laboratory, my fingers shook, so he entered the code on my behalf. The door slid open, and he followed me in.

"Sure you don't want me to give him a good thrashing? Or . . . I don't know. Want some tea, or something?"

I ignored his threat since I believed he was not serious and shook my head, then nodded. I had read studies verifying the calming effects of warm beverages, but before I could say as much, and before I could stop them, unexpected tears slid down my cheeks. They dropped onto my tunic, and I made no effort to blot them away. Turning my back to him, I blinked, unseeing, at the monochromatic print affixed on the wall.

"Nate, I do not understand. I did not . . . Records indicate that kissing is pleasant."

"That wasn't kissing. Doesn't count." The tightness had returned to his voice.

It matched definitions I had read. "It was decidedly not pleasurable."

Nate uttered vilifications I had no desire to rebuke, but he did not understand. This, if nothing else, proved I would not be able to fade into the citizenry. While Elliott had not obtained my consent, neither that nor the disgust I felt for him and for myself was in the forefront of my mind.

"Perhaps . . . perhaps I am truly broken."

"No." His voice dropped. "No more than the rest of us."

"I am no longer a Recorder"—I looked up at him—"but I shall never be normal."

"Normal's overrated." He seemed to be searching my face for something. Then, he pulled a small cloth from his pocket, blotting away my tears and wiping my lips, as if he meant to erase the memory as well. All the while, his green eyes remained steadily on mine. Then he stepped to my side, back to the computers and the posters, and we stood together, staring at the table.

I rested my head against his arm and closed my eyes. When I felt him hold his breath, I realized my gross impropriety, but before I could straighten, he put his arm around me. I allowed myself to lean against him and listen to the comforting beat of his heart. There was something else I could not quite identify, something calming, like the scent of pine. My tears slowed.

I sighed. "I never want to experience that again."

Nate placed a light kiss on the top of my head, which, strangely, did not disturb me at all. "It's not like that."

"How can you be certain?"

"Trust me." The sound of his voice resonating in his chest was soothing. His arm tightened about me for a second, then he let go. "Let's get you some tea. Or maybe hot chocolate. That would do you good."

"It might," I said, accepting the change in topic. I disliked being uncomfortable, but I disliked it even more when I made other people uncomfortable. "I have never had hot chocolate."

His eyebrows lifted. "Never? That's criminal. We'd better fix that oversight at once."

He tucked the damp cloth back into his pocket. We left the computer laboratory and headed down the hall, once more side by side.

We stopped by Nate's quarters long enough for him to "raid the emergency stash" of chocolate, then proceeded to the dining commons, where the sounds of the staff's lunch preparation brought me to a stop. Hunger would have been preferable to facing people, but the words to explain this stuck in my throat. Nate ventured into the galley, from whence he returned carrying a steaming mug. I ducked my head and watched the steam rise over the slightly thick, warm brown liquid. Closing my eyes, I inhaled, then took a sip. Chocolate, I decided, was indeed a good thing, and when I looked up, he grinned.

"Told you."

I finished the drink, and he accompanied me to the cats' storage room. For perhaps seventeen seconds, we stood silently outside the door, but before I was able to summon the energy to thank him, his communications link chimed. Adrienne Smith's nasal whine informed him that Captain North required his presence.

Nate signed off and looked at me. "I have to go. Are you going to be all right?"

I could not manage words, so I merely nodded, like a puppet. The door behind us slid open, and a brief smile flashed across his face. He lifted his hand, then lightly touched my shoulder. "I'll see you later."

Kyleigh stepped next to me as I watched him disappear down the hall.

"Well." Kyleigh put her hands on her hips. "What was that about?"

"I have no particular desire to speak of this morning's events."

A cat tried to sneak past her. She caught it and followed me into the room. "Events?"

I scrubbed my sleeve over my mouth again as the door slid shut.

Kyleigh's eyes narrowed. She set the cat down. "What happened?"

I shook my head and walked over to check their food supply, after which I added water to their bowls and cleaned the litter boxes, while Kyleigh did not move from the door. I could almost feel her watching me.

"What did Timmons do?" she demanded.

I spun back to face her. "He did nothing."

She frowned. "What happened, then?"

"Elliott," I began, then stopped.

"Elliott?" She blinked rapidly. "What in the name of light did Elliott do?"

I sat on the floor. Kyleigh plopped down in front of me. Bustopher nudged my hand, so I rubbed his ears. Still, she waited. The need to hide what happened warred with the need to tell her, all while shame, indignation, and a pervasive sense of failure wove and tangled in my chest. At length, the words choked through my throat. "He kissed me."

Her hazel eyes grew huge. "What? Slow that ship down! *Elliott* kissed you?"

"Yes." Bustopher settled into a ball on my lap. "I did not consent."

"That's . . ." She bit her lip. "He just can't do that. He knows he can't. And, he should've said something, if he likes you."

"He did—does—not. He apologized, even before." No. I closed my eyes. I was a Recorder, or I had been. I could certainly report events clearly. Drawing a deep breath, I straightened, looked past her at the tan walls, folded my hands, and carefully selected my words despite the pounding of my heart. "As I had finished reviewing this morning's selection of recordings and having found nothing of import, I left VVR for my laboratory. Elliott joined me, and while we discussed the probability of Freddie's recovery, he grew increasingly agitated—"

"Don't."

I stopped, my pulse thundering in my ears.

She reached out, as if to touch me, then pulled back. "Don't go all official Recorder. You don't have to say anything else if you don't want to."

My shoulders relaxed slightly, though the tightness in my chest did not lessen.

"You are all right?"

I nodded.

"Good, I guess." Kyleigh's mouth drew down. "I don't understand."

I could offer her no clarification on Elliott's reprehensible behavior. Why would he behave in such a manner if he cared for Kyleigh? I believed he did. I only said, "His behavior was not, perhaps, in keeping with his character."

"No."

We were silent for approximately thirty-seven seconds before I said, "Kyleigh, I did not enjoy it."

Kyleigh sat upright. "I should say not!"

"Nate says it wasn't kissing."

She blinked. "Nate?"

I blushed. "Timmons. He asked me to call him Nate."

"Really?" She drawled the word, a small smile reappearing on her face. "Now that is interesting."

I focused again on Bustopher, who kneaded sheathed claws on my leg. Thinking he might be displeased I no longer focused solely on him, I rubbed his ears.

"Talking can help, you know."

I shook my head. We sat with the cats for ten minutes longer before we walked to the gymnasium for my neglected therapies. Afterward, I elected not to change out of the generic exercise attire. Kyleigh said nothing as I shoved the lavender tunic into recycling. I would not wear it again. Even rose would be preferable. When Kyleigh left to resume her studies in Max's infirmary, I returned to my laboratory, where I washed my hands and face repeatedly at the small sink in the back near the water closet, on the other end of the counter from the charging station.

Finally, when I could delay no longer, I listed the first one hundred prime numbers, then restarted my computers, but before I could track down the footage from the hallway, the door slid open, and Jordan and Nate stormed in.

"Why?" she demanded, hands on her hips, glowering down at me.

"I beg your pardon?"

"Why did you do it?"

I blinked up at both of them. Jordan had never spoken so brusquely to me before. "What am I purported to have done?"

The muscle in Nate's jaw jumped, but he remained quiet. I caught myself wishing for my drone, to read his expression. Then, I unwished.

"We know you changed the records," Jordan snapped. "But this time, you shot yourself. North let him go."

"I have altered nothing," I protested. "I have shot no one." Still, they both glowered at me. "The captain let whom go?"

"Elliott Ross," Jordan spat.

My heart crimped. I wetted my lips and said, "He was in custody?"

Why did everyone's eyes remind me of lasers?

"Of course. I made sure of it as soon as Tim told me what had happened."

"Spacing right," Nate growled.

"I have done nothing, although my intent—"

"Then what happened to the recordings?"

Agitation crawled through me with clawed, insectile feet. I tapped my thigh, then wrapped my arms around my middle again. "Please explain."

Nate, who watched me closely, said, "Sit." He turned to Jordan. "Both of you."

Jordan raised a brow but acquiesced. I followed her to the table, where Nate pulled out a chair for me and took the seat opposite Jordan.

"When Tim contacted me"—she raised a hand to forestall my response—"as he should have done, I commed Genet. He sent security to Julian's quarters, and they took Elliott into custody to investigate the allegations."

A selfish fear shimmered through me. His behavior had not been invited, but had not similar actions led to Gervase Singh's removal and sent the Recorder he loved to death in a medical tank? Would Elliott's conduct further condemn me? And if an Elder saw Nate holding my hand, would there be consequences for him as well?

Nate's voice broke into my thoughts. "Ross went crying to North, and that spacing, void-ridden waste—"

"Ross filed complaints against you and Tim," Jordan interrupted. "He claims you forced unwanted attention on Elliott and that Tim was physically threatening his brother. And"—she glared at Nate—"Ross accused Tim of inappropriate behavior toward a member of the Consortium, thereby biasing the records. North latched onto that pretty quickly."

My selfish thoughts evaporated. *No.* It was difficult to breathe. How could the computer lab be short of oxygen when the fans still thrummed?

Jordan's beads clattered. "That's when North called me in. He threatened to have me written up for filing false accusations and told me to keep my team under control."

Concern for them both made my heart rate stutter. "Are you in jeopardy?"

Nate raised his chin. "It'd be worth it."

"That's the thing." Jordan flattened her hands on the table and leaned forward, eyes on me. "When Nate said it had been recorded, North had Smith pull up the records."

I stiffened. "Such is not her prerogative. Nor his. He has made too many assumptions about his access to Consortium information."

"Maybe, but North insisted you couldn't be impartial, if Julian's accusations were true."

"Seemed right gleeful about that," Nate said under his breath.

"Upon receiving such accusations, the captain should have called for my presence."

"North said you don't have status. Not a citizen. Not a Recorder. No rights." Jordan tapped her fingers with each point. "So, with all of us there, Smith played the feed. Nothing. Only static."

Static? I jumped to my feet and crossed to the computer. Isolating the proper feed, I played it. Long before Elliott and I appeared, the footage pixelated into nothingness. I drew a breath, then dove deeper into the records. The morning's events had been plucked from the computer at the deepest level. I tried to access the camera itself, but it did not respond, not even playing current images. Dimly, I heard Nate and Jordan approach.

"North laughed and refused to investigate anyone's allegations without evidence," Jordan stated. "Why did you do it?"

I watched the static, not her, not Nate. "I did not. I would never delete information so sloppily." Offended they would assume I lacked skill but unwilling to admit that I had planned to alter the records, I pulled up the footage from the lounge and pointed to the timestamp on the projection.

Jordan's brow furrowed. "What's the lounge have to do with anything?"

I shifted uneasily. "This is your . . . the conversation I overheard."

Nate was so close behind me I could have leaned against him. "How? Did you loop the feed?"

"Yes, and added footage of your presence elsewhere." I stared up at the monochromatic print on the wall. "It might be insufficient now. Today's poorly executed deletion could call the entire ship's recordings into question. My alterations may no longer suffice."

"Can you repair it? Get it back?" Jordan reached over and pulled up the static again. "We need proof that Elliott was the aggressor in this situation."

"No."

Nate cursed.

I shot him a glare. "I am not refusing, though I do not completely agree with your analysis. The camera's feed has been destroyed. Perhaps, were I more familiar with computer forensics, I could reconstruct the data, but without access to the Consortium systems, this is beyond my knowledge and ability." Jordan's golden eyes bored into mine as I added, "And, perhaps it is unwise to prove anything, one way or the other."

"He's not getting away with it," Nate said, too quietly.

"If Ross presses his accusations of misconduct, you and Jordan will be in danger. My status remains uncertain." Attention drifting back to the workplace safety posters, my fingers twisted around the white exercise clothing. "While his actions could be interpreted as—"

Nate interrupted with a vivid description of Elliott's personal failings. Jordan nodded once.

"The point is, Recorder"—Jordan stabbed her index finger at my computer—"any act without consent justifies penalties. Mutual consent is the very foundation of law. No one infringes upon anyone else's rights. You can't really mean to let him get away with this. *You*, of all people?"

I paced the room toward the charging station, then turned back to them. "I am still under Consortium jurisdiction. Jordan, you know undermining Consortium representatives carries heavy penalties. My primary concern is not Elliott's future. It is yours. Nate's." I swallowed. "My own."

"How so?" The edge was back in Nate's voice.

I did not answer him. Jordan opened her mouth to speak, but I held up a hand. "I know what happened ten years ago. To your . . . to both of them."

Her eyes grew wide. "How?"

I tilted my head toward Nate.

Her gaze followed my movement. She backed toward the table. For the space of two minutes, no one spoke or moved, and the whisper of air through the vents was the only sound.

Nate's attention shifted from her to me, and back. "J, what's she talking about?"

Jordan angled away from the table to face me, a pinched look on her face. "Fine." She drew a long breath. "I don't like being manipulated, Recorder."

Nate jerked upright. "What! You *cannot* mean we're letting this go?"

"Without evidence, it's your word against theirs, and we already know where the captain's sympathies lie. Let's just focus on getting the Recorder off *Thalassa* and away from the Consortium. But Elliott," she added, "can't be allowed to do anything like that ever again."

"I do not disagree." I lowered my chin but met her eyes. "Speak with him. I do not believe he will."

"Oh, stars, yes," Jordan hissed. "I'll speak to him, all right."

For two seconds, I felt sorry for Elliott.

Nate made a disgusted sound in his throat. "And you'll have company, J."

"No," I said softly.

His green eyes fastened on me.

"Please, allow Jordan to handle this."

I held his gaze until he managed a strangled agreement to leave Elliott alone. My feet felt heavy as I crossed the room again, back to where he stood at my workstation. I returned my attention to the computer.

"If you will excuse me, I must repair the footage."

"I thought you said you couldn't fix it?" Jordan's eyebrows rose, and then she frowned. "You'll only further complicate things."

I gestured to the static still playing at my terminal. "I also said the crudity of this damage could call unwanted attention to my own alterations. I will attempt to disguise it."

Jordan walked to the door but paused before it opened. "I ought to apologize. I should have known you wouldn't do shoddy work. Comm me if you need anything. Anything at all." Then she left.

Nate lightly touched my back. "Don't have anywhere to be for an hour or so. You want company?"

A smile struggled out of me. "I will not be an engaging companion, but yes, that would be a kindness."

I finished repairing the recording twenty-nine minutes before dinner. After locking my laboratory, I stopped at the infirmary, but Max and Williams were occupied with Freddie's tank. The sharp, purposefulness of their movements and the way neither noticed my presence concerned me. Such focus seemed indicative of a potential problem, so I withdrew, resigned to eating alone. On my way to the dining commons, however, I overheard Kyleigh's voice, sharper than usual, and she stomped out of a room up the hall.

"Kye! Wait!" Elliott stumbled after her.

"I am done talking to you," she snapped.

He tripped in his haste and fell against the wall, watching her retreating form. He called after her, "It's not like that."

"That makes it worse, Elliott!" she said despite her assertion their conversation had ended. She spun around to face him, and her eyes met mine. "Oh! There you are!"

Elliott froze and slowly turned. His heightened color faded when he saw me. "Recorder . . ."

"Elliott. Kyleigh." I had no idea what else to say.

Kyleigh flounced past Elliott and wrapped her arm through mine.

"My *friend* and I are going to dinner, Elliott," she said as she drew me past him down the hallway.

I glanced back at Elliott, who slid slowly down the wall onto the floor, his head in his hands.

Dinner was awkward. People threw uneasy, sidelong looks both in my direction and Elliott's when he finally arrived with Ross, proving that even social engineering failed to repress the human tendency to gossip. I cringed inwardly.

Conversation at our table was subdued, and the mood spilled over to everyone else, though some people's behavior puzzled me. Two crew members whose names I did not know stopped by my chair and wished me a good night. A woman from the kitchen edged through the room, her eyes downcast, to bring me another cup of hot chocolate. Edwards, his ash-brown hair slipping in limp, exhausted strands from his short braid, shifted his tray to one hand and tapped me lightly on the arm. His brow furrowed, but he said nothing. I glanced at Kyleigh, who shook her head before returning her attention to her food.

Ross lounged at the opposite end of the table, but his jaw was tight. Although Jordan still sat next to him, it was as if a barrier stood between them. They made no physical contact, even accidentally. At the very end of the table, closest to the door, Elliott stared at his plate, barely touching his food, just shifting it around with his utensils. No one commented on his appearance, though his lower lip was swollen and split. It had not been when he and Kyleigh had argued.

I shuddered. The thought of lips oozing plasma made my stomach clench.

Spanos and DuBois arrived late. He paused by my chair to inquire how I felt but scowled down the table at Elliott and Ross. He even frowned at Jordan, though how she was implicated in the situation, I did not know.

Though DuBois did not speak to me, she smiled briefly in acknowledgment of my greeting. She was, however, blatantly rude to both brothers. Elliott flinched away from her, and I took a degree of pleasure in his uneasiness. Despite having been the frequent recipient of her animosity myself, I felt sympathy for neither of them.

Jordan finished and excused herself to attend to paperwork, insisting that Kyleigh accompany her to review an application for graduate work at Albany City University. Neither Ross brother lingered, but even after they left, conversation was stilted. Nate mashed his vegetables with repressed violence.

DuBois elbowed Spanos, and he set down his glass of water. "You really all right, Recorder?"

"I am well." I rubbed my palms on my thighs, then picked up my tray. "There is no need to exaggerate the situation's severity. It is done. However, I missed quite a bit of work today and need to rest so I can make up lost time tomorrow. I wish you pleasant dreams."

"I'm walking you to your quarters." Nate stood and took my tray, stacking it on top of his, but neither Nate nor I spoke while we walked.

When we reached my door, however, I said, "Thank you."

Nate raised one perfect eyebrow.

"For coming to my assistance this morning, and for listening. For the hot chocolate, and for accompanying me this afternoon. I know you had other things to do."

"Nothing more important than that," he said.

I opened the door and stepped inside.

"Don't forget to lock it."

"I will not forget."

After the door slid shut, I set the lock and rested my forehead against the cool metal. When I heard him walk away, I changed and went to bed.

Sometime in the middle of the night, I woke, my throat raw. I poured myself a glass of water, but it hurt to swallow. Staggering back to bed, I burrowed under the covers. My muscles hurt, but I shivered back to sleep.

While I searched through paper files, the corpse of Dr. SahnVeer materialized out of a datastream and grabbed my hand. Her eyes were not mummified like the rest of her. They were the bright, violet-blue of the recording images.

She stared unblinkingly at me. "It's in my files, but you didn't look in deep storage. They tried to delete it all, but even though they didn't, you missed it. Why couldn't you follow the breadcrumbs?"

Her hand broke off in mine. She shook her head, and her long red braids slithered over desiccated shoulders.

Dr. SahnVeer's corpse said, reproachfully, "First you ripped my jacket, then you abandoned me. And now you break off my hand? What kind of person does that?"

"She's not a person, not really."

Elliott appeared out of nowhere. He grabbed at me, and I dodged his arms as they began to morph into long, insectile legs, and he shifted into a giant cockroach, clicking his mandibles.

"He's not usually like this," Dr. SahnVeer explained. "He has low blood sugar. He needs to eat something."

"I don't mean to hurt you," the Elliott-Roach clicked. "I'm just hungry. I'm so sorry."

I ran, following the directions in the murals I could no longer see, only to wind up in the medical storage bay. The pods began to open, and dead people and cats poured out of them into the darkened hallways. Roaches converged from the shadows to devour us all.

I woke aching and covered in sweat. It took twenty minutes for my heart rate to slow so I could rest.

It was a very long night.

36

"You look awful," Spanos said.

Uncertain of the appropriate response, I thanked him for his honesty and resumed my breakfast.

"No, you do," he repeated. "You should go see Max."

While I did not lose my temper, I responded more vehemently than necessary. "I do not need to visit the infirmary. I do not need coddling. I shall be fine."

Spanos stopped in the middle of chewing and stared at me.

"There's no need to be nasty, Recorder," DuBois said.

"That wasn't nasty, babe. Come to think of it, my mother would've scolded me for being rude. Okay, Recorder. Pax?"

I stared at his proffered hand, momentarily confused. When I reached out and grasped his wrist, he flinched, and I frowned. If he had not wanted to touch me, he should not have held out his hand.

"Pax," I said through clenched teeth.

Spanos withdrew his hand. "Your skin is too hot."

"No, your hands are too cold." I briefly considered suggesting that he wash off any Recorder contamination, but I refrained.

DuBois watched me as I took my tray and left.

Trailing my fingers on the wall for steadiness, I walked to the computer laboratory where I sat down heavily in my chair. While the programs started up, I laid my head on the cool, flat desk to rest for a few minutes. The programs started sooner than I had anticipated. I sat up with a moan and began to sift through the findings uncovered by my search agents overnight.

I had been working for approximately eleven minutes when my communication link chimed.

"Recorder," Jordan said. "Given the urgency of everything, I'm sending Zhen to work with you today. You two play nicely, all right?"

"Are you sure, Jordan, that I am the one who needs the warning?"

"I'll be speaking with DuBois about this, too, if that's what you mean." She paused. "That was pretty snippy. Are you all right?"

"I am tired," I admitted, "and I have felt better. Then, I have also felt much worse."

"I guess so." She chuckled briefly. "I'll be by later to follow up. I—"

I closed the link and rubbed my temples before I resumed digging through the files. It did not occur to me that I had been rude.

When DuBois entered, I had accomplished little. She frowned at me, but that was not unusual.

"Thank you for coming," I said, neither sincere, nor yet dishonest, since my time was insufficient to finish everything on my own.

She shrugged. Even her shrug seemed elegant, and that irritated me, too.

"This doesn't mean I like you." She glared at me over a console. "But with what you're investigating, it's the right thing to do. So. What's on the agenda today?"

My mind went blank. I simply stared at her.

"The virus?" DuBois pointed at the computer. "What are we doing?"

"I cannot recall."

"Moons and stars. Fine. Just send me the files."

I did, and for a while, she was silent. Then, she asked how I felt. I did not respond.

While I struggled through the logs, not analyzing, simply searching for static and deleted recordings, then logging the time and date of the occurrences, DuBois worked at a seated desk. She neither spoke nor clicked her chair's legs on the floor. I had forgotten she was present until approximately an hour later, when she appeared at my side, holding out a glass of water.

"Thank you," I managed.

She watched me drink, then extended her hand for the empty glass. "Are you sure you're feeling all right?"

"My well-being is . . ." My attention riveted on the faint discoloration tinging her knuckles. "DuBois, your hand is bruised. You should—"

She snatched my glass away. "Mind your own business!"

Chagrined, I lowered my head and tried to resume my work. My eyes burned from reading, and my head pounded. I wanted nothing more than to go back to sleep.

Another hour dragged past before Jordan stopped to check our progress. She cocked her head. "Finally playing nicely with our neighbors, are we?"

DuBois huffed.

I pulled up a summary, then moistened my lips. "My morning's efforts have been insignificant. I will endeavor to increase my speed and meet Zhen DuBois's level of accomplishment. She has worked steadily all morning, with good results."

Her face unreadable, DuBois glanced at me. "I haven't found much yet."

I wanted to be fair. "She has been a pleasant working companion. Quiet, diligent, and courteous. She even brought me water once."

"Easy on the sales pitch." Jordan glanced at DuBois, then her beads clattered as she turned to me. "You don't look good, Recorder."

While I could not verify her visual assessment, perhaps she spoke truly. "I am tired."

After a minute of silence, Jordan left us to our work, or more accurately, left DuBois to hers, since my progress was negligible. When I stood to stretch sometime later, I sat back down quickly and tried to log off, but my vision clouded.

"Zhen DuBois, I am sorry to interrupt your progress, but I suspect Alexander Spanos was correct this morning. I shall go to the infirmary. I hesitate to ask, but would you please log me off the computer?"

She did not divert her attention from the recordings. "Log yourself off."

"I am finding it difficult."

She made an impatient noise and turned to face me. Her dark eyes widened. "Moons and stars, Recorder! Yes, I'll shut it down. Go see Max."

"Thank you," I rasped.

"Do you . . ." She hesitated. "Do you need help?"

"I shall manage." I blinked, but my sight did not clear.

"If you're sure, go ahead. I've got this."

I stumbled to the door, then shut my eyes, and when I could not see the room swimming, progress was easier.

"You're sure you'll be all right?" DuBois called after me. "I'll . . . I'll tell Max you're on your way."

I did not respond, since my sole focus was on putting one foot in front of the other. Navigating by touch, I lost my way at one turning, and though my communication piece chimed several times, I did not trust myself to answer. The sound of the infirmary doors sliding open was welcome, indeed.

"There you are." Edwards stepped into the hallway and took my arm. "Max left a few minutes ago to track you down. Let's get you settled."

He helped me onto a bed and placed a cool hand on my forehead. I squinted at him. A deep crease had appeared over his nose.

"You're running a fever."

What were the symptoms of that virus? Had I ever known? I could not remember. I grabbed at Edwards as he administered a subdermal injection of nanodevices and medication.

"Quarantine me."

His pale blue eyes blurred, then came back into focus.

"DuBois." Her name scraped through my throat. "I spent the morning working with DuBois. Quarantine me, Edwards, then check her."

With a quiet rush of lavender and pine, the nanodevices calmed me, and I collapsed into a fitful sleep.

I was not inside a quarantine bubble when I awoke. Edwards had left, but Kyleigh sat by my bed, working on a datapad, and Max was adjusting something on Freddie's tank. Kyleigh saw me move, put down the tablet, and offered me a tired smile.

"I should be quarantined," I managed. "Is DuBois well?"

Max moved to my bedside. "No, it's not necessary. And yes, she's fine. Are you feeling any better?"

"It is not the . . . a virus?"

"No. It isn't."

"I do not understand, Max." It was difficult to concentrate. "What is wrong with me?"

"The cats," he said, "compounded by the fact that you haven't completely healed from losing your implant."

"The cats made me ill?"

Kyleigh sighed. "Well, he's right. Kind of."

"Those cats are worse than useless." Max scowled. "They're health hazards."

"Toxoplasmosis," Kyleigh explained. "You've got a nasty, active infection of toxoplasmosis. It's a single-celled parasite."

"I do not understand," I said. "Are the cats ill? Is Bustopher ill?"

Max rolled his eyes. "The little beasts are as healthy as ever."

He grumbled about having unsafe organisms on board while Kyleigh explained that cats were carriers for the parasites, which were transmitted in their fecal matter. She apologized profusely, as if she had infected them.

"I do not understand. Kyleigh, are you healthy? How did no one know?"

"I'm fine. Max did some simple tests, and it seems I single-handedly defeated the stuff already." She shook her head. "I'm not sure how the powers-that-be let this slip. It seems most cats on Earth were affected, and the parasites came along for the ride."

While I processed her comments, I blinked to clear my vision, though doing so did not help.

"From what I read, it rarely hits humans this hard," Max said in his deep, soothing rumble. "You're on antibiotics and increased folates, and we've managed to synthesize some pyrimethamine. It's an older treatment, but it works. In the meantime, you need rest. The additional nanodevices will assist your immune system, and with all those nanites, it shouldn't take long, although I will have you continue the medications for a ten-day, to be on the safe side. You'll feel much better in a day or so."

I sat up abruptly, and the room spun. "I cannot rest that long, Max."

"I understand, but there's no alternative." He adjusted my pillow. "Lie down. Heal. We'll do all we can."

He tucked me in as if I were a child, then checked my vital signs once more and gave me another dose of medication. His drooping shoulders signaled fatigue.

"Max?" My eyes and body felt heavy, and my throat felt thick, but I said, "I do not mean to cause you so much work."

"Don't give it another thought." He gave me one of his sad smiles. "You're worth it."

Max's suggestion was the most useful course of action, and whatever had been in that injector made me drowsy. I fell back onto the pillow, and sleep soon claimed me.

It was either very late or very early when I awoke. At first, I believed Williams was the only person present, but then I saw Elliott slumped in a chair by the door. Williams shot glares at him as she entered data into the computer. He seemed so miserable his presence did not make me as uncomfortable as I would have anticipated.

"Elliott?" My mouth was dry, my voice scratchy.

"Is this my fault?" he asked anxiously. "Did I make you sick?"

"No," I said. "You are not a cat with parasites."

Williams's usually soft voice carried a sharp edge. "As I already explained. So now you can leave."

"I thought maybe . . . ."

I offered him a weak smile. "Did you believe yourself to be toxic?"

He shrugged then straightened, as if he had experienced a drone's shock. "Is Kyleigh going to get sick, too? What about me?"

"Max tested Kyleigh. She is fine. She acquired immunity long enough ago that her infection is dormant. I suspect your exposure to the cats was sufficient to attain immunity as well, but you should ask Max."

"Everybody's mad at me, Recorder. He won't help."

"That is an egregious misjudgment of his character," I said, incensed. "Dr. Maxwell is an excellent physician."

Elliott's gaze dropped to the floor.

I added, "He would treat you even if he despised you."

He looked up quickly. I nodded. He looked away.

Williams approached my bed bearing a jet injector and something to drink but paused across from Elliott. "Are you *quite* finished?"

"He is not bothering me," I said, although it was not completely true.

She handed me the beverage and administered the injector. "I am under strict orders to ensure you do nothing but rest." She narrowed her eyes at Elliott. "Your presence is disturbing the Recorder's rest and my evening. You have seen that your friend in the tank is stable for the moment. Unless you are a patient, there is no reason for someone of your caliber to be here. Leave."

Elliott winced. "I'll go. I am sorry. Though, I'm glad it isn't my fault. I really am. I didn't know . . ." His voice trailed off, and for approximately thirty seconds he stared at Freddie's tank, and I saw him swallow. At the door, he turned and added hastily, "Not that I'm glad you're sick. I wish you weren't."

He left abruptly without saying goodbye.

"For having attained his majority, he seems very young sometimes," I said.

Williams removed the empty cartridge from the jet injector and disposed of it. "But he is not."

I shook my head and wiped my lips with my sleeve before I thought to stop the motion. "No," I agreed. "He is not."

When I awoke several hours later, Nate sat near my bed, bleary-eyed and sipping coffee. A smile lit his tired face, and he raised his mug. "There you are. You know, you're plenty interesting without the whole invalid thing you've been working on."

"It is hardly intentional. Being ill is inefficient." I stretched, and a sudden influx of memories jarred me upright. "When is it? How much time did I lose?"

"Take it easy," he said. "Only about nineteen hours. You were asleep last night when I stopped by. It's morning now. Well . . . almost morning." He pointed to his mug. "See? Coffee before socialization. I would recommend it, since you don't seem to be quite social yet, but you're jumpy enough as it is."

"Coffee is not drinkable." A yawn stopped me.

"Don't do that. It's contagious," he managed through a yawn of his own. "J wants you to know Zhen has been working through your earmarked files and found a few that seem promising. I'll be going over your logs. Don't worry. We've still got some time."

"If I recall correctly, you do not interact well with computers," I said cautiously, hoping he would not take offense.

"Well, I might not excel at hacking into locked hangar bays while mutant cockroaches attack, but I'm decent with actual information." He set his mug down, stood, and pulled a datapad halfway out of his jacket pocket. "Fear not. Zhen has rigged a Timmons-safe system. Dropped it off about thirty minutes ago when she stopped in to check on you."

He straightened my pillow and I gratefully leaned back into the bed again. Williams shooed him aside, checked my vitals, and administered another injection. It must have included nanodevices, since my discomfort improved and the familiar scents I associated with peace soothed me. She handed me a cup of the green frothy drink Max had given me the day I had overextended myself. I grimaced, drank it down, and returned it.

Williams nodded. "You will be much improved by later today. Now, if you don't mind, I am going to the dining commons to fetch myself a cup of tea. I'll return soon." A smile crossed her face, and she touched Nate's shoulder. "You stay and keep her company."

Waving unnecessarily, she strolled out of the infirmary.

Nate drained the last of his coffee. "I like her."

"As do I." I plucked at my blankets. "But, Nate, I must complete the tasks Jordan has asked me to perform. I cannot simply lie here in the infirmary, doing nothing."

"Healing isn't nothing," he said. "Don't worry. Jordan brought Max, Alec, and Zhen into the discussion about your long-term goals."

"What? No! Nate, no." I jolted upright again. "It is bad enough that I told you and Jordan. No one else should be implicated." I forced myself not to glance at the camera in the corner. My list of things to do and recordings to alter was already weighty enough to crush me, despite the nanodevices' calming lavender and pine.

Nate held up his hands. "I get it. Thing is, you're running short on time. And you can't go back. That means you have to get out of here, and that means we need help."

"She should not have done so," I insisted.

All traces of his usual smile disappeared. "Maybe. But your escape is the priority. Zhen might not be up to your fighting weight when it comes to computers, but she's clever. She has some ideas, and I have full confidence that between the lot of us, we'll figure something out."

"But Nate—"

He touched my fingers, then leaned back. "I'll do all I can to be sure everything is in place in time. I promise. You trust me, don't you?"

Of course I did. Though I felt myself relax, the nanodevices were not my source of hope for escaping the Consortium. I trusted him. At that moment, in the dim light of the infirmary with my friend beside me, I felt completely safe.

Listening to Nate hum tunelessly, I drifted back to sleep.

I settled back in bed after yet another scan in the closet-like medicomputer and said, "Max, I need my datapad."

He only handed me a cup of water. "No."

"Better listen, Max. The nose scrunches when she's mad," Nate put in from the corner desk where he reviewed DuBois's files.

I glared at him. "That is not amusing, Nathaniel Timmons."

Nate had the temerity to laugh. "Think of this as a character-strengthening exercise."

Kyleigh stared at the three-dimensional image of a nanodevice rotating before her. "Your eyes were affected by the parasite. You don't want to strain them."

"The medicomputer will tell us if the cysts on your eyes are gone. Maybe then." Max spoke either in rebuke or in explanation, but I could not tell which. "You can thank Kyleigh for that. She stayed up until after midnight working on the devices that targeted them."

"It wasn't that hard, Max, so don't make it sound genius or anything," Kyleigh said over her shoulder. "It's like the ones Dr. SahnVeer developed for treating the lung growths in miners excavating heavy metals in the inner belt. The devices carrying the meds tag the growths. Blah, blah, blah. I just tweaked it to search out the parasitic cysts and deliver Max's pyrimethamawhatsit cocktail. Tweaked the other ones to act like T-cells and take out the enemy. Simply standing on the shoulders of giants."

"Pyrimethamine." Max tugged his ear. "I never realized SahnVeer was the one who came up with that treatment."

Kyleigh sat back and rubbed her eyes. "She created the nanodevices the first year we were there. Dad, Dr. Johnson, and Ross developed the meds. I remember being boggled that Dad did something unrelated to math, which wasn't really fair of me. Of course, I was surprised Ross helped, too, which wasn't fair, either, but he was always busy flexing his muscles in self-admiration."

"What's not to admire?"

Everyone turned. Julian Ross stood at the infirmary's open door and flexed an arm.

"Stars above, Ross!" Kyleigh's hand flew to her throat, then fisted on her hip. "Don't go sneaking up on people."

"Especially when they're gossiping about me?" Ross lifted the shadow of an eyebrow. "Yes, how very rude."

Kyleigh huffed. "Well, I was going to say—and the emphasis is on *was*—that kids, which I still was then, often don't understand the people around them."

"Did you need something, Ross?" Max asked, his voice flat.

"Just stopping to inquire after your patients. I didn't come yesterday since the first few hours of treatment can be critical. Elliott wanted to check on the Recorder but wasn't sure of his reception."

Nate growled something.

Kyleigh scowled. "Wonder why."

"I spoke with Elliott last night," I said, hoping the information would suffice and Ross would leave. "He knows I am improving."

He frowned slightly. "He didn't say he'd visited."

Nate's eyebrows drew together, and he looked at me. "Neither did you."

"Oh, Timmons, I didn't notice you." Ross smirked. "How easy you are to overlook."

"Knock it off, Ross." Kyleigh glowered at him. "You're a terrible liar."

Nate leaned back in his chair and crossed his arms. "If I wanted your attention, Julian, I'd get it."

"I am much improved," I repeated, to change the subject.

Ross turned to me, the corner of his mouth crimping slightly. "No one told me what laid you out. You aren't quarantined, so it mustn't be anything too nasty."

I reiterated the information I had given his brother last night.

"It never occurred to me to test the cats," Ross said slowly. "I assumed they'd been cleared. We hadn't started experiments, but I wonder if that would have affected results?"

"Doubtful." Max swiveled from his computer to face us. "Discrepancies would have shown up in computer modeling prior to experimentation."

Ross shrugged. "Let's hope so, for the sake of scientific progress. And, of course, I'm pleased the Recorder is not the bearer of something truly unpleasant."

Max grunted. "We're safe as long as we stay away from the nasty little four-legged monsters those two are so fond of."

"The cats aren't monsters," Kyleigh protested.

I added, "They are pleasant, calming creatures."

"They're a useless bunch of parasite-carrying parasites." Max swiveled back to his computer. "Completely unnecessary."

Kyleigh rolled her eyes, and everyone subsided into an awkward silence.

After approximately three minutes, Max stood. "Anything else, Ross?"

"How's Freddie? Has he recovered from that scare night before last?"

I had not heard of a scare, and my attention shifted to Freddie's tank, which hummed quietly across the room.

Max rubbed the back of his neck. "Honestly, he's not doing as well as I'd hoped. I'm concerned he won't hold out much longer, even in the tank. That can happen after a prolonged experience in a liquid environment. His vital signs are slipping, and he's no longer effectively eliminating carbon dioxide. His diaphragm is strained and fatigued, so even with the nanodevices he's having a hard time expelling the fluid from his lungs. I had to insert tubing this morning to help prevent the buildup of CO_2. Whether or not he is ready, we need to get him out of that tank. Two, three days at most."

For eleven seconds, no one spoke. Then, Kyleigh launched into a highly detailed monologue about liquid breathing, from the way fetuses breathe in utero, to the ability to gift unwanted or medically fragile pregnancies to the Consortium, and to the transportation of humans during extended space travel.

Max tilted his head to the side as she talked, and Nate sat back in his chair, a crease between his brows. Even Ross, mouth pinched and hands in his pockets, listened quietly as he leaned back against the cabinet holding heated blankets. She continued to propound on liquid ventilation experimentation and moved on to the maintenance and viability of organs for transplant and to procedures for treating critically injured or ill patients.

A knot formed in my throat as she tapered off and crossed the room to Freddie's tank, trailing a hand in the medical gel. "There's a delicate balance between a thin enough liquid to allow for natural evacuation by the lungs and the thicker viscosity of nutrient-rich gel and nanodevices, though the nanites boost survival rates."

"Yes." Ross pulled his hands from his pockets and pushed away from the cabinet. "They do. Don't forget that. Kyleigh . . ." He waited until she looked over, then said so softly I almost did not hear him, "I'm sorry."

She wiped her cheeks with the inside of her sleeve.

Ross's gaze swept the room, then he announced, "I'll stop by later with Elliott, if you don't mind, Max. They've been friends since we stepped off the shuttle."

Max looked at me, his straight eyebrows raised. I could not tell if he meant me to speak or not. "After dinner should be a good time. Edwards or Williams will be here if I'm not."

Ross nodded and left.

The medicomputer chimed, and Max turned back to his display to review its analysis. "Well. It seems you're healing nicely."

"Does that mean I may again have access to a datapad?" A pang of remorse hit me after I spoke. I should have asked about Freddie.

He tilted his head to the right. "For short periods. You'll stay here tonight. I'll probably release you for breakfast tomorrow."

Nate stretched and yawned. "That'll be it for me. North expects me on the bridge. I traded shifts with Johansen, and she'll finish in a few."

Max shook his head. "You should have slept, instead of sitting in here."

"Nah. That's what caffeine's for."

A frown flitted across Max's face. "It's addictive, Tim. You ought to cut back."

"You know, Max," Nate observed as he fastened his jacket, "you certainly are a killjoy today. No fun at all. Maybe *you* should be the one resting." With an old-fashioned salute, he gave me both the datapad and a smile. "Knock yourself out."

I glanced at Kyleigh, but she was still at the tank, her eyes closed and her lips moving silently, so she could not clarify his meaning. I settled back on my extra pillows.

"By the way," Nate said, leaning backward through the infirmary door. "I did work on those files, but I might have obfuscated a bit about what kept me busy this afternoon." He disappeared with a wink.

Intrigued, I opened the files he had most recently accessed. He had not worked on the problem of the viruses at all.

DuBois and Jordan had done some work with the station's data, searching for information regarding the virus, but since I had fallen ill, the majority of their efforts focused on creating my new identity. Spanos had provided an older, unsecured identification bracelet. Given the model, I suspected it was his mother's, and my eyes watered. I blinked quickly. He should not have parted with something of such personal value, yet I had no other option. DuBois, too, surprised me. She had created a believable set of identification records, coded onto the wristband.

I bit my lip. Jordan had assembled some personal items, from whence I did not know. She and Nate had constructed a simple personal history that explained my scars and short hair. Max had created medical records and gathered enough of my medications to last me several ten-days.

Together, they had accumulated credits in unlinked accounts and coded them to the wristband. The amount more than supplied the price of immediate transportation away from the lunar station to the inner belt. There was enough on which to survive for some time afterward, until I found a way to earn an income.

All their work had been done in my computer laboratory on my secured datapad, so I need not alter any ship's records. Their efforts would only condemn them without an adjustment to the band's markers, which they could not have known. Such alterations required access to my old quarters. But they had completed everything else I had expected to do on my own, except selecting a name.

A name. Two days.

If I could access my old quarters, if all went well, in two days, I would have a name. When I was released from the infirmary, I would find a way. Hope thrummed through me like my favorite subsonic musical pieces had done. I closed the files and stared across the room at Freddie's tank. Unless Max woke him up soon, I would probably never meet him. I might never see any of my friends again. I might not even be able to say goodbye.

Returning to the Consortium was unacceptable. I could not serve a system that had twisted its purpose to strengthen itself at the expense of children. But leaving these people was also unacceptable. The possibility of encountering Nate or the others at some point in the future was depressingly faint. My eyes stung. I wiped them dry.

I did not need to create a new identity, but I needed to recode that wristband, track down a virus, and find a murderer, if only to grant Kyleigh closure. I did not have the time to waste on regret. I opened the files, and time slipped past.

When Jordan stopped by before dinner, Ross accompanied her. Judging by their proximity to each other, they must have repaired their relationship, which was good, although I was disappointed not to be able to speak with her alone.

"Is everything on the mend and in order, then?" she asked.

"I believe it is," I said, confident that she referred to both my health and the work they had done.

She nodded. "I'll see you tomorrow at breakfast."

"Certainly."

Max checked on me once more, before he left for dinner, promising to bring me something to eat. I shut down the datapad after securing it, tucked it under my pillows, and fell asleep.

I slept so soundly I missed saying goodnight to Max. I also slept through Julian Ross and Elliott's visit, when they stopped by that evening to see Freddie. Though I knew I was safe, I disliked having slept while they were there, however irrational my discomfort was.

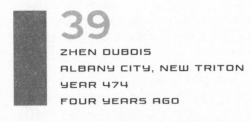

In all honesty, what made Zhen stop in her tracks wasn't his looks, though they certainly didn't detract from the package, as Grandmère used to say. And although his voice—a little growly around the edges—caught her attention first, what held it was that he was singing to his mother.

Outside in the hallway, interns and nursing assistants bustled up and down with trays of food and medicine, but despite the noise, Grandmère finally had fallen asleep. When her breathing grew regular, Zhen tiptoed out of her room, weaving between medpods and service bots, through the narrow corridors that smelled of urine, disinfectant, and the dustiness of age. She needed to sit under the sun lamps in the small garden with living, growing things before she went out onto the dimly lit streets, back to her cluttered dorm room.

Halfway to the garden, she heard a man singing softly in a gravelly tenor. She slowed and peeked in the room.

It was a duplicate of Grandmère's, with cheaply framed art, a small light-window with a retractable shade, a door leading to the water closet, one uncomfortable chair, and two narrow beds, separated by two narrow dressers. He sat facing the bed closest to the window. She couldn't see his face, only the way his dark curls fell across broad shoulders. They were nice shoulders and made curls more masculine than she would've guessed curls could be.

Zhen lingered, listening to him sing, watching the woman's eyes close, her blank stare covered by sleep. The man kissed her hand and laid it carefully on her chest.

"Sweet dreams, Mama," he whispered.

A lump formed in her throat, and she eased away from the door then hurried to the courtyard with the fishpond, where she took a seat on the only vacant bench. His song echoed in her mind.

Zhen closed her eyes. Once again, she tried that therapist's useless suggestion and focused on the faint smells of algae and mildew, on the heat of the sun lamps and the hum of the fans. Once again, her mind wandered.

Stop being selfish and think. If she left school, she could get a second job. Get Grandmère to a place with gardens of grass and flowers, not just ferns and an occasional potted plant. Though, if she stayed in school and graduated, she could find a real job. It was a bet she had to take, balancing her future with her grandmother's. But, Grandmère had pulled her out of a nightmare, years ago. It was Zhen's turn to rescue her, to get her out of this hole and bring her home. As soon as she had a real home to bring her to.

Still . . . It would have been nice to have someone sing to her. She shoved the thought aside again.

Footsteps intruded.

"Mind if I sit down?"

Her eyes flew open. "No. No, of course not." She scooted over.

"Don't mean to bother you. Just need a moment before I head out." He indicated the other occupied benches with a jerk of his chin.

She stole a closer look. His uniform was clean, if a little worn, but he hadn't tied his hair back in a regulation queue. The hint of a beard shadowed his jaw, and fatigue smudged his eyes. He braced his elbows on his knees as he ran a short loop of wooden beads through his fingers over and over again. The breeze from the circulation fans played with one of his long curls. He shoved it behind his ear before he leaned back against the bench.

Zhen blurted, "I'm here to see my grandmother."

He hummed an acknowledgment, keeping his gaze on the pale shapes of the carp moving lazily beneath the lily pads.

"I heard you singing to your mother."

His back stiffened, and his chocolatey eyes bored into hers.

It really isn't fair that a man has lashes like that.

"I sing to Grandmère, too. Songs she sang to me when I was little." The man's posture relaxed.

"I probably shouldn't sing them here," she added. "Children's songs are gruesome. Falling bridges and plucking birds. I ought to find others."

Moons and stars. Stop babbling.

His half smile grew. The hanging ferns tossed lightly in the artificial breeze, casting dappled shadows over his face.

"My name is Zhen." She held out her right hand.

He briefly clasped her wrist. "Zhen. That's pretty." His half smile stretched to a full one. "I'm Alec."

She forced herself to rest both palms on her lap. "Do you visit your mother often?"

His grin fell away. "Whenever I'm planet-side."

"My grandmother has been here for a couple of ten-days. She fell, and medtanks are too expensive since she's older. But I'm not giving up. Once I graduate and have my own place, I'm bringing her home."

He shifted. "Mama's been here for over a quarter. I do what I can, and some friends help. So far, I've been able to avoid anything worse. I don't like leaving her. It's just the two of us now."

What an idiot. You said the wrong thing. Again.

"I'm sorry." Zhen silently resolved to check on his mother whenever she visited. "I understand. Grandmère raised me after— But, I got the better part of the deal, getting to be with her. I visit between classes and work."

"Sounds like she has a good deal, too."

Her cheeks heated. Even if he said it to be polite, the words were as nice as singing.

They lapsed into silence, watching the water together and the shadows. Overhead, the city's dome darkened.

"Oh, moons and stars, I need to go." She jumped up, and he stood, too. "I've got papers to finish and—"

"Would you like to get something to eat first?" He shoved the beads into his pocket. "I'm guessing the cafeteria on campus still serves rice and beans on fifth-days. Although maybe you like beans?"

"Beans," she stated, "are disgusting."

He laughed. "Dinner, then?"

She nodded, and if it was a more platonic evening than she would've liked, it was still a relief to talk with someone who understood. Dark eyes and long, thick curls over strong shoulders could, after all, be appreciated from across the table.

"You're late again, ma chérie," Grandmère said.

Zhen kissed her cheek. "I stopped in on Alec's mom. She was restless again, so I stayed until she settled." She pushed the chair across to the bed, pulled her knitting from her satchel, and leaned back into the uncomfortable, synthleather chair. A quick count told her the stitches hadn't dropped, and the soothing click of needles and gentle slide of yarn worked their calming magic.

"And?" Grandmère asked.

The needles slowed. "And what?"

Grandmère's laugh rustled like paper napkins, and she smoothed her blanket. "Alexander seems like a nice boy."

The needles stopped. "And you would know that how?"

"I met him." Her eyes twinkled.

"But . . . When? He's back?"

Grandmère hummed an affirmative. "I couldn't miss an opportunity to see who has stolen my only granddaughter."

"No one has stolen anything," Zhen protested, her cheeks heating up. "But when we talked last ten-day, he thought the earliest they'd get here was next first."

Grandmère tilted her head. "Oh?"

How does she pack so much meaning into one syllable?

Zhen set the knitting down. "When did he visit you?"

"Yesterday afternoon. He was very complimentary."

"He was?" Zhen sobered. "Did you tell him about Sophi?"

The smile faded. "He stopped to see her first. He knows."

Zhen bit her lip. "If he—"

A knock interrupted, and she turned.

"Zhen?" And there he was, neat as usual, but looking younger without the stubble. "You're . . . May I come in?"

Grandmère answered, "Of course."

He pulled a small potted plant from behind his back and set it on the dresser. "Mama was asleep, so I thought I'd check in."

"You bring me flowers . . ." The corners of Grandmère's eyes crinkled. "Ma chérie, if you are not interested in this young man, I myself will get out of bed and chase him down."

Alec chuckled, but Zhen cringed. "Grandmère . . ."

"Ma chère, if he does not know how to make a young woman happy, then he needs a mature woman to show him what to do."

"Grandmère!"

He grinned. "While it would be an honor to learn from a woman of such experience, since your granddaughter is here, would you mind if I steal her away for breakfast?"

Grandmère winked. "You may steal her, if she *wants* to be stolen."

Alec flushed slightly. "Coffee, at least?"

Zhen stood so quickly her ball of yarn bounced across the floor. He caught it and handed it back.

Grandmère waved a blue-veined hand toward the door. "Go, then. Eat."

Zhen shoved the knitting into her satchel and kissed Grandmère's cheek.

"I like her," he said as they walked out into the morning light, heading toward the cafés on the fringe of the business district. "You know, I'm glad you heard me singing."

Grandmère passed the quarter before graduation, right after midterms. Only a few people showed up at the service. Her arms stiff at her sides, Zhen stood alone in front, next to Grandmère's shell. The traditional green-and-white mourning armband pinched, and she focused on that in the vain hope it would distract her from feeling anything else. A glance through the guests at the Center for Reclamation and Recycling confirmed her mother hadn't come.

As Grandmère would have said, small mercies.

The officiant monologued about circles and cycles and life. Hysteria built in her chest like an overpressurized system, and she blinked back hot tears and raised her chin. She wouldn't cry.

The door opened, and someone hurried in. The officiant paused, and Alec slipped his hand around hers. He didn't say a word, yet his presence was a lifeline.

". . . Dust unto dust," the man intoned, and the conveyor belt shuddered.

Grandmère's shell moved toward the heat rippling from the gaping maw. Zhen's breath caught. She took an involuntary step after her grandmother, but Alec's fingers tightened around hers. The door closed like a guillotine, and Grandmère was gone.

The matron from the home strode past the Center's Recorder and the officiant. She checked her watch and adjusted her armband.

Anger boiled up in Zhen's chest, and she forced herself to turn away. *Hypocrite. Like she cares for anything but another open slot to fill. Like she grants the patients a shred of dignity.*

The light over the door flickered from red to green, and the Center's Recorder verified the time. His drone spat out the small datacard with all relevant information, and he handed it to the officiant, who handed it to her.

The matron coughed politely. When she blathered something trite about Grandmère being in a better place, Alec tensed.

"You're an idiot," he growled. "Being alive would be better." He tugged gently on Zhen's hand. "Let's go."

The other guests parted without a single word, but when she and Alec passed through the courtyard's lush gardens, the living greenery mocked her loss, striking her almost like a physical blow.

She staggered to a halt.

"Zhen?"

"What's the point, Alec? If this is it . . . *recycling* is meaningless. Bringing green to a planet that was supposed to be a barren rock is meaningless." She gestured to the bushes. "What's the point? Reclamation and recycling? Recycling what? If it's just carbon . . ."

Alec smoothed her hair behind her ear. "It can't be."

A tear escaped, and she pulled a handkerchief from her pocket and angrily wiped her face.

Alec hesitated a moment before he drew her under his chin. "I know."

Guests must've come and gone for other services, but she didn't hear them. There, under a ficus tree, beside the spreading ferns, she cried into his uniform, and he sang softly, holding her close.

Grandmère's passing didn't mean life stopped, or classes stopped, or work stopped, or papers wrote themselves. Alec shipped out, leaving Sophi alone, so Zhen continued to visit her, even though she hated that home. Sophi smiled when Zhen stopped in, though she rarely spoke. Zhen would read her novels, or tell her about classes, or pull out her knitting and let the click of the needles comfort them both. Sophi loved plants, so Zhen brought Grandmère's fern and tiny moss garden to her bedside table.

Twelve days before graduation, she took a break from cramming to sit with Sophi. Zhen couldn't sing as well as Alec, but she hummed while she knitted a lacy, olive-green sweater, enjoying the relative quiet and the knowledge she was creating something useful and beautiful.

Sophi grew restless, pushing away the blanket Zhen had made for her before Grandmère passed. Zhen tucked her project in the satchel and settled on the edge of the bed.

"It's all right." A few greying curls had escaped her short braid, and Zhen lifted them off her forehead.

Alec's mother took a stuttering gasp of air, and for several seconds, lay completely still. Fear knotted Zhen's stomach, and she caught Sophi's thin, chilly hand and chafed it. Then, her breathing resumed, just as if she had not forgotten to exhale.

"Sophi?"

Brown eyes, so like her son's, sought the window and blinked slowly.

"Alec loves you."

Those brown eyes lost their focus. Her breaths grew shallower and farther apart.

Zhen whispered, "I love you, too," and hit the call button.

The assistant manager tiptoed in. Wordlessly, he checked Alec's mother, then shook his head. "I've seen this before. There's nothing you can do. You should probably leave."

"*Leave?* I am not leaving anyone." Zhen jabbed her finger at the door. "But *you* can."

He backed from the room without a word. Zhen let go of Sophi's hand only long enough to pull out a datapad and send an emergency message to Alec, though when or where he'd receive it, she had no idea.

Nurses bustled in and out all afternoon and into evening, their shoes shushing on the floor. Zhen missed her last session of macroeconomics. The window grew dark, and the globe-like light on the ceiling, which had never seemed inefficient before, came on. Zhen sat on the bed, cradling Alec's mother's hand, watching her face change in the pale light. Years seemed to slide away as her thready pulse faltered and finally stopped.

The monitor chimed softly, summoning the matron who was followed by the home's middle-aged Recorder and her drone. Zhen didn't rise, and the blood pounding in her ears drowned out their voices.

The matron touched Zhen's shoulder, and her weedy voice finally penetrated the dull fog that seemed to have swallowed Zhen's perceptions. "The Recorder must verify the event, dear, and we need to remove the shell."

Zhen smacked the matron's hand away. "Don't touch me. Don't touch her." Her jaw clenched. "Not yet."

The matron's eyes narrowed. "Now."

"It is my duty," the Recorder said in a dull monotone.

Zhen didn't move. She couldn't.

The Recorder added quietly, "I must verify in order to send notification to the family."

Her drone whirred from the door to hover over Sophi, and Zhen scooted back. The knot in her throat burned away the words she wanted to shout in protest.

She turned away as the drone took scans, temperatures, samples, but she kept a hand on the blanket over Sophi's foot.

The matron's voice intruded again. "Arrangements have been made. Resources will be sent here, to the Center, as final payment."

Indignation overtook the feeling of being lost. "What does that mean?"

The matron straightened. "It means that any material payment from this shell's recycling will be used to offset the cost of her maintenance."

"What? You didn't do that for Grandmère!"

The matron ignored her and moved toward the door, stopping on the threshold. "Recorder, inform the shell's son. DuBois, you should go."

Alec hates Recorders. "No, let me tell him."

"That's not how it's done." The matron's toe tapped the floor. "Contact him or not, as you will, but don't think you have the authority to make an official announcement."

Zhen shot to her feet. "Get out."

The matron's back stiffened, and she glared at Zhen, then at the Recorder. "You're going to let her speak to me like that?"

The Recorder turned to the matron. "It is recorded. You must acknowledge the guest's request." She turned to Zhen. "Bear in mind that she could file a complaint."

"I'll file one right back," Zhen spat.

Spinning on her heels, the matron stormed out.

Zhen tried to sit back down next to Sophi, but the drone edged her away.

"I shall send a priority message to the son after the shell has been removed." The Recorder bent and picked up the satchel of yarn and needles and handed it to Zhen. "I see that you knit. Perhaps you have scissors."

"What? Of course I have scissors."

The Recorder glided past Zhen and touched Sophi's head gently, and before Zhen could demand that she leave Sophi alone, she gestured to the bag in Zhen's arms.

Oh . . .

If Zhen snipped off Sophi's braid, at least the home wouldn't have everything. It wasn't enough, but it was something. Alec had nothing from his father or sister, but maybe he could have a ring made from his mother's hair, like the pendant Zhen had from Grandmère's. And that thieving matron would get a little less. Probably sold off hair and other things stolen from patients to pad her own accounts. *Beastly female.* Zhen gave the Recorder a faint nod.

The drone extended a long tentacle to tap the Recorder's shoulder, and her face changed for a moment, almost as if she were afraid.

Zhen hugged the satchel to her chest.

"My duties require only a quarter hour, should you wish to alert the son before I do." The Recorder hesitated, glancing back at her drone, then said, almost defiantly, "I must step out for a moment."

She strode from the room, and her drone hovered for a minute before it followed her into the hallway. Zhen waited a few seconds, then snuck a look at the door. She pulled out her scissors, cut off Sophi's braid, and hid it under her yarn.

Perching on the side of the bed like she usually did, she smoothed Sophi's curls. "I have to go now. I'll tell Alec first, before they do." Her voice wavered. "I will miss you." She kissed Sophi's cheek and tiptoed out, though there was no longer any reason for quiet.

The Recorder stood in the hall, one of the drone's long tentacles twined around her neck. Her skin seemed ashen, and her breath came in ragged gasps. She pushed herself away from the wall. For a second, Zhen wanted to ask if she was all right. She looked awful. Even for a Recorder.

But then she said, "Zhen Ferguson DuBois. She is not your family. Why do you mourn?"

And like that, that voided Recorder wasn't human anymore.

"Moons and stars. What kind of rotting question is that?"

Zhen tossed the satchel's strap over her shoulder and stormed down the hall to contact Alec. If she never came back to this . . . this *spacing* hole, it would be too soon.

Still in his flight jacket, Alec came straight from the ship to his mother's small service, accompanied by the friend she'd met before, whose name she couldn't recall. Only one other guest attended, a statuesque woman with long black braids who stayed a respectful distance away. The blond man kissed Sophi's forehead, then remained at Alec's side, his face pale. Once in a while, he swallowed, but he didn't say a word.

Zhen stepped back and silently watched Alec at his mother's side, stroking her short, curly hair.

The attendant cleared his throat. "We have another client's service in less than twenty minutes." He glanced back at the Recorder standing near the preparation room. "We need to process the shell and prepare for the next group."

Alec's jaw tightened. The blond man scowled, and the tall woman glared, but none of them spoke.

Zhen rounded on the attendant. "Show a little compassion! Let him say goodbye to his mother, blast you."

Startled, the attendant stepped back, though when the Recorder moved in their direction, Zhen blocked his path, too.

She pounded out her words. "Neither of you will interfere. Leave him alone."

The attendant ducked behind the Recorder and hit the conveyor button.

Alec stood in impassive silence while his mother's shell rode down the belt. The door slid shut. The Recorder verified the procedure, then followed the assistant to the preparation room. They didn't even give him the certificate. Alec's friend glanced at the tall woman, who nodded, her beads clattering loudly in the Center's quiet. She crossed the room and spoke in terse undertones to the assistant, who quailed and handed her the datastick.

"Alec, what can I—" When Zhen touched his hand, he didn't move. "What're you going to do now?"

"Now? After failing Mama?" His eyes were bloodshot and pinched, his jaw tight. "I'm getting good and drunk, then taking painkillers and going back to work."

"Alec—"

He brushed past, out of the building. Zhen darted after him and grabbed his arm. "Stop," she demanded. "Talk to me."

He glowered at first, then his face softened a little. If a Recorder hadn't passed them right then, he might have relented. Instead, his jaw muscle ticced, and he pivoted and walked away, leaving Zhen alone in the middle of the street.

The blond touched her arm as he and the woman followed Alec. "Don't worry. He'll be okay."

Zhen watched them catch up with Alec. There was no point in staying. As she turned to leave, she heard, "Alec, you idiot, she was trying to help."

Oblivious to the hover transports in the road next to her, she watched her feet take one step after another. No friends, no parents. No loss there. But no Grandmère, no Sophi? And Alec just left? Her feet went faster, almost without her consent.

She didn't see the woman until they collided. Zhen helped her up, carefully checking for injuries, but thankfully, the older woman seemed unharmed. Zhen babbled an apology, but the woman only smiled, though it didn't reach her grey eyes, which were striking even surrounded by fine lines. If she used a good moisturizer, she might even be beyond the sixty years she appeared.

From the corner of her eye, she saw Alec turn back. "Zhen?" he called. "Zhen, I'm sorry!"

The grey-eyed woman turned to his voice. "Alec?"

He froze.

"I'm so sorry I missed her service," the woman said. "I left as soon as I could, but I only heard yesterday."

"You came." Alec swallowed. "I didn't expect to see you."

She gave him a sad smile. "I wish I'd known earlier. You wouldn't have had to face this alone. I lost track of you both. One more thing for which I'm sorry."

Zhen scowled. "You don't lose track of people you care about."

Alec took her hand.

The woman shook her head, and loose silver-and-black curls slid over her shoulder. "No. We shouldn't. I can't change the past, but I can prevent it happening again." She hesitated. "Alec, may I take the four of you to lunch?"

Moons and stars, what?

Alec kept his eyes on the woman. "All right."

The blond man stepped up and made an old-fashioned bow. "Thank you. I, for one, am most appreciative of your offer. The food on that last ship was an affront to humanity."

The woman smiled up at him. "Still a voracious eater, Nate? Last time I took you boys out for a treat, I believe you horrified the servers."

"Tim, now," he said, his smile faltering slightly. "I go by Tim."

The woman's expression softened. "Ah. I shall try to remember."

"Charity, this is Jordan," Tim said. "And this is Zhen DuBois." Tim gestured to Zhen, then held out his arm to the woman.

The woman smiled and took it. Amusement and annoyance flickered across Jordan's face. Tim continued to flirt outrageously with the older woman, whose melancholy evaporated into laughter.

"Is he always like that?" Zhen said to Alec.

The corner of his mouth lifted, just a little. "I don't think he can help it."

Charity took them to a small café near the university, one with seating under arbors of hops. The food looked good, but Zhen wasn't very hungry. She watched the others eat while the cup of creamy coffee cooled in her hands, though when Alec glanced pointedly from her to her plate, she picked at her food. When they finished, the woman handed Alec a datastick and left.

"You know who she reminds me of?" Tim asked as they walked Zhen home.

"No," Alec said, clearly uninterested.

"That Recorder a few quarters back, our last run before we left the fleet. Same eyes."

Alec stopped cold, and Zhen bumped into him. "Don't even mention Recorders in the same sentence as her."

Tim shrugged, and they continued walking.

"So, Zhen. Do you have a job lined up?" Jordan asked.

Moons and stars, I hate that question. "I had a few leads, but I lost focus. I still have the year of required service."

"Well," Alec said, "stay in touch. Our team's got good contacts with universities and the government. We need someone good with computers."

Jordan's sculpted eyebrows rose, but she smiled. "True. It certainly isn't Tim's forte."

"After your year, I mean," Alec added quickly. "Like you said, you don't lose track of people you care about."

Zhen felt a smile edge its way onto her face.

The sadness didn't truly leave his, but it lightened. He threaded his fingers through hers. And in spite of everything else, a spark of hope pushed aside the pointlessness.

"Maybe," she said slowly, "I will."

Max walked to breakfast with me. I sat with him and Nate, sipping tea between bites of reconstituted fruit, trying to memorize my friends.

When Elliott and Ross arrived eleven minutes later, the atmosphere changed. Both Spanos and DuBois stiffened, and Nate's laughter vanished. I frowned. The awkwardness with Elliott was not conducive to proper digestion. Truthfully and selfishly, I disapproved of how the altered mood affected my morning. I set down my fork and took a fortifying gulp of lavender-peppermint tea.

I leaned past Nate. "Elliott." Everyone stopped eating to stare at me, and under their scrutiny I forgot what I had intended to say, so I continued almost randomly, "Have you resumed your studies?"

His face flushed a bright red. "No, I haven't."

"If you have any difficulties in mathematics, I am willing to be of assistance this evening during dinner. I would be of little help in literature." I stopped speaking before I began to ramble.

"I don't . . ." Elliott failed to complete his thought.

Next to me, Nate tensed. I placed a hand on his arm, then rose, walked to the end of the table, and extended my fist.

Elliott stood as well, his lashless blue eyes glanced from me to the floor. "Why?"

Life, it seemed, was complicated. I struggled for an answer but could find none. Towering over me, Elliott gently tapped my fist with his larger one, then left.

Julian Ross rose to dispose of their dishes. "I might have underestimated you, Recorder."

"It is quite possible that I am no longer a Recorder, which might explain the discrepancy in your comprehension."

He grunted and followed his brother out the door.

I went back to my seat and stared at my plate. The noise level crept back up, then began to fade as nightshift left for sleep and dayshift left for duty. Soon only Jordan, Nate, Max, and I remained.

"Well," I said, "regardless—"

"Regardless, nothing," Nate snapped. "That blasted—"

"Regardless!" Jordan interrupted.

Nate said through clenched teeth, "I don't trust him."

Max watched me silently. Had I erred? Was I incorrect to extend clemency to Elliott? Max had greater experience. I should have spoken to him first.

"Perhaps not." I folded my hands on my lap to keep them from betraying my uncertainty. "But we can grant him the opportunity to redeem himself. Jordan, if you have time, I am available to review . . . updates."

Before she could reply, her communication link chimed. Captain North requested her presence in his office. She signed off. "Would you mind meeting in your lab after dinner?"

"That is acceptable."

"I'll expect a full report this evening, then." Jordan strode out, her braids making music.

Nate yawned, and Max focused on him. "Tim, you're exhausted. You need more sleep."

Nate groaned and scrubbed his eyes. "Remind me not to do that double shift thing again for a while. You were right. Caffeine wasn't enough. I'll see you both later." He lightly tapped my nose. "You'd better remember to eat."

I could think of no adequate response before he left the room, so I turned to Max. "What does a tap on the nose signify?"

He grinned. "He must like that nose of yours. He commented on it several times yesterday."

Exiting without further explanation, Max left me to puzzle over his comments. I reached no conclusion, so I proceeded to VVR to continue the search for the virus I still hoped was not real.

Standing by the virtual image of the research station console we had used to access the stasis pods on Pallas, where my drone had been destroyed, I shuddered. Leaning through the projected medical bay, I rested against the smooth, solid wall beyond it. I should not have had an adverse reaction to the long hallway, with its cool light flooding spotlessly clean walls and the blue safety lights' dim glow edging the floors. It was entirely different when it was clean and brightly lit.

Once more, occupied pods rested in their ports, but now, the view plates and control panels glowed. Living faces slept behind clear windows. Other people in clean, synthetic robes lined up in an orderly fashion to enter the pods that extended around the hall's gentle curve.

Four of the five young children waited with wide eyes, but the last one clung to his parents, tiny sobs echoing slightly until Dr. Allen administered a sedative. He spoke gently to the little ones before their parents pulled back their sleeves for the jet injectors' quick hisses, then murmured to parents who lowered limp children into the pods. Once or twice, an adult begged for a dose, but most climbed in, panic hidden until they thrashed as their pods filled.

I, too, had panicked when Nate and Spanos lowered me into the liquid environment of a medical tank, but my sympathy was compounded by the heaviness of knowing none of these people, not even the children, would wake.

I drummed my thigh and forced my mind back to the task of viewing the recordings Nate had collected and organized.

Strangely, evidence pointed to the deletion of records *after* the pods had been filled, yet only John Westruther, Georgette SahnVeer, Dr. Allen, and Jean-Pierre Marsden were not listed in the medical storage records. I hoped to ascertain if anyone else had not been in stasis, so I watched people enter the pods, verifying their identification records and unit numbers. It seemed unlikely that Westruther, SahnVeer, Marsden, or Dr. Allen had been the perpetrator, or had deleted records, but unlikely did not mean impossible.

I increased playback speed, and people raced through the lines into stasis. The first group settled, and the pods operated appropriately. The second wave and the third and the fourth progressed as expected. When Julian Ross moved to the front of the line, however, curiosity compelled me to slow the recording.

He was even more handsome with long, dark, wavy hair falling loosely down his back, though his eyebrows were thicker and darker than Nate's.

"No need for the sedative, Allen," he said.

Dr. Allen asked, "Do you want to wait for Elliott?"

Julian Ross nodded and moved to the side. He stood at a control panel and absentmindedly ran his fingers over the buttons, eyes focused down the long hallway as he waited. As if suddenly realizing what he was doing, he jumped back and reset any maladjustments. The sequence replayed at my request, and although his body partially blocked the view of the control screen, the panel was identical before and after he adjusted it. The recording resumed.

Everyone else was in the pods when a shorter and much more substantial Elliott raced down the hall, his long dark hair escaping from the single braid hanging down his back. Two other teens followed him.

Kyleigh's hair bounced in a cloud of tight, light brown ringlets that nearly reached her waist. I was surprised since she had often told me she missed having braids. She was the same height but much heavier. Her face was rounder and softer, and her sandy eyebrows matched perfectly. She was winded, and her hazel eyes, framed by short lashes, were wide. Freddie, too, was much shorter, barely taller than Kyleigh. His face did not have the sharp edges and wasted appearance he had in the tank. He reminded me of my friend, with warm, medium-brown skin, though Freddie's eyes were a pale green. His dark hair was clipped close to his scalp, and his small earrings sparkled, even in the recording.

"Julian, I'm sorry I'm late," Elliott panted. "I have something for you. Freddie just finished it."

Elliott raised his hand and pressed a code into the tiny, waterproof datapad on his palm. A series of images began to play, recordings of the brothers when they were younger, a three-dimensional pixelated sculpture of the two of them with a tall man who strongly resembled Ross, and then a sculpture of Elliott himself, which somehow resembled him more than the recordings did.

Ross beamed at Freddie. "This is amazing. Thank you."

"I wanted you to have it, in case—" Elliott broke off, then swallowed. "Just in case."

Julian Ross placed his hands on his brother's shoulders. "There's nothing to worry about. Westruther has everything under control."

"What if—"

Ross shook him gently. "No what-iffing. You three go say goodbye to the lab animals or something. I'll be right here when we wake up. The supply ship will revive us when they arrive in a few ten-days. We'll be fine."

Elliott swallowed. "I'm glad you're my brother, Julian."

Ross pulled him into a hug.

Elliott held on to his brother, eyes closed, repeating, "Please be all right, please be all right."

"Julian," Dr. Allen said.

Julian Ross glanced at the controls, then climbed into his stasis pod. He held the small recording device to his chest and quirked a smile at his brother, while the lid slid shut and the pod filled with gel. Ross writhed as the liquid entered his lungs, and Elliott turned away.

"He'll be fine." Dr. Allen patted Elliott's arm. "Kids, we need to run a system check before the last group. You'll have two hours until you need to be here. Go change. If you need me before then, I'll be in the control room, double checking the shielding on the algae and plankton tanks. Can't let the nutrient levels slip with everyone going into stasis."

The doctor walked away, consulting a datapad in his hand, talking to Westruther over his communication link.

"C'mon, Elliott." Freddie's voice, which was much deeper than his slight frame suggested, cracked a little. "Kye, let's go say goodbye to the cats."

"I hate that we have to leave them out," Kyleigh said. "What if they get sick? Who's going to feed them?"

"No one," Elliott said. His shoulders, his whole frame, slumped, and he kept his focus on his brother's pod. "I heard Julian talking to Dr. SahnVeer. They're gonna put them down."

Kyleigh gasped.

Freddie took her hand. "I'm sorry, Kye."

When Elliott turned away from Ross's pod, he frowned at their intertwined fingers, but the other two did not notice.

A sudden smile made Freddie's light green eyes crinkle at the sides. "There are extra pods. What if we use them?"

"What do you mean?" Elliott asked.

A grin spread over Kyleigh's face. "That's worth a shot." She grabbed their hands and pulled them into a run. They sprinted past me toward the door.

I paused the recording and paced through the hallway, tapping my leg with my fist. Bias could not be allowed to impact my interpretation of the events, and my current distrust of the Ross brothers might influence my opinion. I needed to know what else had been on that datapad. Was it possible the device held more than memories of their family? Max would have retrieved it if it had been in Ross's pod, so I contacted him over the communication link.

"Max, did Julian Ross have a datapad when he woke from stasis?"

"Yes, he did," Max said. "Zhen checked it out. It had some family portraits on it. According to Kyleigh, Freddie had done some of them. Excellent work."

"Was anything else on the device?"

"No. Why?"

"I had not seen the report."

"It wasn't strictly medical, so I didn't think of adding it. I'll have Zhen send you the data if you need it."

"Yes," I said. "I should review it and add it to the records."

"Agreed, if only to save the artwork." Max paused. "I need to get Freddie out of that tank soon."

I nodded as I disconnected the link, forgetting that he could not see me. I considered contacting him and apologizing for my rudeness, but Max would understand.

VVR resumed the recording. I slowed the program whenever someone entered the medical storage bay.

A technician carefully adjusted the panels over the feedlines from the algae and plankton tanks and to and from the recycling and purification lines. She checked on the backup geothermal power, then notified Dr. Allen and Westruther via communication link that it was fully functional and that the feeds "operated at 100 percent." She left. I increased the playback speed, then slowed it again as two more people, glancing cautiously in either direction, emerged from a storage room. They exchanged a quick kiss and left in opposite directions. I rewound the recording and checked inside the storage room but found nothing amiss.

No one entered the bay for a while, and the recording sped up again until the teenagers returned carrying two bags, similar to those people carried to the gymnasium. They walked down to the antepenultimate pod and ejected it from the wall. Kyleigh watched as a lookout while Freddie unzipped the larger bag, and Elliott the smaller one.

"Are you sure you got the dosage right?" Freddie asked in a quiet undertone.

"Of course," Kyleigh hissed. "Just get them loaded quickly. If Dr. Allen finds out, we're in trouble."

The boys carefully lifted limp animals out of the bags. Elliott lowered the rats, their naked tails dangling, one by one into the pod, and Freddie carefully set the cats on their sides. I recognized Bustopher at once. His white feet and the splash of white on his neck stood out clearly against his thick black fur. He was quite handsome, and a knot formed in my throat when I realized I would not see him after I left. His fur would grow in, but he would not nudge my hand to make me scratch his ears. Smuggling him with me was not possible. I bit my lip and watched the boys, who stepped back as Kyleigh adjusted the controls.

"Hurry up," Elliott urged, looking over his shoulder.

"Shh! And don't rush me. Jenny's pregnant. I have to get this just right."

Freddie glanced over his shoulder. "If she goes into labor in the pod, it'll be bad."

"I know. But we shouldn't be in there too long. It ought to be fine." She sighed and stepped away from the panel. "I hope I did that right."

"We need to get out of here before someone sees us," Elliott said under his breath.

Freddie picked up the empty bags and gave Kyleigh a quick kiss on her cheek. "They'll be fine. We'll all be fine. And when we wake up, they'll figure out about your dad and why people got sick."

Elliott awkwardly patted her shoulder while he met Freddie's eyes over Kyleigh's bowed head. "We need to go. We only have a few more minutes."

She nodded. Then they left.

I already knew Kyleigh had done well in altering the protocol while masking the pod's contents, but I checked all the same, stepping back into the image when Dr. Allen walked over to the stasis pod with the animals and reviewed the controls. A smile creased his face, and he laughed quietly.

The next group of people, including the technician and the couple from the storage room, lined up against the walls, waiting to enter the older pods. The teens stood toward the end of the line, repeatedly offering "cuts" to latecomers. While alarmed at first, I eventually deduced that "cutting" did not indicate lacerations. Rather, it was an idiom indicating stepping ahead of someone else in line.

Elliott was already in his unit, and Kyleigh and Freddie were waiting their turn, when John Westruther rounded the corner. The teenagers were holding hands and watching the pod, where tiny thuds bore witness to Elliott's acclimation. The noise eventually stilled.

Dr. Allen beckoned to Kyleigh. "You're next, Kye."

Westruther stepped forward before she reached the pod. "A moment, Oliver. Kyleigh, I'm sorry. This doesn't mean you won't find out what happened."

"I know," she said in a small voice. "At least I've got the smartest people in the colonies on my side." She stared down the long hall with the protruding stasis pods. "John, does it hurt? Everyone thrashes. The records say what happens, how it works, but it sounds like it hurts."

Dr. Allen answered before Westruther could. "It does, a little. But as you adjust, it is comfortable and soothing. The nanodevices, which you've studied and know how they work, will trigger neurotransmitters, and soon enough you are happy and in a sleeplike state. It might help to recite something."

John Westruther leaned down and whispered in her ear something about never leaving or forsaking her. The recording's quality was not good enough to be certain.

She gave him a weak smile. "Never."

I did not understand how the Consortium allowed such old recording devices on a research station. Whatever else my failings were, the abysmal, poor quality of the records was not my fault.

A tear slid down her cheek, and Freddie wiped it away with his thumb.

She climbed into the pod, self-consciously holding her gown's flap shut.

Although Dr. Allen said nothing about safety, she pulled a long golden chain over her head and untied the gown's sash before she lay back, her fingers wrapped around the necklace and charm.

My anxiety was irrational. I knew I could not help my friend and that she would be well, but I stepped closer all the same.

"Kyleigh!" Freddie reached for her hand as the lid began to shut. "I love you."

She smiled, and held up one hand to him, which he touched.

"Get your hand out of the pod!" snapped Dr. Allen.

He withdrew his hand as the lid began to close.

"Me, too, Fr—" The lid clicked shut. It buzzed and clanked as it filled. I heard her flail briefly.

"Freddie." Dr. Allen motioned to the next pod.

Freddie looked up at his father. "Dad, I love you, too."

John Westruther, who towered over his son, pulled him close. "Freddie, you have no idea how much you mean to me. I know I've pushed you hard in math and science, but I don't care about that, not deep down. You're like your mother, a light to me in the darkness." His voice faltered. "You made my life better."

Freddie pulled back. "Made? Dad, why're you using past tense?"

Westruther shook his head. "It's just unsettling." He gave his son a quick smile. "You're better at the arts. Follow that dream instead. We have enough in savings to get you through any rough years."

Freddie's knuckles whitened as he gripped his father's arm. "What aren't you telling me?"

John Westruther touched Freddie's face. "After your mother died, I haven't been the best father, but I have always loved you. I always will."

Freddie's forehead furrowed. "I know, Dad. But—"

Westruther hugged him again, tightly.

"You'll be here when I wake up, right?" Freddie spoke into his father's chest, his voice muffled.

His father did not answer right away. He hugged Freddie once again and kissed the top of his head. "I love you, son."

Freddie's eyes glistened. "I understand." He blinked away a tear. "Love you, too, Dad. Always have, always will."

He climbed into the pod. Westruther stepped close, and they gazed at each other as the lid slid shut. Freddie did not thrash as the pod filled. The tank retracted into the wall, and Westruther slumped against it, saying only, "Always."

Dr. Allen cleared his throat. "That leaves the four of us, John."

Westruther squared his shoulders. "Jean-Pierre should be here in an hour, after he finishes blasting the tunnels. When he gets here, you two get in the pods. Georgette and I will come right before things lock down. Don't wait for us."

"John—"

"Blast it, Oliver, don't make me risk Jean-Pierre by forcing you into a pod now. You know he won't be able to figure it out himself."

"I know. But I don't like it."

"Who does?" Westruther replied. After a moment, his brow furrowed. "There should be seven pods left here. I'm counting six."

Dr. Allen pointed to the last pod. "The kids smuggled some of the lab animals up to that one. No, no, it's all good. I checked. That clever Kyleigh reprogrammed it to adjust the nutrient uptake. It won't challenge the system in the slightest."

"You should have stopped them. Unauthorized—"

"It won't hurt anyone, and it gave them hope. We all need as much hope as we can get."

John Westruther nodded, only once. After thirty-one seconds of silence, he held out his hand. "Good luck, Oliver. Look to the light, yes?"

Dr. Allen grasped his wrist, but the recording flickered. The quality was insufficient to determine with certainty whether or not he had tears in his eyes. "Yes. Look to the light, John."

As Westruther left the bay, Dr. Allen returned to studying the computer readouts. He left temporarily and returned in his gown, which was oddly long on him. Soon afterward, he received a call from Jean-Pierre Marsden regarding an injury. Dr. Allen said something under his breath and grabbed a small medical kit. He ran out of the bay, explaining the situation to Westruther and SahnVeer as he ran, and the recording cut to static.

Again, I dropped to my knees as the hissing noise and thick, flickering grey light surrounded me. This time, however, it lasted only three seconds, and I recovered quickly. I replayed certain segments again, and then the next recording began.

A virtual Dr. SahnVeer transferred data to deep storage and secure systems at the control panel beside which we had found her body. Although she hummed tunelessly as she worked, there was a rigidity in her posture. I checked the time stamp and switched to another recording.

Jean-Pierre Marsden carefully inserted explosives in the passages leading out of the station. He complained, loudly and profanely, about ruining perfectly good tunnels as he backed out of the one he was in. Marsden screamed as the explosion shook the visual recording, which disappeared into a grey storm of pixels, though the audio still played.

Nathaniel Timmons's notes indicated that visual records did not resume, so I shut my eyes to block the flickering grey static and listened to Marsden swear prolifically, noting again that in no way could his word combinations be applied within either the laws of man or nature. He grunted, something metallic clattered, nearly hiding the muted thud of someone falling, and he swore again through ragged breaths. Fabric rustled as if it were dragged over concrete, and the faint slaps of flesh on the floor made me cringe.

Was he crawling, then? In my memory, I envisioned the tunnels, the length of the walk from the collapse to the control room. Although I did not like him, and although I knew he would not make it to safety, when his communication link chimed as he contacted Dr. Allen, for three seconds, I hoped he would. My fingernails dug into my palms again, and I hit my leg with greater force than usual.

Marsden, his voice terse, stated that debris had injured his leg and he could not walk. I could not confirm the veracity of his claim. Footsteps echoed, speeding up as they grew louder, and I surmised that Dr. Allen had arrived. Dr. Allen spoke of splints and medical tanks, of contacting John Westruther for assistance, and Marsden began to respond. However, even in the recording with the volume adjusted, the following rumble of collapsing cement and rock shook my bones. Another high-pitched scream preceded the hissing buzz of static.

VVR played my next complete selection—an empty hallway near the collapsed tunnel.

"Jean-Pierre? Oliver? Update. Now!" Westruther's voice repeated over and over through the station's communication system.

Marsden half-crawled on one leg and one arm from the darkened hallway, dragging a very still Dr. Allen by the arm, both leaving shining, red trails, which led back into the darkness. He tried to tell Westruther that Oliver Allen was dead, but his communication link must have malfunctioned.

Dr. SahnVeer's voice echoed slightly in the cement corridor as it aired over the station's intercom. "John, you've been trying to raise them for twenty minutes. Neither is in the medical bay. Either we go and find them, or we assume the worst. I don't want to seem unfeeling, but whoever did this cannot be allowed to take that virus out of this station. We already started the countdown. What do you want to do?"

Marsden's arms fell to his sides, and he slumped into a heap next to Dr. Allen. He glared up at the camera and spat onto the floor. "Figures."

"You're right. I know you're right." Westruther's sigh filled the hall. "Jean-Pierre, Oliver. If you are out there, I'm sorry, but we're out of time. We must assume the worst. You know what we have to do. Godspeed, my friends."

The communication link chimed, and everything was quiet. Marsden hesitated, then set his hand on Dr. Allen's head, and after another seven minutes, the feed went black. There was no static, no noise, nothing at all. Despite my feelings about Jean-Pierre Marsden, my heart pinched. To die alone, unheard, in the dark was a terrible thing.

I could not know with certainty what had happened in those dark tunnels. The recordings had been erased. And even had they not been, uncovering them would not change the outcome, would never alter the past. I queued up the control room and checked the time stamp, and both SahnVeer and Westruther had been there the whole time. I watched Westruther and SahnVeer execute the self-destruct order. I saw them try fruitlessly to contact Dr. Allen and Marsden, saw the way Georgette SahnVeer grew pale, saw Westruther's mouth pinch as he pulled up his son's image in a datastream. The recording cut off as abruptly as the other had when the generator imploded.

I wanted to tell him that Freddie was under Max's care, that Kyleigh, too, had survived. But I could not. Resolutely, I shoved the thought aside and focused on the reason I watched any of them at all.

I had overlooked something incredibly obvious, but I did not know what.

Was there a fifth person, someone who had not been counted? No evidence of any other person on the station existed, so an extra person did not seem plausible. Everyone else had been secured in the pods.

I logged out of VVR, carefully deleting my records.

After I reviewed Zhen's analysis of Ross's device and found it did indeed only hold video recordings of family, I walked to the dining commons. I had missed the lunch crowd, but Kyleigh lingered over her empty tray. I selected my food based on availability and nutritional value and sat down across from her. After several bites, I decided to choose more wisely in the future. The combination of flavors and textures was truly unappealing.

"How are you feeling?" she asked.

"I am well enough, thanks to your knowledge and hard work targeting parasites with nanodevices."

She gave her head a shake and shuffled dishes around on her tray.

"Kyleigh." I paused, considering the best possible way to inquire about what I had seen. "I would like to ask you a question, but I am concerned that it will be misinterpreted."

She stilled. "Misinterpreted how?"

"Once before, I meant to help . . ." I stopped before I brought up the autopsy. "It is regarding the medical stasis pods."

"If it's about the pods . . ."

I hesitated before I said, "You had a necklace."

Her hand rose to her throat.

"Why did Dr. Allen allow you to take it in the pod?"

"Because . . ." She hesitated. "Because he understood."

"I do not, however. Do you still have it?"

She slowly pulled the necklace from under her tunic and over her head to show me. The fine chain was gold alloy, with a gold charm shaped like a lowercase T.

I examined it and returned it to her. "If it is a t for Tristram, you should have utilized a capital letter."

She glanced around the empty room then whispered, "It's a cross."

"A cross of what?"

"It's a religious symbol."

"You have a religion? I did not know."

Kyleigh put the chain back over her head and slid it under her tunic.

"Well, Recorder," she said, using my former title, "you aren't supposed to know. It's supposed to be something people see in your life, unless people ask. Or unless they are Recorders, of course."

"And Dr. Allen?"

"He understood. He and Dad would meet to talk and pray. They're dead, though, so they can't get in trouble for it, even if I can." Her hazel eyes met mine. "You won't tell, will you?"

"I would not betray your trust," I said. "Although, it surprises me that you would believe in something as unquantifiable as a god."

She offered me a small smile. "Well, he wouldn't be much of a God if he was quantifiable, would he?"

I did not answer. I returned my tray to the galley and headed to my computer laboratory. Whatever I was missing, it, too, remained unquantifiable.

I had not made enough progress, and I only had one full day left.

42

The unexpectedness of Zhen DuBois knitting in my computer laboratory stopped me just inside the door.

"About time you showed up." She slid a loop of dusky-orange yarn from her left needle to the right, glaring up at me before glancing at the datapad on the table. She pursed her lips briefly and scowled at her yarn.

"Do you require my assistance?"

"No." Her needles made hushed, rhythmic clicks. "Are you just going to stand there?"

I stepped in, and the door closed behind me. If she did not need my help, I could see no reason for her to be sitting at my table, but several ten-days of interacting with Zhen DuBois kept me from saying as much. Instead, I watched while she picked the yarn with one long, blue metallic needle, tucked it through, and slid each new loop over the tip, until finally, the yarn was all on her right side. Her lips moved as she ran her thumb over the loops, then tucked the long, lacy orange triangle in a satchel.

"So." She turned off the datapad before sliding it on top of the yarn. "We reach Lunar One day after tomorrow."

"Yes." I crossed to my workstation, my back to her, my thoughts circling again over what I had seen in VVR and over my upcoming departure.

"You'll need this." She deposited a black and steel identification bracelet on my datapad. "Jordan skimmed it today and says it looks good. She'll be by after dinner. I wanted to drop it off before then. Good thing I ate early. I've been waiting for three rows."

While she spoke, worries for my friends' safety and for their futures shot through me like a reprimand, dwarfing my own concerns. I edged away from her, backing to the table and dropping into a chair. "I cannot use the identification bracelet."

She snatched the bracelet from the datapad and shoved it into my left hand. "Why not?"

My heart raced. "If it is traced to you, you will be in danger."

DuBois leaned her hands on my chair's arms, and her black hair poured over her shoulder. I pressed myself as far away as the chair would allow.

"And if you don't have it—if you don't run—what happens then? You can't possibly be stupid enough to think they'll take you back?"

I shook my head.

She jerked away from the chair and straightened. "I didn't think so. If you return, you'll disappear, just like a citizen. Just like Alec's dad."

I stood abruptly. "Nevertheless, I will not risk you. Nor Spanos. If I am not mistaken, this was his mother's."

Her dark eyes widened at my words, but her lips tightened. "How did—no. Listen, Recorder, I already risked myself. I'm not a fool. I know what I did. I know the potential consequences. I decided to take them. No one *made* me."

Familiar, invisible bands tightened around my chest, and I tapped my fist on my thigh.

Her hand shot out and grabbed my arm. "Stop."

I tried to pull away, but her fingers tightened like a vise.

She stepped closer, so close that our faces were less than thirty centimeters apart. "Don't." Then, her face lost some of its tightness, and her fingers loosened as she leaned in even closer still, and again I detected coffee and lemon. Her voice lowered, yet remained sharp. "Just because a drone used to hurt you doesn't mean you need to hurt yourself."

DuBois released me suddenly, and I fell backward, bumping against the table. Before I could protest about her mistaken belief, she leaned her weight over her heels and folded her arms. "Besides. Maybe I stole it. Our contract, Alec's and mine, expired. He's not connected to me anymore. What I do can't impact him legally."

"No." It was my turn to frown. "I foresee two problems, Zhen DuBois. Primarily, you disregard the potential of personal danger. If an Elder believed there to be a connection, she would find it."

Her face paled. "They can't."

"When you know Alexander Spanos's story"—she flinched at my words—"how can you believe the Elders would not hesitate, would stop at nothing, to prove their case?"

Her throat worked, and her mouth opened, though she did not speak.

"Secondarily, I cannot use this." I extended the bracelet and gentled my voice. "The serial number is linked with the identification number, and that cannot be changed without access to the documentation databases on New Triton. Additionally, it will be missing Consortium markers. Therefore, for all the generosity you have displayed, you must see why I cannot use it. If I gain access to my old quarters, perhaps I could add those layers, but I may not be able to remove all traces of tampering."

She laughed harshly. "Remove my fingerprints, you mean?"

"No." I could not help but smile. "Electronic documents cannot carry oil residue, and cleaning the bracelet itself would be sufficient."

"Moons and stars." She rolled her eyes. "Not that kind of fingerprints, Recorder." She pulled her hair over her shoulder and fingered the ends. "Just get out of here, all right? Even if it means using that"—she pointed at the bracelet—"you get away. I'll be fine. *We'll* be fine. Just find a way to let us—them—know you're safe. Track us down. Stay in touch."

The lure of contacting my friends, of finding a way to reunite with them, would be too strong. It already was. The decorative rim of mica around the bracelet's smooth black face winked at me, and the steel links shone.

"I cannot risk it."

DuBois curled my fingers around the bracelet. "I don't lose track of people—" She stopped abruptly and dropped my hand as though I had reprimanded her. Her lips pinched. "Do it anyway."

She pivoted to pick up her satchel, but before she reached the door, it slid open.

"Told you she'd be here, J," Spanos said over his shoulder. He wrapped an arm around DuBois's waist and kissed her cheek. "Missed you at dinner."

She narrowed her dark eyes at me. "I ate early."

My shoulders drooped. It was hardly my fault if she chose to dine before he did.

Nate, Max, and Jordan followed Spanos through the door, Jordan locked it, and they all turned to DuBois.

"Yeah, I gave it to her, and it's not my fault she's being difficult," DuBois said. "Do I have to stay for this?"

A muscle twitched in Nate's jaw, but Jordan held up her hand. "Simmer down."

Spanos took the yarn satchel from DuBois's shoulder and set it on the table. He leaned over and whispered something in her ear. His arms enfolded her, and a knot formed in my throat. I studied the grey-flecked antistatic flooring and listed prime numbers in my head. Though voices rose and fell around me like music, I did not listen.

Black boots appeared in my visual range. "Hey. Join us at the table?"

Nate was holding out his hand. For a fractured second, I wished to take it, or for him to take mine, but I would not impose. Neither would I tap my thigh in front of DuBois, and my fist tightened in the effort to be still. I turned back to the table with the others.

Nate brought the chair from DuBois's workstation to the table and gestured for me to be seated, but he himself remained standing. "Let's figure this out."

The subsequent silence lasted one minute and thirty-seven seconds, though it felt an interminable length of time. Finally, Nate pulled a paper brochure from inside his jacket, leaned over me, and spread it on the table. It was a map of Lunar One.

Jordan raised an eyebrow. "Your pack rat habits finally pay off, Tim?"

"I guess." He tapped the paper. "We'll probably dock here. Best berth for this size ship. There's a lot of security around there, the admin centers, and shopping areas."

"Your hoarded paper isn't as helpful as you might think," Spanos muttered on my left. He leaned forward, elbows on the table, and rubbed his knuckles. "First step is figuring out how to get her off *Thalassa*."

"No," DuBois said brusquely. "The first step is to give her a name and make her take that ID bracelet."

"What?" Max stared at me. "You don't have a name yet? I assumed I didn't know in case anyone asked."

Anxiety again snuck cold tendrils around my heart and lungs. All I could manage to say was, "I cannot take it."

Jordan drummed her fingers. "You need one to survive out there. And when we dock, you'll have to find a way to mingle, disappear into the crowds. Your hair isn't long enough yet and I don't have a clue how to get around that."

"You're missing the *point*," DuBois snapped. "She refused to take the bracelet."

Nate's hand flattened on the paper, but he said nothing. Max rubbed his neck, and Spanos turned to me, blocking my view of DuBois.

Jordan riveted her gaze on me. "Why?"

"It is a security concern." The words almost stuck in my throat.

"Can we fix it?" she asked.

We.

And at that word, some of the anxious tendrils loosened. Perhaps, after all, I was not alone, even if I knew enough to eschew their aid. "*I shall do my best. I must complete it on my own, and I will not require your assistance.*"

Jordan drew a sharp breath. Nate dropped to a crouch beside me, and I forced a slight smile for him. His forehead wrinkled in response, and my smile fled.

DuBois spoke through gritted teeth. "No, *you* wouldn't."

"Zhen," Spanos said. "Be nice."

"I *am* nice. I made those stellar documents, which could get me sent to the mines, or worse. I even picked out a nice name."

"A name?" I asked. She had said nothing before. "I did not know."

"You are not using that name," Jordan said as Max asked, "What name?"

DuBois glowered at the others. "It's a perfectly lovely name: Chrysanthemum Patel-Tir."

"No." Jordan tapped the table in time with her words. "She needs a quiet, unassuming name. Not a name that shouts for attention."

"I do not know its meaning," I said.

"A chrysanthemum is a flower," DuBois said, "and it's a much better name than 'Precious.'"

A flower. No one had ever likened me to a flower before.

"No one is naming her 'Precious,' either, Zhen. Her name is certainly not going to be Chrysanthemum," Jordan stated flatly. "Like

I said before, it's better to combine a popular name from the year she was born with common surnames."

While DuBois and Jordan continued to argue, I pulled out my datapad and skimmed the five most popular names from 454: Yrsa, Monique, Annalise, Rainbow, and Amira. None of them suited me. I showed the list to Nate, and he made a face and mouthed, "Rainbow?"

A sudden pounding on the door brought Nate and Jordan to their feet, and Max, Spanos, and DuBois seemed as tightly coiled as springs. Nate pointed at my datapad, so I turned it off and slid it under my thigh. Only then did Jordan open my laboratory door.

"There you are—" Kyleigh broke off at the sight of all of us. "Nice. A party, and I'm not invited."

"Or Ross," added Spanos. "Or Elliott."

"Great. Even better. No offense, Jordan, but honestly? To be left off the list with Ross and Elliott?" She frowned. "This isn't a party, is it? It's a meeting." When no one answered her, she sighed. "Okay, fine, I'm uninvited. But I need to talk to Max and Jordan and the Recorder-who-isn't."

"What is it?" I asked.

"It's the nanodevices. I've been studying them all day, and the ones in your bloodstream as of yesterday when Williams drew that last sample aren't the same as the ones in your blood before you got sick."

My stomach twisted. "What do you mean?"

"I'll show you." She pulled out her datapad and held it horizontally. Two lists and images rose above it, side by side. "See?" She pointed. "Different. And it's morphing. Your old nanodevices are physically changing for some reason."

Max leaned forward, eyes narrowed as he reached out and enlarged one image. The other disappeared. "Can you see any effects?"

"No." She froze it and pointed at a section I was too far away to see. "They're completely encapsulated. I haven't found my way in."

Max took the device. His forehead furrowed, and he tugged on his ear. "Thoughts?"

"I don't know." Kyleigh bit both lips. "But I wouldn't be surprised if this was related to her being a Recorder."

"She's not a Recorder," Nate and Spanos said simultaneously.

Kyleigh glared around the room. "She cannot go back to the Consortium."

Jordan said, "I know."

"Well, we can't do nothing! Can't she get off at the next station?"

Spanos met Jordan's eyes, and she nodded slowly. He grinned. I shook my head, but no one acknowledged me.

Kyleigh sputtered. "It's not funny, Alec!"

"Actually, it is."

She studied us all, and a smile dawned. "Oh. It's a *meeting*."

Nate remained quiet, but as Jordan and the others resumed their bickering about names and discussed docking procedures, I realized that their conversation was like music.

And what was life without music?

Once again, I felt as if bands of synthleather bound my chest, restricting my breath. The thought of leaving was almost as frightening as my nightmares of roaches.

"You've got everything, then?" Kyleigh still beamed. "I can help you pack. I'm good at packing."

"Yes." I closed my eyes and exhaled. "No. I must do something tomorrow. And I need a name."

DuBois snorted. "Chrysanthemum is a good name."

"Zhen," Jordan said, "we've been over that."

"Actually, I've been thinking about this for over a ten-day," Kyleigh announced. "I personally like Elle, which means 'she,' so you can pretend it isn't a name at all, if that still bothers you. It could be a nickname for Elinor or Helena, though I guess you could go by Lena, too. But if you like flowers, there's Lavender or Rose. You like lavender, and Rose is my middle name, but I'll share." She beamed at me.

"It won't take long to key in the name." Jordan held up her hand. "At any rate, we should all get some sleep. Including you, Recorder. You've got rough days ahead, not to mention having a few difficult ten-days behind you."

"No," I said quietly. "These have been the best days of my life. While I have experienced challenges, for the first time, I have been able to be myself. It is true I miss my drone's additional input, but I have been able to think and feel and act without reprisal. And, through all of it, I have had friends. It is good. I am thankful."

No one answered, but that was of no concern. DuBois would not meet my eye as she and Spanos departed. When Kyleigh, Jordan, and Max stood to leave, my thoughts returned to Max's question, fourteen years past, in the Consortium's gardens. He might not recall the conversation, but I could not leave without finally responding.

"Max?"

He stopped near the door.

"I must answer your question."

"What did I ask?"

"It was long ago." I searched for the right words. "Occasionally, I have difficulty discerning the relevance of particular statements. Indeed, one of the reasons Recorders are given drones is to aid in the prioritization of information."

Max glanced at Nate, who shook his head. Standing at the threshold, Max asked, "What are you talking about?"

"Fourteen years ago, you asked if I was happy. I was neither happy nor unhappy most of the time."

His eyes widened.

"After my misconduct in speaking to you, I was not allowed out during Tour Days, so I could not find you to explain."

Max took a step toward me, as if compelled by an outside force.

"I was glad to see you when I boarded, but I did not wish our conversation to be recorded, so I said nothing. And then, after my drone was destroyed, it had been too long to speak."

Jordan placed a hand on his arm. "Max?"

He did not seem to notice. "*You* were the little girl, the only one who ever spoke to me. I worried you would be in trouble after . . ." His eyes clouded. "That man, the Elder, did he hurt you after I left?"

I ignored Kyleigh's sharp inhalation and the click of Jordan's beads. Nate's hand on my back steadied me.

"I was disciplined, of course, but—" I stopped. "Yes. He did." Labeling reprimands as harmful rather than a consequence somehow frightened me. Pain should only be for corrections, but what if it were not truly merited?

"I didn't recognize you." Usually so resonant and smooth, his voice sounded hollow. He crossed the room and took my hands in his.

"There is no shame in that, Max. It was fourteen years ago. Children change greatly, and we are not meant to be memorable. We are forgettable, individually. Being an indistinguishable unit in a larger whole aids in maintaining our neutrality. I am not important as an individual."

"That's a lie," Nate burst out and Jordan echoed him.

I shook my head. "I felt it important to answer your question before I leave. We are not taught to value happiness, even though it is a basic human emotion. But I was usually content. And, I apologize for the tardiness of my reply."

"Were you ever happy?" Jordan's face was slightly ashen.

I rubbed my sternum. "Yes, occasionally. I had a friend once. We met three times, near the lavender brook and made boats of lily leaves." I smiled at the memory, but my smile ran its course and faded. "He no longer met me after they gave him his drone. Once assigned drones, training limits free time. Perhaps I was less content than some, but I was content." A thought suddenly struck me, and I was disturbed that it had not occurred to me before. "Max . . . You were looking for someone."

He met my eyes directly as he had years ago and nodded.

Aware that I trespassed by asking, I asked nonetheless, "Did you ever find the person you sought?"

"No," he said, his voice rough. "Neither of them."

"Them . . ." The words felt pulled from me. "Do you seek them still?"

Jordan had stepped to his side and rested a hand on his back. I gripped his hands in mine, staring up into his nut-brown eyes.

"Yes," he said quietly. "And I always will. Always."

He turned and left without another word.

Jordan followed him.

I felt as if I had stabbed his heart, and oh, I wished I had not spoken.

Nate placed his hand on my wrist. "I'm glad you told him."

"Max, of all people, should not be so defeated." It hurt me, that Max was hurting. He had given me a glimpse of what family might have been like. If I had not been gifted away, if I had a father, I would have wanted him to be like Max.

Kyleigh, Nate, and I left together, the silence between us thundering like the roar of a ship's engines. She bade us a teary good night, and Nate walked me to my quarters. I dashed a solitary tear from my cheek and managed a smile before the door closed between us.

As I stood alone in my quarters, without the invisible light which had made life beautiful before I learned of beauty beyond mere color, before I had friends, determination pumped through my veins. I had another reason to break into my old quarters. Whoever they were, I would find them. Max deserved to know.

43

Robert first asked her to marry him when they stood on the hotel balcony, watching Ceres's twin moons set and the sun creep over the ocean.

She turned away from the sky to lean against the railing. The first rays of the new year gilded the black curls tumbling down her back and outlined her slim hands with gold. She shook her head. "You're too young, Robert, and I'm too old."

Chiding himself for getting it wrong, he ran his fingers over her bare arms and tried again.

"Marriage. Such an old word." She wrapped her arms around his neck under his long braids. "Why?"

"Because I adore you," he murmured into her hair, and though she didn't answer, she kissed him.

He didn't mention it again for the rest of their trip, and once home, they fell into their regular routines of work and music and life.

On the symphony's opening night, however, he waited for her near the exit while the other musicians filed out of the hall after the performance, turning his grandmother's pearl ring over and over in his jacket pocket. When she finally arrived, he took the viola case and her arm, as usual, and they walked the two kilometers home. The noise and bustle faded as they entered the residential district, and familiar peacefulness settled around them. The streetlights' soft spheres of radiance created a sense of safety, like the tents he and his dad had made in the dining room after dinner when he was young.

While he'd loved the sky, the stars, the soft touch of real wind on his skin during their trip to Ceres, Albany City's lofty, riveted domes were home. *She* was home.

It was after midnight when they passed the community gardens. He paused and broke off a sprig of night-blooming jasmine to tuck in her hair like stars in a night sky, and a smile lit her tired face.

His hand found the ring in his pocket, small, cool, and smooth. His heart beat faster, but he couldn't manage the words, and the moment passed.

Once the front door closed behind them, she tossed her wrap onto the overstuffed chaise lounge. He set the viola case on the table and watched her pull out the pins that imprisoned her hair. Curls tumbled down in a riot of silky black, and the jasmine fell with them. She picked it up, twirling the stem, and her forehead puckered. Faint shadows under her eyes told him she needed to rest, but her expression suggested something further.

He tucked a curl behind her ear. "What's bothering you?"

She shook her head, and when he placed a light kiss on her palm, an almost imperceptible blush stole across her face. Then, threading their fingers, he studied the way hers tapered delicately between his long blunt-tipped ones.

He drew in a long breath. "I want us to be together forever."

She sighed. "Nothing lasts forever, Robert."

"I love you."

"I know." She averted her gaze. "You know I love you, too?"

"Yes." He lifted her chin and met the silver-grey eyes which had first caught his attention. "Will you—"

"I'm pregnant."

It was as if his heart stopped. He couldn't answer.

"I'm pregnant," she repeated, watching him carefully, "with twins."

A smile broke across his face.

"You're pleased?" she whispered.

He couldn't find the right words, so he lifted her in his arms and spun in a circle, joy bubbling out in a laugh.

"Yes, I am." He kissed her soundly. "Will you marry me now?"

"Maybe." Her smile lessened the worry around the corners of her eyes.

Robert gave her his grandmother's pearl ring, and she wore it to make him happy.

He would have been happier if she'd said yes.

He couldn't go into her appointments since they had no legal contract, but he accompanied her to every single one and waited in the ugly reception rooms. The doctors cautioned her that her pregnancy might be difficult because she had passed the "advanced" age of forty-five a few years before, that there could be complications for her or medical issues with the babies.

Robert threatened mock revenge on the doctors who called her old and teased her back into laughter when she cried as her waistline disappeared. They found out the twins were a boy and a girl and talked about names.

In the mornings, he held her hair back when she was sick.

"I hate you," she groaned, spitting bile into the toilet.

"No, you don't." He wiped her face with a damp cloth. "Not really."

She glared up at him, her eyes bloodshot and skin clammy.

His lips brushed her forehead. "This morning, that's completely reasonable."

She smiled weakly before she threw up again.

They celebrated Robert's birthday at their favorite restaurant, and he made a late-night run for kimchi and ice cream after they came home. He scooped out enough strawberry swirl for two and handed her the bowl and then, dropping to his knee, asked her to marry him again.

She shoved the bowl away. "Why do you keep asking that? And why do you use that archaic term? People don't 'get married.' They have contracts. We live in the Colonies, not Medieval Earth."

He sank into the chair next to her. "I want us to be a family. I want to teach them to be good people. Because I love you, and I already love our children. Marriage is more than a contract. It's deeper, and that's what I want. *You're* what I want. I suppose I'm a romantic at heart."

"Yes, you are," she said, softening. She reached for the bowl, then paused and took his outstretched hand instead. "It's why I love you, but sometimes . . ."

"Sometimes?"

She seemed to be memorizing the sight of her fingers in his. "You are so young."

"I'm not," he protested, rubbing his thumb over her knuckles.

Her gaze fell to the pearl on her third finger. "Robert, I'm more than twenty years older than you. You won't want to stay, and I can't bear it without you."

"Then marry me. That way you'll know."

She shook her head, long curls bouncing in contrast to the tension in her eyes, and after a few moments of silence, she pulled her hand away, moved onto his lap, and traced his jawline with her fingers. He closed his eyes and breathed in the scent of strawberries and jasmine.

She whispered, "Don't leave me," and then kissed him.

The next morning, Robert went with her to the appointment at the new, glass facility and waited for her on the red synthleather chairs in the lobby. The doors slid apart, but she only stood there, her face drained of color, her hands clenched around expensive paper brochures.

Paper brochures, he lied to himself, did not mean anything in particular.

Robert rose from the uncomfortable chair to meet her, and she fell against his chest and sobbed. The other patients and their support partners turned away.

"Let's go home," he said.

When she didn't respond, he scooped her up and cradled her to his heart. The walk would be too long, so he hailed a private transport, and she wept in silent, body-wracking sobs the whole way.

By the time he had settled her on the chaise lounge his heart was beating like a kettle drum. He swallowed down a creeping sense of dread and said, in his most soothing voice, the one he cultivated for difficult patients, "Tell me."

She shot him an anguished look, then thrust the crumpled brochures into his outstretched hand, but the words swam on the creased papers.

"I don't understand."

"How could you not understand that?" she snapped. "Defective. The male is defective."

He wanted to protest that their son was James, not "the male," but he only repeated, "Tell me."

"The tests indicate that he—that *it*—will most likely . . . that it has genetic markers. It won't be normal. They talked about cellular dysfunction and . . . delays." She broke off in tears again.

He waited.

She choked out the words, "People don't have children like this anymore. Not for centuries. The female will probably be defective, too, though they didn't say so. Don't you see? They'll never be normal. They'll *appear* normal on the outside, but on the inside? No."

A little part of him, the hopes and dreams, died, withered, collapsed like a dying star. He foresaw medical appointments, counseling, and therapies. The challenges which would set this pair of children apart from their peers, and which would set the two of them apart from other parents, loomed before him. He foresaw isolation, friends drifting away when difficulties grew uncomfortable. His role as a father wouldn't be the one he'd planned, but he set his jaw in that moment when his dreams died, because his love didn't.

"It'll be all right," he pushed a wayward curl off her high forehead, noting a few twisting strands of silver in her dark hair. He brought the curl to his lips, then let it go. "Whatever it is, we can get through it together. There are behavioral therapies and nutritional therapies and other tests. We have nanotechnology now, and any manner of treatments."

She jolted upright. "You're a doctor, Robert. You understand what genetics mean!"

He drew back, shook his head. "We're more than the raw combinations of our DNA."

"Don't you see? I can't do this. I can't deal with damaged children."

"We'll figure it out."

"I'm too old."

"Stop, just stop." He held out his hand, but she didn't take it. "You're forgetting I'm here, too. I'll do what it takes. *We'll* do what it takes. We'll make it work."

She stared at him, her face swollen and blotchy from tears.

"I love you, remember?" he said. "And I love them. No matter what."

She didn't answer. He could almost see her mind racing, but she gave him no clue to her thoughts.

She stood slowly and rubbed the small of her back. "I'm going to shower and go to bed."

"Do you need anything?" he asked, although he really meant, *do you need me?*

She said, "No."

That night, she turned away from him and cried silently into her pillow instead of resting on his shoulder. Robert lay, arm behind his head, and stared at the ceiling.

How could he feel full of loss if loss was empty? How could a heart be full to the brim of nothingness? That morning, life had held *hope*, and the disparity hurt even more.

Neither of them spoke of the pregnancy over the next few days. She didn't want to be touched, and though he missed the closeness, missed the babies kicking and rolling under his hand, he knew she needed time. When he put in extra hours at the hospital, she didn't protest his absence.

On her birthday, however, he took her to a spa for pampering, then set up dinner on their deck. Since she rebuffed his attempts at conversation, they ate in comparative silence, and after they finished, he brought out the small cake he had ordered from her favorite bakery.

She waved at the candles. "I'm old now."

"No, you're not. And even if you were, I wouldn't care. It's not like I'm getting younger."

She flinched, and Robert groaned inwardly. He'd said the wrong thing. Again.

"You're much younger than I." The candles sputtered out. "I don't want defective children."

"They aren't defective. I know this won't be easy—"

"My second trimester is almost over. In another ten-day, I'll be far enough along to gift."

His blood turned to ice. "What?"

"Yes." She said it in a voice devoid of emotion, but she might as well have hit him. "I can't do this. You're young, Robert. Sooner or later, you'll leave."

"No, I won't." He drew a deep breath, fought down both rising anger and panic. "Why do you think I keep asking you to marry me?"

She pushed her chair away from the small, round table. "You're doing well at the hospital. At some point, you will need to go places, do things. You won't want an old woman with you, and I will not care for these on my own."

"You won't need to, because I'm *not* leaving," he repeated.

Her belly rolled, and she absently rubbed it, then stopped. Her hands curled into fists, and she stood and shoved them into her tunic pockets.

Robert also rose, his pulse thundering in his head, but all he could manage was, "Don't do this."

She rounded on him in fury. "You can't tell me what to do! It isn't like we're contracted or *married*!"

He tried to keep his tone even. "These are my children, too."

"Without a contract, they aren't. You have no say." Her voice was tight. "This is my decision."

He swallowed down bile. "You can't give our children away. We can figure this out."

"I can." Her jaw clenched, yet her silver eyes glistened with moisture. "And I will." She removed his grandmother's ring and dropped it on his empty plate. The faint chime of platinum hitting china faded, and the pearl shone like a tear. "There is no 'we.' Not anymore."

"I can afford a medtank for them," he pled.

Her lips pressed into a firm line, and she walked to the door.

He sprang up and caught her arm. "Don't destroy my children. I love them. I love you."

But the truth hit him like an electrical shock. His heart had fractured, and his love for her was fracturing, too. And she saw it. A single drop fell and splattered on her tunic, but she didn't move. He dropped his hands.

"This is not destruction. Destruction is both illegal and immoral." Her voice, though calm, reverberated in his ears. "This is giving life. The Consortium exists to serve and to save. If I gift them . . ." She faltered, waving her ringless hand at her swollen belly. "They will be cared for. They will have the guidance they need, the support they require, and they'll serve a higher purpose for the common good, holding a place in society, whether as service staff or Recorders or whatever role they *can* fill."

"But"—his voice broke—"they won't be loved. Let me have them. Let me love them."

For a moment, he thought she wavered, but then she sighed. "It's a good thing I never said yes." What might have been compassion, though the idea mocked him, shone in her silvery eyes. "It's a good thing we never entered into a contract. You won't want this burden, Robert, not after you consider the matter. They will *never* be truly functional and would crush you like a black hole. I will bear this on my own, but you can start again with someone else. I am sorry."

She touched his face, then, slinging her satchel over her shoulder and hugging it close to her chest, walked to the door and picked up her viola. "You can do what you want with my things. I have what I need. I won't be back. Even though I'm right, you'll never forgive me."

The door closed behind her, and his world shattered.

Sleep eluded me, so I went to the kitchen for water and some fruit, then headed to work on the drones. There, in the partially lit storage bay, deep in the ones and not-ones, I searched for patterns that would allow me access to my old quarters. If I could find it, if I could but unravel the codes, I could add the layers to the identification bracelet. I could escape without endangering my friends.

I could, perhaps, locate the people Max sought.

Nate found me eventually. He adopted his typical pose against the doorframe, watching silently for several minutes, while I tried to ignore him.

"Did you even eat breakfast?"

"Yes."

"Then I need you to come with me," he said. "We'll reach Lunar One tomorrow, and you've a few more things to do."

Realization struck. He was correct, and the list of things I needed to finish stretched before me like pi. I had not disabled the camera in the hangar. My tampering with an AAVA drone was recorded. My friends' presence going in and out of my laboratory had been documented. So many things . . . I rubbed the heels of my hands against my eyes. True, I could reprogram the recording devices after I finished here, but I needed to disable the devices randomly in other areas as well. I had too much to accomplish. "I cannot, Timmons."

"Nate, remember?"

I turned, resting the small of my back against the table. "I remember. Using your surname was an attempt to express displeasure at your command. You have no right to issue me orders."

His dimple peeked at me. "If you have to explain what you meant, your word choice wasn't effective."

"What is it you need, Nate?"

"I need you." He flushed. "I mean, you need to come with me."

"I beg your pardon?"

"You have lessons." He stepped into the hangar and joined me at the table. "Why are you messing with these blasted drones again?"

"What lessons?" I asked.

He glanced at me, then glared at the drones. "Self-defense."

"Because of the incident with Elliott?"

"In part." He picked up a broken piece of my drone, turning it over in his hands. "To use archaic language, you need to be able to 'fend off unwanted advances.'"

"I know what to do."

He put the piece down carefully, as if precise movements would make his point. "You need to react automatically, without thinking."

"That type of response takes time I do not have. My current knowledge and training must suffice." I glanced up at the recording device I needed to disable. "I have other priorities."

"Not good enough." His voice was sharp. "If someone got too close, what would you do?"

"I would ask him or her to leave."

Nate grabbed my wrist and stepped into my personal space.

I tried to pull away. "Let go of my wrist. You are distracting me from something truly important."

"What would you do?"

"This is not amusing, Nathaniel Timmons." I glared up at him. "I must finish my work."

"If you are out on your own, and if no one is with you, you have to act." He took hold of my shoulders. "If I were Elliott, what would you do?"

"You are not Elliott. You would never . . ." I looked up into his eyes and promptly forgot what I had meant to say. I should have been thinking of the coding, of Max, of securing the systems, but I wondered again what Nate's hair felt like or if he had shaved right before he came to find me. His cheeks appeared smooth, touchable. Was touchable a word? I could not recall. His grip changed, loosened but drew me in.

"That's not going to help." His tenor dropped in pitch.

"What will not help?" My own voice sounded strange to my ears.

"Stars . . ." His hands slid from my wrist to behind my back, and it occurred to me that he had nice, solid arms. "When you look at me like that—"

"Not interrupting anything, am I?" Spanos asked.

Nate's arms stiffened and he released me. Pink suffused his cheeks, and heat rushed to mine, as well.

"Maybe it's a good thing Zhen agreed to go over those self-defense lessons, Tim." Spanos's mouth quirked. "Don't know that you'd be able to keep on task."

Nate growled.

Spanos gave a bark of laughter. "Recorder-who-isn't, do you need a safe escort?"

"I do not understand. Do you and Nate intend to accompany me somewhere?"

"Nate?" Spanos asked, eyes wider than usual. "I haven't heard that since university. She gets to call you Nate?"

"Shut it, Alec."

I glanced from one to the other. "I assure you, I could walk by myself, if I needed to go anywhere, but I am not leaving. I am currently occupied."

"Yes." Spanos arced a thick brow. "I can see that. You certainly looked occupied."

Nate shot him a glare. "If you aren't . . . I'll head back over to the chem system. Make sure everything's in place."

Spanos grinned. "Coward," he said, just as his communication link chimed.

DuBois's disembodied voice said, "Tim hasn't shown up with the Recorder yet. Could you track them down?"

"Found 'em. Interesting story, too." Spanos laughed, denying DuBois the chance to respond.

"Fine." Nate turned to me. "I'll accompany you to the gym."

"I did not agree to abandon my work." I gestured at the table. "It is of utmost importance."

Spanos scowled at the drones. "What're you doing with those voided things?"

DuBois's voice was slightly tinny over the communications link. "What things?"

"She's messing with those drones. There's no good reason to be dealing with them anymore."

"Yes, there is," I said. "But I do not wish to discuss it."

Spanos started toward me, and Nate moved between us. "Back off, Alec."

I stepped around him. "I will tell you, Alexander Spanos. I must find a way to access my old quarters if I am to leave. All evidence of any work done to enable my escape *must be* erased. If I fail in this, you all are at risk. If I succeed, however, then even if the work is discovered, blame will be solely mine. Mine alone. This is more important than self-defense, so I will decline your offer. Thank you all for your kind intentions." I did not allow myself to look at Nate. "This is essential. Most essential."

"Moons and stars," DuBois exclaimed. "Is that what you were trying to tell me earlier?"

I sighed. "I do not know if I can gain access to my old quarters, which would allow me to utilize the Consortium's network to connect to the databases on New Triton. If I can do that, I can reprogram the bracelet."

Spanos whistled, and DuBois asked, "In real time? I thought we'd lost that tech."

"The Consortium has the capability. But perhaps I should not have told you."

Nate scowled. "How much trouble did you just get in by saying that?"

I focused on the blank wall behind Spanos. "I will have no trouble at all once I delete everything, including this conversation. This is the only self-defense I can afford right now."

"Don't like it," Spanos muttered.

"Self-defense lesson cancelled." DuBois paused. "Would you like my help?"

I hesitated. "While I am grateful for the offer, not only am I faster than you are, but I do not want your—how did you say it?—your fingerprints on this."

Spanos glanced at the drones, then at the doors. "This place isn't secure enough if you're messing with stuff like that. I'll add an extra lock. I'm pretty sure I can make up an excuse for that. I'll get to it before lunch."

"I will not be joining you," I said.

Nate glared at the wall. "You'll forget to eat. I'll bring you something."

"Thank you, but please tell Kyleigh I shall not be able to visit her with the cats today." The likelihood of seeing them again was small, and the knowledge pulled at me like a whirlpool. "Although this is the correct course of action, I find it difficult to leave you all."

I found it disheartening when the communication piece chirped as DuBois disconnected the link without replying.

Spanos cleared his throat. "I'll let Jordan know what we've been talking about, then start the paper trail for the new lock."

"Should the necessity of discussion arise, my computer laboratory is the most secure location." I rubbed my palms dry on my leggings. "Please excuse me. I have work to do."

Nate put a hand on my arm but said nothing, and I felt as if I had lost something indefinable when he left. Spanos and I stood in momentary, uncomfortable silence.

"I ought to trust you by now, but it's hard, you know?"

"I know," I said quietly. "I understand. It is well."

When Spanos left me alone with the defunct drones, the hangar felt larger and emptier than before. It took seven minutes to refocus, then the work swallowed me.

My concentration was interrupted again when Spanos returned with the additional magnetic lock. After he finished, he pulled out his string of beads and ran them through his fingers.

"Recorder?"

"Yes?"

"I'm sorry about all this."

"It is well, Spanos. None of this is your doing." I returned my focus to the disassembled drone.

"I didn't make it easy for you, though. It isn't your fault either. Can we start over, for the time you've got left?"

"I do not understand your meaning."

He pushed a long curl behind his ear and blew out a gust of air. Then, a brilliant smile stretched across his face and filled his chocolate-brown eyes, and he extended his right fist. "My name is Alec Spanos. It's nice to meet you."

When I did not move, he reached out, folded my hand into a fist, and tapped it with his own. "You know, you need to work harder at this whole social interaction thing."

"Spanos," I began, but he interrupted me.

"Alec," he said. "Call me Alec."

He nodded once and left me staring after him with my mouth open, like a tilapia from the Consortium's ponds. It took me another thirteen minutes to immerse myself again in my work.

Long after I normally retired, Nate and Jordan found me working on the drones.

"It's late," Jordan said without preamble. "You need to be functional and alert in a few hours. You've got to get some sleep."

I held up one hand as I finished reading the glowing projection of green, amber, and cyan, and a minute later I stepped back, rolling my neck to relieve the tension and smothering a yawn. "I have it."

"Good," Jordan said. "Now get some rest. Work later."

"No, I have too much to do." I transferred the information to my blue datapad and began wiping the drone's memory clean. "With this, I can hide all traces of your assistance and can adjust the invisible light markers on the identification band. You will be safe, and I can disappear."

Jordan rested her hand on my shoulder. "We've already been over that."

"Additionally"—I hesitated—"I have another purpose."

While Nate merely raised one eyebrow, Jordan folded her arms. "What do you mean?"

"It is also for Max." I kept my eyes on hers. "I wish to locate the people he seeks. The Consortium's records are excellent, so when I access them to add markers to the bracelet, I can search for them. Max deserves to know—" I yawned again. "I must finish before we reach the station. I will rest later."

"All right." Jordan nodded slowly. "If that's what you need to do."

"Unacceptable." Nate ran his fingers through his hair. "If you don't rest, you won't make it out of here tomorrow."

"If I cannot hide everyone completely, Nate, I will not go. I will not sleep until I finish clearing the records."

A muscle in Nate's jaw twitched. "You don't get to go making grand statements, saying you're not going if you don't finish."

"Actually, Tim, she does. It isn't that I agree with you, Recorder," Jordan said, "but I will support whatever you decide."

"No." He did not even glance at her, but kept his gaze locked on me. "You're not going back. You are getting out of here if I have to knock you out and carry you off this ship in a bag."

Jordan shook her head. "Tim, don't bully her."

I tapped my thigh. "Please, *please* understand that I do not wish to return. I have had a rare glimpse of freedom, and do not wish to lose it, but it is not worth your safety. Not to me. My entire childhood, I dreamed of a family and friends." I swallowed and picked up my datapad, holding it to my chest as if it could shield me from my words. "I realize you are not my family, that I will never have family, but you are my friends. I cannot leave you unprotected." I glanced up at Nate, then back to Jordan. "Do not allow Nate to act mistakenly as Gervase Singh did. It is not the same, I know, but the consequences would be similar."

Color drained from her face. "I've never told him," she whispered. "I've never told anyone."

Nate's eyes narrowed as he glanced between us. "What are you talking about?"

She did not answer, and somehow, she looked smaller, younger.

"Ten years ago"—I ignored her faint noise of protest—"her cousin became involved with a Recorder while finishing his senior year at Albany City University. They were documented together after hours while her drone charged. When they attempted to flee, they were apprehended. The Recorder was tried for her betrayal. Gervase Singh was convicted of undermining and corrupting the records and of subverting a Recorder. He was, of course, removed."

"Stars, J." Nate pushed his bangs back. "That's why he vanished?"

She closed her eyes and nodded.

"You could've told me."

She shook her head. "They threatened my family if anyone said anything. I couldn't. It's not your fault. Not mine. Maybe not even Gerry's or his Recorder's." She looked past us. "I've been going over that in my head for the past ten years. The night Gerry disappeared, the night I left

Albany City, my father said a few things that I hope meant Ger was just sent to work in the mines on the belts."

It was likely, though I did not share my thought.

Nate's green eyes fastened on mine. "What happened to her? To the Recorder?"

"She was—she has been . . ."

"She's been what?"

I looked away. "Suffice it to say his fate was preferable to hers."

"What could be worse than being removed from everyone you know, and your identity stripped away with no chance to escape? To a life of hard, dangerous, unpaid labor?" Jordan's eyebrows pinched together, and perhaps she paled further. "What did happen to her?"

Pushing away the unwanted memory of rows of medical stasis pods extending into the shadows, my stomach knotting, I tried not to think of it. "Primary reclamation."

"What does that even mean?" she asked.

Nate studied me. "Are you risking that, whatever it is?"

I could answer neither of them. The white noise of the circulation fans was very loud.

Jordan straightened, and her jaw clenched. "That settles the question, then. You need to get off this ship as soon as you can."

I forced a smile. "Believe it or not, I intend to be on the first shuttle. I do not wish to return to the Consortium."

"You don't have a name yet. You need one." Jordan nodded toward the door. "We should let you work."

"You didn't answer my question." Nate made no move to depart. "We have a meeting first thing, but you can't leave without saying goodbye. Tell me then."

And, moons and stars, I did not want to leave him. "Please do nothing that will arouse suspicion, Nate." It hurt to say them, but I forced the words out. "Even if it means not saying goodbye."

His chest rose and fell quickly. I could see the pulse in his temple. "I'll find you as soon as I can."

"Please do nothing rash. I could not bear it."

I spun abruptly on my heels and left them in the hangar.

The ship's general communication system startled me awake three hours later. I had dozed off standing at my terminal. Fortunately, I remained standing while I slept and had not collapsed onto the computer. Even more fortunately, I had logged off, so I did not transmit bizarre, illogical information, which could have revealed me after all.

Officer Smith's nasal voice twanged over the ship's communication system. "While docking, artificial gravity will be offline. Secure yourselves, and any liquid or loose substances. Damage incurred will be levied against your personal accounts. Meals will resume after artificial gravity is back online. Personnel approved for two-hour leave may board the shuttles after decontamination is complete. Have papers and identification ready before departure. Refueling will take between eight and nine hours, and all business must be concluded within that time."

Not even unsettled emotions could push away my fatigue. I stretched before retrieving my magnetic blanket, which was exactly where it should have been. After ascertaining the cleaning bots were stowed properly, I attached the blanket before strapping myself into my seat, and the magnets clicked into place on my other side. The fractals on the walls and the puzzles on the sliding tiles still undoubtedly glowed in ultraviolet. The aphorism projected on the polished steel opposite my bed would have changed from *Clarity of mind is the gateway to personal peace* to some other saying. And while I could still feel the rhythm of the subsonic music, the nuances were lost to me. The faint scents I associated with my old dormitory were, most likely, wafting through the room, beyond my perception.

Without my drone, it was an empty, barren room. It was no longer mine.

In a few hours, I would have neither my identity as a Recorder nor my friends. But I would be free. Sleep claimed me immediately. I did not even notice when artificial gravity resumed its steady purr and ushered in the three-hour decontamination process.

My communication link was chiming. Hoping I had sufficient coherence to answer, I slid my arm up under the blanket to tap it.

"Recorder," Adrienne Smith's disembodied voice said over the link. "Your presence is requested in Captain North's office."

I blinked to clear the sleep from my eyes and struggled to unfasten the magnetic clasps. "Very well. Eight minutes." I terminated the link.

The designation of "Recorder" no longer felt like who I was, but I centered myself to become her again. I splashed water on my face, hoping fatigue would not be too obvious, but when my fingers touched the hair on my scalp, I paused. No mirror hung over the small sink, for a Recorder needed none. I ran my fingers through the two-and-a-half-centimeter growth and over the welt-like scars. The memory of John Westruther's disordered curls, not much longer than my own hair, made me dampen it down. Straightening my tunic, I left my datapad and the recoded identification bracelet in a drawer under clean clothes and took a deep breath.

It was time.

The door whispered shut behind me, and I headed to the captain's office. People spilled into the hallways on their way to duty, meals, or the shuttles, though this time, a few met my eyes and even smiled.

When I entered the room, Captain North swiveled his blue synthleather chair to face me. Officer Genet was not present, but the communications officer stood by the captain's chair, fidgeting.

Without salutation, Captain North said, "Genet and Smith have noted discrepancies with our ship's recordings."

Somehow, I neither flinched nor lifted my eyebrows. He would have discerned neither my elevated heart rate nor my fluctuating skin temperature. He would not have noticed my pupils dilating or contracting. The quality of the records here would be insufficient to lay evidence against me. Perhaps I would have time to alter them as well. I told myself he could not know of all I had done.

Suppressing my agitation, I said, "This is simply information. Do you wish me to record it?"

"No," he snapped. "I'd hardly need you for that!"

"Sir!" Adrienne Smith interjected.

The captain ignored her and glowered at me. "Since you have nothing else to do, I want you to look into the matter."

"I shall investigate it," I said. "However, I have been working with Venetia Jordan's team, sorting and reorganizing the data from the research station, which is hardly 'nothing.'"

"Oh, I know all about that." His chin jutted forward. "And don't think that information won't find its way where it belongs. We've let it go, but don't think you, or Jordan and the rest of her—"

"Sir!" Officer Smith said again. Her eyes flitted around the room, landing on everything but me. "Recorder, we realize your accident has altered the way you . . . altered everything. We've included this information in our reports."

"Out of line, Smith," the captain barked, and she subsided, seeming to shrink back down into herself.

Forcing down the trepidation his threat inspired, I set my jaw, caught his eyes, and spoke without inflection. "Regardless of my injuries and the disastrous nature of this expedition, you must recall that until such a time as I am relieved of my duties by the Eldest, I still bear the full weight of the Consortium's authority on this voyage. Your attitude reflects disrespect toward the Eldest herself and will be logged as such." Grasping the opportunity he had inadvertently offered, I added, "Since I have no drone, after we have cleared decontamination, I shall disembark and take the records to a secure location, transmitting them to the proper authorities for internal adjudication."

Officer Smith blanched. Captain North's face took on a greenish tint.

I left.

I truly was not a Recorder, for despite my fear, speaking as one and witnessing the captain's discomfiture had granted me more pleasure than it should.

I selected only a mug of tea at breakfast. Nate and Max would have chastised me had they been present, but after the meeting with North, I was uncertain of my ability to take the first shuttle off *Thalassa*, and my stomach would not tolerate food. I made my way to my usual table, and DuBois nodded at me, her eyes glancing at my bare wrist, then away.

Kyleigh lethargically shoved food around her plate. Her color was good, and she seemed well rested, but she did not speak, only threw sidelong glances in my direction. Elliott entered alone and made his way to the table.

"Can I sit here?"

"No," DuBois snapped. "There's an empty chair in the back." She slid her tray down the table next to mine.

Elliott mumbled an apology and left for the other side of the room.

"My apologies, Kyleigh, but I cannot assist you with the cats this morning." How did I tell her goodbye or tell her my plans had changed, if only slightly? "I must check something for the captain."

"Oh." Her eyes watered, and she pushed her tray away. "It's all right, I checked them already." She paused. "You weren't around yesterday. You might not have heard about Freddie?"

A separate anxiety grabbed me, and I set my tea down. "Is he . . . ?" I could not bring myself to ask.

"Oh, no," she said quickly. "It's just, his vitals are still slipping, so Max has to get him out of the tank today. Lunar One has better medical facilities, so this might be the best chance he has."

I did not know whether to be relieved or more concerned.

Alec set his tray down next to DuBois, who was studying me as she might a challenging zoological specimen. I stood to leave, but I needed to let someone know of the altered plans.

After thirty seconds of consideration, I addressed DuBois. "This morning I was summoned to a meeting in which North requested I investigate apparent records tampering. I must relay some information through a central node, and although I intend to board the first shuttle in approximately two hours, should the investigation take longer, I hope to take the one after that."

She shrugged slightly. "Fine by me. I don't want to be on a shuttle with you anyway."

Alec winced. "Babe . . ."

I had not meant to antagonize her. Ignoring the omnipresent lump in my throat, I picked up my empty mug. "I wish you a pleasant excursion."

"Wait. Here." Alec shoved a protein bar into my hand. "You shouldn't work on an empty stomach."

I thanked him and left. How could a protein bar make me want to cry?

Decontamination procedures completed, the first shuttle was boarding by the time I finished reviewing the information Smith and Genet had uncovered, and I fought the urge to neglect my duties and run from my old quarters to the shuttle bay. Every second ticking past was one step further from freedom.

Yet, the captain's assertion that someone had tampered with the records was more correct than he knew. I had not been alone in deleting information. Someone without my finesse had erased clusters of data, starting on 478.1.8.07, fifteen days ago. I leaned back away from the console, my hands clenching and unclenching at my sides.

The deleted material was primarily focused on the infirmary, the small lab that processed the samples from the station, my computer laboratory, the sleeping quarters near mine, and hallways. Data was crudely erased and replaced with violent static, as had been done with the station recordings, though not as crudely as the deletion from the hallway on seventh-day past. It was the simplest method of altering records but was too great a coincidence to be coincidence at all.

On a whim, I accessed the infirmary recordings of Ross emerging from stasis. He had the datapad Elliott had given him, and I watched DuBois test it. It contained his family images and nothing else. So that was not evidence.

Why would anyone, other than I, seek to delete ship's recordings? What was there, other than my own illegal activity, to hide?

I paced and reviewed what I knew, what I had viewed in VVR: the discovery of the virus, the likely link to Kyleigh's father, John Westruther's meetings, the station's inhabitants climbing into the stasis pods, the four people who remained behind . . . I opened the files to review those recordings again.

They were gone.

In the space of time it took to pace through my old quarters five times, someone had deleted them. I tried to pull up all the ship's data, but every recording—every single one—was damaged, and all devices were offline, only generating static. Who would have—

I froze. I could not have been so imperceptive. Tapping my communication link, I contacted Jordan and Nate.

Jordan said, "DuBois just told me about your new investigation—"

"I require your presence, and Nate's, in my computer laboratory," I interrupted. "At once. This is important, Jordan."

After a brief pause, she said, "We'll be there, but we have to finish inspecting the backup chem systems."

"And I have to secure them when we're done," Nate added. "Shouldn't be more than ten, fifteen minutes."

I said nothing more, merely terminated the link.

With recording devices throughout the ship disabled, I ran to my laboratory unconcerned that my actions would be documented. Mentally berating myself for obtuseness, the cramp in my side made me slow at the final corner, holding my side.

But review and verification were essential. I needed to check my own computers.

When I reached the laboratory, neither Nate nor Jordan had arrived. However, the voices of Elliott and Julian Ross were audible through the unsealed door, a foolish mistake if they required privacy. I pressed against the wall and purposefully eavesdropped.

Julian Ross snorted. "And whose fault is that? You grabbed that Recorder and mauled her for no good reason. I hope *you* at least enjoyed it. She didn't, and now no one trusts you, even given her bizarre attitude."

"It's not like I wanted to kiss someone like her!"

"Well, you can't go around kissing people without consent. Good stars above!"

Indignation burned through my chest. I had not wished Elliott's attention, but his assertion somehow made the incident worse.

"I didn't see you asking Jordan first."

"Ah. That's entirely different. She wanted it."

My hands curled into fists.

"You practically told me to kiss her—"

"No!" Chair legs scraped across flooring. His words flew out sharply, like weapons' fire. "I never wanted you to risk yourself like that! The others would take care of it. They'll have a way to introduce the devices via some kind of fluid that—"

"You said blood or saliva or—"

"I said that they had a plan, a plan which you nearly ruined. The timing was all wrong." Ross's voice slowed slightly as he continued, "Though if she'd gotten sick, it might've been all right."

"But you didn't say anything about making her sick. You just said it would stop them, and that's all I wanted."

"Elliott. How else did you think it was going to work?" Footsteps paced the room. "Something must be wrong with the delivery system. Just sit tight until I have a good lab to finish work on your blood sample."

The pulse pounding in my ears drowned out the next words he spoke. I blamed myself for not tracing the deletion of records to Julian Ross sooner. How had I missed so broadly?

"Blast it, Julian." Elliott's distinct footsteps indicated he had risen to his feet. "You can't leave me. You're all I've got!"

There were indecipherable noises before Ross said, "Calm down. I'll find you when it's done, when we're safe."

There was a pause. "You'll make it back?"

"I'll do my best."

"You're sure?"

Ross's tone sharpened. "Stop questioning me. They'll get me a lab, and I'll figure it out. The captain granted me shore leave to report the necessary data to the *university*. You stay calm. No one will think twice about you, although I'll say again that mauling the Recorder was supremely stupid."

Elliott mumbled something.

"Venn's distracted. That will give me a chance to get out of here."

Unfamiliar rage burned inside me while I backtracked down the hall and tapped my communication link, asking for Captain North.

"Captain," I said in an undertone, "I have discovered the individual who has altered your records. The perpetrator is Julian Ross. He is currently in the computer laboratory on Deck B. Send security immediately."

I signed off without waiting for a response, then tiptoed back to the doorway. The brothers' disagreement seemed to have resolved, for their tones had changed.

"Yes," Ross was saying, "I know, but her assets make up for it. Haven't enjoyed that kind of athleticism in some time."

Manipulating Jordan, however reprehensible, was insignificant compared with his other actions, but I could not let it stand. Without stopping to consider the rash nature of my decision, I slammed the door into its pocket and faced the pair of them, seething. If emotions alone could have triumphed, the Ross brothers would have had no chance.

Elliott spun around, and Ross jumped up from my chair, his handsome face flushed.

"Step away from my computer," I commanded. "Security officers will arrive shortly, and you, Julian Meredith Ross, will turn yourself over to the authorities for your crimes here and on the research station."

Ross's blue eyes burned like fire. His jaw clenched. He towered over Elliott, whose mouth opened and closed soundlessly. Ross moved carefully and precisely toward me.

I glared up at him. "You are charged with illegally creating a virus for the purpose of endangering and killing citizens. For behaving as an accessory in the willful murder of Dr. Charles Tristram."

"Liar!" Elliott shouted.

"For the destruction of records at the research station and here on this ship. For altering the safety protocols and killing seventy-nine people. For encouraging another to act against the general codes of conduct and assault a Recorder. Turn yourself in. Anything you say or do will be entered into the Record and may be legally used against you."

The laboratory was so quiet that our breathing was audible.

"No." From less than a meter away, Julian Ross sneered down at me. "You might not realize it," he clearly enunciated each word, "but I've deactivated the security recordings on this deck. There is no record. And you, Recorder, have no drone. You can do nothing. Turn myself in? I don't think so."

"I do not want to hurt you," I said, sincerely, if dishonestly.

Julian Ross laughed and then lunged. I ducked under his arms, spun behind him, and swung a kick at the back of his right leg. It buckled. He fell to his knees, and I kicked again. He pitched sideways, head connecting with the door frame in a hollow thud. Ross pushed himself upright and got to his feet, blinking rapidly against the blood running in scarlet ribbons from his hairline.

"Julian!" Elliott dashed past me to his brother.

I realized then that I had erred, and disgust at my multiple mistakes battled fear. My primary error was not making the connections earlier. My secondary error was confronting them alone. My tertiary error was missing my opportunity to leave, since they stood between me and the door.

Backing away from my computers, toward the charging station, I kept my eyes on the two men.

Julian Ross dashed blood from his eyes and spat it from his mouth, then shoved Elliott in my direction. "Stop her."

I picked up a chair and threw it. Elliott ducked, raising his right arm to protect his face, but one metal leg caught him on the shoulder. He stumbled. The chair dropped, shattering the largest computer's projectors. Fragmented glass flew across the room. The Consortium's security feature activated, and chemicals combined in a noxious gas as they melted the memory center. Yellow, sulfurous clouds billowed, and Elliott coughed, though the clouds dissipated quickly. Thin red lines streaked his cheek.

I grabbed another chair and held it ready. "Stay back."

Elliott froze.

For a tierce, I saw everything in absolute detail, as if time slowed, and I still had my drone.

Blood fell from Elliott's face and splattered like a crown on the floor. His pupils constricted. Ross's tunic slowly changed color as its fabric wicked up blood. His facial muscles tightened.

"I do not know for certain if you killed Kyleigh's father," I said to Ross when time resumed. "But as you deleted all the files on the station, you know who did and have been protecting him. Or her."

"You liar," Elliott said through clenched teeth. "He wouldn't kill anyone."

"When you altered the medical stasis bay protocol, you effectively murdered seventy-eight people." The stitch in my side returned, and the chair, too heavy, dipped toward the floor. "You did so to redirect the feedlines to ensure you and your brother survived, should Westruther trigger the self-destruct."

Julian Ross watched me closely. I could sense him measuring my capabilities. "You have no proof."

Elliott's head jerked over to his brother. "Julian, what? Please tell me all you did was erase—"

"Elliott!"

"Tell me you didn't hurt Kyleigh's dad!"

"Of course not."

"What about the pods? You were in a different group—"

"I would not make baseless accusations, Julian Ross." I ignored his younger brother and exaggerated the facts as I never would have been able to in my drone's presence. "You simply failed to cover your trail of evidence as well as you might have supposed."

"There was no trail to cover." He carefully picked a path around shards and slivers from the console.

"Your erasure of the ship's data is easily verified. And while your personal ethics are not actionable, your treatment of Jordan is wrong. She deserves better than you."

Ross did not answer, but Elliott did. "He didn't mistreat her."

"And you." I shifted my attention to him. "You nauseate me, Elliott Ross. I was willing to grant you a second chance. I did not file a report against you. Perhaps I should have. Perhaps I will."

Ross dove at me. I did not move quickly enough to evade him, and the chair dropped, banging against my shin. He grabbed my left arm and twisted it behind my back. I refused to make a sound, though my eyes watered in pain.

"You will not, you vile little—"

"Recorder. Ross. Explain!"

Peering past Ross's shoulder, I glimpsed Captain North at the door. My eyes closed for a moment in relief. "Julian Ross is the perpetrator, Captain."

"I'm correcting a mistake." Ross twisted my arm. He paused, and with a smile as charming as any he had ever given me, he added, "You were wrong, Recorder. The Consortium, not the citizenry, is my target."

"Move it, Julian," snapped North. "We've got a shuttle to catch. No time to waste."

I stiffened. So. Security would not be coming.

Ross slapped me, and my ears rang. Blood trickled from my lower lip.

"What are you going to do to her?" Elliott asked.

"Whatever I need to."

"Blast it, Julian." Elliott's voice shook. "Don't hurt her. She doesn't deserve that."

"She's a Recorder, Elliott. They're not human. It doesn't matter what we do." He smiled and pulled a jet injector from his blood-soaked jacket pocket. "I've got a perfect use for her."

I had no desire to be of any use to him or anyone like him. "Are you aware repeated exposure to electrical shock reduces perceived pain in subjects but does not impede the flow of electrons?" I asked. "To provide a sufficient reaction, you must increase . . ." With my free hand, I reached behind me, flipped off the safety, and grabbed the charger in the wall.

Julian Ross's hand tightened on my arm. He screamed. My back arched, and everything went black.

47

Kyleigh cried out. She needed help.

I forced myself to sit up, and I winced. My muscles cramped, my vision blurred, and my hand throbbed with every heartbeat. Everything hurt.

She knelt next to me, crying. I heard footsteps, and then Nate was holding me.

"Sweet stars above! What happened here?" Jordan exclaimed.

Nate kissed the top of my head and touched my cheek. "Can you speak?"

My tongue felt thick in my mouth. I blinked, and my laboratory came into focus. Blood glistened on the doorframe, the floor, on the counter next to me. The liquid computer's console was irreparably damaged, and shards of glass littered the floor. Chemicals had dissolved the carpet, the acrid stench still tainting the air. A chair lay on its side, one leg bent, and the table had been knocked askew.

Memory rushed back. "Where is Ross?" I forced the words out. "Captain North? Elliott?"

"Ross?" Jordan knelt in front of me. "Julian?"

"Has the first shuttle departed?"

"Yes. The first boarding call for the second shuttle just went out." Her voice sharpened. "What happened?"

Without answering, I tried to use my communication link. It was dead. Cradling my throbbing right hand to my chest, I tapped Nate's with my left, demanding to speak with Archimedes Genet. When he responded, Jordan interrupted me to describe the destruction in the computer laboratory.

Within two and a half minutes, First Officer Genet arrived, out of breath, with a security team. Once he saw the chaos, he ordered security to record the scene, lock down the ship, and contact Lunar One to hold all inbound shuttles and stop all outgoing flights. His prompt action gave me momentary hope, which was dashed when the bridge informed him all external communication systems were down. So, although witnesses verified that the captain and Elliott had taken Ross onto a shuttle, they could not be apprehended.

Leaving another officer in charge, Genet stormed out of the room. Additional security personnel arrived to help contain the laboratory's disaster.

Jordan studied me. "We'd better get you to Max. Never in my career, in my whole life for that matter, have I met someone who needs medical attention as frequently as you do."

"No, I shall be fine." I paused, unwilling to say what I needed to. "Jordan, Julian Ross was not sincere in his affection for you." When she did not respond, I pulled my uninjured hand from Nate's and touched her arm. "He is not a good man, but I am sorry."

"It doesn't matter." She stood abruptly. "You need to get to the infirmary."

"But it does matter," I said. "I cannot leave yet. I must file a report, then contact the Consortium."

Nate's hand tightened on my arm, and Kyleigh gasped, "*No.*" Jordan spun around, but I did not find the sound of her beads comforting.

"What will you report?" one of the security officers asked.

Looking at the recording device in his hands, I carefully selected my words and summarized the incident, even revealing the threat of the virus. The security team grew still.

Jordan began to pace, but the debris in the room stopped her. She stood, face tight. "Did you know this before you got here?"

Staring at the shattered console, I said, "Right before, yes, which is why I contacted you. The truth was before me the whole time, but I did not assemble it. I should have known. He lied. And, Kyleigh, I am sorry about your father."

I wished to lean against Nate, who had stayed silently beside me, but we were being recorded. I drew a deep breath. "Julian Ross was originally secured in a different stasis pod, which he reprogrammed, not the one in which we found him. I should have noticed it much earlier." I glanced at Kyleigh, then at the disaster around me. "I have only those facts. I suspect Julian Ross was involved in Dr. Tristram's murder, even if only by covering the perpetrator's trail, but he *did* reprogram the medical supply lines, directing resources to that last cluster of pods, ensuring that he and Elliott had sufficient resources to survive. He must have suspected John Westruther would activate a protocol to prevent escape. I believe he would have done anything to preserve his life and his brother's."

The security officer cleared his throat. "You think it's possible there's any evidence left on the station? He destroyed all this." He gestured at the shattered computer.

I nodded. "If it is in deep storage, data might yet be retrieved, which I shall recommend in my report." I wetted my lips. "Jordan, he viewed your acceptance of his attentions as advantageous. He seemed to believe your relationship added to his credibility."

The emergency lights flashed, and the klaxon sounded. I should have been prepared for it since Archimedes Genet had put the ship on alert, but I startled and would have fallen had Nate not steadied me.

"I'm taking you to the infirmary." He guided me out the door, and the security officer did not protest.

In the hallway, with the alarm sounding and the recording systems damaged, Jordan finally spoke. "Was Elliott in on it?"

"He seemed horrified at my accusations. However, he knew Ross had deleted evidence, and he knew Ross had designed something, though Ross denied telling him to . . . to contaminate me." Nate's grip on my arm tightened. "When Elliott protested that Ross had indicated whatever was in his system could be transmitted by blood or saliva, Ross insisted 'they' had another plan, and that Elliott's actions were not helpful, that since I did not become ill, the delivery system had failed. He is targeting the Consortium."

"Bodily fluids." Kyleigh pinched her lips and stared ahead. A single tear fell onto her pale pink tunic, and she dashed her sleeve across her cheek. "He engineered it to be transmitted through bodily fluids."

"Yes," I said. "This explains Elliott's reaction when he visited me in the infirmary and expressed concern that he had made me ill."

Kyleigh's eyes grew huge. "But that makes what he did attempted murder!"

I slowed, trying to catch my breath, and Nate swung me up into his arms. When I protested, he was firm. "Let me do this much, all right?"

I looked up into his eyes. "I do not agree with the Consortium's methodology, but I must warn them."

"No." Jordan's voice was harsh. "We'll patch you up, then get you out of here. Let someone else tell them. If they're so smart, they'll figure it out."

I rested against Nate's chest. "Do not be irrational, Jordan. Genet has placed the ship on alert. Both the military and the Consortium will have been notified. When they arrive, restrictions will only increase. I have nowhere to go. Additionally, no matter how I feel about the Consortium, I cannot allow them to be completely destroyed."

"Why not?" Nate demanded.

For a few seconds, which I did not count, I listened to his heartbeat. "You cannot mean that. How many millions of people could be harmed if no one tells them? And consider how much scrutiny they will direct at you, and effort they would expend to find me, if they uncover the threat after I depart. They would punish anyone with whom I have associated. It is a flawed plan, in which I will not participate."

Jordan rubbed her temples while she walked. "There has to be something. Tim, have Max double check everything. *Everything.* Run that blasted medicomputer a couple times." She increased her pace. "I don't like the idea of viruses and genocide in general, but I specifically dislike it when people try to murder my friends. I'll head to the bridge and see what Genet needs. I'm not giving up yet. I don't know if there's a way to get you out of here, but . . . wait. You said Ross altered the ship's records?"

"Yes. He also deleted everything from the station. All of it."

"Well, there's that," she said, but did not clarify her antecedent.

My throat tightened at the look on her face. I craned my head to Kyleigh. The red emergency lights cast a weird sheen to the tears on her cheeks. "Kyleigh?" I asked. "Are you well enough to accompany me so Nate could, perhaps, stay with Jordan?"

His eyebrows rose. "I'll join her *after* I leave you with Max."

Jordan gave a short laugh, though nothing was amusing. "Don't give me that look, Tim. I'm fine. Mark another tally on your 'I told you so'

card. Give yourself several extra points for murdering psychopath. Go."
She placed a gentle hand on my shoulder. "Get her to Max to work his
magic." She strode off to the bridge.

"Comm the infirmary, Kyleigh," Nate said. "Let Max know we're
coming. My hands are full."

She tried, but Max did not answer. After several attempts her face
grew pale. She whispered, "Freddie," and broke into a run.

I curled thankfully against Nate's chest, but fatigue and pain blurred
the rest of our short walk. When we arrived, I noted the red emergency
lighting was offset by bright, white lights, all aimed at a bed in the back.
The medical tank no longer glowed in luminescent green. Nate carefully
deposited me on a chair near the door and our attention was drawn to
the bedside where Max was giving terse commands to Edwards and
Williams, and Kyleigh stood, hands clasped together and her index
fingers at her lips. My good hand sought Nate's, and he held it tightly.

I did not count the minutes we watched the still figure on the bed at
the center of their activity, but he did not thrash, as Elliott had. Whether
the faint movement of his abdomen was my imagination or not, I could
not tell. Finally, Max noticed Kyleigh and nodded to her. Williams
moved away, allowing Kyleigh to take her place. My friend stepped
close to the bed and touched the young man's cheek, then she simply
stood there, holding his hand.

While Max focused on his datapad, Edwards reached for another jet
injector, so Williams saw me first. Her involuntary cry made the others
look around. They froze for a moment, and for some reason, things
were a blur until Williams stripped off my burned, bloody tunic, leaving
me shivering in my tight undershirt until she handed me a robe.

"Blast it all! What in the six colonies did you do this time?" Max shot
me a glare as he inspected my hand.

"It was but an electrical shock. I am not that badly injured," I
protested.

"Do you *want* to go back in the blasted tank?"

"No. I certainly do not."

"Trying to electrocute yourself?" He frowned at me. "Did you think
being a Recorder made you immune?"

"I was not thinking. I simply reacted when he spoke disparagingly of Jordan."

Max grew still. "What?"

As I saw no reason to maintain silence, I described the incident.

Max's mouth was a thin line. "Yes, you're definitely going in the medicomputer. I need to determine if you've damaged your heart . . ." He paused a moment. "SahnVeer figured out the encapsulation for those tumors. Could Ross have used that to hide the virus?"

Of course. I had heard Dr. SahnVeer say as much. Yet another piece of information I had missed. "Yes. That would be what Ross meant, then. Nanotechnology as a way to hide a virus. He did say that the delivery system must have failed."

"That means Elliott tried to kill you." I had never heard that tone in Max's voice. "Stars . . . Williams, we'll need blood samples. Kyleigh, pull up the nanodevices you found the other day."

"In a minute, Max." Kyleigh's voice sounded hollow. "I'll get started then."

The room grew still.

Edwards said, "Perhaps, I can?"

"No." Her voice caught. "I'll do it. But Max . . . Freddie?"

Max closed his eyes and exhaled through his nose. "Only God knows right now, Kye. Freddie's holding. We do our best, and we wait."

"We won't leave him, Kyleigh," Edwards said.

"All right. I'll . . . I'll pull up those devices and take a look." She bent to lightly kiss Freddie's hand, then returned to her computer.

Williams applied a gel pack to my left cheek where Ross's hand had apparently left an imprint, and to my split lip, then encased my burned hand in a mitten full of gel and antibiotics. She and Edwards helped me into the medicomputer for analysis.

Before they closed the door behind me, I heard Max ask, "Tim, is Venetia all right?"

"She'll put on a good face. Always does."

Max's response was hidden by the medicomputer's low hum.

For ten minutes, I sat on the narrow cot while it scanned me, then its calm vocalization program announced, "Electrical burns. Abrasions.

Contusions. Remnants of parasitic activity. Subject clear of viral infection."

When the medicomputer's small scanning room door opened, the dull red cast from the alert lighting had disappeared. Edwards did not smile, but he ruffled my short hair. Williams had retreated next to Freddie's bed, watching everyone. Max, Nate, and Kyleigh were reviewing a slowly rotating representation of a nanodevice. The medical tank gave a final chug as the purification cycle ended, and it stood empty, ready for its next patient.

"I am sufficiently recovered," I said. "I should return to file the report."

"No." Max straightened. "I'll run another scan, recheck your hand. That was an incredibly stupid thing you did, grabbing that charger. Someone must have pried you off it, or you wouldn't be sitting here. What on any known planet made you do it?"

I stared down at my boots. "I was determined not to be of use to him. I did not care what happened, as long as he was stopped."

"What?" The words shot from Nate like weapons' fire. "Didn't *care*?"

I tapped my thigh, caught myself, then held out my hands. "He made it clear he meant to target millions of people. I know many do not see Recorders as human, but we are. He targets Edwards and Williams, and the staff that serve in housekeeping and the kitchens, as well as our younger brothers and sisters at the training centers." I blinked back sudden moisture in my eyes. "The little ones, Nate. The little ones."

Kyleigh's hand flew to her throat. Nate took a step toward me but stopped.

"He mistreated Jordan, and if I am not mistaken, he orchestrated the deaths of nearly everyone on that station. I wanted no part in his plans."

The sounds of mechanical systems somehow exacerbated the quiet in the room.

"I ate with him." Kyleigh's chin quivered. "And Elliott was my *friend*."

"He did not understand what Julian Ross intended to do." Irritation with myself for defending him made me nauseous.

Nate's communication link chimed.

"Tim?" Jordan's voice seemed unusually loud. "Is she okay?"

"She'll be fine," Max answered before Nate could. "Venetia. How are *you*?"

"I've still got security cleaning up this mess. Can the Recorder get to a secure computer and write that report? Genet needs it five minutes ago. We haven't sent out shuttles on time. Someone will figure out about the emergency alert pretty soon, which means we need to have it ready as soon as communication is up and running."

I fought to keep my voice steady. "My datapads are in my old quarters. I shall begin work on that immediately."

Nate shook his head, and his bangs fell over his eyes. "You need someone to watch over you."

But without responding, I left the infirmary, fleeing my friends and Nate.

This time, the plain, white walls of my original quarters were oppressively bright, and their eerie lack of connection to the morning's events made the room strange and uninviting. I sat heavily on the bed and scooted back against the wall, with the now-barren room closing in on me like a trap and my hand throbbing. I had no future with the Consortium, no escape route, no hope.

At least my headache had receded, and my face no longer stung. To use Jordan's imprecise phrase, there was that.

With the datapad balanced on my lap, I entered my report with my good hand, the injured one tucked against my stomach. Providing all the information they needed without telling them everything was a singular challenge. The last report I transmitted had described only my preliminary theories about the virus.

I continued from that point but left out the incident with Elliott four days ago. Had it only been four days? I closed my eyes, but darkness failed to alleviate my concerns. By the time I had finished, *Thalassa*'s crew had repaired the communication system, so I transmitted the report through the ship's secured channel, then reclined against the wall and stared blankly in front of me.

Julian Ross had the virus in his possession, ready to release and destroy the Consortium. His escape would force authorities to publicly disseminate the information, which could trigger widespread panic. Someone must return to the station and retrieve the backup files. They might prove Ross's guilt, but more importantly, they might reveal critical information about the virus and its delivery method. Surely, Ross did not intend Elliott to run around the system kissing Recorders.

No, I would not tell the Consortium what Elliott had done. I pulled my knees to my chest and did not cry.

My alarm woke me from a dull, heavy sleep. Pushing myself up from the crumpled bedding and rubbing my eyes, I stretched, then reached for the datapad to access the Consortium's network one last time. My empty stomach knotted.

An Elder would arrive with my replacement in five and a half standard hours. To take me. The Elders' displeasure had trumped protocol. They intended to deny me a tribunal and send me directly to adjudication. I told myself my fate had not been sealed, that primary reclamation was not guaranteed, but deep down, I knew such hopes were false.

I read on to determine if anyone else was implicated and would face the full weight of the Consortium's ire. The disaster Alec's family had faced, that Jordan's cousin had faced, could not threaten my friends.

Please, please. I could bear it if only they were safe. It seemed clear. Nevertheless, I ran another search to be certain all evidence of their complicity had been removed, which, with the more powerful Consortium system, took a splintered fraction of the time.

Sagging back against the wall, my eyes closed in relief. When I opened them, a flashing symbol in the upper right-hand corner indicated two results on my search for Max's people. I opened the first packet, and my heart sputtered.

Missing: Presumed Dead. A storm on Ceres had devastated Trinity North and had taken her with it. They had found her tunic on a grate and her tracking device inside a fish. I could not tell Max, not now. Why could the universe not grant me some small hope? I wiped away the moisture accumulating in my eyes.

The remaining packet blinked from the screen. I did not want to open it but did anyway, and after I skimmed it once, then twice, I actually laughed a proper laugh, not bothering to stop the tears that streamed down.

Thank you.

In my mind, I saw him, his smile, his eyes, the thoughtful expression on his face when he concentrated. My first friend, and Max. How had I missed it? Wiping my cheeks with my good hand, I leaned back against the wall, balanced my datapad on my knees, and searched. Now that I knew my quarry, I knew where to begin.

There was no way under any sun, moon, or star I would not find him. And I did. My stomach lurched again. *No.* I viewed his files, both the Elders' verdict and the ones they had forcefully downloaded through his neural implant. I read how he had acted, had interfered, lost his neutrality. For a minute, I sat, eyes scrunched tight, and remembered the Hall of Reclamation with its medical tanks of deceased citizen donors and living Recorders sentenced to serve with their very selves. We only saw it once, and that singular time was enough. My happiness evaporated.

When my communication link chimed, I ignored it. My head in my hands, I ran through scenario after scenario. Then, with shaking fingers, I began an addendum to my original report, with new recommendations, suggesting the Consortium send Recorders to retrieve the backup data and the dead Recorder's body and drone from the station. Given the potential virus, only expendable personnel should be sent. Recorders awaiting adjudication or tribunal might be given the opportunity to redeem themselves. I bit my lip and added the suggestion that as a potentially contaminated Recorder, I should be sent as well. I placed a priority on the message and sent it.

It was far from the safest option, but exposure to the virus was worth the risk, offered more hope than ending his life in a medical tank. He could turn it down if he wished. I hoped he would not. The virus which could destroy us all might ultimately save him, and to me, even a small chance was better than none.

Fear of reclamation exceeded my fear of the station, though nausea rose at the memory of the roaches, but the miniscule hope that they would give me a chance flickered, struggling to stay lit.

I could not tell Max. But if my actions saved my first friend, perhaps someday he would know. The possibility was bittersweet.

On impulse, I emptied my favorite datapad, the one with the smooth blue cover, and used it to back up my discovery and the coding I had used to break into the Consortium's network, filling the memory to capacity.

I added several layers of encryption but only a simple password, one that almost made me smile. Almost.

Taking a deep breath, I violated all my training and ruined the rest of the ship's security footage, copying Ross's blunt methods, and erased the coding for the recording devices. Satisfaction curled through me as every feed on *Thalassa* went dead. I set the bots on a heavy cleaning cycle and erased all evidence that I had returned to these quarters. It would all be Ross's fault, which granted me a degree of satisfaction. Should he be caught, no one would believe his protests that he had not caused the entire system to crumble.

The Recorder on the station, with her drone, would have known he lied. Had she been killed, too? My chest hurt, and I rubbed my good hand over my sternum.

I would not need to find a name after all. That opportunity had passed when I confronted Ross instead of taking the shuttle. If I had known of his deception, I could have stopped him, though if I had known, I would not have chosen differently.

I might not be free, but my friends, perhaps even my first friend, would be safe. It was the least and the best I could do, but I was afraid.

An assistant strapped the Recorder into a chair before administering the memory uptake devices via jet injector. The Recorder gritted his teeth. The devices, which extracted memories from his neural implant and displayed them on his visual cortex and those of the Elders, only required a small electrical current, but the tribunal had warned him that current and the devices could cause convulsive movements and pain.

There was nothing he could do. Tribunals cleared very few Recorders. He closed his eyes to reduce extraneous visual information and watched the disaster of his last assignment unfold.

He stood at the intersection, his drone hovering nearby. Above the tenements' grimy exteriors, the riveted dome glowed with the colors of a programmed sunset, highlighting the dull buildings with orange. Three scraggly trees grew on the patchy lawn, and eight children played under them.

A group of citizens dressed in the flowing, colorful clothing of more affluent districts disembarked from a private transport, and the children ran to meet them. As the new arrivals handed small boxes to the children, one woman knelt to speak with a little girl. The woman's movements were fluid and strong, though silver had overtaken black in her long, loose hair. The little girl hugged her and tucked the small package into her pocket before running past the Recorder toward the buildings. The woman watched with a smile, but when she saw him, she sprang to her feet, grey eyes wide. She gasped. His drone did not reprimand him when he inclined his head to acknowledge her attention.

The ground jolted. After a flash of confusion, he found the name: earthquake. Screams sounded as the pavement continued to roll. He staggered, then fell to his knees, tearing his pants and skinning his palms. Irritation rippled through him, stronger than his fear. No alarms had sounded before the quake had struck, even though he had notified the council last quarter of problems with the sensors. They should have listened.

With an ear-splitting screech, the metal structural supports in one of the tenement buildings crumpled. Glass shattered, and debris flew as the walls collapsed.

The Recorder regained his balance and sent his drone above the treetops to better document the disaster. Panicked cries joined the rumble of concrete and sharp noise of buckling metal. He started toward the crying children and screaming adults, and his drone dropped quickly and tapped his cheek with one long tentacle, reminding him not to interact, only to observe.

Accessing the building's schematics, residency files, and video recordings from the lobby, he determined seventy-four of the building's residents had returned that evening. Some of the children had departed to play outside, so only sixty-seven residents were inside when the building collapsed.

Sixty-seven residents. He forced himself to remain still. His duty was to observe and record. He would do his duty.

The woman with silver-and-black curls ran past him to the fallen building. Her companions collected the children and moved them away from the leaning structures and spreading fires.

"Not again, oh stars above, not again!" She spun around, and her silver-grey eyes sought him. "Help me! There's a child here—you must help me!"

He stood frozen while the woman tried to shift debris off the small body of the girl with whom she had spoken moments ago.

"Not again," she repeated, tears streaming down her cheeks.

Almost without knowing how, he was at her side. "Move," he said.

Muscles straining, the Recorder shifted the beam off the little girl's leg before he lifted her carefully in his arms. He carried the child across the street to the woman's companions. One of them snatched the girl away from him and settled her gently on the ground where another woman checked her pulse and respiration.

The Recorder's breath came in bursts. The pounding of his heart grew so loud he could no longer hear, but he could feel the screams, pressing in, stabbing his skin like needles. The trees' shadows stretched long claws, squeezing the air from his lungs.

A reprimand shattered his panic, and the drone triggered a flood of neurotransmitters. He closed his eyes and exhaled. He would be fine, momentarily, and truly, his drone's reprimand was not unwarranted.

The woman had approached him. She touched his arm. She did not seem frightened of him, though citizens were. "Please," she murmured. "There are more people."

Her eyes, silvery-grey like his, studied his face, and he looked away. Then, together, they carried eight more survivors from the rubble and laid them on the patchy grass. His drone reprimanded him several times, but he used the rebukes to focus on the people they saved.

The woman started back to the disaster, but as he deposited an older man under a tree, the man reached thin, veined fingers to catch the Recorder's face. He froze. The man wheezed, "Thank you, my son, my brother. Go in peace."

One of the affluent people shooed the Recorder away, but as he turned, an aftershock rippled the ground. A crash and the grey-eyed woman's cry of pain rent the air.

The panic started again, but he summoned neurotransmitters and ducked under twisted metal to find her pinned beneath a wall. He knelt at her side, evaluating which piece to move first.

"No." Sweat, tears, and dust combined in rivulets of fine mud on her cheeks. "Don't."

She was correct. If he moved the debris, she would bleed to death. The anxiety which circled like a whirlpool bit him again. His fingers twitched until his drone hovered behind him and laid one gentle tentacle across his neck.

Once again, its weight and its reprimand centered him.

The woman struggled to speak. "I did what I . . . thought . . . best.""

"You have done well," he said. "I do not believe anyone would have performed with greater alacrity to save these citizens."

"No—" Her eyes squeezed closed, and she drew a shuddering breath. "Tell him I'm sorry."

The Recorder hesitated, then held out his hand as he had seen citizens do.

His drone twisted a tendril around his neck, but he pushed a curl from her forehead so he could better see her face. She rested her cheek on his palm.

"I am here." Though why his presence mattered, he could not say. Other than rescuing those people, when had his presence ever been beneficial?

She cried out, and her face contorted. "It hurts."

Emergency rescue crews arrived, their sirens and calls drowning out other noises while they coordinated their efforts. He wanted to send his drone to summon assistance, but it would not leave him while he exhibited this much distress.

She labored over each breath. "Forgive . . . me."

"You did your best."

". . . for gifting you."

He froze. His tiny reflection stared back from her silvery eyes, and the drone's weighted arms settled around him. Finally, he managed to say, "Yes."

Her breath caught in the middle. Not knowing what else to do, he raised her hand to his face. Serenity flooded her features. Her gasps grew more ragged, and her grip weakened.

"Thank you . . . so like your father . . . He was near . . . your age."

His drone did not reprimand him for emotional disturbance since he held her hand and touched her face, but he knew he would be punished later.

"He wanted . . . to name you . . . James . . ." Her voice trailed away to nothing.

The Recorder knelt at her side, still cradling her face, in the gathering dark. The programmed sunset faded as the light in her silver-grey eyes went out.

And then, he was punished.

The playback stopped.

"Recorder." The Elder's words creaked, like metal under pressure. "This verifies your failure to maintain proper distance and objectivity."

The Recorder lowered his gaze. "I have no defense against the accusation."

"You did not maintain the integrity of your calling," she continued.

"I did not."

"It is within our jurisdiction to attend a dying citizen," the short Elder said.

The remaining Elder slowly, thoughtfully stroked the tendril around his neck. "It once was."

"In responding to a request by a citizen," the short one added, "he was within our original scope of service."

The Recorder could only assume they continued the discussion nonverbally, because after a severe reprimand, while he shook in the chair, the three Elders spoke simultaneously.

"We are not united."

Two of them recited together, "You lost objectivity. We recommend you continue your service through primary reclamation."

The dissenting Elder said, "You acted without objectivity, but you attended a citizen's request, which lies within our original contract. You should be warned and reassigned. A repetition of these actions will not be considered acceptable."

Together, they finished, "You shall await Final Adjudication with the Eldest in one ten-day. Until then, you shall minister in the Hall of Reclamation."

They stood. Two left. The dissenter sent one of his slave drones to unbuckle the straps that secured the Recorder to the chair. Three long arms from its soft underbelly steadied him when he slumped forward, still panting from the discipline.

"Use your time wisely. Do not dwell on what she told you. At the end of life, many people wish to atone for gifting to the Consortium. Though it is a noble gift, they experience guilt. Three women and one man have begged me for forgiveness in gifting me, though none of them spoke truly. Like you, I extended it. At the end of life, one should find peace."

"Her eyes were like my own," the Recorder said.

The Elder inclined his head. "It is possible she spoke the truth, but your primary concern is to prepare for meeting the Eldest. She does not tolerate aberrations. You have my condolences. You may contact me, should you need to do so."

Once in his holding cell, the Recorder disconnected from his drone to allow it to charge, and he sat on his cot in the dark, shoulders slumped.

Without the visual input that made the world beautiful, shadows raced through his mind.

Even if the woman spoke the truth, it changed nothing.

He would face the Eldest in a ten-day. The Eldest did not tolerate personal interaction with citizens, and she would not dispense mercy. Recorders who lost their objectivity—aberrations—were reclaimed. If they did not serve with their actions, they served with their selves, saving the lives of citizens from inside a medical stasis pod.

And that reclamation was the sum of the problem.

He ought to have been grateful for the reprieve, but it was a pointless delay.

James. Perhaps his name was James. Hands clasped on his chest, he lay down and stared blankly at the paneled ceiling and returned to memories he had hidden away.

No drone oversaw his emotions while he remembered silver-grey eyes and their reaction to his forgiveness or remembered the feeling of carrying the people away from the fallen building and the way the old man had placed shaking hands on his face and blessed him. The drone did not punish him for thinking of his first assignment and the girl with earnest, hazel eyes, who had indignantly defended him.

He summoned his favorite memories. The sound of a cello chasing a melody. Fresh apples. The mouse in the biology laboratory falling asleep on his palm, its tiny ribs moving with each breath. His one friend's coffee-brown eyes, fringed with long dark lashes, watching him intently as he taught her how to shape a boat of lily leaves and lavender. When she had smiled, she reminded him of light.

He had nine evenings left to remember. Although he did not want to waste his time sleeping, eventually, sleep claimed him all the same.

Quiet filled the dining commons. Everyone except my friends had left, so I pulled the identification bracelet from my pocket and placed it on the table in front of Jordan.

"Please wipe the memory." DuBois leaned over her and took it, and I gave her my datapad as well. "Keep this safe."

When a single tear trickled down her cheek, I suspected I was wrong to burden her. I held out my hand. "I am sorry. Please return it. I have time to wipe the memory, then destroy it."

She hugged the blue datapad to her chest, ignoring my outstretched hand. "No."

Kyleigh, however, took my hand in hers. "I don't want you to go."

"Neither do I," Max said quietly.

"I must thank each of you for your assistance and friendship." I withdrew my hand from Kyleigh's. "No Recorder has ever been as fortunate as I in his or her companions."

"You're not a Recorder." Nate rose, slammed his chair under the table, and stormed from the room.

I stood to follow, but when Jordan touched my arm, I sat back down. She shook her head, and her braids played their staccato music. "Let him go."

A longing for braids with beads swelled in my chest. If only the familiar sound could travel with me. If I were incredibly fortunate, it would not be long before I was bald again, and I did not truly mind, although I found I did not wish to lose my eyebrows.

Alec had been leaning his chair back. He sat up straight, and its legs smacked the floor. "You're not one of them anymore. You shouldn't have to go."

DuBois's knuckles whitened as she gripped both the datapad and the identification bracelet. "He's right, you know."

"There is naught you or I can do. Thank you, DuBois, for your efforts. I have triple-checked the computer logs, and they are now as clean as they can be." I tried to smile. "I was well trained. You should all be safe. Of course, Ross's more obvious interference might have rendered my efforts immaterial. His disappearance should keep the focus away from what I have done."

Alec walked around the table and knelt before me, his eyes boring into mine. "You're not like them. Don't let them take that away from you."

DuBois followed him and rested one slim hand on his shoulder.

"I'll miss you, you know." Jordan said. "We all will."

"I did not know." I held my breath for three seconds, then lied, "Do not worry. My work identifying problems on the station will redeem me."

Max leaned forward. "Redeem you, how?"

I only shook my head in answer.

DuBois broke the uncomfortable silence. "When I was rude earlier, I didn't mean it. It's just, you were so blasted *obvious* in trying to warn me off that shuttle. I had to say something. I had to be rude, but I didn't mean it."

I bit my lower lip. "I am afraid I did not understand your intent, but I thank you. Your consideration is a gift." What insufficient words. "The new Recorder . . . he or she will run a thorough check on the systems, so be extremely cautious in conversation and personal record keeping."

"Can you–" DuBois blinked rapidly. "Is there any way to let us know if you're safe?"

I debated another lie, then said, "No." I stood again.

"Wait," she said in a rush. "I want you to call me Zhen."

"Zhen," I repeated, meeting her dark eyes. She nodded twice. I glanced around the table. "Please do not come to say goodbye."

"I wish we could send something with you." Kyleigh's voice trembled. "To remember us."

"You are all here"–I tapped my head–"and here." I tapped my chest. "As long as I am myself, I will have you."

Kyleigh made a choking sound, and Max rose to enfold me in a hug. He placed a kiss on the top of my head, like a benediction.

Jordan went with me to the doorway. "We won't forget."

"Goodbye," I said, and left.

What I truly wanted was to find Nate to bid him farewell, but I did not know where to begin. Out of habit, I followed the familiar path to the computer laboratory before I headed to the docking bay to wait. The room was not sealed. Security had finished processing it, and the door stood open.

There he was, at the table where we had shared sandwiches, head in his hands. I paused at the doorway, watching him, before I spoke.

"Nate."

His head came up as the door slid closed behind me, but he said nothing. His jaw was tight, his mouth a narrow line.

"You are angry with me, are you not? I cannot go if you are angry with me."

"Good. Then you'll stay."

"That is not what I meant."

"Well, what did you mean?" His voice was harsh.

"Nate." How could I make him see? "If I resist, it will go poorly for you, Max, Kyleigh, Jordan, for everyone. You will be in danger."

"I don't care."

"You *should* care. If I resist, I would have jeopardized you all for nothing."

"You actually believe that?" he snapped, but his eyes softened. He stood and crossed the room, then reached out and gently touched my cheek. "You're more precious than anything."

His hand dropped. I wanted to catch it, but I did not.

"I cannot risk you," I managed as a lump filled my throat. "I must cooperate."

His breath quickened, but he did not move.

"Max says whether we are stardust or creation, our uniqueness is valuable. This, I am learning, is true, and I cannot risk the value of all of you, merely for me."

The corners of his mouth drew down. "That has to be the stupidest thing you've ever said."

"Please, Nate." I placed my hand on his arm, but he turned away. "Nate, look at me."

"What?"

"That is the wrong response." When he said nothing, I attempted to sound stern. "The correct response is 'I am looking.' We will try again. Nathaniel Timmons, look at me."

He turned around, and a muscle ticced in his jaw. "I'm looking."

I wanted to stare into his eyes until they became the world all around. He tilted his head. "What is it?" he asked at last.

"I need to finish memorizing you. I need one more memory to carry with me." Before I lost my courage, I added, "I have a favor to ask."

His eyebrows rose. I would miss seeing them jump. When had eyebrows ceased being strange and become so very important? "You said it would be . . ." I hesitated. "You told me . . . They will soon arrive with their drones." The fear of reclamation shook me, and I lost my way through my words. "Nate, I am frightened."

He closed the distance between us.

"If they reinstate me, I hope to lock away my memories. It is also possible that they will not, that they have another fate for me. In all honesty, I do not wish to be reinstated, but I would rather die than face the alternative."

"No." His eyes held mine, and he put a finger to my lips. "Don't."

I caught his hand. "Even if I—if they take me back, I will not see you." His fingers tightened around mine, and I ran my thumb over the faint scars on his knuckles. I drew a deep breath. "Would you mind, Nate? I would like you to kiss me."

He did not move.

I rambled on. "Because I cannot stay, and you cannot come with me. Because when I am alone, the thought of you comforts me. Because I would like to have that extra memory to keep in my heart . . . If you do not mind."

The intensity of his gaze stopped me. His hands slid up my arms and traced the bare skin of my neck, then cradled my face. Breathing became difficult.

"Nate, I—"

"Shh." He brushed his thumb over my lower lip.

This close, I could see tiny flecks of blue and brown in the green of his eyes, which I had never noticed, even when I had studied him before I lost my drone. I closed my eyes, but my heart pounded.

His lips brushed mine for a moment. I could smell the spiciness of his breath, of cinnamon and cloves. His lips touched mine again. I had not expected them to be so soft. With a slow exhale, I leaned into him, and my arms went around his neck of their own volition. I felt him smile, and then he kissed me.

The world disappeared, and stars above, but I wanted to kiss him forever.

When he drew back, my lips tingled, and I could not quite catch my breath. He rested his forehead against mine, then enfolded me in his arms. I did not count the moments we stood there, and I listened to his heartbeat.

"Cinnamon."

He laughed, the lovely sound rumbling in his chest. "Cinnamon?"

"You taste of cinnamon. I have always liked cinnamon."

He lifted my chin, and his fingertips traced my cheek again.

"And pine," I added.

"I did have cinnamon this evening, but I don't recall eating any trees." His eyes twinkled, like stars.

"Do not be ridiculous. You smell like pine."

He shook his head but grinned. "You don't make sense."

"Nathaniel Timmons, I make perfect sense." I ran my fingers through the hair on the nape of his neck and peeked up at him through my lashes. "Absolutely perfect sense. You were indeed correct. This is pleasant, and I would very much like to do it again."

His smile broadened, then his lips teased mine for a moment while I traced the faint stubble on his jawline. Then, I kissed him like all the stars in the universe burned inside me.

He pulled back and cupped my face. His breath caught. "Sweetheart, I don't want you to go. I need you to stay. We can find a way. I know we can. Stay, please."

"I cannot."

"You must know . . ." He rested his forehead against mine for a moment. "You have to know I love you."

How did I breathe again after he said that? "Truly?"

"Truly." His dimple reappeared. "And I've been wanting to kiss you for the longest time."

"I did not know."

He gave a small laugh. "Well, just about everyone else did."

"Everyone? Perhaps I am not as observant as I had thought. You would not mind if I told you, then—oh, I do not have the right words." I whispered so quietly that he might not have heard me, "Nathaniel, you are my heart." Then, I stood on my toes and pulled him to me.

His communication piece chimed. I must have hit it accidentally, because Jordan's disembodied voice said, "Tim?"

We broke apart.

I heard a smile in his voice when he answered. "Kinda busy, J."

Jordan said, "They're docking."

The magic of the past minutes was almost dashed by those words. Almost. It could never be completely dashed.

"If I ever could, or can, I will return," I managed despite feeling as though the floor had fallen away from under me. "But I cannot stay."

"Moons and stars." Zhen's voice was fainter, as if she were further away. "Recorder?"

"I am here," I said, perhaps a little breathlessly. "Do not remain sad for long. I have this much, now."

"No," Nate said, his voice husky. "We'll keep you safe."

"You two know we can hear you?" Kyleigh seemed to choke on the words.

"Tim, tell me you weren't—" Max swore softly. "Where are you?"

"Computer lab," Nate said, the green of his eyes strangely bright.

"Nate, you need to step away. Now." Alec lowered his voice. "They're here."

Nate did not move, so I self-consciously tapped his communication link to turn it off. I lifted my hand to memorize the feel of his features and smooth his worries while I could. His eyes closed when I pushed back his bangs.

"Your hair is as soft as I imagined."

A shadow of a smile flitted across his face. "You've been imagining my hair?"

"Yes." I touched his lips softly, then pulled away. "Before I even knew I did. For what seems to be the longest time."

This was not enough, but it was all there was, and all there could have been.

The door slid open again, and Max charged into the room. "That's what I was afraid of." He handed me a vial of gel and scowled at Nate. "Good night, Tim! You ought to know better. Are you trying to get her killed?"

Nate blanched.

I clutched the vial to my chest. "What is wrong?"

"Your lips are slightly swollen, and you'll have traces of his DNA on your skin, not that they'll necessarily be able to see that. You'd know better than I. That's dangerous to you both." His concern sent a shiver of fear through me. "Apply that to your face. Then swallow some. Now. They're docking."

"I did not know." Though I did not want to lose the taste of cinnamon, I complied, even swishing the cool, thick, minty gel in my mouth before swallowing. I spread it over my face, the chill of the menthol seeping through my skin to my heart. Nate took the tube and did the same.

"Under different circumstances, Tim, I'd say it's about time." Max shook his head. "If you'd done that earlier, we might not be having this conversation now. Maybe we could still figure something out."

"No!" Panic slashed through me like a reprimand. I could no longer regulate my neurotransmitters, but years of experience with shadow drones aided me in slowing my breath. I closed my eyes, focusing on their safety and the possibility the Elders might save my first friend.

Nate's communication piece chimed again, and Zhen's calm, melodic soprano said, "Timmons, please locate the Recorder and take her to the hangar. Her transport has arrived, and Consortium reps are loading her—the drones. The replacement Recorder has already boarded and taken possession of her old quarters."

"On my way." He logged off.

The quiet in my computer lab resounded like a symphony.

"I must go."

Nate picked me up and held me tightly, his head against my neck, then put me down.

I backed away but refused to relinquish his hand. "I must be good at dissembling. I have not hidden truth before, so I shall need wishes and prayers to do this. I erred in giving DuBois, I mean, Zhen, a datapad this morning. She must destroy it."

Max nodded.

Glancing down at my fingers intertwined with Nate's, I thought perhaps Max was correct. If I had summoned the bravery and the honesty sooner, perhaps I would not be leaving now. Perhaps I could have held his hand forever.

Before I lost my courage and the opportunity, I met Max's eyes. "*She* is gone, and I cannot help her. But he—I have done my best, have done everything in my power, such as it is, to protect him and to keep him safe."

Max startled.

"Who are you talking about?" Nate asked.

"My first friend." I tightened my fingers around Nate's, because I needed to let go. "We made boats."

"What do you mean?" Max's deep voice was hoarse.

"I think . . . I think perhaps, you know." I set the empty vial beside my computer and turned to Nate. "But you, my Nathaniel, you are my heart. You will always be my heart." I dropped Nate's hand then and walked briskly from the room, tucking the memory of his kiss into the furthest corners of my mind.

Their footsteps sounded behind me, and I did not acknowledge them until we reached the doors. Schooling my features into position, I glanced back over my shoulder and spoke as flatly as I could, "It would have been better had you not come."

The doors parted. I found myself face-to-face with an Elder, two Recorders, and five drones.

"Elder," I said, bowing to the appropriate depth.

The Elder blinked slowly. He was young in his calling; the faint shadow of his irises showed under the grey nanodevices spreading across his corneas. Two slave drones flanked his personal drone, which hovered directly behind him, its two longest tentacles wrapped around his neck. The Recorders took up positions on either side of me.

Whether prayer or hope was the right word, I did not know, but with all my being I hoped or prayed that the exact measurements of skin temperature and pupil dilation would not betray us. That any unusual variation would be attributed to the presence of an Elder, his drones, and the other two Recorders. That my accelerated heartbeat would be perceived as anticipation of punishment or personal disappointment about my failures.

"Recorder, your appearance is completely unacceptable," he rasped. "Offer civilities to the citizens, then board."

"Yes, Elder." I bowed again. "My thanks, Dr. Maxwell, for your knowledge and persistence. For saving my life."

Max's deep voice rumbled, "You're welcome."

"Nathaniel Timmons"—I made my voice as distant as I could—"I appreciate the assistance you have rendered. If it is not inconvenient, please inform the remainder of Venetia Jordan's team of my gratitude as well."

The two Recorders led me toward their shuttle. When the desire to look, to speak, one last time rose inside me, I quelled it as ruthlessly as any drone and did not turn back.

I followed the Elder into the shuttle, the Recorders behind us. The doors closed, and the locking mechanism snapped shut. I did not doubt but that I would be punished. My best and only hope rested in the Eldest's mercy, and she did not tolerate aberrations.

Once aboard CTV *Agamemnon*, they escorted me to a small room stripped of all furnishings. Even the safety harness had been removed, in violation of the regulations on the posters in my computer laboratory. The Recorders took my boots and my tunic, even my socks, leaving me shivering in my leggings and undershirt, while the Elder waited in the doorway, issuing a warning against taking my own life, as others facing tribunal and adjudication had done. I wanted to protest that taking my clothes was unnecessary, that I would not surrender my sliver of hope. But I knew better. I kept my back straight and held my tongue as the two Recorders filed out.

"We are considering your report," the Elder said. For thirty-seven seconds, he stood at the door, his grey-shrouded eyes locked onto mine. He stepped backward without a glance, and the door slid shut. The magnetic lock's click reverberated in my bones.

I wrapped my arms across my bare midriff.

Prime numbers... two, three, five, seven, eleven, thirteen, seventeen...

A woman's voice broke my concentration and recited the standard announcement for leaving dock, the same warnings Officer Smith had given. How long ago had it been? Less than eighteen hours? I could not remember.

Without the harness, I had little choice but to brace myself in the small bunk built into the wall. My weight disappeared, and the light over the door flashed red as *Agamemnon* pulled away.

I could have sworn I felt it. That the distance stretched my heart to a thin thread, threatening to snap with the strain.

Artificial gravity resumed, the light turned green, and I dropped onto the bunk's spongy surface.

I was alone. The thought echoed. I was nothing, and I was alone. Perhaps it was good that I did not have a name.

No.

The circulation fans beat a low rhythm, and air whispered through the vent over the door. I stood and dug my bare toes into the antistatic carpeting. I thought of Nate. Of Max and Kyleigh and the others. Of stardust and creation. Of lavender and cinnamon and pine.

I straightened, dropped my hands to my sides, and breathed deeply.

No, whatever loomed in my future, I had a name. I might not have found it yet.

But I would.

ACKNOWLEDGMENTS

Once upon a time, a girl loved stories. They were a part of her, but when the girl grew up and wrote a book, she found it wasn't as easy as simply telling a story, after all.

My first thanks goes to you, reader, for taking time to dive into the world of my imaginary friends. It is such an amazing thing to share these people with you.

If I listed off everyone who has been a part of this process, the book would be too long, so I must summarize instead. I appreciate the many people who have encouraged and prayed with me, with a special shout out to Bethany. Thank you to the people on ISI, Realm Makers, WS, and Inklings. To DCS, Friday Crit, and *especially* Peaklings. I cannot list everyone, but you are in my heart as I write this.

Beta readers, those courageous souls who dive into the hot mess of earlier drafts, make the end product better, and I must mention Pam, who braved this first. A special thank you to Sherry, Kate, and Laura.

Julie, words are not enough. You inspire me, my friend. All those nights talking in the library parking lot led here. Thank you for listening.

Jenn and Laura, your steadfast friendship makes me a better writer and a better person.

Angie, what can I say? You are a blessing.

Daniel and Laura, your feedback and ongoing support have been water in the desert.

Angel, my midnight writing buddy, your cheering and crit keep me going.

Anne, please keep bribing—I mean, rewarding—me with chapters.

CJ, you are amazing—thank you—no words!

And Patrice ... Where on earth can I start if saying thank you is insufficient? Because it is insufficient. Thank you for your wisdom, prayers, and faithfulness.

I don't know where I'd be without my family. Gratitude unending to my children and husband. A particular thank you to both my sisters, especially for insight into knitting. Mary Beth, I miss you.

Publishing is a daunting task, but Enclave is amazing. Thank you to Steve for making this possible; to Lisa, for *everything*; to Trissina; to Lindsay, Katelyn, and Jamie. I appreciate you all!

Finally, to the One who granted me the words in the first place, the Author of the best story ever written, unending thanks for words and life itself.

ABOUT THE AUTHOR

Cathy graduated from Biola University with a degree in English Literature and a love for stories. She and her husband, whom she met while writing letters to soldiers, have five children and currently live within the shadow of the Rocky Mountains. While writing is one of her favorite things to do, she also enjoys reading, long hikes and long naps, gluten-free brownies and raspberries, and crocheting while watching science fiction movies with friends and family. Most of her imaginary friends are nice people.